Stalker's Creek and Genesis Rider

Two Full Length Western Novels

Cameron Judd

WOLFPACK
PUBLISHING
— EST 2013 —

Stalker's Creek and Genesis Rider: Two Full Length Western Novels
Paperback Edition
Copyright © 2022 (As Revised) Cameron Judd

Wolfpack Publishing
5130 S. Fort Apache Rd. 215-380
Las Vegas, NV 89148

wolfpackpublishing.com

Paperback ISBN 978-1-63977-701-3
eBook ISBN 978-1-63977-700-6

STALKER'S CREEK AND GENESIS RIDER

STALKER'S CREEK

CHAPTER 1

L ike his father had before him, Jeff Cornwell had begun to go nearsighted about the age of ten. So he squinted hard into the ravine for a full minute before persuading himself that really was a dead man he was looking at.

A dead man! The boy pulled back from the edge of the ravine and debated what to do. There was no one at the house just now to fetch, and besides, the house was more than a mile away. He could try to drag the body out of the ravine himself, but it would probably be too heavy for one thirteen-year-old boy to handle. And what if he'd been dead long enough for there to be maggots and stench and all that? Jeff was glad to leave this duty to the grown men.

He decided to run home and simply wait until someone showed up. His father should be back from Pactolas by noon.

He'd only gone a short distance before he reconsidered. What if the man wasn't dead, just hurt? Jeff paused uncertainly. He really didn't want to have to approach a body that might be all gruesome and bird-pecked. He also didn't want to be guilty of leaving an injured man to die.

Screwing up his courage, he went back to the ravine and

began to carefully climb down its steep wall. He kept a grip on stones and roots, a toehold in every crevice and hole he could find, and half an eye turned on the body below.

He fell about halfway down. He was lucky in that the ravine wall was much less steep at that point, unlucky in that he tumbled and rolled right toward the body.

Jeff landed not five feet away from the corpse. The breath was knocked out of him so thoroughly that he couldn't even yell. He scrambled up onto his rump and crabbed backward, away from the cadaver, his eyes and mouth wide open.

The cadaver rolled over and looked at him. Jeff's lungs found air again and he let out a long, piercing yell.

———

It took Jeff only a moment or two to recompose himself and grow embarrassed. He was glad there was no one around, except the injured man himself, to have heard his yell. For a second there he'd actually perceived this man as an animated corpse, ready to rise up and eat him alive like some wicked ghost in one of those ghastly stories his late grandfather used to tell him when he was little, then laugh about when Jeff's mother scolded him for "scaring the poor boy."

Jeff knelt at the injured man's side. The poor fellow was so bruised and dirty that Jeff couldn't even guess his age.

"How'd you get so banged up, mister?"

A groan came in answer. Then he whispered coarsely: "I had some help."

"Did you get robbed?"

"I did."

"Mighty sorry. At least they didn't kill you."

"I'd feel better right now if they had."

"Any broke bones?"

The young man moved a little, experimentally, slowly and with evident pain. He shook his head. "Don't think so."

"That's good. Let me take a look at your eyeballs. My father, Will Cornwell, who you've probably heard of, told me you can tell from looking into somebody's eyeballs whether or not their skull has been cracked." Jeff pried open the man's eyes and stared into them. Dark blue eyes, the kind that probably would be rather piercing under normal circumstances. A little bit bloodshot at the moment, owing to the beating. Jeff frowned like some evaluating physician, then shook his head.

"Your skull ain't cracked, I don't think," he said. "You're lucky there, too."

"Where am I?"

"A ways from the town of Pactolas, which I'm sure you've probably heard of."

"Sorry, young fellow, but I ain't heard of either Pactolas nor your father."

"I'm surprised. Everybody's heard of Will Cornwell. Well, most everybody. And them that ain't at least know his brother Bax." He proudly added: "Bax Cornwell is my uncle."

"Good. Boy, you going to get me some help? Is there a doctor around here?"

"There's one in Pactolas, though he ain't a doctor all the time. Sometimes he's just a miner like everybody else."

"I'd like to meet this man, soon."

"You stay there. I'll run home and get help as quick as I can. My father's gone to Pactolas, but he'll be back soon. I'll bring him here. He'll know what to do. My father always knows what to do. What's your name, anyway?"

"Matthew. Matthew Fadden. Most call me Matt."

"Fadden! Same name as old Temple Fadden!"

"That's right."

"I bet I've heard a thousand stories about Temple Fadden! They say he could outfight an army of wild Indians, all by himself, and that he once gunned down a whole nest ' of outlaws, twenty of them, all by himself."

"Don't believe everything you're told."

"I wasn't told that one, I read it. I still got the book at home. Yellow-backed novel. I keep it hid from my mother because she says dime novels are trash. But I don't think they are. I like 'em. Read every one I can get my hands on."

"You ought to be obeying your mother. What's your name, boy?"

"Jeff Cornwell. I'm one of *the* Cornwells."

"Reckon you could help me sit up against that tree there while I wait for that help you're going to bring me?"

"If you want to try."

They did try, and succeeded, though Matthew Fadden suffered some in the process.

"Thank you, Jeff," Matthew said.

"Yes, sir, Mr. Fadden."

"Call me Matt."

"You ain't kin to Temple Fadden, are you, Matt?"

"Matter of fact, I am."

"No! How are you kin?"

"He's my father."

"You're a-lying!"

"No. Honest to goodness. My father is Temple Fadden himself."

Jeff Cornwell stared at Matt in awe. Without another word he turned and scrambled up out of the ravine, and ran hard all the way to his house.

CHAPTER 2

Riding in the back of a jolting wagon through this rough portion of the Montana Territory made Matt Fadden feel like he was being beaten all over again.

He was self-conscious as he rode through Pactolas, which was a much bigger and more developed town than he'd expected to find in this part of the territory. Sitting up in the back of the wagon, he felt like some odd and interesting specimen deliberately displayed for all to see—a thoroughly beaten and bruised specimen on his way to the local sawbones, probably perceived by those who stared at him as some kind of no-account brawler who came out on the worst end of his last fight. Which, come to think of it, was pretty much exactly what he was.

Will Cornwell was much the image of his son, though of course much older, and a little more stoutly made. When Jeff had brought him down to meet Matt, the man had seemed more than a bit skeptical about Matt really being the son of Temple Fadden, one of America's most famous frontiersmen since Crockett. But he'd been friendly and helpful, and used his miner's muscles to give battered and hurting Matt some good assistance out of the ravine and into the wagon.

The wagon at last lurched to a stop outside a cabin with a shingle above the door, upon which was one word:

PHYSICIAN

The doctor was a crusty gent, older than Matt had anticipated, with thick hair that once had been blond but now was mostly white, retaining only enough yellow to make it look faded and sickly. His callused hands bore testimony to the fact that he was as much miner as doctor.

When he'd finished Matt's examination, he stood back a pace or two and simply stared at him with brows knitted. "Son, how in the devil do you come to be so battered up?"

"I told you. I got jumped by some fellows who had a grudge against me. They beat the stuffing out of me and threw me in a ravine, and took everything I had."

"That accounts for the current injuries. But you've got plenty of old ones, too. What do you do for a living?"

"Mostly I drift around, here and there. Do whatever work I can find, that mostly being fighting."

"The behind-the-saloon variety, I suppose."

"Generally. My father happens to be a famous man with a reputation. There's plenty of people interested in seeing if they can get the best of the son of a man the tall tales say can throw a lariat around the hook of a quarter moon."

"Uh-huh. Your famous father being Temple Fadden, I take it."

"That's right."

"Hmph."

"I take it that you don't believe me."

"You're who you are, and not who you aren't, whatever I believe about it. What you are to me is a patient I need to give some stern advice to: Quit this fighting. Find another way to make a living. You're doing some significant damage to yourself, son, and that's just judging from what I can see outside. If I could look inside you I daresay I'd find you none the better there."

"A man has to make a living however he can."

"There's better ways. Don't you grow weary of being beaten up all the time, sore and wore out?"

"I'd say I feel no worse than the average miner. And I'm not sure mining is any safer way to make a living than what I do. Besides, I win most of my fights, Doc."

"You didn't win the last one. If they'd beat you much more, you might be on the undertaker's slab instead of here."

"This last fight wasn't really a fight. It was an ambush. They robbed me, too."

The doctor would argue with him no further. "Took everything you had, I guess?"

"Afraid so."

"Nothing left for such things as paying doctor bills, eh?"

"I'll pay you, Doc. But you may have to give me a little time to find a way."

"Don't worry. Will out yonder already told me he'd pay if you couldn't. He's a good man, son. You're fortunate to have been found by the Cornwells. They're not a perfect family, nobody is, but much good has been done in this town for people they take a liking to."

"If they've taken a liking to me, I'm glad. But I'm not fond of taking anybody's charity."

"Then you can work for him or do something to pay him back."

"I will. And when I find the ones who beat me, I'll do some paying back on their account, too."

The doctor shook his head. "I'll say this: Whether you're really Temple Fadden's son or just some drifter making wild claims to stir things up, you've surely got the same kind of recklessness about you that folks attribute to old Temple. Now let me pack you up some salve for those bruises and cuts. On the house. And you go find yourself a bed and rest up until you've healed a bit. Don't go trying to track down and pay back anybody just now. The shape you're in at the moment, my little granddaughter could whip you. You got a place to stay? Then you are indeed on the Cornwells' good side. Take some advice: Stay there."

"What are you getting at?"

"Just giving wise counsel. Stay on the Cornwell's good side. Around here it's where you want to be."

———

Matt finished his last bite of beef and dabbed at his lips with a checkered napkin.

"No, sir, I just can't do that," he said to Will Cornwell, who was seated across the table from him. "You've already done too much for me. You took me to the doctor, paid my bill there, brought me here to your home and fed me—mighty good victuals, by the way, Miz Cornwell—I can't have you doing even more without being overly beholden to you."

"We've got room, Mr. Fadden. You'll not be in the way. There's a bed in that back room that never gets used. You're welcome to it until you've healed up some."

"I can't keep imposing on the kindness of strangers, sir."

"We ain't strangers anymore. We know each other. Besides, where else would you go? Your money's stolen. You can't afford a hotel room."

"I got a few dollars left that were stuck in my boot."

"If that's all you have, you don't need to spend it on some hotel."

"I wasn't raised to make myself an imposition on good people, Mr. Cornwell."

"Please, call me Will. And quit arguing with me. We're putting you up for a while, and if you just can't bear to have folks be kind to you, you can pay me back later, when you're on your feet again. That fair enough?"

Constance Cornwell, Will's dark-haired wife, chimed in her support. "You may as well give in, Mr. Fadden. If my husband decides to do you a kindness, he'll find a way to do it whether you want it or not."

"You folks are mighty kind to a sorry old drifter who don't deserve it."

"We try to be good Christian folks. Now, let's hush about all that. Connie, we got some of that pie left? Let's all have a slice, and then we'll get Matt here back to bed. Let him get started with that healing up."

Matt decided to argue no further. The truth was he really didn't have means to pay for his own lodging just now, and he badly felt the need of bed rest. His body was beginning to seriously hurt, and it was all he could do to sit in his chair and eat. His body was punishing him not only for this most recent beating but for all the others he'd allowed to be inflicted upon it in the name of making a living.

He made it through only half a slice of pie before he had to give up. He headed for bed with Jeff Cornwell propping him up on one side and Will on the other.

CHAPTER 3

H e slept. But the aching of his body made sleep fitful, and full of dreams.

In his dreams he was fighting. Fists swinging, pounding flesh, sweat running and flying, mixing with blood. Men gathered all around, hooting and calling and roaring.

Even in his sleep he was living out the life he knew, and if it wasn't much of a life, at least it was a living. There weren't many who could defeat him man to man, not with the fighting skills his father had taught him. But even the progeny of an American frontier legend couldn't defeat men who attacked him three at a time.

He groaned and rolled over, trying in vain to find a position that took away his pain. But nothing he could do could ease his discomfort, and his rest was fitful the whole night through.

———

When he woke up he found himself staring into the intent and frowning face of a girl of about eight. She was kneeling beside his bed, studying his face closely. She had an open and forthright look about her, and it didn't seem to bother her at all when he opened his eyes and looked right back at her.

He knew as soon as he saw her that this was another Cornwell. The girl strongly resembled Jeff.

"Hello," Matt said.

"So you're the son of Temple Fadden," she said without a trace of meekness.

"That's right."

"I don't know that I believe that. That's a pretty dadgum wild story to come telling folks."

"It's the truth."

"My father ain't so sure about it either. But he says it don't really matter, that we'll be good to you no matter whether your father's famous or not."

"Your father, I'm guessing, is Will Cornwell?"

"That's right."

"I thought so. I can tell from your looks. You bear a resemblance to Will. People say I look like my father, too."

She gave a little snort. "You don't look like no picture of Temple Fadden I ever seen! You got some muscle on you, but Temple Fadden is as stout as a barn, big as a grizzly bear, and three times as strong."

"You've been seeing a bunch of dime-novel pictures that don't look anything like the real man. And yes, he's strong, but even a small grizzly bear would say grace over him and have him for breakfast. What's your name, young lady?"

"Florence. Florence Maria Cornwell. How'd you get beat up so bad?"

"I get beat up for a living."

"No you don't!"

"Well, no. Mostly I beat up other people. I'm not proud of this, Florence, but I make my living going from place to place and fist fighting for money. There's a surprising number of folks out there who are downright eager to try their hand at beating the fire out of the son of an American legend."

"My father says you probably claim to be Temple Fadden's son just to get attention and to make people want to fight you so you'll make more money. He says he's seen your kind before. But he also says he kind of likes you."

Matt could see now whom he needed to turn to if ever he wanted the straight truth about the Cornwell family. This fearless young lady minced no words.

"I can see how he might think I'm a fraud. But I'm afraid it's really true. Temple Fadden really is my father."

"You must not be as strong as he is, then. He'd have never gotten beat up like you did. There ain't nobody that could beat up Temple Fadden. Except maybe Davy Crockett hisself, if he wasn't dead."

"Temple Fadden's been beat up many a time, Florence. I've hauled his drunk and battered carcass back from many a barroom when he'd had too much to drink and boasted a little too much to them not in the humor to hear it. Temple Fadden is as human a man as they come. Despite everything those dime novels say, I've yet to see him really throw a rope around the moon."

"Shows how much *you* know. You can't print it in a book if it ain't true, mister. There's a law about that. Jeff's got a book that says Temple Fadden once defended a whole fort against an Indian attack, all by himself. And he killed three Mexican outlaws with one bullet."

"Honey, Temple Fadden is a talented man, and his biggest talent is selling himself. You know who wrote the first dime novel about Temple Fadden?"

"Yes. Mister Leroy V. Ketchum. He writes them all. My father says he must be able to crank out books like he was churning ice cream."

"Temple Fadden *is* Leroy V. Ketchum. Or he was. He wrote the first three books himself under the Ketchum name, then hired himself some writers to keep it all going. They all use the name of Leroy Ketchum. But there's really no such fellow. Those books are such lies that they don't even tell you the truth about the author's name."

Florence shook her head as if saddened by this poor, misled wretch now speaking to her. She clearly didn't buy a thing he was saying. "Momma's right. She told Pa that it's a shame that somebody has to go around fighting and brawling just to keep himself fed, and make up big tales about himself, too."

"Your momma said that?"

"Yes."

"So I reckon she's not persuaded that I'm really Temple Fadden's son."

"I think she's got her doubts. But she says it don't matter, that you're still one of God's wayward children and we're obliged to care for you."

"Well, you know what I think about your momma? I think she's a fine woman to have taken in a man like me, and fed him and put him up to heal. And I think your father's a fine man for the same reason. And I understand why folks are slow to believe me when I say who I am. And you know what? I agree with your momma in part of what she says about me. It is a shame that I make a living the way I do."

"Then why do you do it?"

"Because it works. Because it's what I'm used to. I ain't found much other way. A man gets off track with his life sometimes and just can't figure out how to get back on it again. And the truth is, most of the time things go pretty well for me. I win most of my fights."

"You sure didn't win your last one. You look like you've been run over by a coal train."

"That's because I was trailed by three men I'd whipped the fire out of in three fair fights, one after the other, and they didn't like it. They tracked me and ganged up on me. I can whip about anybody in a fair fight, but three against one ain't odds anybody can handle. Two of them held me while the biggest one pounded me to a pulp. Things like that happen sometimes. It's a hazard of my profession."

"Momma says she's going to pray for you so that you'll turn away from living such a sorry and dangerous life."

"I'd appreciate that. Maybe you can pray for me too. I'll bet the good Lord will listen extra hard to the prayer of a fine young lady such as you."

"I will pray for you."

"Thank you." Matt thrust his hand out from under the covers and offered it to Florence to shake. The girl grasped it and shook it firmly.

"I like you, Florence Cornwell. Pleased to have made your acquaintance today."

"Likewise."

"Tell me something: Is your momma unhappy with me being here? Because if she is, I'll crawl out of here right now and do my healing up in somebody's barn loft. It wouldn't be the first time I've done that."

"You don't need to do that. Momma's glad to have you here. She likes to take care of folks in need. It's the Cornwell way to do that. We ain't mean trash like the Packards."

Matt didn't know who the Packards were, and didn't ask because he was growing weary of talking. But he liked this forthright little girl and hoped she'd come around for more conversations. He decided that the Cornwells must indeed be a very fine clan. It showed in their kindness to a drifting stranger, and in the cleverness and self-confidence of their offspring. If Florence were a few years older, she might be just the kind of female who Matt Fadden could consider courting for a wife.

"You come around and visit some more," Matt said. He sniffed the air. "What's that wonderful smell, by the way? You're young to be wearing perfume, ain't you?"

She laughed. "You silly thing! That don't smell nothing like perfume. That's the oven you smell. Momma's baking biscuits. She makes them big as a cat's head."

"Well, bless her heart. Maybe you can sneak me one when they're done."

"I will. Good day to you, Mr. Matthew Fadden, or whoever you really are."

"Good day, Miss Florence Maria Cornwell."

CHAPTER 4

THREE DAYS LATER

Matt fidgeted on the hard pew and squinted at the hymn-book in his hand. His lips moved, but it was mostly for show. The hymn the congregation was singing all around him was strange to him. Simply being in church felt strange.

He could tell he was receiving a lot of subtle attention from those around him, and this was no surprise. Though three days of rest and healing had made him feel better, it had done little for his appearance. His bruises were at their darkest; he looked like a matador who'd challenged a train instead of a bull.

He held up the hymnbook and continued pretending to sing, meanwhile casting his eyes around the church and taking note of an oddity of this congregation: Most of its members resembled one another. He could tell by mere observation that this was a congregation with a preponderance of Cornwells. Given what he'd learned about this town during his time in the Will Cornwell home, this was not unexpected.

He'd learned that Pactolas was dominated by the Corn-well family. In particular, it was dominated by Will's older brother, Baxter, or "Bax," who was at this moment booming out the bass line to the hymn from the front pew. Bax Corn-well was a big man, broad and muscular, and possessed of a dominating presence that marked him as king of his clan. He was virtually king of the town, too, Matt had gathered. Bax Cornwell possessed the best claims and owned quite a few of Pactolas' businesses besides. And his brother Will was appar-ently not far behind him in local prominence.

However, the Cornwell dominance of Pactolas was apparently due mostly to Bax, not Will. Florence, who had become Matt's best source of information about the family and town, had told him how Bax was the first man to strike color here in these mountains, and made the first and best claims. He'd then moved swiftly to bring in his kin to join him. It was a major effort, transplanting dozens of Cornwells all the way from their native Arkansas Ozarks to this mining region of the Montana Territory, but Bax had pulled it off. Suddenly a family that had struggled with poverty in Arkansas was an established clan in a town mostly their own, and though Pactolas was small and rough, it showed promise of moving beyond the mining-town stage and becoming a real and maybe permanent entity. Should that happen, and should the gold hold out and the various Cornwell business concerns hold out along with it, this family was poised to become truly wealthy and powerful, the kind of family to generate senators and congressmen and governors. Matt was duly impressed.

The congregation at last reached the final verse of the seemingly endless hymn. Matt shifted his weight and looked forward to abandoning this uncomfortable pew— though that would happen only at the far end of a sermon that hadn't even started yet, and which would probably run even longer than the singing.

He felt the eyes upon him and knew he was watched for more reasons than his colorful bruises. People here now knew that he was indeed the true son of Temple Fadden, and that alone made him fascinating. Even Florence was treating him with deference now that the truth was verified.

It was Bax who had settled the issue. Bax, it seemed, had actually met the famed old frontiersman Temple Fadden a few years ago, and when he saw Matt for the first time had declared that his resemblance to the man was too remarkable to be coincidental. A few questions, a few answers from Matt, and any lingering doubt had been put aside: Matthew Fadden really *was* the offspring of America's most famous living legend. Once Bax declared it so, all the other Cornwells believed it, and Matt's status in their eyes rose. He went from being a drifting saloon brawler who foisted off a false identity for the sake of money, to being the blood kin of a celebrated man, and therefore a celebrated man himself.

The hymn ended, a prayer followed, and the Cornwell-dominated congregation sank down onto the wooden pews. The pastor went to the pulpit and smiled out across the congregation. His look, too, was that of a Cornwell; when he spoke his accent was that of an Arkansan. This was a family church, no doubt about it. A Cornwell minister overseeing a Cornwell congregation.

The jovial preacher greeted the congregation and embarrassed Matt a little by singling him out as a "most welcome and noteworthy visitor." Matt nodded his thanks for the smiles and greetings that followed, then sank farther down into his pew.

The preacher's joviality diminished significantly as the sermon began. Matt's mind wandered initially, but eventually the preacher's words began to register with him and he noted that the sermon seemed dominated by the theme of troubled times, danger, worry, and the need to do justice when a wrong has been done. It was the kind of sermon that might be preached somewhere where war had just broken out, or some major crime had been committed. As Matt looked around, he noted that the congregation was solemn, many frowning, some of the women dabbing at their eyes, the children looking disturbed and uncertain.

At last the service ended, with Bax Cornwell called upon to pray. He stood and prayed for five minutes straight, and though Matt had not heard an abundance of prayers in his life, this one seemed a little odd to him. Bax implored the Almighty repeatedly for protection from the "enemies who wrongly beset us," and the "evil that follows us, Lord, like an undeserved curse." Many a murmured "Amen" and "Yes, Lord" rumbled through the congregation as Bax prayed.

Later that day, after a good meal at the Will Cornwell family table with Bax and numerous other Cornwells present as guests, Matt joined the menfolk out in the yard for cigars and pipes. At one point the group headed for Will's barn to look at a colt born the week before, but Matt stayed behind, Jeff lingering as well.

"Jeff, let me ask you something: Is everything well with your family?"

"What do you mean?"

"In church today, it just seemed there was a burden there you could feel, something big and worrisome. The sermon and prayers and all seemed focused on trouble and enemies and so on."

Jeff grew uncomfortable to hear this. "We don't talk a lot about family business with strange—uh, with outside folks, you know. It really ain't nothing you should have to concern yourself with."

"I ain't trying to intrude into your family affairs. I don't believe in doing that. I just felt some concern for you folks, that's all. You've been mighty kind to me, and I hope nothing bad is wrong."

"There ain't nothing wrong except the same kinds of

problems we've always had, even before we came to the Territory. I really ain't supposed to talk about it."

"That's right," a young female voice said from behind Matt, startling him. He turned to see Florence, who had drifted up from somewhere, silent as a ghost. "When we talk about the feud with folks outside the family, Pa gets upset about it."

"Florence!" Jeff scolded. "Watch what you say!"

"I didn't say nothing I shouldn't have."

"Yes, you did. You mentioned the you-know-what. Now you'd best hush."

Feud. That's what she'd said, that was the "you-know-what," and Matt had taken due note of it.

Florence grew flustered; she realized that she'd made a blunder. She tried to brush it off. "It don't matter. Everybody knows about the... the you-know-what anyway."

"If I told Pa, he'd be mad."

"Don't tell him, Jeff. Please don't."

"I think I will."

Matt spoke up. "Jeff, I hope you won't tell. It was my fault for being too inquisitive. I was wrong to poke my nose into your family's business. I didn't even really catch what Florence said." The latter statement was a lie, but Matt wanted to help out Florence.

"See? He didn't even hear! Ain't nothing for you to tattle about," Florence snapped at her brother. She turned haughtily and headed on around the house and away from them.

"That dang sister of mine drives me loco," Jeff said. "Can't keep her mouth shut to save her life. It keeps her in trouble with Pa. If there's one thing Pa don't favor, it's Cornwells talking too much about family business with folks from the outside."

"She seems a fine girl to me," Matt said. "A lot of spirit and life about her."

"She just don't know when to shut up, that's all. And you really did hear what she said, didn't you?"

"No. No, I didn't." But Matt could tell Jeff knew better.

Matt almost wished he hadn't heard, though, because now he was intrigued but wasn't free to ask questions. A feud implied trouble between two rival groups. One was obviously the Cornwell clan. Who would be the other? Another family, maybe? Matt had heard all the old cliches about feuding Ozark families. But this Ozark family was now in Montana, a long way from their home environment.

Matt picked up a twig and chewed on its end. He knew just enough to be intrigued, and to realize that he'd intruded into territory in which he wasn't welcome.

"Can I ask you something, Matt?" Jeff said.

"Ask away."

"When I found you I didn't find no horse, no bags, no guns. But there were horse tracks on the ground near there. Did the folks that beat you steal your horse, too?"

"They did. Not only my horse but also my saddlebags, my bedroll, my guns. Everything."

"Reckon your stolen stuff is still close by somewhere?"

"I doubt it. I'd say it was took back to Big Fork. That's where I'd come from when I was followed and jumped."

"Will you go back to get it?"

"I doubt I'd find it. It's probably been sold off and taken away by now."

"Makes you mad, I bet."

"I ain't happy about it. But there's only one thing I lost that I care much about. That was my Henry rifle. It was a gift to me from my father. I'd sure like to get it back."

"Do you and your father get on well with each other?"

"I'll be truthful, Jeff: It ain't easy sometimes to be the son of Temple Fadden. He's a good man, maybe not the big hero that the dime novels make him out to be, but still a good man... though a hard one. He won't put up with nonsense—and I gave him plenty of it growing up. I guess that's why I took off like I did, and struck out on my own."

"Ain't it hard, just going from one place to another and getting beat up?"

"I don't get beat up often. I win most of my fights. It's a talent I seem to have."

"Don't you make a lot of enemies?"

"A few. But most of the ones I beat end up being friendly about it, believe it or not. Because of who my father is. They kind of take pride in having fought with the blood kin of Temple Fadden, even if they lose. I guess it kind of confirms the myth for them. They go off telling how bad I whipped them, and how if Temple Fadden's son is that good a fighter, old Temple himself must be everything they say he is, and they seem to like believing that. Jeff, I've beat the very pulp out of a lot of men and had them turn around and buy me a round of drinks right after, slapping me on the shoulder and all that. There ain't no stranger a creature crawling over this earth than the human creature, Jeff."

They were silent awhile. Jeff spoke next. "You ought to ask my Uncle Bax to put the word out about your rifle. If it does still happen to be around these parts, he might be able to find it for you."

"From everything I can see, your Uncle Bax has most of the power and influence around Pactolas."

"He does. He's the powerfulest man in town, and the closest thing to a rich one. By now I reckon he really *is* rich. Hey, want me to ask him to put the word out that you're looking for your stolen rifle?"

"Couldn't hurt, I guess. Why, does he have connections to help such a thing be found?"

"He's got connections to do about anything he wants. Tell me about the rifle."

Matt described it, particularly noting a peculiar nick in

the stock and the initials "T.F." that his father had scratched onto the butt plate back before he gave the rifle to his son. "I figure that I ain't likely to get it back," Matt said. "But I'd sure like to. It's one of the few good things my father ever gave me."

CHAPTER 5

Matt, still sore and injured, retired early that night. Just before he reached over to extinguish his light, Jeff stuck his head in the door.

"I told Uncle Bax about the rifle and he's going to put up a reward for its return," Jeff said. "He says he don't think it will be easy to find, but you never know."

"I appreciate it, Jeff. Maybe I'll get lucky and get it back."

"Good night, Matt."

"Good night."

Matt lay in bed thinking about the missing rifle, then about his stolen horse and possessions. He was accustomed to owning little, but now he owned virtually nothing at all. And he wasn't sure what he could do about it. Even a drifter needed a horse and saddle, weapons to protect himself and hunt with, a change or two of clothing, personal goods, and such as that.

It looked like Matt Fadden was going to have to rebuild, as it were, from the ground up. Find some work, make some money. But how long would it take to earn enough to buy a horse and saddle? The few dollars he had made for a mighty meager pile; he'd have to rebuild his humble fortunes almost from the ground up. How could he earn enough to replace his rifle and pistol? He'd have to win a lot of fights behind a lot of saloons to get that kind of money... and how could he travel around to do that without a horse? Besides, he'd not be in shape for fighting for some time yet.

He couldn't impose on the Cornwells forever. They'd already been saints enough just to give aid and lodging to a stranger for as long as they had.

Matt's mind raced, and sleep was slow in coming.

A WEEK LATER

Bax Cornwell, Ozark mountain man turned rising mining town mogul, kept his offices above the big mining supply store that bore his name. Matt, by now much recovered from his beating but still a bit sore and with fading but lingering bruises, paused at the front of the Cornwell Mining Supply Enterprise and pondered the potential future of Bax Cornwell. Should Pactolas prove to be one of those fortunate mining realms where the gold did not run out too quickly and where other forms of commerce had time to develop a toehold, Cornwell could be well on the way to major riches. Or, if the gold played out, he might look back on these days as the peak of his success.

Either way, Bax was better off than Matt himself was. At least he was making progress in life, something Matt hadn't begun to do at all. *You're plumb sorry,* his father had often said to him. *Have you got no ambition about you at all? Are you going to bring down my good name by being no more than a lousy saloon brawler?*

It was not easy to be the son of Temple Fadden.

Well, maybe he was indeed "sorry," as his father put it,

but he did believe a man should try to pay his own debts. It was that conviction that had led him here.

An exterior staircase led up to the second floor office.

Matt trudged heavily up the stairs, deliberately making noise so that Bax would know somebody was coming. He reached the landing and rapped firmly on the door.

Bax had already seen him through the window.

"Come in, Mr. Fadden!" he called. "Door's open!"

Matt entered a plainly decorated but nicely built office that took up virtually the entire upper floor of the building, home to one of several Cornwell businesses in Pactolas. The walls were made of heavy sawn lumber, painted white; the ceiling was white as well, but the floor was a milky yellow. The paintings and ornamentation that hung about the walls were not artwork selected by a man of refined tastes, and in fact looked like the same kinds of paintings that typically decorated the saloons Matt knew so well. Even so, they had been placed by someone with an instinctive sense of aesthetic balance, and their overall effect was appealing.

Bax Cornwell was in the midst of lighting a large cigar. He waved Matt over toward a chair that sat atop a heavy bearskin rug spread in front of the big and battered desk. Matt sat down and waited for Bax to finish firing up, and got the feeling that the cigar-lighting was being done for his benefit—Bax using the cigar as a prop to enhance his image as a big and important man of business.

Bax smiled at him through a cloud of aromatic smoke, then pushed back in his chair and propped his feet up on the desktop with practiced casualness.

"Good day, Mr. Fadden. To what do I owe the pleasure of this visit?" Bax Cornwell, noted Matt, sounded like a man trying hard to throw off his natural accent, in his case the backwoods tones of an Ozark resident. It wasn't working very well.

"Morning, Mr. Cornwell. And please just call me Matt."

"Matt, then. What can I do for you?" Matt noticed that Bax hadn't invited him in turn to call him by his first name.

"Well, sir, I came to see you because of your brother and his family."

"Something's wrong?"

"Oh, no. It's just that they've been mighty kind to me, taking me in and giving me lodging and care, and me being nothing but a stranger to them. And because of having had all my possessions stolen, I'm a penniless stranger, and can't do anything to repay them. And until now I've been too beat up to really do any work. Now, though, I'm a good deal better, and..."

"And maybe you're interested in finding some work to do," Bax finished for him.

"That's it, sir. I thought if by chance there was work for me, I could earn a bit to recompense your brother for his kindness, and get myself a bit of money laid aside so I could eventually get myself back on my feet again."

"Well, that's noble. What kind of work are you looking for?"

"Anything I can handle. I'm still trying to get all my strength back, but I believe I could clerk in a store or do something along that line, and before long I'll be healed up all the way and able to do anything. And I ain't asking for charity, sir. Not a bit of it. I'm looking for a real job. I can go back to saloon fighting before long, but the truth is, I'd like to try something a little less hazardous. I came to you because I know you're a successful man, with a large share of business in this town. I figured maybe you'd know where I might find what I'm looking for."

Bax seemed to like hearing himself called successful. He took a slow drag on his cigar with a look of satisfaction on his face, and leaned back to blow smoke at the white ceiling. A circle of discoloration directly above him bore testimony to many prior cigars smoked in this same spot.

Bax sat with head tilted back for nearly a minute. Matt actually began to wonder if he'd fallen asleep. But suddenly Bax straightened, put his elbows on his desk, and leaned intently toward Matt.

"Ambition, young man. Ambition! It's a fine thing, ambition. It's what leads a man out of the hills of Arkansas and all the way across a nation so he can find himself the first gold strike in a region. It's what makes that man secure all the finest claims, hire himself an army of miners to work them, and also establish himself as the first and leading merchant of the services needed to make a town a town. It's what leads him to bring scores of his own kin after him and reestablish them in a place where they can make a fortune for themselves, and—it was hoped, at least—live with some measure of peace and security not known in their home region. Ambition! It has built me into what I am, and I see the spark of it in you. I like that!"

"Thank you." Matt wondered where this pomposity was leading. He'd asked for work but so far was getting only an inspirational talk. It was slightly amusing: His own father had spent most of Matt's younger years informing his son that there was nothing good in him, no drive for success, no hope for a good future, no potential at all. And now here was a man Matt hardly knew telling him what a fine and ambitious fellow he was.

"I'm intrigued by you, son," Bax went on. "Your father is a famous man indeed. Quite a famous man!"

Matt said nothing. Bax, like everyone else, wasn't really intrigued by Matt, but by his parentage. Even here in this remote corner of the continent, Temple Fadden inevitably overshadowed his son.

Amazing how a few tall tales and exaggerated dime novels could lend such fame to a man who Matt knew really didn't fully deserve it all. Temple Fadden was a capable hunter, had managed to do a couple of heroic things during the war with Mexico, and had the innate skill of self-promotion, but beyond that he was an average man, a bit of a drinker, and certainly not a particularly good father.

"Tell me a bit about your father," Bax said. "I have a reason for asking."

Matt drew in a slow breath and readied himself to lie again. He'd gotten used to it, though he'd never enjoy it—but he'd learned that people didn't want to know the truth about legends. They simply wanted those legends reconfirmed.

"He's a powerful, wise, capable man... pretty much what you've heard," Matt said. "I've never seen so fine a shot, so good a fighter, or so brave a soul. But he doesn't think of himself as anything special. Just an average man."

Matt mentally added: *An average man who sits and reads through the dime novels about himself time and time again, never growing tired of them and eventually coming to believe everything they say.*

"Where does he live now?"

"Back on his spread in Texas. He raises a few cattle, trades horses. Puts flowers every day on my mother's grave whenever they're in bloom."

That anecdote was true. Matt pondered with some bitterness the fact that Temple Fadden had made his wife's life so miserable that she'd actually not much dreaded going to the grave he now somewhat hypocritically festooned with daily blossoms. Death was an escape from an insufferably self-centered man.

"Does he ever travel? Might he come to the Territory here, for example?"

Matt began to see where this was going. Bax probably wanted to open a new feed store, or something, and have Temple Fadden himself there to stand around in his fringed buckskin coat, grin at folks, shake hands, and show off the pistol he used to single-handedly win a fight against twelve

Mexican soldiers, and the knife he'd used to finish off a Comanche warrior about to kill an entire family. Matt knew the truth about those tall tales, but kept it to himself.

"He pretty much stays put in Texas," Matt said.

"Ah. I see. But you... you're his blood kin, and you're here, very far from Texas."

"Yes."

"*Um-huh.*" Bax rubbed his chin thoughtfully.

Matt winced inwardly. He could see it now:

MEET THE SON OF TEMPLE FADDEN! SHAKE THE HAND OF THE PROGENY OF AMERICA'S GREATEST LIVING HERO! BUY FEED AT DISCOUNTED PRICES TODAY ONLY!

Bax drew on the cigar again, then through the aromatic cloud said, "I think I might be able to find some work for you, Matt. I'll give it some thought and get back to you. I know where to find you, and I'll let you know."

"Thank you, sir. It would be a pleasure to be able to recompense your brother and his family for all the kindness they're showing me."

"Will wouldn't demand it. Thanks in large part to me and my business successes, he does well for himself. And he's the kind of man to be good to the downtrodden and make no demand of recompense."

"That's good of him." Matt hid the disgust that Bax's arrogance roused in him. Bax reminded him in some ways of his father, though even Bax's swollen view of himself didn't reach the proportions of Temple Fadden's conceit. Temple Fadden had the art of self-worship perfected to a level never before achieved by humankind.

Matt rose to leave. "I'll not take any more of your time, sir. Thank you for seeing me this morning."

Bax waved the cigar at him as if to dismiss it all—Matt

had the impression that it was a practiced gesture, the kind of move a big and important man makes when performing before the downtrodden. "Glad to be of help to a man of such a famous bloodline. Family is important. A man's first duty is to his heritage and his kin."

Matt said nothing but tried to at least look agreeable. He supposed Bax was right, but given his own family experience it was difficult to work up much emotion about family loyalty. The only good things his father had given him were a strong physical constitution and a name that made it easy to earn money through saloon fighting.

"Good day, Mr. Cornwell," Matt said, turning to go.

But Bax wasn't finished. "About this matter of family, Matt: Keep in mind that when you work for a Cornwell, you should think of yourself *as* a Cornwell. .. and shape your personal loyalties accordingly."

A cryptic statement, but Matt dutifully nodded. Right now he was ready to go along with about anything.

"Just keep those loyalties in mind. It's an important thing in this town . . . and especially in my family. I've paid some high costs for the welfare of my family. Those who work for me are expected to give my family its due respect and loyalty. While you are with Will and his family, think of yourself as a Cornwell and behave accordingly."

"I'll keep that in mind, sir."

"I'll be in touch with you, Matt."

"Thank you."

Chapter 6

On the street, Matt leaned against a hitchpost and wondered exactly what had just happened. What he'd undertaken as a straightforward search for a job had turned into something a little odd and vague... He had the sense that he'd just earned himself some work, but he had no clue about what it was or when it would start. He did have a feeling in his gut, however, that he probably wasn't going to like it much.

What was all that about family and loyalty? Was Bax making some veiled reference to the feud that had come up in Matt's conversation with Jeff Cornwell's children?

Matt's attention was suddenly diverted by a loud thump out on the street, followed by a burst of rough laughter. A man had just fallen on his rump and landed squarely in a puddle, and a couple of other men, probably friends of the unfortunate, were having quite a good laugh over it. The fellow sitting in the manure pile didn't seem amused, however.

The man began to get up, and one of the pair laughing at him shoved him back roughly with his boot, making him splash down into the puddle again. The second laughing man laughed all the harder.

Matt lost his perception that the laughing pair were friends of the unfortunate. There had been too much roughness in that kick and too much vindictiveness in the tone of the laughter. Matt was now willing to bet that the fellow in the manure pile hadn't fallen in by accident.

"I'm getting up now," the victim said. "And don't you kick me again!"

"What'll you do about it if I do?" the other replied. "Whip on me with that peg-leg?"

Peg-leg? Matt noticed only then that the fallen man was missing his left leg from just below the knee. In its place was a wooden replacement.

The man rolled out of the water and away from the other two. He was just about to get upright when the man kicked him once again, making him fall. He missed the puddle this time, landing in the dirt. Grit stuck to the muck coating his trousers.

Someone hollered from the far boardwalk. "Here now, John, can't you leave him be?"

John turned and aimed a finger at the speaker. "You mind your own affairs, Henry. This ain't none of yours."

Matt decided right then that he'd do a little butting in of his own. He'd never been able to abide seeing someone mistreated. If these men intended to do their harassing in public, they'd get an equally public response.

The man with the missing foot tried to rise again, but his pegleg had loosened and turned out from under him. He went down hard, evoking roaring amusement from his highly entertained tormentors.

"You need to learn to tie that stick on a little better, Frank!" John said.

Suddenly John's partner leaned down, grabbed the loose

pegleg, and pulled it away. He held it up in his hand and waved it around, its leather straps dangling and flapping.

"Let me have that!" Frank said, scrambling up and balancing on his one foot.

The other man held it out toward Frank, then yanked it away and tossed it onto the top of a flat-roofed, false-fronted cafe. It clunked loudly as it landed there.

"Climb up and fetch it, you sorry dog. And next time, you watch your mouth before you talk smart to your betters."

Matt was somewhat apprehensive about doing what he knew he must do. Normally he wouldn't feel this way, but his situation was not normal: He was still feeling the effects of the beating he'd taken. Was he up to doing what it might take to deal with these two?

He'd find out soon. Matt took a deep breath and walked up to them. All three men, aggressors and victim together, looked at him warily.

"Hello, gentlemen," he said cheerfully. "What are you up to here?"

"Minding our own affairs."

"Really? What kind of affairs might they be? Seems to me you're being might unfriendly to this crippled man. Did I not just see his wooden leg get thrown up there on that roof? Now, how is a crippled man supposed to get back his pegleg when it's been thrown onto a roof?"

The man who'd tossed the leg stepped up and looked Matt in the eye. "Don't I know you? Didn't I see you in the church house on Sunday?"

Matt noticed something just then: There was about this man's face, and that of the other, something familiar... that Cornwell family resemblance. A glance at the second bullying man revealed the same. And the mention of church further indicated they were likely to be Cornwells.

Oh boy, Matt thought. *I may have stepped in it now. I've just shaken my fist in the face of the very family that's been so kind to me—right after getting a sermon from Bax about loyalty.*

He couldn't back down now, though. If the Cornwells had been good to him, they certainly weren't being good to this man, and him a cripple at that.

"I *was* in church. I seem to recall the preacher read from the Bible, which I think says we ought to be kind and tender-hearted to one another."

"You're the fellow who's been staying with Will."

"I am."

"Will's been mighty good to you."

"He has."

"He's kin of mine. He's kin of John here, too."

"Then let me say I have a high appreciation for your family. But what I see you doing here to this man doesn't fit with what I think of the Cornwell family as being. Will and his brood have treated me a lot better than you're treating this man. I'm asking you to leave him be."

"There's a reason for what we're doing."

The one-legged man spoke up. "It's because I work for the Packards. They hold me to be no more than a dog just because of who I work for."

"Shut up, you!" John commanded.

In normal circumstances Matt would lay out the two Cornwells and be done with it. But his sense of obligation to the family made this diplomatically clumsy. "Listen," he said. "I'm not here looking for trouble. I find trouble aplenty without looking for it. But I'd like to ask you as decent men, part of a fine family, to leave this fellow alone. It ain't right to pick on a man who's got but one foot and can't hope to defend himself against two able-bodied men like yourselves."

"There's things here you don't understand, son," John said, somewhat condescending. "There's history between Cornwell and Packard that goes way back many years, and many miles. A man who works for the Packards has no place in this town. There's a place for them on up the mountain a ways, and them and their hired help ought to stay there."

Matt almost wanted to back down. Bad blood between himself and the Cornwells was the last thing he needed. But he glanced at the pitiful crippled man and knew he couldn't back down. He couldn't live with himself if he did.

"Gentlemen," he said, "it's not my place to interfere with your family affairs. But I'm not the kind who can merely stand by while this sort of thing happens. I'd like to ask you, as friendly as I can, to leave this man alone. Please."

Soft-spoken words of that sort clearly were not what was expected, and it threw the two Cornwells off balance. John seemed to deflate a little bit before Matt's eyes.

"All right," he said. "Out of respect to a guest of Will's, we'll let this go for now. We've already made our point. This cur dog here knows he'd best not be seen on our streets again. Don't you, dog, huh?"

The cripple looked like he wanted to kill right now. Matt couldn't blame him. But the man swallowed his pride and made no response at all.

"Come on," John said to his companion. "Let's get on our way."

When they were gone, the crippled man hopped over to the boardwalk, with Matt's help, and sat down on it. He was red-faced—angry, embarrassed, humiliated. But he put out his hand toward Matt, who shook it.

"Thank you, sir," he said. "You probably saved me from a pretty bad trouncing. Name's McGeeter. Thomas McGeeter."

"I'm Matt Fadden."

"Why'd you do what you just did?"

"I never cared for bullies."

"But you're a friend of Will Cornwell's?"

"He and his family have been kind to me. I owe them a

debt for that. Whether I'm truly a friend in their eyes is hard to say. Maybe even harder after today."

McGeeter nodded, and glanced around him. The row on the street had drawn some attention, and even now a few gawking folks were eyeing him and Matt.

"Embarrassing, you know," he said. "It's a sorry thing to be a cripple and not able to stand up for yourself. There was a time when I'd have had both of them laid out on the street, spitting out their own teeth."

"I don't doubt it," Matt said. "How'd you lose the foot?"

"Mining accident, two years ago, over near Stalker's Creek. That's where I live."

"And you work for the family that the Cornwells are feuding with?"

"I do. Which, as you heard, makes me nothing more than a dog to them. The Cornwells think they own this town. I guess they *do* own it! Bax Cornwell especially. And that means anybody even associated with the Packards ain't welcome here."

"Thomas, I'm going to see if I can't get your pegleg back. You just sit here and I'll see about getting up on that roof."

"Too embarrassing to sit here in the public gaze," McGeeter said. "I'd buy you a whiskey if it wasn't so early. Would you let me buy you a cup of coffee instead?"

"Coffee would be mighty good. Come on. I'll help you into the cafe."

Matt left McGeeter safely seated at a table, then inquired of the proprietor about how to get to the roof. There was no staircase, he learned, but there did happen to be a painter's ladder leaned up against the back of the building. Matt went out, climbed the ladder, and found the peg-leg where it had landed.

As he stood atop the roof, he glanced over the rise of the false front toward the office of Bax Cornwell.

The glare on Bax's window made it hard to be sure, but

he believed he saw Bax on the other side of the glass, looking back at him.

Bax had probably watched the whole thing. Watched Matt butting into Cornwell business. Watched Matt befriending an employee of the Packards, foes of the Cornwell family.

He might have just shot his chance for finding a job. Oh, well. A man had to do what was right, sometimes, even at a cost to himself.

Matt descended the ladder and returned the peg-leg to Thomas McGeeter.

CHAPTER 7

The coffee was good, but demanded something to accompany it. McGeeter ordered biscuits and jam for each of them and they ate them slowly, washing them down with a third round of coffee.

It was inevitable, of course, that McGeeter would note that Matt's surname was the same as that of the famed Temple Fadden, and inevitable that he would react with astonishment as soon as Matt revealed that he was Temple's son.

"Are you joshing me? Temple Fadden himself?"

"Yep."

"I'll be! I'm all the more honored to know you, then, sir! Temple Fadden! Greater even than Crockett, in my book!"

"In his book, too. The only problem being that his book is of the dime-novel variety, where everything is exaggerated."

"Are you saying he's not the man people believe he is?"

Matt had long ago stopped trying very hard to set the record straight about his father. It just wasn't worth it, and made him look petty besides, so he let it go.

"He's a great man who's done some great things. Not an easy man to be son to, but there's no law against that."

"Well, I admire him. I wish I had half his grit."

"You do. I can tell you that Temple Fadden wouldn't be able to abide having but one foot with anything near the grace and attitude that you've got."

"Kind of you to say. But tell me something: Do you find it helps you to be the son of so famous a man?"

"In my line of work, I guess it does."

"That being?"

"I go from saloon to saloon, asking big idiot drunks whether they think they can outfight the son of America's most famous frontiersman. They take me up on it, I beat the stuffing out of them, take my money, and move on to do it all over again at the next town."

"You always win?"

"Almost always. The last round I had, though, I didn't. But that wasn't a fair fight." He briefly described how he'd been followed by a band of disgruntled losers and beaten half to death.

"Young Jeff Cornwell found me lying there half senseless," Matt said. "He and his family took me in and tended to me, put me up like I was one of their own kin. They've been good to me, which makes it all the more troubling to see how they are regarding this feud. There's two sides to that family, I guess. The good side that they showed me, and the bad, which shows itself anytime the matter of the Packards comes up."

"I hope that you helping me today doesn't cause you trouble."

Matt shrugged. "If it does, it does. You know, I'd just come out of the office of Bax Cornwell himself when I saw you having your encounter. I was asking him for work so I could have means to repay Will Cornwell for his kindness."

"Did Bax see what happened?"

"I think so."

McGeeter looked troubled. "I'm mighty sorry for it,

then. Bax Cornwell won't take kindly to you helping the likes of me. I've become a source of trouble for you."

"I did the right thing. I couldn't have walked away. Like I said: I despise bullies."

"You know, it's an odd thing about this feud. The Cornwells and Packards have a long history of hating each other, but for a good while they had a sort of peace between one another. They left each other alone. A year ago, you'd not have seen nothing happen like happened today. The Cornwells would have known me to be associated with the Packards, and they wouldn't have liked seeing me in their town, but nobody would have said nothing nor done nothing. But it ain't the same anymore."

"What's made the difference?"

"The death of Henry Packard. He was a grandson of the Stalker Packard, over in Stalker's Creek. He was found shot to death on a roadside. Of course, it was figured that the Cornwells were involved, especially in that Henry had argued with a couple of them a day or two before. Just some minor little squabble. Then, after Henry turned up dead, somebody took a shot at Joe Frank Cornwell when he was out hunting. Missed him by a good distance, and it could have been an accident with somebody else hunting, but the presumption was it was the Packards. Ever since then, things have been tense. A few more shots have been fired, and one Packard cousin slightly wounded... a shot fired from a distance. The feud seems to be breaking out again. Things could get mighty ugly if something don't happen to settle matters down again."

They talked a little more as they finished their biscuits, the subject drifting away from the unpleasant topic of the Cornwells and Packards. Somewhere along the way, Matt mentioned the rifle that had been stolen from him when he was beaten.

"You know," McGeeter said, "there's a man in Stalker's

Creek who I know deals in stolen guns. Give me a good description of that rifle and I'll see if I can't find it there."

Though the chances seemed slim to Matt, he gave McGeeter a thorough description. Even though his relationship with his father wasn't particularly good, it did trouble Matt greatly to have lost the rifle that his father had given him. It had always represented to him the best of their relationship, a mark of a time when the pair of them had gotten along.

"If I find it, I'll get word to you," McGeeter promised.

"Thank you," Matt said. "It would mean a lot to me to get that rifle back."

They finished their biscuits and coffee, shook hands, and went their separate ways.

CHAPTER 8

M att felt vaguely depressed after parting from McGeeter. What kind of town was this, where a crippled man could be abused right on the street in open daylight, with no one but an outsider like himself responding?

He took a walk around town, thinking about this place, the feud, Bax and the other Cornwells, and whether he ever really would get his missing gun back. He doubted it, in fact doubted if he'd ever run across McGeeter again. Best to go ahead and write off what he'd lost, and prepare to move ahead.

Matt decided that Pactolas would never be a town in which he could stay for the long term—not if what he'd seen today was typical of its ways. Nor were the Cornwells people he could become truly friendly with, if they were so mean and low as to victimize even cripples. Not if they were so intimidating to the people of the town they'd built that no one dared step up to protect the unoffending out of fear of drawing down the wrath of the Cornwells.

Matt decided to stay around this town only long enough

to fully heal, and to earn enough money to repay the Cornwells for their hospitality. Then he'd gladly move on.

Too bad, really. There'd been a part of him, barely acknowledged, that had been mulling over what it might be like to settle down. Give his roots time to grow into one patch of soil and stay there. Perhaps meet a good woman and marry, have some children.

Odd thoughts for a drifter like him. But they carried a certain enticement.

Not here, though. Not in Pactolas.

"Sir! A moment of your time?"

Matt turned at the sound of the voice and saw a tall, broadly made man lumbering toward him across the street. The fellow didn't look like a miner. Maybe a merchant. Then Matt noticed the pad of paper in his hand and the pencil behind his ear.

"Good day, Mr. Fadden," the man said, putting out his hand for a shake. "Robert Day's the name. *Pactolas Bi-Weekly Post*. Editor, chief writer, and printer, all rolled up into one package." He pumped Matt's hand a few moments. "Awfully pleased to meet you, sir."

"What can I do for you, Mr. Day?"

"Talk to me, I hope," he replied, yanking the pencil from behind his ear. "I was told about you by a few folks who said the son of America's most famous hero was visiting Pactolas. Quite a good story opportunity for my fledgling little newspaper, if you'll only agree to talk to me a few minutes."

"What is there to say?"

"Why, your father, of course. What it's like to be his son. What *he's* like. Your favorite anecdotes about him. All that kind of thing. You've done it before, I'm sure."

"Afraid not, sir. I don't tend to talk to the papers." Talking to the papers made it easier for his father to keep up with where he was, a process Matt didn't want to accommodate.

"But you'll make an exception for me, perhaps?"

"Sir, I make a practice of not talking about my father."

Day cocked his head and gave him a skeptical look. "Really? I was told that you talk about him a lot, and in fact use his reputation to get people to fight you in saloons and so on."

"I don't deny that. It's just that I prefer to do the talking on my own, and not in print."

"You're a famous man, sir—well, the son of a famous man, anyway—and you'd be of great interest to my readers. And I'm told you have become a good friend of the Cornwell family."

Matt wondered if this man was in the pocket of the Cornwells. Probably so, or he wouldn't be running a newspaper here.

"The Cornwells have been very kind to me."

"Can I quote you?"

"No. No story. Sorry."

Day lost his grin and his joviality. "Very well, then. If you won't cooperate, you won't cooperate. Even so, you can't control the news, sir. I can write about what I wish, you understand, with or without your permission."

"What's that supposed to mean?"

"That I can write about anyone in this town—straight from the horse's mouth, or if not, then from the mouths of other horses."

"Is that some kind of threat to make up a bunch of nonsense about me and print it?"

Day grinned in a way that made him look downright wicked. "There's been plenty of nonsense written about your father. Why not you?"

"You'd best write the truth if you write about me."

"Then you'd best tell me the truth."

"There's nothing to tell. I'm a drifter who minds his own business and likes to have other people mind theirs."

"I hear you were minding business other than your own a while ago. Quite bold of you, coming to the defense of a Packard man in this town."

"1 came to the defense of a crippled man who was being mistreated. Who told you about that, anyway?"

"People talk. Especially when they see things that surprise them. Like a man putting his neck on the line for a Packard, right in broad daylight on the street in front of Bax Cornwell's own headquarters."

"That man wasn't a Packard. His name is McGeeter. He works for the Packards, that's all."

"That makes him as good as a Packard in the eyes of the Cornwells. That's the way it is in this town."

"I'm beginning to think I ain't too fond of this town, then."

"You got to let it grow on you some. You got to get comfortable with the notion that one family calls the shots."

Matt pondered silently a moment or two, then decided firmly that he'd not remain in Pactolas any longer than it required to get all his strength back and earn enough money to pay the Cornwells properly for their kindness, and to get him sufficiently back on his feet financially to replace the essentials he'd lost.

All that could take a good while, he considered unhappily.

"Come on, sir. Give me my interview. People around here would be tickled to death to read about the living and breathing son of old Temple Fadden himself."

Irritating though this man was to him, Matt decided to be friendly, even if he couldn't really say yes to his request. "Mr. Day, I appreciate your interest, but there's good reason for me to say no. I'm still trying to get the lay of the land around here, and I'm awfully beholden to the Cornwells for all they've done for me. They took me in when I was as down as a man could be."

"So I've heard. Don't worry—I'll give the Cornwells due credit in any story I write. Hell, I have to live in this town, too. Why would being beholden to the Cornwells make you not want to let me interview you?"

"Because of what I did this morning. I don't know how they'll feel about me helping out a man who works for the family they apparently hate so much. And I have a sneaking suspicion you'd not be content to let that subject go by."

"I think your suspicion is correct. But the Cornwells know about it already. A lot of folks witnessed you intervening."

"Then let's not make it worse by putting it in the paper. Good day to you, Mr. Day."

Day gave a little salute and half-wink, sighed slowly, and turned away with a shrug.

Matt hoped sincerely that the man would write nothing about him. The life he lived wasn't one he was particularly proud of or eager to publicize.

On the other hand, if his actions of today ended up costing him his good standing with Will Cornwell and lost him the chance at a job, he'd have to turn back to saloon fighting again, and publicity would help.

He headed back toward Will Cornwell's place. Out on the main street he cast a glance up toward Bax Cornwell's window, wondering how what he'd done today would affect his status with the leader of the Cornwell family.

He decided it didn't matter. He'd done the right thing, and under the same circumstances, he'd do the same again.

CHAPTER 9

W ill Cornwell looked up over the edge of his newspaper and peered through the smoke of his pipe.

"1 believe I hear Bax coming," he said.

"How can you do that, Pa?" Jeff asked. "I don't hear nothing, and you already know it's Uncle Bax." Jeff looked over at Matt, who was finishing the last bite of a slab of excellent apple pie. "Pa always can tell when Bax is here."

"It's because they're brothers," Florence said. "Sort of like family magic."

Will put his pipe and paper aside and went to the door. By now everyone could hear the soft hoofbeats of an approaching horse. Will opened the door.

"Hello, Bax.... What brings you out this evening?"

"Will, I've come to see your guest."

Matt's brows arched upward in surprise. He glanced over at Constance Cornwell and was surprised again: She was frowning deeply, shaking her head.

Jeff sidled up to Matt. "Uncle Bax is tipsy again. You can tell it in his voice."

Matt couldn't tell it, but then he didn't know Bax all

that well. When Bax appeared in the doorway and shook his brother's hand, though, it was indeed evident he'd been drinking. His smile seemed too broad, his gaze a little bleary, and he was slightly unsure on his feet.

"Bax, you've been tipping the flask tonight, ain't you?" Will said, glancing warily toward his obviously unhappy wife. "Connie will run you out of here with a broom!" He chuckled, but nervously.

Connie made a faint grunting sound and abruptly headed for the next room, from which she did not re-emerge.

Bax ignored his brother's references to his drinking, and instead focused his attention on Matt. "Well, Matt again we meet today!"

"Yes, sir."

"I've come to talk further with you... I've been thinking about our conversation today."

"Come sit down, Bax," Will said.

Bax grunted and headed for a chair near the fire. He waved toward a stool nearby it. "You sit there, Matt. Let's you and me have some private conversation."

"Come on, young'uns," Will, taking the hint, said to his brood. "Let's see what your mother's up to, and let Bax talk to Matt here by himself."

When the others were gone, no doubt in the next room with ears pressed to the door, Bax smiled benevolently at Matt.

"I drink some, you should know," he said.

"I see."

"My sister-in-law in yonder strongly objects. She says it's hypocritical of me to worship in the church and then get drunk on occasion. What do you think?"

"It's your business, not mine."

"A good answer. Besides, I see hypocrisy as a sort of spice for life. A touch here and there gives it some flavor."

He threw back his head and laughed, sending out great

gusts of whiskey-scented breath. He pulled a soiled handkerchief from his pocket and swiped at the moist corners of his mouth, then put it away again.

"Matt, I've been thinking about that job you came to me about. I want to hire you, and I know just how I want to use you. And it will benefit both you and me—adding to your fame and reputation, saving you from having to fight for a living, and for me, drawing new crowds all the time. Especially newcomers to Pactolas. My stock will be upped considerably... and it will be to the welfare of my kin to have the son of America's most famed frontiersman associated in these parts with the Cornwell clan."

So, Matt thought, *he wants to use me to in some way up the Cornwell advantage in this foolish feud. Or at least the Cornwell public image.*

"Exactly what would I be doing?"

"Just being yourself. That's all. Just being yourself, talking to folks, shaking hands, signing your name. That kind of thing. You'd be at my general mercantile store most of the time. I might move you about some, business to business, but mostly it would be at the mercantile. Easy job, easy job."

But the very kind of job I hate, Matt thought. Preening and posing and playing up my famous surname—the one part of saloon fighting that was worse than the fighting itself.

"I don't know, Mr. Cornwell..."

"You don't know? Dang, son, wasn't it you who came to me today, asking for any kind of work?"

"Yes, sir."

"Then why you getting picky all at once? I'm talking about work that ain't work at all—work that you can do right away, even before you're all the way healed up from that beating you took. And I'll pay you well enough to let you recompense my brother for his hospitality. You do want to do that, don't you?"

Matt felt an inner deflation. He had indeed gone asking for work, and he did indeed owe Will Cornwell and his family. Like it or not, it was going to be hard to justify turning down Bax's offer, whatever it turned out to be.

"I'm listening, sir."

Bax launched into a description of everything Matt had hoped he would not hear. A coonskin cap, fringed shirt, moccasins... shaking hands and giving endless "Howdy, partner" greetings to everyone who came by...

Matt felt almost ill. But he nodded obediently, hearing Bax out even as he promised himself that he would not linger long in this particular job. He'd earn what he needed to repay the Cornwell family, then he'd be gone.

When Bax finished the job description, he looked piercingly at Matt. "You don't appear too happy about this job offer, Matt."

"The truth is, Mr. Cornwell, I'm grateful for it... but it's not the kind of thing I take to very naturally. I don't much look to publicize myself... my father and I are very different in that way. He always wants all the attention he can get... I want only enough to let me earn my living, as rough a living as it is. There was a man who came up to me today, for instance, a newspaperman wanting to do a story about me. I told him to forget about it."

"Newspaperman!" Bax exclaimed. "Mr. Day, I assume?"

"That's him."

"Well, Matt, there will be a newspaper story. Has to be. We can't afford to pass up that kind of publicity. I was intending to go speak to Mr. Day about it myself, not having any notion he'd already approached you on his own! This is mighty good fortune. We'll go talk to him together, me and you. You can tell him all about your famous pap, talk about how you can't wait to meet the people of Pactolas, talk about the help that my kin have been to you.. . . The newspaper will be the thing, yes sir."

Matt couldn't believe it. This was almost funny... though not really. It was he who would be displayed before all Pactolas like some circus performer. He who would have to stand there grinning like a dime-novel caricature while people came by to gawk at him not for who he was, but for who his father was.

But what the devil? Work was work... and Bax was right: This was a job he certainly could do. He'd go along with Bax, and put up with whatever he had to do for as long as it took to settle his obligations.

"Well, sir, if you want me to be in the newspaper, I'll be in the newspaper," Matt said.

Bax grinned. "We have an arrangement, then?"

"Yes sir, assuming there is some pay involved in this. We haven't talked about that yet."

Bax laughed. "So we haven't."

They did talk pay, and it was more than acceptable. Matt was surprised at Bax's generosity. Indeed, he had no option but to take the offer. The kind of money Bax was going to pay would be worth a bit of showmanship, even embarrassment.

Matt put forth his hand. "I'm pleased to accept your offer, sir," he said.

Bax shook his hand—but did not let go of it. His expression became intense, and he pulled Matt toward him slightly and shoved his own face closer to his.

"The deal is done, then. You work for me now. And that means you work for the Cornwell family. You never forget that, son. You're on our side now, and that means you better be damn careful from now on what sorry cripples and such you help in the street. You understanding me?"

Matt was so stunned, he couldn't even react.

"Answer me, son. You understand that from now on, you got nothing to do with any lousy Packard nor any who work for them or befriend them. The Packards are the enemies of the Cornwells, and we have naught to do with them. Do you understand me?"

"I understand, sir. But if you're talking about me helping out that man on the street today, there's something *you* should understand. He wasn't a Packard. His name is McGeeter."

"He works for them! Same as being one of them, in my book."

"Not in mine, but we may just have to agree to differ on that. I helped him because he was a man in trouble, same as I would have helped any other man. What I did had nothing to do with any trouble that has existed between your family and the Packards."

Even now Bax did not let go of Matt's hand. He gripped it so hard, it hurt. "From now on, son, you don't think that way no more. Not while you work for me. You have nothing to do with the Packards, nor with the town of Stalker's Creek, nor with anyone who has aught to do with that bunch of murderous scoundrels."

Matt almost changed his plans right then. He almost told Bax to forget about the job. Almost, but he held back. He needed the work. And he'd only stay in it for a short time. Odds were this nonsense between the two feuding families would not become an issue for him again. So he merely looked Bax in the eye and held his silence.

At last Bax let go of Matt's hand. "Just so we know where we stand now."

"You've made yourself clear enough," Matt said.

All at once Bax was jovial and friendly again. His eyes lost their piercing edge and became again merely the bleary eyes of a good-humored man who'd had a touch too much to drink.

"I'll see you seven in the morning, Monday morning,"

Bax said. "First thing we'll do is talk with Mr. Day, to get that story in the paper. Then we'll get you outfitted. I've got some old buckskins that will do just the trick. I believe they'll fit you just fine."

CHAPTER 10

When Sunday morning came, Matt declared that he felt a cold possibly coming on and used it as an excuse to miss the church service. The prospect of a couple of hours away from the Cornwells was too enticing to pass up.

Come the next morning, he'd turn into Matthew Fadden, the Honest-to-Goodness Living Son of Temple Fadden, America's Most Famous Frontiersman. A public spectacle, displayed for the sake of Bax Cornwell's commercial interests. He'd enjoy a bit of solitude and anonymity while he had the chance.

As soon as the Cornwells were gone from the house, Matt shaved, washed up a bit in the basin, dressed, and headed out for a long walk.

He was pleased to note how well he was recovering from his beating. However ambivalent he might feel about the Cornwell family, he had to credit the hospitality, shelter, rest, and good food they'd provided with giving his body a chance to get better. In a day or two he'd be completely fit again.

Matt walked into the mountains north of Pactolas, walking for walking's sake and following a path he'd found at random. The farther he went and the higher he climbed, the better he felt. His strength indeed was returning, helped along by the exercise and fresh air.

He lost track of time and distance, but did not worry about it. He'd slipped a couple of biscuits out of the house in his pocket to nibble on if he grew hungry. He could stay out all day if he wanted, telling the Cornwells later that he always dealt with oncoming colds by burning them out through physical exertion... and he considered this possibility strongly, in that the next morning would be the beginning of what he perceived as a sort of slavery to the Cornwells, Bax in particular.

Matt climbed to the top of a crag and paused to rest. The view was spectacular, broad and rugged land spreading all around him. The town and the assorted mines were admittedly ugly, man-made mars on an otherwise splendid landscape—yet with the sunlight spilling across it all, bathing every surface in light and every corner in shadow, there was somehow even beauty in the ugliness. Matt sat down at the base of a scrubby tree and relaxed. He pulled one of the biscuits from his pocket and nibbled at it, and felt peaceful as the gentle toll of a church bell made music across the town below.

Matt finished the biscuit, pulled his hat down over his eyes, and lay back. Before long he slept.

He wasn't sure what wakened him with a start. A noise, a movement?

It happened again, and Matt came to his feet. What had wakened him was a gunshot.

The noise of the shot had come from the east. Judging as best he could, he determined it had been fired at least two or three hundred yards away from him.

It was probably just a hunter, but it was still worth knowing exactly where the shooter was, to avoid becoming an accidental target.

Below the precipice on which he stood, movement drew his eye and he saw a man scrambling off a footpath and into some brush. The man's frantic manner made Matt instantly sure that he was the target of whoever had fired the shot.

Matt froze, unsure what to do. Was this some sort of assassination attempt? He scanned the landscape in the area where he thought the shooter must be, and saw motion in a rocky, overgrown area. Someone was there—but no. A couple of stray dogs bounding around, that's all it was.

Another shot. Matt caught the flash of it in the corner of his eye. It came from the rim of a brushy ridge east of him and almost at the elevation of the ridge he was on. It appeared to have been aimed in the general direction of the man he'd seen below, a man now completely out of sight in the natural cover.

Apparently the shot had been made in too much haste, the shooter not well-positioned, because right after it sounded, Matt saw something tumble over the edge of the ridgeline and clatter down the rocky face into the crevice below. A rifle! The shooter had actually dropped his rifle, perhaps knocked from his hands by the recoil. Maybe that last shot had been triggered accidentally.

Matt found his voice. "Hey! You there—why are you shooting at that man?"

It was dangerous to expose his presence in this way, but he felt he had to do it, and now was the best time, with the shooter having lost his weapon. Perhaps he'd be frightened away, especially if he thought he'd been seen.

Or perhaps he had more than one weapon up there. Matt might become a second target.

Matt stepped behind a tree, just in case, and kept his eye on the ridge. Nothing. No movement. But probably the gunman was watching him from hiding, maybe drawing a bead.... So Matt squeezed in a little more squarely behind the tree.

No shot came. He saw nothing, heard nothing. Whoever was there either was holding very still and staying under cover, or had already left the scene via the far side of the ridge.

Matt edged around the trunk and looked below in time to see the apparent intended target of the shots come out of hiding. The man looked furtively up toward the place where the shooter had hidden, then toward Matt. Reflexively, Matt shrunk in behind the tree again. Not knowing what this all was about, he preferred being anonymous, if possible, so that no one else's trouble came looking for him. Of course, he'd already drawn attention to himself. Both the shooter and the intended victim might have seen him when he shouted. But was he close enough to either that he could have been identified? Probably not. Not many folks hereabouts knew him anyway.

Not until tomorrow, at least. Not until he put on buckskin and a big hat and went around shaking hands and howdying and talking about how fine it was to be the son of the great Temple Fadden, who was, yes sir, every bit as marvelous as everyone thought he was.

The man below scrambled away, and despite the distance between them Matt found something familiar in his general look and way of movement—something that reminded him a little of Bax, and also Will. But of course he was not either of them, both of them being in church right now, hearing about how God favored the Cornwells and despised the Packards. But he'd bet that the man was one of the other many Cornwells of these parts.

A Cornwell, being shot at from hiding, Matt theorized that he'd just stumbled into the latest incident in the Cornwell-Packard feud.

Matt wondered if the shooter would appear, looking for the lost weapon. Matt decided to wait and see.

Ten minutes passed, then fifteen, then twenty. No

evidence of anyone moving around anywhere in the vicinity, no sign of a continuing presence on the ridge. The failed assassin had moved on, it seemed, probably leaving the ridge by its far, unseen side.

Matt came out of hiding and moved down the ridge, heading for the place where the rifle had fallen. Meanwhile he kept an eye on the ridge above and the terrain all around, in case the sniper was simply hiding, waiting for him to leave. But he saw no sign that this was the case.

Matt poked about in the rocks and brush until he spotted the rifle. Carefully he made his way toward it, though he had to proceed with great caution because there was much loose stone around, ready to give way under foot.

The rifle was a Winchester, scratched and scarred from its fall, but apparently undamaged. The lever worked easily. Matt looked it over and found no markings beyond those of the manufacturer. The only thing that made the rifle distinctive was that it had a brand-new butt plate, very shiny and clean, standing out from the rest of the worn and scratched rifle.

He looked around again, above and below, wondering if the sniper maybe hadn't already gone and was still watching him, hoping he'd leave and not take the rifle with him.

Matt had no intention of leaving the rifle behind. He was persuaded he'd just witnessed an attempted murder, maybe feud-related. The rifle was going with him, in case it was ever needed for evidence.

Matt tucked the rifle under his arm and descended. He found the trail he'd followed there and began working his way back toward Will Cornwell'. He'd show Will the rifle, tell him what he'd seen.

By the time he was within sight of Will's place, he had changed his mind. This was a feud situation, inherently explosive. What if the Cornwells overreacted, got vengeful, maybe hurt the wrong person? The rifle might be stolen.

The true owner might be innocent, but wrongly accused if the rifle was examined and identified.

Matt veered toward an old, unused shed that stood at the edge of a meadow near Will Cornwell's. Inside he chanced upon an old but usable oilcloth, and wrapped the rifle in that. He put the bound-up weapon in a corner and hid it behind some assorted trash. Checking through a knothole to make sure no one was around to see him, he left the shed and headed toward Will's, pondering how odd a Sunday morning this had turned out to be.

Half an hour later, as the Cornwell family came riding up the road on buggy and wagon, Matt was seated on the front porch swing, waiting for them. For now he would say nothing of what he had seen.

D ay the newspaperman had a look of smugness about him while he interviewed Matt, or so Matt fancied. He answered questions glumly, and had most of his answers superseded by Bax, who sat behind his big desk, feet upraised and resting on the desktop, his face dark with thought, fingers steepled over his lips. Nothing, of course, was said of his brave intervention to help out McGeeter, even though that act certainly fit the image of heroism attached in the public mind to the Fadden name. But no valor extended in the direction of the Packards or their associates would appear in a story being controlled and engineered by the Cornwells.

"No, Matt," Bax was saying in the wake of one of Matt's uninspired answers about his father. "You need to build your father up much more than that... this is Temple Fadden we're talking about here! People want to think of him as ten feet tall. Describe him as a really big fellow, Mr. Day. Say he towers over his son, but his son makes up for his small size in muscle."

Matt looked down at himself. His "small" size? Matt had the build of an average man, didn't he? The more these fellows built up the mythical version of Matt Fadden and his father, the more the real Matt Fadden was diminished. But there was nothing new in that—he'd felt diminished by the great Fadden name since he was a boy.

They talked for nearly an hour, Day enjoying every minute of it because he was getting the very interview Matt had earlier denied him. He told them the story would appear in the next edition, to be published Wednesday.

Matt pretended not to see Day's extended hand as he turned to leave.

"Too bad we'll have to wait before the story appears," Bax said as they headed toward the store where Matt would be displayed. "But we can get some attention without it. Dress you up, put you on the porch, waving at folks..."

And within half an hour, the process was under way. Matt stood in buckskins and a broad-brimmed hat, leaning on an old flintlock Bax brought up from the back of the store, waving like an idiot at people who looked back at him as if he was just that—until Bax appeared with a hand-lettered sign to place beside him:

MEET MATTHEW FADDEN, SON OF THE GRATE TEMPLE FADDEN HISSELF.

Bax was not much of a speller or grammarian, but the sign did its job. People began to appear, gaping at him, seemingly afraid to approach him at first, then warming to him.

"Are you really Temple Fadden's boy? *The* Temple Fadden?"

"Why are you way out in these parts if you're Temple's son?"

"Where's your pa? Is he here too?"

Matt smiled at them all, shook hands, signed his name a few times. Children, mostly boys, soon surrounded him, accompanied by the inevitable canine companions. A photographer appeared from some studio down the street, dragging out heavy equipment that he set up before the store porch. Powder flashed and Matt's image was preserved forever, dressed in full, clownish, embarrassing splendor.

Matt endured, keeping his smile going with extraordinary effort. Bax was beaming in the background of it all, everything going just like he wanted.

Several of the people who stopped to meet Matt also dropped into the store. A few bought things. Bax's plan was working. He rubbed his hands together in glee.

The embarrassed Matt comforted himself with the thought of the money he was making, and reminded himself that, if nothing else, the clock would go around like always. He'd be free of this in a few hours... until tomorrow, anyway, when he'd have to do it all over again. And the day after that, and after that...

CHAPTER 12

Midday brought a welcome break and a meal carried over from the nearest café. Matt ate in the back of the store, glumly dreading the afternoon and wondering how long this job could really hold out. He was drawing a crowd right now, but eventually folks would be used to seeing him. The novelty would wear off. Once he ceased to be a draw, Bax would no longer want to keep him at this.

Then he remembered having read in a newspaper somewhere that Pactolas was one of those towns that drew scores, even hundreds, of newcomers every month, people following the fortunes of mining. There'd always be new folks in town eager to gawk at the offspring of America's greatest hero.

Dejected by this thought, Matt finished his food, put his hat back on, and headed back to the storefront to serve out the afternoon half of this day's sentence.

An hour into it, a man emerged from a saloon across the street, swiped the beer suds off his lips with the back of his hand, and staggered down off the boardwalk onto the street. Matt watched him closely, finding him familiar and for some reason vaguely disturbing. The man, quite drunk even though it was only midafternoon, staggered toward the mercantile. As he grew nearer, Matt realized why he seemed familiar.

This was the man he'd seen shot at in the mountains yesterday.

The man climbed onto the porch, swayed on the final step like a tree about to fall over, then righted himself and pushed his way past Matt into the store. As he went by Matt he looked at him with a glaring frown for a long moment.

Bax had gone to his office a little earlier in the day but had returned fifteen minutes ago to make sure his costumed prize was still drawing in the customers. Inside the store talking to the clerk, he'd spotted this man coming and intercepted him just inside the door.

"Jimbo Cornwell, you're drunk. What do you mean getting drunk in the middle of the day and coming to my store like this?"

Matt thought to himself that this Jimbo Cornwell wasn't the only one of his family who got tipsy during daylight hours. Bax himself had been quite into his cups by suppertime the day last week that he'd visited Matt at Will's house to offer him this humiliating job.

"Bax, I got to talk to you. I know I'm drunk, but I've had me a scare, a scare to shiver the very life out of a man. I was shot at yesterday morning, Bax, out in the mountains. Shot at serious!"

"No lie?"

"No lie. And it wasn't no hunter, neither. There was somebody up on Pate's Ridge, shooting at me to kill me. A Packard, no doubt about it. Had to be a Packard."

Matt was listening closely, his heart beginning to race a little. He wondered if Jimbo had recognized him from his own appearance on that ridge, when he'd yelled and tried to stop the shooting.

He thought about that rifle he'd hidden, and worried about it. Should he have turned it over to Bax?

"Jimbo, let's not talk about this here," Bax said. "This ain't the place. Come over to my office. We'll talk there."

"I been so scared and shaky since I was shot at that all I can do is drink," Jimbo whined. "I'm scared to death, Bax. The Packards nearly got me!"

"We'll do whatever needs doing to deal with it, Jimbo. Now hush and come with me."

Bax and Jimbo emerged from the front door. Matt tried to look nonchalant and act as if he'd heard nothing.

Jimbo stopped and glared at him again. "I know you," he said. "I seen you before... somewhere."

"Maybe you have, Jimbo," Bax said, hand on his shoulder to urge him on. "He's been a saloon fighter, and God knows you've been in every saloon in the territory once or twice or maybe fifty times. Come on, now. Let's get over to my office."

Jimbo continued, but he looked back at Matt one last time, his liquor-clouded mind clearly turning, trying to figure out where he'd seen this fellow before.

Matt hoped he wouldn't remember. He'd been a good distance away up there on that ridge, and possibly Jimbo had not gotten a clear look at him, only a general impression. Jimbo had a slight squint... a touch of nearsightedness, if Matt was lucky. He watched Jimbo and Bax walk across the street and head into an alleyway that provided a shortcut over to where Bax's office stood.

Matt was distracted by the approach of a boy with a battered Temple Fadden dime novel in his hand, shyly extended, accompanied by a muttered request for an autograph. Matt smiled at the bashful young man, whose mother stood to the side with a look of uncertainty about the appropriateness of letting her beloved make contact with such a worldly type. He scribed out his name, and beneath it the identifying phrase "Son of Temple Fadden," and handed the book back to the boy.

The boy grinned and for the first time had the courage to look Matt in the eye. "Thank you, sir," he murmured, turned, and scampered back to his mother. They walked away.

Matt watched them go and sighed. Not much different from being a monkey on an organ grinder's leash, this job. But it was paid, and that's all that counted right now.

He looked across in the direction of Bax's office, not visible from here, and wondered if Jimbo would remember where he'd seen him. He thought of that stashed rifle and wondered if he should have shown it to the Cornwells after all, and how they would respond if they learned he'd witnessed the attempted shooting of one of their own, and said nothing about it.

———

An hour later, Bax returned. Matt was busy at that time, talking with four men who, like all good Americans, were eager to see Temple Fadden as something just under the level of an Olympian god. Matt gave them what they wanted, found himself actually beginning to get into the spirit of this whole strange business, and entered a purely fictional oration about Temple wiping out an entire band of Apaches—a variety of Indian the real-life Temple had never even met—using only a faulty pistol with three bullets and a broken Bowie knife. But when Bax came by, face grim, Matt's attention shifted and the story dwindled away.

Bax approached his clerk. Matt said goodbye to his four admirers and edged back toward the door, wanting to hear what Bax said to him.

He was sending the clerk on an errand. "Go to my brother's place. Bring Will back here ... tell him it's important. Tell him there's been trouble again. We may have to act."

"What kind of trouble?" asked the clerk.

"Never mind that. Just hurry. And if you can't find him right off, track him down."

Matt's stomach lurched. Something serious was afoot.

More people appeared, eager to meet the son of a hero, and Matt was busy for the next forty minutes. But when he finally was free again, he saw the clerk and Will coming down the street. Will looked very somber.

"Hello, Matt," Will said as he climbed up on the porch. "How are you doing with the new work?"

"Doing fine," Matt said, smiling.

"Good. Drawing the crowds, I guess."

"Quite a bit. Looks like I've drawn you, too."

"I'm here to see Bax, Matt. Some sort of a situation has come up. Family thing." He smiled tightly and went inside.

More people approached, eager to meet him, eager to shake his hand. Matt slapped on a fresh smile and pondered the salesman's savvy of Bax Cornwell. Putting the son of the famous Fadden out here to perform like a dressed-up bear was working better than Matt would have anticipated. He rather dreaded what the crowds might be like after Day's work of journalistic fiction came out on Wednesday.

CHAPTER 13

That night, Matt joined Will on the porch. Will had headed out there after a quiet, tense supper during which he had seemed preoccupied and solemn.

"Howdy, Will," Matt said. He did not sit down. The brooding Will might want to be left alone.

"Matt. Have a seat."

Matt pulled up a chair and drew a cigar out of his pocket. "Want a smoke?"

"Don't mind if I do."

Matt handed him the cigar, then produced another for himself. They bit off the ends, rolled the smokes around, settled them in place. Matt struck a match, lit Will's cigar, then his own.

"Business looked brisk today," Will said.

"I did all right, I guess. It's probably the first time I made money off my name without having to throw punches at some drunk to get it."

"That's good."

They drew on the cigars and blew smoke into the evening air, holding silent for a minute or so. From inside they heard the clank and clatter of dishes being washed, the sound of Jeff and Florence arguing about something, the ticking of the clock on the hand-hewn mantelpiece.

"Everything all right with you, Will?" Matt ventured.

"Not entirely. Bit of trouble with the Packards. More than a bit."

"The 'family thing' you touched on today when you came to the store."

"Yes." Will looked at Matt. "One of our kin was shot at in the mountains Sunday morning. It appears to be an outright assassination attempt."

"You're sure it's the Packards?"

"Who else would it be? Jimbo Cornwell is a harmless soul. Not much money, nothing anybody would want to rob. No wife, no woman friend, no mining claim. He makes his living sweeping up stores and hauling rubbish. He stays drunk half the time. The only reason anybody would try to kill Jimbo is because of his last name. And the only folks who would do that are the Packards."

"But why? It was my understanding that this feud you folks have has been... not gone, maybe, but sort of cooled off."

"It had been. But not now, it seems. The heat is coming back."

"I'd heard talk, Will, to the effect that there's been shots fired earlier. Some of them at the Packards. I ain't saying that it was Cornwells doing the shooting but if the Packards think it is, maybe one of them is retaliating by shooting at Cornwells."

Will looked at him wryly. "Do you think you're telling me something I don't already know?"

"No, sir. I guess not." Matt reddened, knowing he'd simply stated the obvious. He wanted to say more, to talk about what he'd witnessed and bring out that rifle—but something was still holding him back. Some warning bell was ringing in his brain, something telling him that involving himself in this muddle would bring about nothing good.

"We've been patient, we Cornwells," Will said. "We've had the Packards accusing us of shooting at them, feuding them again—and I swear, Matt, it ain't the truth. The Cornwells have no love for the Packards, never will, but we are willing to leave them be if they'll do the same to us. But they won't do it. Having Jimbo shot at is the last straw. We got to do something. Bax thinks so, and so do I. Got to do something."

"Do what?"

"That's the big question, son. That's the big question."

"And who do you do it to? Maybe there's just one or two folks causing the problem."

"Maybe. But we can't sit back and let those one or two, if that's all it is, go shooting our people from hiding. One or two folks can bring harm to dozens of others."

"So what can you do?"

"I don't know. Bax is thinking about it. I reckon he'll be the one to decide."

"He's pretty much the leader in such situations, I guess."

"He's the leader. He's a strong man, Matt. You're lucky to know him. You're lucky he likes you. Just make sure you keep it that way, and you'll be fine as long as you're here. Stay on his good side... because he's not a man you want to cross."

"I'll keep that in mind."

"You do that."

———

Matt awakened the next morning and made his way to the breakfast table downstairs. Constance Cornwell was down there, busying about as usual in the mornings, but this time with a very solemn manner and a pinched look about the eyes that made Matt wonder if she'd been crying. Florence was in the next room, engaged in trying to teach herself to knit. Through a window Matt saw Jeff heading for the chicken coop, doing his morning chores. But Will was not present.

Matt said his good mornings and verified to himself that Constance was indeed upset about something. She was friendly and trying hard to seem her usual self, but it was all forced and distracted. She cooked Matt eggs and bacon. While he waited for it to be done he nibbled a biscuit from the basketful already on the table, and sipped strong coffee.

"Is Will still in bed?" he asked. "Not feeling poorly, I hope."

"Will is already gone. Up and about on his day's business. Oh, and I was told to tell you that you might not see Bax today. They're busy today, Will and Bax both."

"I see. Well, I didn't expect that Bax would necessarily be hanging about while I do my work." It felt odd to use the word "work" to describe what amounted to no more than standing around in a clownish outfit, saying howdy to a bunch of gawking strangers who were caught up in the dime-novel mythology of Temple Fadden.

She put the meal before him; he praised her skills and thanked her for the thousandth time for all the hospitality she and her family were giving him, and she smiled and said it was nothing. Then she turned away and he sensed that the clouds around her darkened a little more.

He finished his breakfast without much enjoying it, his own mood being affected by the thick atmosphere in the room. He eyed Florence busy with her knitting needles in the next room and thought that she, too, seemed thoughtful and quiet. Usually she was engaging in rather animated conversations with him this time of the morning. He noted that she took long glances at her mother from time to time.

Matt thanked Constance for the breakfast again, then went up to his room, cleaned up at the basin, took a cold shave, and dressed for the day. He felt as absurd as ever in his frontiersman getup, and reminded himself anew that paying work was paying work and not to be scorned.

Maybe he'd write that down. Create a whole book of pithy, wise sayings. Call it "The Wit and Wisdom of the Honest-to-Goodness Son of Temple Fadden, Greatest American Who Ever Walked the Soil." He'd put a picture of himself on the cover, buckskin-fringed arm extended in greeting, with his image saying the words, "Howdy, partner.. . come shake my hand and be sure to buy some dry goods and such while you're here."

Matt left the house and headed in the direction of town and the store. He wondered if his patronage would be down today, with the first-day novelty now worn off, and Day's journalistic tall tales still a day from publication. Probably so. Bad, in a way. At least it made the day pass quickly when there were folks to talk to.

He considered going over to find Jeff and see if he knew what Will and Bax were up to today. Probably it had something to do with the feud and that assassination attempt in the mountains. But Jeff was out of sight somewhere.

Matt initially headed toward his work place, but once out of sight of the house, paused. He cut through the woods and headed back around toward the rear portion of Will's land, and entered the little shed where he'd hidden the rifle.

The rifle was gone. It was startling and unnerving, and he wondered if one of the Cornwells had found it.

No. More likely, that hidden shootist in the mountains had followed him on Sunday, seen where he hid the rifle, and removed it. The thought that he'd been tracked all the way back here by someone he had not known was even there, someone of the character to shoot at others from hiding, gave him a cold chill and shiver.

At the same time, he was relieved that the rifle was gone. It lifted a burden from him.

Deciding to involve himself no further in feuds that belonged to others, he headed out and back toward the store, ready to shake hands and sign his name on dime novels for one more day.

CHAPTER 14

H e was slightly surprised to find himself even busier than he'd been the day before. Apparently word of mouth had spread, and people were actually waiting for the son of Temple Fadden when he got there.

"Howdy, folks," he said, touching his hat. "Mighty good of you to come out."

A little boy was already pushing a dime novel at him, with a pencil, eager for the Great Man—well, the son of the Great Man, which would have to do as a substitute— to put his name on the cover.

Matt did the job, talked to the boy a few moments, then turned his attention to the next in line. And so it went for the longest time, until before Matt knew it, the morning was past. He'd hardly had a moment to think, Bax Cornwell's clerks had sold a wagonload of dry goods and hardware, and Matt had actually enjoyed himself to a degree. He took a break to eat a bite at midday, then came back ready for an afternoon of more of the same.

The crowd had dwindled, however, and time passed more slowly. Matt spent quite a bit of time simply standing around, or sitting on the porch bench. The arrival of visitors was welcome as a break from the boredom. And he worried that Bax would return from wherever he'd gone, see him idle, and decide to dismiss him from service. As inherently temporary and somewhat embarrassing as this job was, he didn't want to lose it right away.

Shortly before four o'clock, Matt dozed off sitting on the bench. He lifted his head when he realized someone was standing before him.

It was McGeeter, looking furtively about. Matt straightened his hat and took a glance about as well. Bax, if nearby, would not be pleased to see his prize display talking to a Packard associate.

"McGeeter... what brings you here?"

"I'm in town on an errand, but I want to tell you something. Some information about that rifle you lost."

For half a moment Matt thought he meant the rifle that had vanished from the shed, then realized that of course he was referring to Matt's own Henry, stolen during his beating.

"I know we can't speak long here," McGeeter said. "Meet me in ten minutes in back of the store—say you're heading for the privy, if anyone asks—and I'll talk to you there."

McGeeter turned and left the porch, crossing the street and stumping along down the boardwalk until he rounded a corner and went out of sight.

An absurd town, this one, Matt thought. Two grown men, forced by circumstances to meet in hiding simply for one to convey information to the other. It went against his grain... downright angering, when he thought about it. It was the Packards and Cornwells feuding, not himself and McGeeter.

He made his way around to the back of the store at the appointed time, and found McGeeter already there.

"I've located your rifle, I think," McGeeter said. "You recall I told you that I know a man who deals in stolen ones.

There's a Henry there that I think may be yours." McGeeter described it in some detail.

"That's it, sure enough," Matt said. "How can I get it back?"

"Well, you'll never get him to give it back to you. He'll deny it's stolen and give you a long history about how it came to him, and believe me, from what I know, there's no point in trying to talk him out of it. The only way you'll get that rifle back from him is to buy it."

Matt looked away thoughtfully. "Or steal it back."

"Steal it? You're looking for trouble, my friend."

"It's not really stealing when you own it already."

"As far as Roland Kelsey is concerned, he owns it. And he's the kind who'd shoot a man he caught stealing from him."

"Like I said, it ain't stealing when you own what you're taking."

"I wish I hadn't told you. You'll go get yourself killed and I'll feel like it's my fault."

"Don't worry, McGeeter. I don't know what I'll do— I'm just talking big talk. Tugging on my rope a little because I'm tired of being tied up to other people's plans and problems and schedules. I've always been used to freedom, and I don't have a lot of it now."

"Talking about your new job, I take it."

"If you can call standing around looking like a dressed-up fool a job, then yes, that's what I'm talking about."

"Don't like it much?"

"It's not so bad, I guess. And when I get a payday I can recompense my hosts like I should." He paused. "But I got a problem now. I got to try to get my rifle back, before somebody else gets it."

"I can take you to Kelsey's place tomorrow. It's in Stalker's Creek."

"I'm supposed to work tomorrow. And it's a big day— a

story in the newspaper will be coming out, all about me and my wonderful father. It would be a bad day for me to not be there."

"That rifle won't linger long. Kelsey moves his guns fast."

Matt swore quietly to himself. He shook his head. "I don't know what to do. I'm not willing to let that gun get away from me again."

"Then let me know where to meet you, and when, and I'll take you to Kelsey."

"I appreciate your help."

"After what you did for me, I owe you."

"Tomorrow, then. I'll meet you at the crossroads just west of where Will Cornwell lives, just after sunrise."

"I know the place. I'll be waiting at the big tree."

CHAPTER 15

W ill was at home when Matt arrived there. Bax, too. They were talking quietly, serious but not somber, and Matt could tell right away that nothing major had happened that day. He'd been fearful that they'd gone off somewhere to retaliate violently against the Packards.

"Glad to see both of you safe and sound," Matt said, leaning over his cup of coffee.

"Thank you. How'd it go at the store?" Bax asked.

"We did right well." He described the day's business, emphasizing the parts that were brisk.

"Good. And the newspaper story comes out tomorrow. That ought to bolster things even more."

"Reckon so." Matt had to talk to Bax about tomorrow... and the fact he'd not be on the job that day. He hadn't figured out the best way to broach the subject, though.

"Bax and I made some family calls today," Will said. "Some Cornwell-to-Cornwell visits."

"This shooting business," Bax offered helpfully.

"Yes, sir." Matt grinned. "I'm glad it was just family visits. I had some fear you might be out... well, feuding."

"It may come to that," Bax said. "That was the reason for

our travel today. Conferring with the other men of the family, to see their thinking on the matter."

Matt didn't suppose Bax had really done much real conferring. More likely his own mind was made up and as family head he'd simply told them the way things were going to be.

"I hope you found them all safe and sound."

"Yes. But very concerned. A lot of rumors out there. Trouble coming to our family by way of Stalker's Creek and the Packards."

"I just wish we knew who'd took the shot at Jimbo," Will said.

At that, Matt's conscience surged painfully. A moment for truth-telling had just presented itself.

"I need to tell both of you something about that," Matt said. "I should have told you before now, I guess. I witnessed that shooting attempt." He fought the impulse to hang his head. Confessing this made him feel like a little boy caught stealing sugar.

"You witnessed it? How the hell..." Bax's face was instantly red.

"It was Sunday morning, remember? I didn't go to church with you. Instead I went walking in the mountains. While I was out there, I spotted Jimbo down below. I didn't know him, but it did seem to me he had a Cornwell way of moving, a Cornwell build. Then somebody shot at him from a ridgetop, I hollered, they dropped the rifle, and that was that."

Both men stared at him, taking a few moments to absorb and understand this.

"So it was you!" Will said. "Jimbo said there was a man who got involved, tried to stop the shooting."

Matt felt hopeful. If this was the attitude in which they would judge this, he might come through all right. "I didn't know what it was all about, but I couldn't stand by and see a man gunned down from hiding."

"You didn't see the shooter?" Bax asked. His tone was harder, nearly gruff.

"No."

"What's this about them dropping a rifle?"

"That's what happened. The shooter must have gotten spooked when I yelled, and dropped the rifle. It fell down the bluff. Or maybe he was just clumsy."

"Did you go get the rifle?"

"Yes."

"And you haven't said anything? Damnation, boy—don't you know we might be able to identify the shooter with that rifle? Where is it?"

"Gone. I brought it back with me and put it in the shed at the edge of the back field. The next time I went to look for it, it was gone. I suppose the shooter followed me back on the sneak and saw where I put it."

"So you led a would-be assassin right back to my home?" Will exclaimed.

"I didn't know I was being followed. And besides, I expect it's no secret in these parts where you live," Matt said. "I doubt I revealed anything that wasn't already known."

"You sure as hell didn't reveal anything to us, that's for cussed sure!" Bax said, on his feet now. "How could you sit here amongst us, eat our food, hear our talk, know we're worried like we are, and not even speak up?"

"I was wrong. I know that now, and that's why I'm telling you this. It took me a while to figure out the best way to handle this."

"You handle it the only way there is to handle it! You tell us what you saw! You bring the rifle straight to us so we can identify it, not hide it in some shed where the shooter could take it back! Damn, son! Did Temple Fadden not put any sense in your head? Didn't he give you no notion of duty?"

"Any duty I've learned I've learned on my own. Any

sense I've got came from some other source than my father. And I'll tell you why I didn't bring that rifle straight to you: I figured a man aiming to shoot another man might do so with a stolen rifle, so as not to be traced if the rifle was found. I feared I'd show you the rifle, that it would be identified in some way, and you'd go after the owner and maybe lynch him to a tree before finding out that the rifle was stolen from him and used by somebody else."

"That's a stretch. You expect me to believe that?"

"Yes, sir, I do. I'm pretty aware of stolen rifles right now, you know. Mine was taken when I was beat up. If that had proved to be my stolen rifle that shot at Jimbo, would you have strung me up because of it?"

"Nobody's said anything about stringing anybody up ... yet. The point is you had information and you held it back from us. I don't forgive that easy," Bax said.

"I didn't ask for forgiveness. I just told you what I did, and why, and that I figure I was probably wrong to hold it back until now. But I did have my reason for it, and I've told it to you for whatever it's worth."

"It ain't worth much. You messed up, boy. And after all this family has done for you, it's pretty damned sorry of you to have done it, too."

It took all Matt had within him to keep from rising up right there and letting Bax know, by word and maybe fist, that what the Cornwell family had done for him was really no more than any decent family would do for an injured stranger, and that it might be argued that it was he who was going beyond the call of duty by allowing Bax to use him like a trained monkey on his porch store to sell dry goods. And it wasn't his feud, nor was there a reason for him to make it his feud.

Somehow Matt held all this back. "I did what I thought was right. If it wasn't, I apologize for it."

Will, calmer than his brother, asked him, "Was there anything about the rifle that made it distinctive?"

"Not really. It was a Winchester, pretty battered and worn, but with a new butt plate. The butt plate was shiny, much cleaner than the rest of the rifle. That was the main thing I noticed about it."

"No marks? No initials or name on it?"

"No."

Bax drew in a deep breath and calmed down. "Well... not much harm in what you did, then. There's probably hundreds of battered Winchesters in this town. But it was still wrong. Hell, you witnessed a shooting, knew it was one of our kin, and said not a word!"

"I'm sorry."

Bax glared at him, gave his hand a little wave of disgust and dismissal, swore again, then said, "Well, you're drawing a crowd for me. I guess you ain't completely worthless."

"I need to talk to you about that. I can't be there tomorrow."

"What?"

"1 can't work for you tomorrow. I've got some information about the rifle that was stolen from me, and I need to go track it down."

Bax was red and blustering again. "The hell you say! Tomorrow is the day the paper comes out, son! There'll be all kinds of people heading over just to see you! You can't be gone tomorrow!"

"I can't wait to do this. That rifle will disappear if I don't go after it right away."

"So what am I supposed to tell the folks who come to see you?"

"Tell them I'm off looking to recover a rifle that was stolen from me—a rifle that my father gave me, and that I'll be glad to let them look at and hold once I get it back."

That last part caught Bax by surprise and threw a new

light on the situation. "Huh," he said. "Huh. Yeah. All right. I see." He cleared his throat and lost some of his redness, thinking about what a draw it would be if customers could actually hold a rifle that had belonged to Temple Fadden.

Matt congratulated himself for having thought of that angle. He'd turned his stolen rifle from a problem to a carrot now dangling before Bax's nose.

"Go on, then. Find your rifle," Bax said. But he thrust a pointing figure right in Matt's face. "But remember what family you work for. Remember what family has helped you, took you in, given you work. And when you get the chance to help that family, you don't fail to do it. You understand me?"

It was right then, with Bax's finger wagging under his nose and his big, angry face looming over him, that Matt decided his time with the Cornwells would be very short indeed. He'd not abide this much longer, maybe not any longer at all. He could find some other way to repay Will Cornwell for the help he'd given.

He said nothing at all in reply to Bax, simply staring back at him with no expression.

"I asked you if you understood me."

"I do speak the language, sir."

Bax flared a little at the sarcasm, but bit off whatever he'd been about to say. He looked away, then after a moment or two said, "You just be sure to be back on the job all the earlier tomorrow ... and when you get that rifle back, be sure to bring it with you."

CHAPTER 16

McGeeter stood beside the big tree that marked the crossroads and squinted into the morning sun, watching for the arrival of Matt Fadden. Beside him were two horses, one of them his own usual mount, the other a saddled mare he'd brought along for Matt. The horse was old and slow and belonged to his cousin, who'd been happy to let him borrow it when he learned that it was to be used by the son of the famous Temple Fadden.

Matt strode up to him, his shadow stretching out before him, and shook his hand. "I didn't expect to be brought a horse," he said. "Kind of you."

"A man of your stature ought not to have to go to Stalker's Creek on foot," McGeeter said. "And a man of my pegleggedness goes on foot as little as possible. I figured we could ride in together." He explained how he came to have the mare and so on.

"Tell your cousin I appreciate the use of his mare," Matt said, checking out the battered but serviceable saddle. "I've felt plumb hobbled since my own horse was stolen."

"He'd sell you that mare at a good bargain."

"Unfortunately, I can't even afford good bargains at the

moment," Matt said. "I'm still waiting for my first payday from Bax Cornwell."

They mounted and rode. "What do you do, McGeeter? Your work, I mean."

"Well, I mined until I lost the foot. After that the Widow Packard looked kindly on me and hired me as a kind of general help to her and anyone else she wants to help out. I drive a wagon, some, hauling things for folks, and I do errands and odd jobs ... that's pretty much the way I live. I guess the best thing I do for the Widow is making trips into Pactolas when need be. It saves her or other Packards from having to go into the belly of the beast, you see."

"If I recall, the beast has a taste for you, even if you aren't a Packard yourself."

McGeeter shrugged. "Work for the Packards, and the Cornwells will treat you like a Packard. I get a bit of trouble every now and again from them, but then there's always folks like you to help me out." He grinned.

"What if I hadn't?"

"Then they'd have harassed me and embarrassed me and I'd have had to put up with it best I could. A man has to make a living, and for me that involves occasional trips into a town where I ain't welcome."

"This feud is the biggest bunch of nonsense I've ever run across," Matt said. "Seems to me that all could have been left behind in Arkansas." He paused, then chuckled. "Kind of funny, two feuding families winding up in neighboring towns all the way across the country from where the feud began."

"It is funny... sometimes. But I'm afraid it will get uglier. There's bad things in the wind. Somebody on one side or the other, or both, is trying to stir this thing up to full-scale war again."

"Why?"

"Who can say? Like you said, feuding is nonsense. So you

can't expect folks to do sensible things when they're involved in it. If they'd just let it sit for a few years, it would all die away on its own. Feuds and hating and all can't live without being fed."

"There's been a recent turn or two in the situation that you probably don't know about," Matt said. He told McGeeter the story of the shooting attempt he'd witnessed, the dropped rifle, the reaction of the Cornwells, everything.

McGeeter gave a long, slow whistle when the story was done. "So now the Cornwells are having family meetings about it all! That's bad. Bad."

"You think a Packard tried to shoot Jimbo Cornwell?"

"Who can say? It might have been somebody else who had a grudge against him. I've heard of Jimbo Cornwell. He drinks, fights, steals—sorry character. He could have any number of folks mad at him at any given time. But you can rest assured the Packards will get the blame."

Matt was weary of thinking about the Packards and Cornwells and let the conversation lapse. He studied the rugged landscape and listened to the aging mare heave and wheeze as she lumbered up the steadily rising elevation toward Stalker's Creek. The day was pleasant, the air fresh, and it was very good to be on the move, as he was used to, and not standing on the porch at Bax's store, playing the village idiot for the sake of dry goods commerce.

He was considering not going back. He'd decided last night to give up working for the Cornwells as soon as possible, but had figured he'd give a decent notice. Now he wasn't certain he'd bother with it. He could quit, have Bax give his due pay to Will as hospitality compensation, then move on. Some saloon fighting, and he could earn a few more dollars to send Will's way, then forget the Cornwells and begin working toward getting himself back on his feet again with a new horse, new saddle, and so on.

The possibility had gelled into something approaching a

solid plan when they topped a rise and came into view of Stalker's Creek. Matt pulled the mare to a halt, letting it get some rest, and looked over the panorama before him.

The town was ugly, uglier than Pactolas—but Matt instantly liked it. There was an atmosphere about it, a rugged sense of freedom and potential, that appealed to him. Maybe it was because this was a Cornwell-free town, or because it reminded him of countless other towns of the type where a man who made money with his fists could do well for himself. Whatever it was, Matt knew right away that the next small phase of his life would probably be spent in and around Stalker's Creek.

"Nice town you got here, McGeeter," he said.

"Nice? Ha! It looks like the furnace scrapings of hell, and you know it."

"That's the kind of town I like. Bet you got a lot of saloons and gambling halls, eh?"

"More than enough."

"Bet a lot of the folks who frequent them wouldn't mind sparring with Temple Fadden's son, right?"

"You thinking of going back to the very way of living that got you beat nearly to death?"

"I am. Better to be beaten, bloody, and proud than to stand on a porch store dressed like a fool, pumping the hands of strangers who couldn't care less about you and only care about who your father is."

"What's the difference? You think those folks who fight you out behind saloons are fighting you for any other reason than who your father is? The reason they want to whup you is that it's a way of whupping *him*. The next-best brag to being able to say, 'I'm tougher than Temple Fadden himself.' "

"You're probably right. Maybe I just like punching folks in the face better than shaking them by the hand. Now come on, McGeeter. Show me your town."

CHAPTER 17

They rode down the middle of a street that was dusty at most spots, muddy with horse urine at others. The town was dirty, haphazard, somehow looking old even though it was not, and it stunk with every kind of human and animal reek one could think of. Matt rode through the middle of it all with a smile on his face.

"I feel invigorated, McGeeter," he said. "This is the best I've felt since I took the beating. Where can I find this man who may have my rifle?"

"I'll take you straight there ... and at that point, you and me will part ways for a spell," he said.

"Why?"

"Because I figure you'll go in there and threaten and cuss at Kelsey, and tell him what a sorry piece of trash he is for dealing in stolen guns, and if he sees me with you he'll figure I'm behind it all and I'll be on his list from then on. Kelsey ain't forgiving, and when he gets down on somebody he does all he can to make life miserable for them."

"What kind of hold does he have over you? What can he do to make your life worse, other than refuse to sell you a gun if you want one?"

"He deals with the Packards a lot, and knows I work for the Widow. If he gives the Packards trouble, then it works its way down to me."

"So how do you propose I deal with Kelsey?"

"That's up to you. As long as it don't involve me. If I was you I'd pretend I was a lawman and go in there and threaten him for selling stolen weapons. But I doubt you'd fool him."

"You leave me with little direction, McGeeter."

"Hey, I got you here, didn't I?" He pointed. "Yonder's the shop, the one with the blue door. Kelsey's a short fellow, stocky, no hair on the top of his head. Looks at you sideways a lot. Good luck."

"Where will you be when I come out again? I'll need to return the mare to you."

"Not right away you don't. You use that mare until you can get a horse and saddle of your own. Unless you leave the vicinity, of course. My cousin might look askance at that. But as long as you're in Pactolas or Stalker's Creek, you're welcome to keep the horse."

"Your cousin is generous."

"He's only doing it because of who your father is, and because you helped me."

Matt wondered if there would ever be anything in life he achieved or received on his own, not for the sake of his parentage. "Well, I'd still like to give you a report on my success or lack thereof," he said. "Meet you a little later?"

"I'll be at that cafe yonder in an hour," McGeeter said, pointing at a hole-in-the-wall they'd just ridden past. "Come find me, and show me that rifle, if you're able to get it back. Maybe I can hold it and look down the sights."

"Because it used to belong to Temple Fadden."

"Of course." McGeeter grinned.

"See you in an hour. I'll have either the rifle or Kelsey's head."

———

Kelsey had a sour look on his face and a short cigar smoldering in his mouth when Matt walked in. He was cleaning a disassembled Colt on a worktable that stood behind a long counter case full of assorted handguns. Rifles and shotguns of all varieties lined the room in wall racks.

"Howdy," Matt said.

Kelsey grunted in response and chewed on the cigar, vigorously rubbing the pistol barrel.

"Looking for a rifle."

"I got plenty. What kind you want?"

"A Henry."

"Got several. Yonder." He tossed his head toward the rifle rack on the west wall.

Matt went over and inspected the rifles for a minute or so. Kelsey watched out of the corner of his eye, confirming McGeeter's description of him. "Any others besides these?"

"I got a few in the back."

"Can I see them?"

Kelsey laid down the pistol, hopped down off the high stool he'd been perched upon, and revealed how short he really was. He waddled through a door behind him into the back room, then came out with four Henrys in his arms. These he laid upon the counter.

Matt looked down at a familiar old friend, which looked to have suffered no harm since it was stolen from him. He picked it up and smiled.

"This is the one. I'll take it."

"Fine. The price is on the tag."

Matt looked at the tag, yanked it off, and shook his head. "No. This one's free. If anybody pays, it will be you."

Kelsey turned his head to the side, squinted, and looked at Matt sideways. "What are you saying?"

"This rifle was stolen from me. It's mine."

"The hell! I bought that rifle myself at an auction in Helena six months ago!" He reached across the display case, trying to grab the Henry from Matt's hands. Matt deftly pulled it out of reach.

"You didn't buy this rifle at an auction and you and I both know it, so drop the pretense. This rifle was a gift to me from my father, who happens to be Temple Fadden, if you've ever heard of him. It was stolen from me when I was attacked and beaten up some several days ago over on the far side of Pactolas, and I figure you bought this rifle from the same ones who stole it from me. It wasn't theirs to sell and it isn't yours to keep. I'm walking out this door with it, and there's not a thing you're going to do about it."

Kelsey's head was a bald, red ball on top of his meaty shoulders. His eyes were red and his lips quivering, and Matt thought he'd never seen a human being so mad—until Kelsey spoke again, and he realized that Kelsey was no longer mad at all.

"Did you say your father is Temple Fadden?" His voice was an awed whisper.

"Yes."

"I'd heard... somebody told me that... I mean, I had been hearing that Temple Fadden's son was in the area. Shaking folk's hands at a store over in Pactolas. That's *you?*"

"That's me."

Kelsey waddled out from behind the counter, thrust out his hand at Matt, and they shook. It was one of those endless handshakes in which one party pumps the other's arm up and down for an inordinately long time.

"I'm honored to have you in my store, Mr. Fadden, and I apologize to you about the rifle. I had no notion it was yours. If I'd known, I'd have brung it to you myself. Closed down the shop and rode all the way to Pactolas to hand it to you personal, I would have."

Matt figured what he'd really have done was put the rifle

on special display with an absurdly high price tag in hopes of selling it to some other blubbering Temple Fadden worshipper.

This was all very surprising. Kelsey was beaming now and still pumping Matt's hand.

He couldn't help but ask: "Don't you wonder if I'm telling you the truth? Anybody could come in here and claim to be the son of Temple Fadden."

"Oh, your face is your proof, sir. I've seen far too many pictures of your great father to doubt you're the authentic offspring. Come here—let me show you something."

He led Matt back into the rear room. He had a rough and cluttered office there, one wall of which had several sketches and photographs of Temple Fadden, clipped from newspapers and magazines. Temple Fadden shakes hands with members of Congress. Temple Fadden displays the skin of the bear he killed with only his bare hands and a broken Bowie (a bruin that, Matt happened to know, had actually merely been found dead in the woods, natural causes, and hacked upon by his father so as to provide evidence to back up a wild story of having killed the beast). Temple Fadden meets a delegation of famous Indian chiefs. Temple Fadden stands on a riverboat at the beginning of his famous Mississippi River excursion and lecture tour.

Matt looked closely at his father's pictures, and realized that indeed he did resemble him a lot. More than he'd known, or wanted to know. As much as he'd banked on his father's famous name to make his own living, he really didn't like the notion of bearing the man's image around on his own person. When he was older, he'd be reminded of his father every time he looked in the mirror—not a pleasant prospect.

Below the pictures was an entire library of Temple Fadden dime novels. From a cursory glance Matt ascertained that Kelsey had nearly the entire lot—a whole shelf full of literary lies and rubbish, fawningly depicting the mythical version of the Great Man that the whole country seemed to somehow need to believe.

"I see you are a man very appreciative of my father."

"He's a great American. The very image of everything this country needs more of. Bravery. Goodness. Valor. Purity of heart. Toughness. Temperance. Good old-fashioned honesty. I keep these pictures here to remind me every day of those values, which your father embodies so well."

Odd words to come from a man who made part of his living selling stolen guns, but Matt let it pass. He looked at one of the images of his father and grudgingly gave mental thanks to the man. Once again his fame and reputation had allowed Matt to squeeze through a potentially difficult situation as easily as if he'd been greased from head to toe.

"Again, Mr. Fadden, I'm sorry about the rifle. If I'd known it was yours—"

"Yes, I know. Thanks for keeping it in good condition."

"I've had in my store a rifle that actually belonged to Temple Fadden! I can hardly believe it! Oh, sir —could I impose on you to sign your name on my collection of novels? I'd surely be obliged to you."

Matt looked at the long row of books and sighed. "All right. I reckon I can do that."

Kelsey scrambled back into the front room to fetch a pencil from off the counter. Matt stared at a photograph of his father, simultaneously appreciating and resenting the way his life and his father's were forever entwined.

As Kelsey reentered the office, Matt glanced at a small stack of rifles laid on a table in the corner. His eyes narrowed and he went to it.

"Here's your pencil, Mr. Fadden," Kelsey said, coming through the door.

"Mr. Kelsey... this rifle here... have you had it long?"

"Oh, no, sir. Just got those in yesterday, and they haven't been cleaned yet. That's why they're still back here."

Matt picked up one of them, a battered Winchester with a bright new butt plate. Another familiar rifle, one he'd last seen when he stashed it in that shed on Will Cornwell's property.

"Do you recall who brought these in?"

"Nobody brought them in. I bought them off a traveling gunsmith who came through town yesterday. He buys and sells from folks along the way, and then resells to me and other gun sellers. That was among the lot."

"Is he still in town?"

"Left this morning, going I don't know where."

Matt nodded and laid the rifle back in place. If Kelsey wondered why Matt was so interested in that Winchester, he didn't show it or ask it. He merely smiled and handed him the pencil.

CHAPTER 18

Matt left the gunshop with his rifle cradled in his arm, wrapped and tied in a soft cloth. For once being the son of Temple Fadden was not something to complain about. He knew that if he admitted the truth, most of the good things that had come to him had come because of his father's fame.

It was too early to meet McGeeter at the cafe. Matt chose to take advantage of the time to walk around town a little and look around. He liked this place. He liked the very dirt and smell and grit of it, the sense of freedom that it somehow gave him—a feeling perhaps associated with the fact that nobody here expected him to dress up like some imitation Crockett and say howdy on a porch store to every gawker who came by.

When he was finished with his obligations in Pactolas, he'd definitely spend some time in Stalker's Creek.

He wandered over to where the creek that gave the town its name flowed right through the middle of it all, at one point cutting right across Main Street. A rough, wide wooden bridge allowed the street to go on. Matt went to the edge of it, looking down into the rushing water, noting the trash that flowed along with it, including sewage from the many outhouses that were built right out over the creek itself.

"Well!" a voice said from the other side of the bridge. "If it ain't the famous Temple Fadden himself... oops, no, just his dear little boy."

Matt turned. Two hardcase types were there, grinning at him, both of them ugly and rough and looking like trouble trying to find a home. They seemed vaguely familiar.

"Why, it *is* him! Imagine that, Jess—two times in our lives we get to meet such a noted man! Ain't we just the luckiest ones there is!"

The speaker's voice and sarcastic tone were beginning to stir some recognition in Matt's mind. Also the mention of the name Jess. Ah, yes. This was a pair he'd fought at a saloon... where was it? Denver, he thought. All the way back in Denver. And now, by sheer chance, here they were again.

"You remember me, Fadden?" the speaker said. Matt had the impression he was slightly tipsy, even though the hour was early.

"I remember you. How you faring?"

"Oh, I'm fine. Took me a while to get over that little row you and me had, though. You knocked a tooth so loose that it had to be pulled out. Done it myself with farrier's tongs. See?" He pulled up his lip into an exaggerated snarl and revealed an empty place.

"Sorry. I didn't mean to do permanent damage."

"Hell, I don't mind it. Not much, anyway. I just tell folks that that there tooth was knocked out by the living, breathing offspring of Temple Fadden, and they seem right impressed. Had me a saloon girl so excited about it that she stuck her finger right in there to rub the gap. How you like that, huh? She done more than that after I took her upstairs." He chortled idiotically and elbowed his grinning companion.

Matt gave him a vague smile and nod in return, then touched his hat. "Good to see you again. Better be moving on now."

"What? You don't want to fight again? This time I'd whup you."

"You probably would. Have a good day, gents." He walked away, but kept these fellows in the corner of his eye. Both were wearing gunbelts, and the silent one had an unnerving tendency to rest his hand on the butt of his Colt, as if he might yank it out at any moment.

"Hey, Fadden!" the man called after him. "Let me tell you something: There's other folks than you and your pappy who can be famous! You can get famous all kinds of ways. Jesse James got right famous, didn't he? Did you know that women like a bad man? You can make a name for yourself just by robbing a bank, or holding up a train, or cleaning out a gunshop safe!"

Surely he was drunk. All this sounded to Matt like so much babble. He ignored it and went on.

The man hollered a little more nonsense after him, then at last went his own way, in the opposite direction, his companion with him.

Matt glanced back. There was something nagging at him —some odd sense of warning or threat. These two were trouble for certain.

He stretched his legs a little longer, then headed back toward the cafe. He paused to check on his horse at the hitchpost, then clumped down the boardwalk toward his destination. He wondered if McGeeter would be buying. Having not yet been paid by Bax, Matt was still hoarding the few dollars that hadn't been stolen from him when he was attacked.

He glanced up the street, looking for the two hardcases. He saw them at the door of a saloon across the street, the loud one arguing with the proprietor, who apparently hadn't opened yet for business and who was trying to send them on their way. Matt watched a few moments, that same bad feeling nagging at him. Then he went into the cafe to find a table and await McGeeter.

———

"That easy, huh?" McGeeter said, sipping coffee and grinning, his peg leg stretched out under the table in a way that looked like it would be uncomfortable but which apparently wasn't. Matt was leaning back in his own chair, also sipping coffee, and feeling quite full and satisfied. His emptied plate was scooted to the side, near McGeeter's, and both men were slowly working on slices of apple pie that had been brought to them five minutes earlier. McGeeter hadn't offered to pay Matt's tab, but the food was so good that Matt didn't really mind parting with some of his own cash.

"He all but knelt down and bowed his head when he gave it to me," Matt replied. "I went in expecting to have to argue like the devil. It surely didn't go like I expected."

McGeeter shook his head, grinning. "I didn't know old Kelsey had any streak in him except a mean one. And I surely didn't figure him for a dime novel reader. You never know, huh? Some folks ain't entirely what they seem."

Matt was looking out through the checkerboard-paned window. "And some are. Like those two there." He pointed at the pair he'd encountered earlier, now making their way past the cafe, heading up the street again.

"You know them?"

"Fought with them. Trounced them in a saloon fight a long, long way from here. And now danged if we don't turn up in the same town."

"Kind of like the Cornwells and the Packards."

"I guess so, now that you mention it."

"Have they seen you here?"

"Ran into them out on the bridge. Had a few words with some edge to them, but that was all. But those two are trouble. You can smell it on them."

"Well, let's hope they go somewhere besides Stalker's Creek if they do cause trouble."

"Why? You got you a tough-knot lawman here or something?"

"Nope. No law at all. Not for about a month now."

"What happened?"

"The town marshal got sick and left. The town ain't replaced him yet. Nobody willing to take the job."

"Why?"

"This can be a rough town, Matt. Miners and all ain't known for their Sunday-school behavior, especially in Stalker's Creek. It's just the town reputation, I guess. You know how some towns just get known for being rough."

"Yeah."

"You know, Matt... you ought to consider becoming the town marshal here."

"Me? A marshal?" Matt laughed.

"Why not? The son of Temple Fadden would have the respect of everyone. Nobody would want to mess with you."

"You're forgetting something, McGeeter. People mess with me all the time. They pay me for the privilege of fighting me."

"Yes, and you whip them nine times out of ten, right?"

"Reckon I do."

"Then you've got what it takes. You could have that job, Matt. If the Widow put in the word for you, you'd have it."

"The Widow Packard?"

"Yep. She pulls a lot of weight in this town." He glanced around and grinned coyly. "And she's got plenty of it to pull."

"I don't want to be a town marshal."

"Would you rather spend the rest of your days grinning on a porch for Bax Cornwell?"

"No."

"Then you'll spend them fighting behind saloons?"

"Not forever, no."

"You've got what it takes to be a lawman, Matt. I can tell it."

"You've got a nose for lawmen, huh?"

"Some things a man just knows. You ought to do it, Matt. Let me talk to the Widow. Come meet her. She'll get you the job if you want it."

"How did the Widow Packard get so much power?"

"Her husband, God rest him, was Stalker Packard. He was the one who made the first strikes around here, and you can see where the name of the creek and the town come from. He was a good man, a hard worker, but it was the Widow who had the sense in the family. She had a business mind, a lot of common sense, and she's hard as stone, that woman. Tough as she has to be. When Stalker passed on, she just sort of fell into the role of town leader. Nothing official, no title or nothing, but everybody here respects her. The town board listens to her, tries to do what she says. She wears the pants in this town, that's for certain." McGeeter snickered just after saying this.

There was evidently a hidden meaning to the comment that Matt had missed. "What?" he said, finding McGeeter's smile contagious.

"You meet her, you'll know what I mean," he said. "Come on, Matt. Go with me and we'll talk to her. You'd make a good lawman. The way you stood up to them two who was bothering me, why, you'd do just fine at it."

"I told you, I don't want to be a lawman."

It was just then that they heard a gunshot. Outside, down the street somewhere, but still startlingly loud. Matt and McGeeter looked at each other, then rose, along with everyone else in the cafe. They tried the window, found they could see nothing but people on the street also shifting positions and craning their necks, looking up the street. So they tossed money onto the table, went to the door, and exited— Matt still holding his wrapped-up Henry rifle— just as another gunshot sounded and a woman somewhere along the street let out a scream, and men's voices here and there rumbled and thundered.

Then, loudly and abruptly, two fast gunshots echoed down the street.

CHAPTER 19

"They've robbed it!" somebody yelled. "They've robbed it, in broad daylight!"

"The bank?" Matt asked McGeeter.

"Not in this part of town. . . . Look out!"

The two hardcases Matt had talked to earlier suddenly appeared at the doorway of Kelsey's gun shop, blasting away in all directions, sending people scrambling. They cut around the side of the store, ducked back into an alley. Right behind them, Kelsey came staggering out, bloody, holding his head, yelling for help, then collapsed onto the boardwalk. A crowd converged on him, kneeling to help.

"Dang!" Matt muttered. "That just plain riles me!"

He had the Henry out of its wraps in two seconds, loading some of the cartridges Kelsey had given to him when he returned the weapon.

"What are you doing?" McGeeter asked.

"Going after those two bastards. They can't go busting the head of common merchants and get away with it."

"I didn't think you wanted to be a lawman."

"I'm not being a lawman. It's just that I kind of liked old Kelsey. I don't like folks hurting people I like."

"You better move fast if you aim to catch them. They probably got horses waiting."

Matt was already on his way before McGeeter finished his words. He ran to the nearest alley and turned back in the same direction the pair had gone, loping along, fighting the disadvantage of unfamiliarity with the layout of this town. But like most mining towns, it was simple, and he quickly found his way to a smaller back street, and saw the pair running along, one of them dropping cash as he ran, the other trying to retrieve it and cussing loudly.

Matt ran hard right at them, and was nearly upon them before the money-grabber—the same half-drunk man who had babbled so much at him before—noticed him coming. Something about Matt's onrushing, fury-driven form must have been terrifying, because the man let out a yell of alarm and dropped the money he'd picked up.

He had enough presence of mind, however, to raise the pistol he carried in his other hand and take a nearly point-blank shot at Matt.

Somehow the bullet missed. Matt heard it strike a pole-mounted bell somewhere down the street with a loud clang, and sing off in a wild, dangerous ricochet. Matt swore beneath his breath, swung the Henry, and caught the man in the jaw with its butt, laying open flesh all the way to the bone. The man screeched and fell.

The other thief, meanwhile, was leaping onto a horse that was loosely hitched to a porch rail a few yards ahead. He was dropping money worse than ever now, bills flying everywhere. Matt marveled to think that Kelsey kept that much cash in his place.

Matt stepped over the fallen man and reached the mounted one just as he was pulling the horse away from the post. Matt swung the Henry again and hit the man hard on the right thigh, making him howl. Then he pounded him again, again, and with a wide swing hit him in the gut with the full weight of the rifle, plus the force of Matt's muscle. The man folded up and fell off the horse.

Matt was hit from behind by a mass of solid force. The first man had managed to get up and attack him wildly, blood flying from the open wound. Matt went down and the man went down atop him, flailing and pounding, but disoriented enough that he lacked any effectiveness. Matt heaved upward and rolled him off, then came to his feet.

The man kicked out aimlessly, and as luck would have it, kicked the rifle right out of Matt's hands. The second man, meanwhile, was up and now joined the attack, coming onto Matt from the side just as a second lucky kick took Matt's feet out from under him. He went down as the newer attacker drove two hard punches against his jaw.

At the same time, the first hardcase was going for the dropped rifle. When he reached it, Matt was back against, and onto, the low porch behind him. He fell back onto the wood, head reeling from the blows he'd received, and the first man leveled the Henry and fired at him. Matt felt the sting of the powder blast and the heat of the shot as something nipped through his hair, not an inch from his scalp. The porch absorbed the bullet. Matt heard the lever being worked. The second shot would probably not miss.

He rolled and pushed upward, deftly coming to his feet, and did a spinning kick that caught the rifleman in the elbow, hard. The rifle went flying, clattering onto the street, as the rifleman was driven by the force of the kick back against the building. Matt moved in, fists accurate and hard as hammers, pounding the man's face, head, chin, then driving into his gut. A knee to the groin finished him off, taking him down as a half-senseless, helpless heap.

Matt turned his attention to the second man, who at the first shot had lost his interest in fists and was now thinking again of escape. The man turned to run, but Matt was upon him, throwing an arm around his neck from behind and pulling him into a choke hold, lifting him off the ground and twisting him down. The man was strong, though, and somehow kept his footing, and with a surge of power gained the advantage. He let out a massive roar and threw Matt against a big-paned window facing onto the porch. The glass shattered and Matt tumbled inside the building, a lawyer's office. He heard exclamations of surprise and anger from behind him, and a woman's scream, but didn't even bother to look around. He got to his feet and literally dove back out the window he'd just come through, and caught the man who'd thrown him right around the waist. They fell off the porch together, coming to rest against a hitchpost. Matt, driven by anger and determination, got the man by the hair and pounded his head three times against the hitchpost, very hard. But the man did not collapse, as Matt had hoped he would. He wrenched free, turned, and hit Matt hard on the chin. Fortunately it was a somewhat glancing blow, or Matt would have been down for good.

Matt was vaguely aware that the fight had by now drawn a crowd. Through a ringing in his ears he heard the howls and hoots of men rooting him on. He heard the name "Fadden" called more than once and knew he was recognized. There well could be people in this crowd who had been in Pactolas in recent days and seen him on Bax Cornwell's store porch. Or there might be others here whom he had fought before in saloons, as he had his two current opponents.

It was not his watchers who compelled his fighting now, though, but his own determination not to let these two get away. This was not his problem, not his town, but it didn't matter. He'd prevail here or die trying.

The fight was in the center of the street now, a hard-slugging battle of blood, sweat, and aching muscles, bruises and flying saliva—two men doing their best to pound one another senseless and both refusing to give up.

Matt's vision was focused as if through a tunnel; for the

most part, he saw nothing but the face and form of his opponent. Around the periphery was a blur of human forms and
the background of a mining town, but little specific or clari-
fied came through the murk. Occasionally, though, he was
conscious of one particular face or another, watching him,
shouting at him with a voice that couldn't be heard through
the din ringing inside his head. He saw McGeeter, pumping
his fist and shouting encouragement. He saw three strangers,
restraining the first man he'd taken down, who now had no
fight left in him and was nothing but a mass of bloody weari-
ness. He saw a man, wearing an oversized, rumpled suit,
smoking a cigar and standing on the same porch that had
hosted part of the fight. And once, he thought, he saw Jimbo
Cornwell himself, mounted out on the street, watching the
fight with great interest. But Matt figured he'd just imagined
this. Why would a Cornwell be in Stalker's Creek, the home
of the enemy?

The world suddenly changed, becoming wet, cold. The
ringing in his ears became muffled and his vision went gray
and blurred. It took him a moment to realize that his head
was submerged in dirty water. His opponent somehow had
managed to knock him down and shove his head into a
watering trough. Matt felt the man's hands close around his
throat, choking him...

He brought up his leg and kneed him in the crotch, but
even that didn't immediately break his hold. Matt balled up
his fists, estimated where he needed to aim, brought the fists
together like the twin prongs of a vise, and hit his enemy on
each ear at the same time.

That did the job. The choke hold loosened and Matt
pulled his head out of the water. He shook his head like a wet
dog shaking its body, and found that the dunking had actually done him some good. The ringing in his ears was lessened his vision became clearer, and the cold sting of the
water had given him a burst of new vigor.

Time to end this thing. He went straight at his opponent, who was now temporarily deaf from what Matt had just done, and hit him in the face again and again. The man staggered backward, somehow managing not to fall even though it would be better for him if he did, so the pounding would cease. Matt punished him fiercely, driving through his fists every ounce of rage he could muster. The man at last went down and Matt went down as well, still hitting, until at last strong hands pulled him off and it was over.

"Here now, Mr. Fadden, you don't want to be killing him!" an Irish miner said in his right ear.

"You've done a right fine job on them two pieces of rubbish!" another voice, this one sounding like a Georgian, said in his left ear.

He was only dimly aware of his surroundings as he was half-led, half-carried to the nearest porch and sat down upon its edge. Hands pounded his back in congratulations, and through the murk of his still-slackened consciousness, Matt detected a general air of joviality prevailing all around. He began to realize that he'd just made himself a hero in the eyes of his watchers.

It didn't matter. All he wanted at the moment was a cool drink of water and someplace to rest. He asked for both. In moments a cold cup was in his hands, and he drank deeply. His strength was coming back fast, and some pain with it. He knew he'd be hurting for a day or two, and hurting badly. He doubted he'd be up to standing on Bax's porch, or for that matter going back to Pactolas at all for a day or two.

He didn't much care. He was too tired... but also satisfied. He'd done a good thing here.

"What will you do with those two?" he asked a stranger near him. "You have no law here."

"No, but we've got a jail, and we'll lock them up and place some volunteer guards. We'll deal with them, no worry."

They helped him up. McGeeter joined him now. "Come on, Matt, you loco, knotheaded hero, you! What the devil made you jump in like that?"

"Where are we going?"

"To meet the Widow Packard. And you can rest there, and we'll have the sawbones come in to look you over. You took a good beating there."

"I gave a worse one back."

"I reckon you did! That's the finest fight this town has seen in a long time—and it's seen a lot of fights!"

"Thank you," Matt said. "How's Kelsey?"

"Cracked skull, but he'll be fine."

"Good. Good."

They went on, Matt letting McGeeter lead the way.

CHAPTER 20

T he doctor was younger than the one at Pactolas, and smelled like horses. Matt suspected that most of this man's patients had four legs rather than two.

He swabbed the last crusted blood off Matt's face, looked over the bruises already starting to appear, and shook his head. "My friend, if you don't change your way of life, you're going to be dead before your time. You've got the most battered-up body I've seen in all my years of practicing medicine."

"Does that include both human and horse bodies?" Matt asked.

"What?"

"Nothing. Forget it. Am I going to be all right, Doc?"

"Oh, you'll heal up. But the body never forgets. You beat and batter it enough times and eventually it turns on you. You'll have aches and pains that won't go away for the rest of your days, and if you just keep on taking beatings, you very well may wind up with damage to the brain or the internal organs, in which case you'll be needing ministerial services rather than medical ones."

"All I do for a living these days is stand on a porch and

grin at people." Matt turned slightly in his chair, felt a stab of pain, and groaned.

"I'm told you're a saloon fighter."

"I have been."

"You need to quit it. Keep on standing on the porch, but don't get in more fights."

"I got very little money to pay you, Doc. Will you set me up on a tab so I can come back and pay you later?"

"Mr. McGeeter has already paid your bill."

"I can't let him do that!"

"If you want to repay him, that's between you and him. Meanwhile, I've done all I can do. Go thy way and sin no more, Mr. Fadden. Go lay up somewhere for a couple of days and heal up."

"Thank you, Doc."

Matt left the office, hobbling like an old man, looking for McGeeter. McGeeter had brought him here, then vanished while he was being examined. Matt didn't know where he'd gone, or why.

Matt slowly crossed the street, and noticed that people were looking at him, talking to one another. He saw one woman smiling at him with such obvious interest that at first he thought she was a prostitute singling him out for a proposition, then realized she was standing beside her husband and daughter, and both of them were looking at him in just the same way.

A couple of boys of about thirteen came to him and told him they'd seen part of the fight and thought it was the finest thing they'd ever witnessed. One babbled on about Temple Fadden, and the other offered to go fetch his crippled father's walking cane and give it to Matt, if he needed it until he was over being sore from the fight. What the crippled father would do in the meantime without his cane didn't seem to concern the boy.

"Boys, all I need you to do for me is to tell me where Mr. Thomas McGeeter might be. Do you know him?"

"I know him!" one of them piped. "I seen him talking to the Widow Packard."

"Yonder he comes!" the other boy declared, pointing.

Indeed, McGeeter was peg-legging it up the street toward Matt. He had a big grin and eager manner.

"Doc finish up with you?" he asked, looking Matt up and down and checking out the bandages and bruises on his visible portions.

"Told me I was going to die unless I quit fighting."

"He's probably right. Come on. I want to take you to meet somebody who can help you do just that."

"Do what?"

"Quit fighting for a living. Make a real living in a real job."

"If you're talking about what you were talking about earlier—"

"Don't go prejudging things before you've heard everything out."

"Listen, McGeeter, the doctor said you paid my bill. I appreciate it, but I can't have you doing that for me."

"It ain't really me. It's the Widow. She's got plenty of money to cover it, and believe me, after what you did today she's more than happy to pay that measly bill. There's hardly a soul in this town who wouldn't pay it for you."

"Where's the two I fought with?"

"Locked up. The town council is getting together this afternoon to set up a temporary jail guard, probably volunteer, and to talk about replacing our missing marshal."

Matt realized something all at once. "My rifle's gone!"

"No, it's not. It's over at the Widow's place, waiting for you. Let's go. Can you make it?"

"I can make it if you can. I sure won't be outdone by a man with a wooden prop."

"Hey, I can move on this thing like a leaping antelope. Let's go see the Widow. I think you'll find meeting her will be very interesting, and maybe a little surprising."

"What are you talking about?"

"Just come and meet her."

———

McGeeter led Matt to a simple small cabin, standing on a side street and not marked in any way to indicate it was anything but some impoverished person's dwelling. But as they entered, Matt saw that the cabin was actually furnished as a business office of some sort, though an untidy one to be sure. Shelves drooped under the weight of maps, documents, and other materials; a desk in the center of the single room was piled with papers and books. On the wall hung a slate board like one that might be used in a classroom, and a piece of chalk dangled beside it on a string. Scribbled on the board were various almost indecipherable notes and numbers, most of them seeming to relate to mining claims, rents due and rents received, mine productivity reports, and so on.

The chair behind the desk was turned backward as Matt and McGeeter entered, so that all Matt could see of the man who occupied it was slumping shoulders and a rounded, lowered head with thick gray-black hair. He was wearing a faded, very threadbare business suit that seemed a little ill-fitting. Smoke curled from somewhere in front of the unseen face, filling the room with the stench of a cheap cigar.

For some reason, that ill-fitting suit looked familiar.

The chair turned and Matt's eyes widened as he saw the strangest-looking man he'd ever encountered. The face seemed oddly clean, childish-looking... and then Matt realized that the look wasn't so much childish as feminine.

This cigar-smoking, business-suit-wearing being before him was not a man but a woman.

"Mizz Packard, I've brung him like you wanted,"
McGeeter said. "This here is Matthew Fadden. Matt,
meet Mizz Packard."

The Widow Packard stood slowly, examining Matt up
and down, chewing on the reeking cigar stub in her mouth.
Matt couldn't help but stare back at her, astounded at this
unexpectedly androgynous human being.

Something McGeeter had said flashed through his mind:
She wears the pants in this town, that's for certain. He'd
laughed when he said it, and told Matt he'd understand the
humor once he met the Widow.

Matt did understand—though he didn't understand
why.

The Widow had a hard, almost masculine quality about
her, but as she looked at Matt an astonishing transformation
occurred. The masculine quality softened, faded away
entirely, and for a moment she was as womanly as any female
Matt had ever met—reminded him of his late mother, in
fact, so much so that it jolted him.

"You are Temple's boy, no doubt about it. I see him so
clear in your face—just like him, you are. Just like I
remember him so well."

Matt was taken aback by the implications of her words,
and himself could not find an immediate response.

She went on: "I saw you fight today, Mr. Fadden, and
your motion and grace were Temple Fadden all over again. It
was just like watching him the time he fought off two of the
biggest and meanest Cornwells of the lot, way back in
Arkansas more years ago than I care to remember."

"You knew my father?"

"Still do, I daresay, unless the worst has happened and I
haven't learned it."

"He's still alive... or was as of five months ago, which was
the last time I had any contact with him. I sent a wire to him,

checking on him, and got one back. But how... when... what was... how did you know him?"

She threw back her head and laughed. "He never talked about it to you, I'm sure. It was a long time ago, son, when your father was hunting in Arkansas, back when he very nearly was what the dime novels make him out to be. He was yet single and I hadn't married into the Packards at the time, though my kin were close to theirs and the Cornwells viewed us as part and parcel with them. Your father and I were close to each other. Very close. Had things gone different, had he not been so restless, I might have been your mother, young man." She laughed again, and all the femininity vanished. She was again a sexless, cigar-smoking, undefinable, and uncategorizable human entity.

"It's a day of surprises, huh, Matt?" McGeeter observed from the side.

Matt wouldn't dispute that. This whole affair was quite surreal, but intriguing. He wondered how his father, a man whose eye for the ladies had been very evident since he was a widower and perhaps, Matt always suspected, before that as well, could have been attracted to such a female as this.

Perhaps the way she presented herself today was different from how she had in her earlier days. Surely this was the case —the Temple Fadden that Matt knew would be astonished, and not positively, by such a spectacle as the Widow Packard.

"Well, I've given you a lot to justify that look on your face," the Widow said. "Come over here and sit down. Can I offer you a cigar?"

Matt nodded, and went to the nearest chair and settled into it. The cigar, unlike that smoked by the Widow, was a good one. He bit off the end and she fired it up for him, then went around her desk and sat down in her chair again, leaning on the desktop with her elbows and looking firmly at Matt. The whole thing was more than a bit uncomfortable for him.

"You know, I reckon, what I might talk to you about."

"I think so. McGeeter has been saying you might want me to be—"

"Our town marshal. Yes."

"I don't know that I could do that job."

"From what I saw today, I believe you could. From what you did for Thomas over in Pactolas, I believe you could."

"All I did was intervene to keep a crippled man from being wrongly treated."

"That's the very kind of trait a lawman needs. And the fact that you went up against Cornwells makes you shine even brighter in my eyes."

Matt saw where this might be heading. "I need to tell you, Miz Packard: This feud between your family and the Cornwells is your feud, not mine. I work for Bax Cornwell because his brother was kind to me at a time I was down, and Bax offered me a way to make some money to repay that kindness." He paused. "Of course, Bax doesn't seem to see it that way himself."

"He's told you that if you work for a Cornwell, you are a Cornwell," she said.

"Something like that."

"Do you see it that way?"

"No."

"I can offer you work, too, Matt. May I call you Matt? I can pay you better than Bax Cornwell. And if you want to use that money to repay this debt of yours, that's fine. If you become the town marshal of Stalker's Creek, you don't work for the Packards. You don't work for me. You work for the law."

"Beg your pardon, Miz Packard, but if you're so in control of this town that you can decide all on your own who the marshal is and what his salary will be, it seems to me that I *would* pretty much be working for you."

"I won't deny to you that I have a lot of power in this

town. But I'm not Bax Cornwell. I don't treat Stalker's Creek as my personal kingdom, as he does Pactolas. I don't think like he does."

"But he does think like he does, and if I went to work in Stalker's Creek, especially at the behest of the patriarch, uh, the matriarch of the Packard family..."

"He'd consider you a vile traitor and an enemy. The moral equivalent of Judas Iscariot. And in the current climate, your safety from the Cornwells could not be assured."

Something about the Widow beyond her odd mode of dress was striking Matt as unusual, but only now did he realize what it was: This backwoods Arkansas woman was remarkably well-spoken. Not in a citified, formally educated manner, but she presented herself with a certain degree of articulateness.

A glance around the room revealed something he hadn't noticed before. Mixed in with the maps and papers and general clutter were books of many sorts—novels, history, essays, reference works, even volumes on philosophy and religion. This woman, though probably lacking a formal education, had done much on her own to fill the gap.

"Ma'am, I won't lie to you. Right now the work I'm doing, not real work at all, in my way of thinking, doesn't much suit me. And though I've never thought of being a lawman, I admit to being attracted to the offer. But I do need time to think about it, and to tell the Cornwells whatever needs telling."

The Widow looked very pleased. "I'm glad to hear this. I would be honored to have the son of my old friend Temple Fadden helping oversee the safety of this town."

Chapter 21

This was all moving ahead much faster than Matt had anticipated. In fact, Matt hadn't come here really expecting to let it move ahead at all. But he was growing more intrigued by the moment. Options that didn't seem options at all an hour before were suddenly worth considering.

"Would I work alone?" he asked.

"I believe we could attract you a force of deputies, at least one and probably two. I would be willing to fund the salary of at least one myself, and perhaps both."

"Why are you being so kind and helpful to me?"

"I've explained that sufficiently, haven't I? You were kind and helpful to McGeeter. You intervened today when a crime was committed, even though it was of no personal consequence to you and you easily could have done what the rest of the town did: nothing. And you are Temple Fadden's son. You would have the respect of the public. And hiring you would enable me to do a kindness, however indirectly, for an old and dear friend I would love to see again someday." She puffed her cigar and squinted at Matt through the smoke.

Matt asked more questions. Pay, hours, the general function of the office, how he would fit into the town's governance system, to whom he would directly answer, and so on. She had all the answers, and none of them provided him a reason to shun what was being offered him.

"I have no horse," he said. "Mine was stolen from me, and the one I'm riding today is borrowed from McGeeter."

"When you leave today you'll be riding a good horse and it will be yours. I'll also provide you a pistol and holster, which I note you don't have on you today. Do you need one?"

"Truthfully, yes." Matt was stunned to think he was to be given a horse outright. And a pistol, too?

"You do shoot well, I assume?"

"I'm a good marksman with both rifle and handgun."

"Being Temple's son, what else could you be?"

Matt had to smile. "My father isn't quite the human god he's made out to be. I've seen him miss many a shot."

She laughed. "I'm under no illusions about your father, Matt. I knew him well, and human he is. But in his younger days, he was extraordinary. I knew few men who could approach Temple's capabilities, with the exception of my own husband Stalker, God rest him." She tilted her head and looked at Matt closely. "Pardon me, but I'm continually astonished by how much you look like him as he was when I knew him."

Knowing his father's taste for beautiful women, Matt had to assume that the Widow had changed dramatically over the years. He couldn't picture his father being attracted at all to the Widow as she was now.

"The horse is yours whether or not you take the job. The pistol and gunbelt come as part of the enticement."

He drew a deep breath, then made his decision. "I'm inclined to take the position. Don't hold me to that firm just yet, but I think in a day or two you'll have a final answer from me, and it will be yes."

He could hardly believe he was saying it. A town marshal! It was one of the last things Matt Fadden had ever expected to become.

The Widow beamed, rose, and thrust her hand across the desk. Matt rose, wincing a little from the lingering pain of his fight, and shook her hand.

"I don't know if you should try to return to Pactolas today," she said. "You took quite a beating."

"I'm accustomed to it. I'll make it."

"Then Thomas here will take you to get that horse right away. And I'll call Kelsey's brother to go reopen his gun shop so that we can get you a pistol."

"I haven't finally accepted the job offer."

"No, but you will. I think you and I both know that now."

"Yes."

"I'll get the town council together and we'll make the offer official and final within the next day or two. Meanwhile, you go tell Bax Cornwell and his ilk whatever you need to tell them."

McGeeter pounded Matt on the shoulder, generating another wince and a grunt of pain. "Pleased to have you coming to Stalker's Creek," he said.

Matt nodded. Despite his bruises, he had a good feeling just now.

He was glad to be coming to Stalker's Creek, too.

———

The sun was low on the horizon when Matt rode slowly into the stable yard near Will Cornwell's house. The evening was quiet and pleasant, smoke drifting lazily from Will's chimney, the scent of a recently cooked supper lingering in the vicinity. He hoped that Constance had saved some of it for him, because he was half starved.

He stabled the horse and put away the saddle, a saddle he'd obtained today through a special arrangement conceived and backed by the Widow. He'd pay back the cost of it in small increments, taken out of his salary. And Matt had the suspicion that the Widow had deliberately set a salary with just enough extra in it to cover the saddle's cost, so that in effect he was getting it free.

It was all strange and unexpected, but good. The Widow was treating him with the deference she might give a son.

What a strange, interesting woman! After parting company with her today, Matt had asked McGeeter why she dressed as she did, and smoked cigars like a man.

"It's strange," McGeeter said. "She's always smoked the cigars—lots of women do, though not many do it right out in the open—but the clothes are something she started doing after Stalker Packard died. Those are his old suits she wears, redone to fit her."

"But why?"

"She's never said. Some of her kin swear up and down that she does it because Stalker himself, his spirit, at least, is living inside her now. They say she invited him to go on living through her after he died, and that's why she wears his clothes."

"Sounds like a spook story to me. Do you believe it?"

"No," McGeeter had answered after a pause. "I think she wears his clothes because it reminds her of him, and makes her feel like he's with her. And it reminds the rest of us that she's the one in charge now. She's the one wearing Stalker Packard's old mantle of leadership in Stalker's Creek, just like she's wearing his old clothes."

Matt saw Will Cornwell in the shadows of the porch as he walked out of the stable and toward the house. Matt had his Henry rifle in hand.

"Evening, Matt," Will said, his face becoming barely visible for a couple of seconds as he drew on a cigar and caused the tip of it to cast a feeble red glow all around it. "Glad you're back safe and sound."

"Glad to be here."

"Got your rifle back, I see."

"Yes, sir." He hefted up the weapon. "This was my father's rifle once. I'm glad to have found it."

"Where was it?"

"In a gun shop. The men who stole it from me apparently sold it to the shop owner for him to sell again. He didn't know the history of the rifle... just another Henry to him."

"How'd you persuade him to let you have it?"

"It was easy, to my surprise. When he found out who I was, and that the rifle was once Temple Fadden's, he just gave it to me in exchange for me signing my name on a bunch of dime novels about my father."

"He just believed you when you told him your story?"

"Yes. He said he recognized my father's looks in my face. And he'd heard that I was in the region, working for Bax."

"News does travel between these towns. Can't have something happen in Pactolas without people in Stalker's Creek knowing it a heartbeat later." He paused—meaningfully, it seemed to Matt. "And vice versa," he said, a little more slowly.

He was getting at something, but Matt wasn't sure he wanted to see what it was just yet. He was too hungry to banter words.

"Is there anything a man might eat, left from supper?"

"There's four or five pieces of leftover chicken. Some biscuits and beans. All cold by now."

"Cold is fine by me. Might Constance spare me a plate?"

Will gestured him toward the door with a wave of his cigar. Matt walked past him on the porch and Will stared out into the gathering night without even looking over at Matt as he went by.

Something indeed was going on here, some undercurrent that Matt couldn't yet make sense of.

But Will spoke just as Matt was by him and opening the door.

"Where'd you get the horse?"

"I got it today."

"I could guess that. But where?"

"A stable in Stalker's Creek."

Will looked at him. "How'd you pay for it?"

"I didn't have to."

"What?"

"It was given to me."

Will said nothing for a couple of moments. Then: "What about the saddle?"

"Got it on credit, I guess you could say. I'll pay for it over time."

"Somebody gave credit to a drifter from out of town?"

"Yes." Matt could have told him that he was no longer to be a drifter, and from the perspective of Stalker's Creek would soon not be an out-of-towner, either, but all that would open up matters best discussed with a full belly and some renewed mental energy.

"Who gave you credit?"

"Somebody who had horses available."

Will frowned at Matt through the darkness; Matt could feel the burn of it.

"You didn't steal that horse, did you, son?"

"That's a question a man could take a lot of offense to," Matt replied. "That's a serious thing to say."

"Sorry, then. But the question stands."

"I didn't steal the horse."

"Then who sold it to you?"

"I'll talk to you after supper."

Matt went on in, knowing that he was being presump- tuous and a little rude, considering that he was still a guest in this house. But Will had a rude manner tonight as well, and Matt sensed that some learning was going to take place on all sides before this evening was out. Will would learn that Matt was soon to be the town marshal of what the Cornwells saw as enemy territory, and Matt would learn whatever it was that had Will all intense and angry even before Matt had showed up.

He found the food, dished out a plateful, and ate hungrily. Then he ate a second plateful, not quite as much, and washed up his dishes. His belly was full and that was good, but he'd not even tasted the food.

While he had eaten, Will had come back in the house and was in the front room. Someone else had joined him there, coming in from the door leading off to the hall. Matt could hear them talking, low and intensely. Judging from his voice, Matt suspected that the other fellow was Jimbo Cornwell.

Jimbo, whom Matt thought he'd caught a glimpse of in Stalker's Creek today in the midst of the big fight with the gun-shop robbers.

Matt was not disturbed by any others of the household while he was in the kitchen eating and cleaning up afterward. All but Will had gone to bed, and the fact that Will had not seemed significant. Typically the entire clan were early-to-bed types, Will included.

Matt dried his hands on the dish towel and was about to join Will and Jimbo in the front room when he spotted a copy of the newest copy of the *Pactolas Bi- Weekly Post* lying on a stool by the back door. He picked it up and found, right on the front page, the highly anticipated article about Bax Cornwell's latest achievement, the very living and breathing son of Temple Fadden, right here in Pactolas, talking and walking and shaking hands just like the best-trained ape, and anyone is welcome to come by and meet him!

Matt read the article quickly, groaning several times. It was worse than he'd feared. Day had written a gushing, fictionalized, exaggerated, absurd piece of nonsense, full of wrong information, outright lies, and quotes ostensibly from Matt but which obviously had been contrived by Bax and Day, working in conspiracy. Matt read himself praising Bax, praising the Cornwell family, praising Pactolas, and even insulting, in veiled manner, anyone who might be on the Cornwells' wrong side. Journalistically, at least, Bax and Day had engaged Matt Fadden in the feud, taking their side against the Packards and bringing with it all the credibility the public associated with the Fadden name.

Matt felt his face redden, his blood surge in anger. He almost slapped the paper down hard on the stool, but held back. *Calm down,* he counseled himself. *This is just what you thought would happen—maybe a little worse than you thought—but still the same kind of nonsense you knew would be printed. Let it go. It doesn't matter now. You'll be leaving Pactolas and the Cornwells behind and none of this will matter at all.*

Matt scanned over the article again and actually managed to chuckle at it. And it helped him seal irrevocably his decision to take that town marshal's job. No more trained-monkey work. No more playing the clown to sell dry goods. He would have a respectable profession, one that paid well.

Even if that marshaling job didn't pan out, he decided, he'd quit his job with Bax. He'd work a few days more, just to be decent about things, but then he'd be gone. A man could take only so much humiliation.

CHAPTER 22

Matt walked into the front room, carrying the newspaper. Sure enough, Jimbo was there, and the way he looked at Matt could have curled the paper into a crispy ash.

Matt ignored the glare and held up the paper. "Interesting story here," he said. "Talking about some fellow with my name who works for Bax. I need to meet him... I sure don't know the man this article describes."

Oddly, Will seemed to take offense. Matt had the feeling the man was predisposed tonight to take offense at anything Matt said or did. "Are you saying that paper doesn't tell the truth?"

"I'm saying the story about me is about as accurate as a Temple Fadden dime novel. Call it lies if you want; I'll be kind and just refer to it as fiction."

"That paper is Bax's," Will said. "He doesn't advertise much that it's his, but it is."

"I'd gathered that."

"You're insulting Bax when you insult what he owns."

"You have my apology, then."

"Tell me what happened today," Will said, more like a challenge than a question.

"I went to Stalker's Creek. I found the gun shop where I'd heard my stolen rifle might be. Indeed, it was there. I talked to the owner, signed some dime novels about my father, and got my rifle. Now I'm back."

"That took all day?"

"Will, what kind of explanation do you think I owe you?"

"Is there something you don't want to tell me?"

"Don't take offense—though I know you will—but I don't know that I'm obliged to tell everything that I do."

"I know what he did today," muttered Jimbo.

"How'd you get them bruises?" Will asked.

"I helped out a man who'd been robbed."

Jimbo snorted and turned away, muttering something Matt couldn't make out.

"Helped a man? You're quite the hero, ain't you?"

"What are you talking about?"

"Why, you helped out that peg-legged Packard the other day! What are you trying to do? Live up to your father's reputation?"

"The man I helped out the other day is no Packard. His name is McGeeter."

"He works for them. That makes him a Packard."

Matt was beginning to comprehend which direction that dark undercurrent was running, and with Jimbo here, he could guess what Will had been told.

Will went on: "When you associate too close with a Packard, you get their stink on you. You become no more than what they are. I hear you had a fight today, Matt."

Matt looked at Jimbo. "I had a notion I saw you there."

Jimbo, shorter than Matt, suddenly faced him and shoved his homely face close to Matt's. "I seen you, all right, I seen you fighting, and I seen you going about with that peg-leg. And I seen you going in to jaw with the Widow Packard herself, too!"

"And then you came running back home just so you could spread the word before I got back, huh?"

"All I told was what I seen."

"I'd think you might not be so eager to spread hurtful word about a man who might have saved your hide."

"You never saved nothing."

"If I hadn't sung out when you were being shot at, you might not be here today."

"I got shot at again," Jimbo said.

"What?"

"I got shot at, just like before. And it happened today. On the way back from Stalker's Creek."

Matt thought for a moment. "If you were shot at today, I know it wasn't from the same rifle that shot at you before. I saw that rifle in the gun shop today."

"I don't care what rifle shot at me, but what person. I notice you got a rifle now! Got it today, in fact."

"Are you saying I shot at you? I wouldn't waste the bullet."

"I'm saying that it's only your word against nobody's that it wasn't you who took the shot at me the first time. You talk about rifles that fall off cliffs, then disappear, then show up miles away in gun shops. Sounds made-up to me. You could have shot at me today, too, for all I know."

"Why would I want to shoot you, Jimbo?" Though at the moment the idea seemed appealing.

"Hell if I know! Why would you sneak off to Stalker's Creek and pay call on the Widow Packard?"

"You already know why I went to Stalker's Creek. I paid call on the Widow Packard because she asked to see me. I reckon she was pleased that somebody actually took time to stop a couple of thieves instead of just letting them run loose."

"It was her who gave you the horse, ain't it!" Will said.

"Yes."

"And sold you the saddle? On credit?"

"That's right."

Will swore. "She done all this because you fist-fought with two robbers?"

Matt was growing tired of answering questions that he really shouldn't even have to hear. He glared silently at Will.

"I'll tell you what she's doing," Jimbo said. "She knows he works for Bax, and she's buying his loyalty. Hell, she may have give him all that truck as pay for him promising to do in every Cornwell he can!"

"That's nonsense," Matt shot back. "I owe the Cornwells every gratitude for the kindness they've shown me."

"You're right on that," Will said. "And gabbing with the Widow Packard ain't no way to show it."

"You want me out of here, Will? You want me to go?"

Will's eyes were dark fire, and he said nothing.

"Send him away, Will," Jimbo said. "You can't trust him."

But Will shook his head. "No. No. Bax's newspaper story just came out today. If he goes away now, there'll be no benefit from it."

"I'm glad to feel so welcome," Matt said, unable to squelch the sarcasm.

Will studied him, and as he did so, it seemed the flame of his anger began to die, as if its intensity had burned out its own fuel.

"Jimbo, why don't you go now?" Will said, still looking at Matt. "I need to talk to Mr. Fadden in private."

"All right. Maybe I'll go visit Bax. He'd sure like to hear about all this."

"No," Will said firmly. "Not a word of this from you to Bax."

"But Bax would want to—"

"I'll deal with Bax. You leave it be. I mean it, Jimbo."

Jimbo muttered something and turned away, grabbing his hat from the coat stand as he headed for the door. He turned and glared back at Matt a moment. "I still say you could have been the one who shot at me."

"Just go on, Jimbo. And thank you for coming to see me," Will said.

When Jimbo was gone, Will faced Matt. "For the sake of your work with Bax, I'll say nothing to him for now of this meeting of yours with the Widow Packard. He'd be furious to know of it. Your job would be lost."

Matt, disgusted by all of this, was ready to announce that the job didn't matter anymore anyway. One thing made him hold his tongue, though: the fact he was very tired and looking forward to the bed that awaited him. He didn't want to be thrown out of the house tonight.

"I appreciate it," he said. "I have no desire to offend you, Bax, or anyone else. But there's something you have to understand, Will. I know you folks tend to think that everyone around you should be taking your side in this old feud of yours. And the feud is your business, and the Packards' business, not mine. But still, you have to realize that folks like me can't embroil themselves in somebody else's fight. The Widow Packard invited me to see her because she appreciated what I'd done with those two robbers. And it ends up she knows my father from years on back. It would have been right rude of me to refuse to see her."

"Bax won't see it that way."

"I can't help that."

"The old hag knows your pa, eh?"

"She didn't seem a hag to me."

"No, I guess not. I don't know what the word is for a woman who thinks she's a man and dresses up in her dead husband's clothes."

"She was kind enough to me today. She didn't hold it against me that I work for Bax. She don't seem to have the kind of hatred for you folks that you have for her and her kin."

"Somebody on that side has got some hatred, or else Jimbo wouldn't have been shot at twice now. Joe Frank Cornwell wouldn't have been fired upon, nor the others of my kin who have also been shot at."

"But it goes two ways, don't it? I remember being told that the Widow's own son was killed. Henry, I think his name was."

"He was. But I defy anyone to prove a Cornwell did it."

"You don't have proof that the Packards are the ones shooting at you, either."

"Who else would it be? They feuded this family for years back in Arkansas. Now they just won't let it die, even though we're hundreds and hundreds of miles away."

Matt was weary of words. He could hardly wait to get away from this family, this town. Though he'd be willing to work out some more time for Bax before moving on to Stalker's Creek, he knew that he'd never be allowed to stay once they learned where he was going and who had offered him the job. He'd be lucky, in fact, if they didn't shoot him down on the spot.

Perhaps the thing to do would be simply to write a letter, leave it behind, and disappear.

"Will, I'm sorry I've riled you so. I wasn't trying to. I'm tired now and ready to go to bed. Is there anything more you need to say to me?"

"I reckon I'm through. For now."

"Good night, then. And thanks once more for all the hospitality your family has given me."

"Just remember that we were giving that hospitality before the Widow Packard started handing out free horses and such."

"This ain't a competition between rival families, in my mind," Matt said. "I'm just trying to live my life and get along with everybody I can."

Will shook his head. "It don't work that way. When it comes to the Cornwells and the Packards, a man has to choose. It's like that Bible verse: You're either for us or against us."

Will turned away and headed for his bed. Matt watched him go, then moved his battered body wearily and winced. The day's beating had revived some of the aches and pains that had gone away before. Realizing just how tired he really was, he headed for his own bed, and was asleep not two minutes after he collapsed into it, having removed nothing but his boots and his belt.

CHAPTER 23

With his recovered Henry in hand, Matt showed up early the next morning on the porch of Bax's store, clad again in his makeshift costume and ready to make the best of things until he had a chance to talk to Bax and tell him it was over. He'd decided for a time not to tell Bax what his new line of work was going to be, or where, but had changed his mind because it felt unmanly, downright cowardly, to hide the facts just because Bax wouldn't like them.

There was a small crowd already waiting for him at the store when he arrived, most of them bearing clipped-out copies of the story from the newspaper, and copies of Temple Fadden dime novels for him to sign. He cheerfully set about to fulfill their requests, and had just finished dealing with the final member of that initial crowd when he looked up and saw Bax approaching, his face as dark as a storm cloud.

Matt knew right away that Jimbo Cornwell had ignored what Will told him. He'd talked to Bax.

Matt quickly finished signing the dime novel in his hand and handed it back to the little boy who'd brought it. He tousled the boy's hair, smiled, and sent him on his way with an admonition to "be brave and true and honest in everything you do, just like Temple Fadden."

Matt watched Bax stride straight toward him. He braced himself for an explosion, but it didn't come. Instead, Bax stomped up close to him and stared at him from six inches away, eyeball to eyeball, dead silent except for hard breathing brought on by exertion and anger. Matt wanted to shove his looming presence away, but for the sake of the public setting, held back.

"Anything I can do for you, Bax?" Matt said.

"You damned traitor," Bax said back through gritted teeth. "I should knock you off this porch."

"1 don't suggest you try it. You've talked to Jimbo, I guess."

"Oh, yes. I've heard all about your little adventure, and about your visit to the Widow."

"I take it you don't like it."

"You know where I stand on such things. I had a bad feeling about going along with the notion of you going to Stalker's Creek at all. I shouldn't have let you."

"Let me? Just who do you think you are, Bax? You think that because I agreed to stand on your porch a few days you have control over everything I do?"

"You know that when you work for me, you abide by my rules."

"Just how much are you paying me, Bax?"

"I told you what I'm paying you."

"No, it must be more than that. You don't buy my life for so low a price as you said you were paying."

"I ought to cut you off right here. Send you on your way."

"Better not do that, Bax. Your little newspaper story just came out yesterday. You can't promise people the son of

Temple Fadden and then give them nothing but an empty porch."

"I can do whatever I choose in this town. I'm the authority here. Don't forget that."

"Bax, let's you and me both calm down. And just listen to me for a second. I didn't go to Stalker's Creek planning to do what I did. I didn't expect to talk to the Widow Packard, and I didn't expect her to offer me work."

"Work? What the devil are you talking about?"

"I've been offered the job of town marshal for Stalker's Creek." Matt knew this was an exaggeration; he'd received only the Widow's offer so far. But if she had told him the truth, that was merely a technicality.

Bax was so taken aback he wasn't able to speak for a few moments, and when he did, all he could say was "Town marshal?"

"That's right. And I've accepted the job."

"Accepted the..." Bax's voice faltered away.

"Yes. But I'll stay on here awhile, if you want, to fulfill my obligations to you."

Bax's face began to redden. "Stay on..." He faltered away again.

"Yes. If you want me."

"You're... you're getting ready to work for the Widow?"

"No. For the town of Stalker's Creek."

"Same thing! Same damned thing!"

"Not as I see it."

Veins in Bax's temples and neck became visible. He lifted his arm and pointed in the direction of Stalker's Creek. "Go," he said. "Go now."

A little boy with a pencil and piece of paper in his hand wandered up, big-eyed and nervous. "Mr. Fadden?" he said softly.

"Just a minute, son," Matt said.

"You sorry son of a—"

"Bax, we got young ears present."

"Don't you lecture me, you sorry Packard!"

"You're right, Bax. I do need to go now. There's no point in continuing this any longer." Matt took off his fringed coat and tossed it to the floor. "Thank you for the work. It's been mighty fine."

It was then that Bax made his mistake. He made a liquid, retching sound in his throat, filled his mouth, pulled his head back . . .

Matt's hand shot to Bax's throat and grasped it, hard. He squeezed down while looking Bax squarely in the eye. "You won't spit on me, Bax. You can talk to me as you like, call me whatever you want, send me on my way, cuss my father and mother and everybody I ever cared about, and throw rocks and mud in my direction ... but you don't spit on me. No matter who you are. No matter how big a man you think you might be."

Bax's eyes were big and growing as red as his face.

"Do you understand me, Bax?"

As best he could, Bax nodded.

Matt let him go, giving him a little backward shove at the same time. Bax stumbled backward and fell back onto a bench beside the door, somehow managing to keep his seat if not his pride.

He sat there, spraddle-legged, gaping at Matt with a look of pure hatred. But he dared not speak a word.

Bax Cornwell had just been humiliated on his own property, in the heart of his own town. And there were several witnesses, people attracted by the argument. . Matt kept Bax in the corner of his eye as he signed the little boy's paper. "Thank you, son. And take a tip from me: Watch out who you go to work for when you're older. You don't want to waste your time working for a fool."

"Yes, sir. Thank you, sir."

"You're a fine young man."

As the boy walked away, Matt strode up to where Bax still sat. "I'm sorry it ended up like this. No reason for it. If you and your kin had more sense about you, none of this would have had to happen. You're good folks, in your way. You were kind to me, helpful, and I appreciate it. But you can't think you can run the lives of everybody around you, nor expect the rest of the world to take up your own private feuds. Give whatever pay I'm due to Will. Meanwhile, I'll take my leave. I'm off to Stalker's Creek."

"Off to fight with the Packards," Bax said, hatefully.

"No," Matt replied. "Off to enforce the law and keep the peace."

CHAPTER 24

Deputy Jack Bail was finishing off the last of the apple pie as Matt walked into the office. He had eaten it right out of the baking dish, which he was holding to his face and licking clean as Matt came in.

"Oh, oh!" Matt exclaimed. "I was counting on eating that myself. I had my thoughts set on that piece of pie all morning!"

Jack put down the crockery dish and dabbed a stray bit of sugary apple off the end of his nose. "Sorry, Marshal. But a man can resist such a temptation only so long. Ain't nobody can bake a pie like *she* can. Not even my dear departed mother could come close."

From the rear cell block a voice called out: "Ain't right, eating pie when there's a hungry prisoner with nothing but dry corn bread! I could smell that pie the whole time he ate it! I'm dying back here, Marshal!"

Matt called back: "Ronald, if you want pie, you quit coming into town and getting drunk and rowdy every week, so I don't have to lock you up so much. Stay home and have Rowena bake you your own apple pie."

"Rowena can't bake nothing. That woman is no 'count around a stove nor a dish."

"I guess that's what drove you to drink, eh?"

"That and a million other miseries."

"Hush and eat your corn bread, Ronald."

Matt took off his hat and flipped it expertly through the air. It came to rest on a wall peg. "Up from the desk, Jack," he said. "I got some paperwork to do and two tired feet to rest."

Jack rose and put the pie plate on a nearby shelf. "Any particular place I should patrol?"

"North end of town. I spent most of my time on the south side this morning."

Jack nodded, took his own hat from a peg beside the one that held Matt's, and went out the door into the sunshine. Matt settled down in the creaky chair and leaned it back against the wall. He removed a gleaming Colt from the holster on his hip and laid it on the desk, eyeing it with satisfaction. He loved that pistol, a gift from Kelsey down at the gun shop, and wished it needed a cleaning just so he could have an excuse to fiddle around with it. Kelsey, who had not had much use for lawmen before, was Matt's most devoted supporter, grateful that he had brought down the two who had robbed him. They had been sent on to higher legal authorities weeks ago, and Stalker's Creek was glad to be rid of them.

Matt grinned to himself and glanced at the empty pie dish, the thought having risen that losing out on that last piece of Annie Wolfe's apple pie was the biggest disappointment he had yet experienced as town marshal of Stalker's Creek. A man so satisfied that his biggest letdown was something so trivial as that was a man who ought to be grateful, and Matt was.

On the other hand, there was really nothing trivial about Annie Wolfe's apple pie. She had a talent with cookery that Matt doubted had any rival. And to his good fortune, he and Jack Bail, the deputy he'd hired two weeks earlier, had enjoyed the benefits of that talent several times. The lovely Annie Wolfe, like Kelsey down the street, had cause to be very grateful to the town marshal of Stalker's Creek.

Matt had encountered her the first time at the edge of town. She'd been as pale as milk at the time, her skin like alabaster against the highlight of her auburn hair, her attractive face full of pain and fright as blood streamed down from a serious knife wound in her left arm. Matt had gotten to her just as she collapsed.

He'd carried her into town in his arms, finding the doctor quickly and staying nearby until the wound was patched and the bleeding staunched. He'd talked to her briefly, found out the circumstances of the robbery attempt that had brought about her wounding, and set out to find the culprit.

It hadn't taken long. He'd tracked down the man, a drunken failed miner from Texas, and sought to arrest him at a little saloon on the outskirts of town. The man would have none of it, bringing out the same big Bowie he'd used to cut Annie Wolfe. Her bloodstains were still on the blade even as he waved the knife menacingly at Matt with one hand, the other hand sneaking toward the pistol thrust into his belt. He'd just cleared the pistol and was swinging it up when Matt drew and fired. The bullet had clipped the Bowie blade right in half on its way into the scoundrel's heart. The man fell dead right there on the saloon floor.

Matt had just killed his first man, and it did bother him some. But after a couple of days he made peace with it, realizing he'd done only what he had to do. And in a way, the thing had an added value: Word quickly spread about the fast-shooting new marshal at Stalker's Creek—the very son of the legend Temple Fadden himself, no less—and before long Matt was at the front end of some legend-building of his own. The shooting incident earned him the respect of the rough breed that inhabited this town. When he patrolled the streets, he did so with an authority he would not have had otherwise. So far he'd had surprisingly little trouble in Stalker's Creek. Most of the time his arrests consisted of little more than hauling in rowdy drunks like Ronald Fletcher there in the back of the jail with his dried and unwanted corn bread.

Still, the town council that had hired Matt wanted full reports on all arrests and other activity of the marshal's office, so Matt pulled a pad of paper from the desk and began to write. He was a week behind on his reports and determined to catch up today, as much as he despised paperwork.

He worked as Ronald munched his corn bread and Jack walked the streets of Stalker's Creek out there somewhere.

———

Noon. The battered old clock on the office wall chimed it out, and Matt stirred awake. The office was empty, Ronald was snoring back in the cell block, and Matt was glad nobody had been there to see the town marshal of Stalker's Creek snoozing at his desk in broad daylight. Thank heaven the curtains were drawn so no passersby could look in—and that the clock had wakened him before Jack got back. He'd never hear the end of it if Jack caught him sleeping at his desk.

He rubbed his eyes and checked out his report, finding to his disgust that he'd drifted off before finishing it. He scrambled to get it done now, hoping to be through before Jack got back in. Otherwise he'd be questioned sharply about what was taking him so long to do a simple weekly report... Jack was like that.

He swore under his breath as the door began to open.

Jack had returned and he was still scribbling. But when he looked up, he was pleasantly surprised to see not Jack, but Annie Wolfe. In her hand was a covered tray, precariously balanced as she pushed the door open.

Matt scrambled out of his chair and helped her in, taking the hot tray and setting it on the desk. The delicious smell of beef and potatoes rose through the cloth that covered the tray.

"Miss Wolfe, I swear, you shouldn't be walking about carrying such loads as that with your arm still hurt. You might damage yourself."

"My arm's doing well, Marshal. It's because it's doing well enough that I can carry things now without any problem that I decided today would be the day for me to bring you and your deputy a hot meal. It's something I've been wanting to do ever since you were so helpful to me."

"You've already brought us two pies, Miss Wolfe. You needn't have done this." But Matt was awfully glad she had. "Where is your deputy?"

"He ought to be back anytime."

"We'll be sure to save him some."

Matt peeked beneath the cloth. "My goodness, miss. . . there's enough to feed five people here. That is beef stew, I believe? And biscuits? Oh, lands. That looks fine and smells better. You'll have some along with us, won't you?"

"Thank you. I will, if you don't mind it."

"It'd be an honor." He paused as he heard Ronald snort and grunt and abruptly quit snoring. The food aroma had probably awakened him. "And would you mind if..." He cocked his head in the direction of the cell block.

"You're a kind man to be so good to a prisoner," she said.

"Ronald's harmless. Just gets drunk and a little reckless sometimes. I'll give him a small serving. It'd be torture to smell food this good and have not even a taste of it."

Ronald took the food with gratitude. "Don't let this give you the notion that this jail is the place you want to be," Matt told him. "This here is a special gift, courtesy of Miss Annie."

"Obliged, ma'am," Ronald called out to Annie in the office. "You're a fine cook. And pretty. You wouldn't marry an old drunk, would you?"

"You needn't answer that, Miss Wolfe," Matt said. "Don't eat too fast, Ronald. Take time to enjoy it, because there ain't going to be no seconds." He left and closed the door between the cell block and the office.

The outer door opened as Matt closed the inner one. Jack walked in, nose twitching. "I knowed I smelt something," he said. "Good day to you, Miss Wolfe."

"Hello, Mr. Bail."

"Call me Jack." He took a deep whiff of the stew. "Or, if you're willing to have me, you can call me husband."

"That's the second marriage proposal Miss Wolfe's received in the last five minutes," Matt said.

"You beat me to the proposal?"

"No. Ronald."

"Hell you say! Oh... sorry, Miss Wolfe. But lordy, don't marry Ronald. You'd be throwing your life away."

Annie Wolfe blushed shyly. The banter didn't seem fully comfortable to her, though, and Matt detected it. "Let's shut up the talk and use our mouths for eating these good victuals," he said.

They fell to eating, and it was a soul-cheering experience. Annie was obviously pleased to watch the men enjoying her cooking. As he ate, Matt wondered why Annie had no husband. She'd been married when she came to Stalker's Creek, he'd heard, but her husband had died of some unknown cause, the local doctor speculating that a blood vessel in his brain had burst. That had been a couple of years ago, though, and it surprised Matt that such a catch as Annie hadn't been claimed by some other worthy fellow since then.

Ronald began singing in the back, an improvised bunch of atonal nonsense about Annie Wolfe being an angel come down to cook heavenly dishes for mere mortals. Annie looked embarrassed, and Jack rolled his eyes, finally ordering Ronald to shut up.

When Annie had gathered her dishes and left, Jack gave Matt a wry and knowing look and said, "That woman's got her heart set on you, Matt Fadden."

"That's nonsense."

"No it ain't. You can tell."

"She's grateful to me for helping her, and for shooting the man who cut and robbed her. That's all."

"Uh-uh. I can tell such things. That woman's besmitten with you. She's finally found a worthy successor to her lost husband."

"You're a fool, you know that, Jack?"

"You just don't want to admit I'm right."

Matt sighed. "Tell me what you know about her. Did you know her husband?"

"I met him once. He seemed a good enough fellow. Kind of rough and backward... not the kind of man you'd expect to snare a beauty like her."

"Where'd they come from?"

"Eastern part of Texas, I think."

"He was a miner, I guess."

"Yes. But he didn't live long enough to have much success."

"So how does Annie make a living?"

"She's a seamstress, and she keeps the books at the dry goods store. At times she's been a cook at the Stewart Cafe down the street, but I don't think she's doing that now."

"She's an impressive woman."

"Matt, you ought to see if you can court her. I'm serious.

She thinks the world of you, and it shows. Bringing in food, being so doting and kind... that ain't just gratitude."

"I'm too sorry an old drifter for so fine a woman as her."

"You're not a drifter now. You're a lawman. Settled down and respectable. Supported by the Widow Packard, the most powerful individual in this town. Why, you're a prize, my friend. A real prize. I've seen the young ladies of this town watching you walk down the street. Their hearts get all aflutter and their eyes fill up with admiration. Annie Wolfe most of all."

"Ah, it's been too long since I courted any woman that I'd hardly know where to start."

"I can tell you where to start. You start by asking her to accompany you to the dance down at the livery this coming Friday evening."

"In case you don't realize it, you and me have to be at that dance in a working capacity, Jack. From what I've heard of prior dances in this town, there's always a fight or two, or worse."

"You can work the dance and keep company with the lady at the same time. I'll be there, remember. I ain't taking nobody with me. I'll keep watch on the rowdies and you keep watch on Annie Wolfe. If I need your help I'll call for it."

Matt thought it over. "Sounds tempting, I'll admit. It would be fine to escort such a pretty lady."

"Go ask her. I can tell you how to find her place."

"It might raise questions for me to call on a woman who lives alone."

"My goodness, but ain't you turned into a worrier about propriety and all that!"

"I've got a public job. I've got to watch my step. I'd not want to make the Widow regret having put such faith in me."

"I'll go with you to Annie's place. I'll stay off to the side and you can talk to her, right outside in the open. Nobody can wag a tongue over that."

"I'll think about it."

"Don't think long. You ought to ask her this very afternoon."

"I'll think about it."

CHAPTER 25

Matt knelt beside the prone, unmoving body, using his folding knife to carefully cut the bloodied cloth away from the area of the exit wound, located just to the left of the dead man's right shoulder blade. He pulled the cloth back and exposed the ugly hole.

Jack, leaning over beside Matt, said, "Good lands ... that's the worst I've seen, ever. I'm amazed he dragged himself this far before he died."

"He must have been determined to live if he could. Poor fellow! I wonder why he was shot?"

"I can take a good guess. This is Bill Packard."

"I should have known," Matt said. "Another feud death, then."

"Probably. I can't figure any other reason. Bill Packard was a good, decent man. No enemies... except the Cornwells, of course. But Bill never was a feuder himself. He didn't regard the Cornwells as enemies, though no doubt they looked on him as one. Just being a Packard makes you an enemy in the eyes of the Cornwells."

"Help me roll him over."

They heaved the corpse onto its back. Bill Packard's dead

eyes gazed like glazed marbles at a sky they could no longer see.

"Here's where the bullet went in—no powder burns around the hole. So he wasn't shot point-blank. But from the violence of that exit wound, I don't think the shooter was too far distant."

"So he probably saw who shot him."

"Probably."

"Not that it helps us. Bill ain't talking."

"That's for certain. How close kin was this one to the Widow?"

"I think he was a cousin several times removed." Jack glanced up, then whispered, "Speak of the devil..."

Matt looked up to see the Widow Packard striding toward him on her rather short and thick legs. A burned-out cigar hung on her lip and her face was as grim as that of a fire-and-brimstone preacher.

She squatted beside the dead man and looked into his face for a long time, as if trying to find answers in it. At length she shook her head and said, "Poor Bill. God bless his wife and children."

"I'm might sorry, Miz Packard," Matt said.

"Curse this feud," she murmured.

"Amen," Matt said. "Ma'am, that dance is tomorrow evening. Given what's happened here, maybe it should be called off."

"No," she said. "I'll not let this feud start dictating how this town runs itself or how we in it live our lives."

"Jack heard talk that some of the Cornwells might show up and cause trouble."

"If they do, it will be your responsibility to deal with it. If need be, you can deputize some men temporarily to help keep the peace. Ten dollars apiece for the night's work, paid directly by me. Hire up to six men if you want. I'll not see us start running scared of every whispered threat coming out of Pactolas."

"Yes, ma'am."

She sighed. "Poor Bill," she said again.

"Ma'am, one more thing regarding the dance: Perhaps it would be best if you didn't attend. You'd be the prize target."

"I'm not planning on attending, but not because of this. Since Stalker passed on I have no desire to attend such events. But I'll be hanged before I'll see the people of this town deprived of all pleasures."

Jack, attempting to tighten the somber mood of the moment, said, "Matt is taking a woman to the dance. Annie Wolfe. He asked her yesterday afternoon, and she agreed."

The Widow frowned at Matt. "You shouldn't take anyone to that dance," she said. "Not after this. Your full attention needs to be on keeping the peace."

Matt felt a burst of offense. This kind of ordering about seemed a little intrusive, something like the kind of over-control that Bax Cornwell had been prone to force upon him. But this time Matt had to agree. He had a bad feeling about that dance. He truly did not need a distraction such as Annie Wolfe to keep him from giving full attention to his paid duties.

"You're right, ma'am. I'll speak to Miss Wolfe today."

She nodded and rose. "Get Bill's body over to the under-taker. I'll go speak to his family myself."

When she was gone, Jack said, "Sorry, Matt. I'd not have mentioned Annie and the dance if I'd had any notion it would lead to her saying that."

"Don't worry about it. It's for the best. Annie will understand."

"I'm still sorry."

"Don't be. I'm not sure I even want her to go to that dance. I have a feeling there may be trouble there. I wish it would just be called off."

"Maybe it will rain. They'll call it off if it rains. They hold the thing right out in the open, in the middle of the stock pen. It takes them most of the day before just to get the manure all shoveled away."

"Pray for rain, then. I don't want this dance to happen."

"When will you talk to Annie?"

"As soon as we deal with this body. You come with me again. I don't want anybody talking about me paying calls on her, and spreading lies to hurt her reputation."

"You think she'll be angry, you backing out of taking her?"

"I hope not. I'll try to make it up to her later, if she'll let me."

"You're fond of her, I think."

"Yes. I believe I am. You stay here with the body, Jack. I'll go tell the undertaker to bring his wagon."

Jack sat in his saddle, rolling a cigarette and ignoring Matt and Annie, who stood in the yard of her small cabin, talking intently.

"I'm mighty sorry to back out on you this way," Matt was saying. He'd just told her about the shooting, the rumors of the Cornwells causing trouble during the dance, and his worries that the dance might become a dangerous affair in the current volatile atmosphere. He hadn't told her, though, that he was altering their plans at the behest of the Widow Packard. "I hope you understand why."

"Of course I do. I understand that you have to see to your duties first and foremost. And if things do get bad at the dance, maybe I wouldn't want to be there, anyway."

"Please be aware there's no one else I'd rather have accompanying me than you. I'd have been honored to escort you, and have to admit I resent having to back out on it."

"I do understand. I'm not offended." She smiled, but it seemed to Matt she was trying to put a good front on hurt feelings. But he wasn't sure; reading women had never been his gift.

"Who do you think shot the man?" she asked.

"I have no way to know. I suspect it is part of the feud, though. They say Bill Packard was not the kind to make enemies."

"I hate that feud. It's so wrong, and foolish."

"I agree with you. But it ain't going to end. I can tell you from what I know of the Cornwells that they'll never give up hating the Packards."

"The Packards are as bad. They hate the Cornwells just as much as the Cornwells hate them."

"I have to say my impressions from the Widow Packard, at least, are that the Packards are less responsible for keeping the feud going than the Cornwells are. I think she'd like to see it all come to an end—very different than Bax Cornwell, who I worked for briefly in Pactolas."

Annie turned her face away and stared out toward the horizon a moment. "I despise them all," she said softly.

Matt was surprised to hear this from a woman who struck him as so gentle and soft. "Why?"

"Because of how their feud intrudes itself into everyone else's life. It's dangerous to live in a place where people shoot at each other. People here just want peace, but all the Cornwells and Packards give them is that cursed feud."

Matt gazed at her, and felt he'd just learned something. In the quiet anger of Annie Wolfe he'd just gained perspective on how trying it was to live in a place where violence could break out without warning, where anger and bitterness prevailed over reason. Even someone such as Annie, unconnected to whatever old issues sparked the feud, could become embittered and angry in such an environment.

What if others were the same? What if men of the region

who had no connections to either the Packards or Cornwells decided they were tired of putting up with a private war that involved only some but endangered all? What if they decided to put an end to it by putting down both warring factions? This feud could expand into a full-scale local war.

Annie spoke again. "With ail respect, Mr. Fadden, you're not right about the Packards. They are just as hateful and grudge-bearing as the Cornwells. And the Widow is no better than anyone. She may talk peace, but behind the scenes, you can be sure she's helping keep the feud running."

"You know the Widow well enough to know that?"

She hesitated. "My husband knew things about the feud and the two families. I'm just saying what I heard him say."

Matt nodded, and instantly gave lessened heed to Annie's judgmental words. Unless he had some firsthand insight that Matt was unaware of, probably Annie's late husband had merely been repeating local gossip, which had precisely the value of a bucket of old dishwater. Even so, Annie's words were a clue to local attitudes. They told Matt that the respect and deference given to the Widow Packard in this town might not be as universal as it first appeared.

"Annie, I'll make up to you for the dance. Maybe, if you want, we could take a meal together at the cafe."

She smiled. "Not the cafe I work at sometimes, I hope," she said.

He grinned. "Why? Is the food not good?"

"It's very good. Just too familiar."

"Then we'll go to the other one."

"I accept your offer."

"Good. Good." He smiled back at her. "What will you do about the dance?"

"You mean, will I go alone? No. I don't think so."

"I'd feel it a shame for you to miss it just because your escort let you down at the last minute."

"If there's a likelihood of trouble, I think I'll stay home."

She paused, her face clouding. "I hate the feud. I hate it. It killed my husband, you know."

"What? I'd heard he died naturally."

She looked down. "I suppose the feud didn't kill him directly. But it worried him so much. He talked about it a lot, all the time. I sometimes think it was his worrying that caused him to die."

"Was he kin to one or another of the families?"

She held silent, toying with a gold locket that hung around her neck. Matt wondered if it was a gift from her late husband. She spoke. "Listen . .. I'm sorry I said what I did. Don't listen to me. Some things make me feel upset—I say things then that I shouldn't say. I exaggerate things, I think."

Matt smiled and touched the brim of his hat. "Miz Wolfe, you don't worry about that, or anything else. I'll call again and we can discuss when to have that meal."

"Thank you, Mr. Fadden."

"I've got an idea: Why not call me Matt?"

"Fine... and I'm Annie."

They shook hands, and Matt went to his waiting horse.

"Well?" Jack asked.

"She took it just fine. We're going to get together another time and maybe take a meal somewhere."

"She going to the dance alone?"

"Nope."

"Probably a good thing. I don't have a good feeling about tomorrow night."

"Don't say that."

"Why?"

"Because I feel the same way, and I don't want to be right."

They rode silently back into town. "Tell me something, Jack: Did Annie's husband have any ties to either the Packards or the Cornwells?"

"Not that I know of. Why?"

"Nothing. Just wondering."

They rode past the livery, where the dance would take place. Workers were busily shoveling heaps of manure into wheelbarrows, to be hauled off and dumped out of range of eye and nose. Off to one side, a crude but sturdy stage was under construction, just big enough to hold the fiddler, a guitarist, and a dance caller.

"Good place for a dance," Matt observed.

"Yeah. But I hope it rains like Noah was going back in business," Jack said.

"So do I."

CHAPTER 26

J ack and Matt knocked on doors, asked questions, observed again and again the area where the body of Bill Packard had been found. They uncovered nothing. No witnesses, no one who had even heard a shot. They were able to find the place Packard had been standing when the bullet hit him, and track the route he'd taken as he first staggered, then dragged, his mortally wounded body back toward town in vain hope of help. They determined the likely area from which the fatal shot had been fired and explored it thoroughly, but found no clues.

"Maybe we can find the bullet," Matt said. "Figure out what kind of gun it came from."

"Odds are it was a rifle," Jack said. "What's the point, Matt? We can't learn that much from a bullet."

Matt shook his head in disgust. "If these two fool families are going to feud, I wish they'd do it in the open, not shooting at each other from hiding, or off where nobody else can see."

"You're thinking about that shooting back at Pactolas, the one with the dropped rifle."

"I told you about that? I couldn't remember. Yes, that is

what I was thinking of. I'll bet you anything this one was just like that—sorry, outright assassination. Bill Packard going along, minding his own affairs, and somebody pops a bullet through him from behind a tree. Maybe a direct retaliation for that shooting attempt against Jimbo Cornwell. Huh... maybe it was Jimbo himself who did it! He seems the kind, and I know he's around Stalker's Creek sometimes. I saw him here myself."

"Maybe we should ask around, see if anybody saw him about the time of this shooting."

"I guess we should. But we can't be too direct about it. We can't just accuse him out of the clear blue because we just happened to think of him."

"Speaking of the clear blue ... I sure wish it would rain," Jack said.

"Me, too... but it ain't. Not a cloud in the sky. Looks like the dance is going to go on."

Matt had not known that McGeeter was a fiddler. It was with surprise that he watched McGeeter hobble up to the little stage at the end of the surprisingly clean livery pen, open up a flour sack, and pull a battered violin from within. He tuned it up while a dour-faced guitarist did the same, then warmed up his fingers with a fast reel that sent perfect, pure notes soaring up past the paper lanterns and into the clear but darkening sky.

Matt was impressed. He'd tried to play a fiddle once and could only pull from it something like an imitation of a dying cat. He stood listening to McGeeter a few moments, then put his fingers in the corners of his mouth and whistled his applause.

Now that the night of the dance had come, Matt was less worried than he had been. But McGeeter serving as the fiddler did pose one problem Matt had not expected. He approached his one-legged friend.

"McGeeter, you're a man of more talents than I knew, but if you're going to be fiddling tonight..."

"Yes, Marshal, I know: You've deputized me, and how am I going to guard the place and play fiddle too? Don't you worry. Morgan Kench plays fiddle, too—he's better than I am—so if there's any trouble, all I have to do is lay the fiddle aside and go help out. The music will go right on. And if you'll notice, there's no better place than this stage from which a man can see everything that's going on.

"Where's your pistol?"

McGeeter pulled back his coat and showed a stubby Colt holstered in a subtle shoulder rig.

"Well, I guess you are ready, then. But listen: If you see anything happening out in or beyond the crowd, don't you get shy about singing out, right from the stage. All right? Tonight keeping the peace is more important than being a good fiddler. You savvy?"

"Of course I do. Don't you worry, Matt. I'll keep a vigilant eye out."

Matt watched as the crowd began to assemble in the twilight. The good weather would bring out a big group this Friday night, Matt had been told by the Widow. Apparently these occasional town dances, though officially frowned upon by the three churches here, were always big draws. Even many from the churches attended, some of them doing no more than standing to the side, frowning, shaking their heads at the morally questionable practice of dancing—but their feet were always tapping while they glowered, the Widow had noted.

"A town like Stalker's Creek, where new people come in a lot, can quick become a town of strangers," she had said. "Having these here dances makes folks feel like they're part of a real community. That's why the town sponsors them."

"This time I wish it would be called off," Matt had replied. "This feud seems volatile enough right now that there could be trouble. Do Cornwells ever show up for these things?"

"I've seen some of the rowdier ones from time to time, yes," she replied.

"That's what I was afraid of."

"Don't be afraid, Matt. Just be a lawman. That's why you're here: to make sure that the misbehaviors of a few don't destroy the right of everyone to enjoy the normal pleasures of life."

Matt saw Jack out at the far end of the pen, meandering through the gathering crowd, smiling, tipping his hat, but his eyes always alert and moving. Matt nodded to himself. Jack Bail was a good man, and he was mighty lucky to have him as deputy given how little he had been authorized to offer the man. The money for Jack's salary came directly from the Widow rather than through the official town budget, though Jack didn't know that.

Leroy Green and Carson Foster, two trusty local men who had, like McGeeter, agreed to be deputized for the night, were on either side of the pen, talking to folks and keeping an eye out, not looking quite as vigilant and confident in their work as did Jack. But Matt was glad they were there, and wondered if he should have deputized even more like them.

He didn't really think so. Now that the dreaded event had finally arrived, things didn't feel quite so threatening. He believed there was every good chance they'd all make it through the evening without anyone from Pactolas even showing up.

If so, Matt would be glad of it, though admittedly disappointed that he had been forced to break his date with Annie Wolfe. He thought of her there alone at her cabin, missing out on all the festivities. It was a darn shame, especially for one so pretty as she. Annie Wolfe belonged at a dance. She'd have looked very pretty by the light of the encircling paper lanterns. Maybe next time.

Matt looked about for the Widow. She'd told him she'd not be at the dance, but he wondered if she'd really hold to that. She had told him that her late beloved Stalker had been a great lover of dances like this, and since his passing she could hardly bear to be around them. Furthermore, she didn't want her presence to lend the perception that this was the Packard clan dance, when in fact it was for all. For her to be there would be to make trouble more likely, she had said.

It certainly seemed to Matt that the Widow made sincere efforts to squelch the feud and the bitterness that underlay it. Her vision, unlike that of Bax and the Cornwells, seemed broader than her immediate kin and concerns. And so he was somewhat puzzled by the harsh and biting words that Annie had said about the Widow. He just couldn't believe for a moment that the Widow was secretly putting bellows to the feud even while publicly trying to douse it. Annie's husband must have been something of a speculator and story spreader.

The crowd grew quickly. Matt saw no one immediately identifiable as a Cornwell, and felt good about that. Not that he knew them all by any stretch, but he had gotten good at identifying that certain Cornwell look and stance.

The darkness blackened, the lanterns seemed to brighten, the second fiddler arrived and tuned up, and the torchlight around the stage cast a golden aura over the little orchestra. A broadly made man in a very old-fashioned waist-coat climbed onto the stage and called for the dance to begin, evoking cheers. He cleared his throat as the first notes sounded and the dancers assembled. This was the caller, whose booming voice would steer the dancers through their entwining patterns.

Matt watched the dancing only a few moments, then

turned full attention to the crowd. He paced around the perimeter, again and again, conferring at times with Jack and the other watchful deputies. He saw McGeeter keeping a close watch on things as well, even while he expertly fiddled. Good thing he played by ear and not note. No sheet music to require his attention.

The music soared, the dancers reeled, and Matt Fadden and his little force of peacekeepers patrolled. So far no trouble, nor any sign it was coming. If things stayed like that, Matt would be satisfied.

CHAPTER 27

T he dancers had been going hard for an hour, and energy was beginning to wane and the caller's voice to grow somewhat hoarse. He took a break and slipped off for a few sips from a flask. Whiskey was against the rules at this dance, but Matt ignored the flask. In the case of the dance caller, a little whiskey was simply medicinal—voice repair and maintenance.

Jack and Matt stood side by side on the west side of the crowd of watchers that leaned on the fence, eyeing a particular fellow Matt had spotted a minute before.

"He sure looks like a Cornwell to me," Matt was saying. "I'm right sure I saw him in their church meeting."

"If he ain't a Cornwell, he's surely a good imitation of one," Jack replied. "And I don't like the way he's looking around. Kind of conniving and conspiratorial."

"Lord, Jack, where did you learn such two-dollar words as that? I'm impressed. And I agree with you. Hey, look-did I see the flash of something under his coat just then?"

"A flask, maybe."

"Or a pistol." Firearms, like liquor, were not allowed at public dances in Stalker's Creek.

"Hey... look there. That's Jimbo Cornwell, ain't it?"

It was indeed. Jimbo had appeared as if out of a fog, and was talking to the other Cornwell-looking man whom they had just been watching.

"Ira," Matt said abruptly. "The one with the flask, or the pistol... that's Ira Cornwell. I remember it now. I was introduced to him once by Bax. He's Bax's cousin or something."

"There's others there with them, too," Jack observed. "There's something going on here, Matt. Them Cornwells ain't come all the way to Stalker's Creek just to listen to McGeeter's fiddling."

"Nope. Hey, where's Ira going?"

"I don't know. But it looks like he might be following Joe Packard. See him? He just left... heading in the direction of his house, it looks like."

"You stay here—keep an eye on Jimbo and the others. I'm going to follow Ira and see what he's up to."

Matt circled around the crowd's rear, keeping away from the torches and lanterns so he wouldn't be readily observed. Ira Cornwell had just departed the scene, and if Matt had to bet on it, he'd bet Ira was indeed tracking himself a Packard. That was probably why he had come, and Jimbo, and the others with them. This was Packard-hunting night for them.

Matt moved out onto the street and looked for Ira Cornwell, whom he had momentarily let slip out of sight. There, moving down a stretch of boardwalk... into an alley... looking out now, down the street...

No question about it. Ira was following someone just as Matt was following him. No doubt it was the Joe Packard whom Jack had named, a man Matt himself did not know. Matt couldn't see far enough into the darkness to detect just who Ira was following... but he saw Ira clearly enough to recognize the object he pulled from beneath his coat. It wasn't a flask. It was a pistol.

Ira left the alley and trotted down the dirt street. He was

obviously unaware that he was being tracked by the marshal of Stalker's Creek. He was intent on his own tracking—intent as well on murder, Matt felt certain.

Not in my town, he thought. *You fight your feud if you want, Ira Cornwell, but you don't fight it on the streets of Stalker's Creek!*

Matt drew his own pistol and speeded his pace, closing in silently on Ira Cornwell. The farther he went, the farther behind fell the brightly lit livery enclosure, and the thicker grew the darkness.

Ironically, clouds were rolling in, darkening the already meager moonlight. The bad weather Matt had wished would come and halt tonight's dance altogether was at least beginning to roll in—too late to be of benefit.

It was very, very dark. Matt could hardly see Ira at all ahead of him. His foot kicked something unseen on the ground. It was a loose horseshoe. It made a dull, metallic thud as it skidded over to bump up against the base of the boardwalk. Matt froze, wondering if Ira had heard it. After a couple of moments, he advanced again.

He'd lost Ira. No sign of him at all... and if he didn't find him again, right away, there would be no way to stop him from ambushing Joe Packard.

———

Jack Bail glowered, concern rising. He wished Matt hadn't been forced to leave when he did, because now two of the men who'd been loitering around with Ira Cornwell were now slipping away on their own, moving in a manner both purposeful and covert.

They were heading uptown, and Jack could think of no good reason for them to do so. Shops were closed. Many of the houses were at the moment empty, people being down here at the dance instead of at home.

Jimbo Cornwell was not with the pair. He remained back in the shadows, barely visible to Jack, watching the two move off. That alone was enough to make Jack worry.

A gang of Cornwells comes into Stalker's Creek and blends in while everyone is distracted, then scatters in a covert way. Not a good thing, in Jack's book.

"Let's go," Jack said to Leroy Green. "We're following them two. Carson, you stay here and keep an eye out for any trouble out of Jimbo over yonder."

"I'll do it."

Jack wasn't confident. Carson Foster was not the sharpest knife in the drawer, and Jack had been doubtful about the wisdom of deputizing him. But he'd not said anything to Matt. Surely the man could manage to keep track of one fellow, though.

"We'll be back soon, Carson. Remember that McGeeter over there with the fiddle is deputized, too, and he can stop playing and help you out if there's any problems."

Carson nodded. He didn't seem much worried about his suddenly heightened responsibilities. Jack took a surreptitious sniff, thinking he detected a touch of alcoholic aroma about Carson. But he wasn't sure.

"We'd better go before we lose sight of them, Jack," Leroy said.

Jack and Leroy left the crowd and began following the pair up into town, trying to be as quiet and unnoticed as possible.

Carson watched them go, grinned to himself, then pulled a bottle out of his pocket. He turned his back, tilted the bottle, and took a quick swig.

He looked around, watching the crowd, the dancers, the musicians. Then he remembered Jimbo Cornwell. One more quick swig, and the cork went back into the bottle. He looked around for Jimbo.

He was gone.

———

McGeeter had played the fiddle so long that his fingers danced on the strings by almost pure muscle memory—which was a good thing, because right now McGeeter was so distracted that he was only half conscious of what tune he was playing.

He'd seen it all across the bridge of his fiddle, Matt and the assorted deputies scattering to follow the sneaking Cornwell intruders. He'd also seen Carson forgetting his duties and remembering his bottle. And he'd seen what Carson had not: Jimbo Cornwell sneaking away in a direction entirely apart from ones the others had taken.

McGeeter sawed out the last note, swore beneath his breath, and laid the fiddle aside. "Got to go for a few minutes," he said to his fellow fiddler. "You can handle the next one by yourself, I reckon."

"Where you going?"

"Got a quick errand to run. I'll be back."

McGeeter adjusted the fittings of his peg leg, which had loosened some while he was sitting and fiddling. Then, quietly, he glanced under his coat at his pistol, just to reassure himself it was there.

Wishing he could move as efficiently as a man with two feet, McGeeter set out after Jimbo Cornwell. He'd already guessed where the sorry old devil was going.

Jimbo was heading toward the house of the Widow Packard.

CHAPTER 28

Matt felt like giving himself the most thorough cussing a man could ever receive. He couldn't believe he'd let Ira slip away. Every instinct told him the man was up to no good—and now Matt had no notion at all where he was.

He actually considered simply yelling out, *Ira, I know you're here and I know you're looking for trouble... so if trouble comes, I'll know who to come looking for!* But he didn't do it. He just kept trying to see through the darkness like an owl, and tune up the keenness of his hearing to pick up sound of him. Nothing. As dark and silent as this part of town seemed just now, he might be the only human being in the vicinity at alt

All he could hear was the faint and distant whine of the fiddles... no, wait. Only one fiddle played now.

He wondered if McGeeter had left the stage. Had he seen something that had made him forsake his musician's duties and take on his deputy role?

Matt couldn't worry about that now. If there was real trouble back there, a fight or something, the music would have stopped altogether. Besides, there was Jack and the others present, too. McGeeter had probably peg-legged over to the outhouse.

Footfalls... Matt heard them, over in the darkness, softly echoing out of an alleyway. He followed, silently as he could.

It crossed his mind only then that Ira—assuming that it was Ira he now heard ahead of him—was leading him in the general direction of Annie Wolfe's home.

———

"All right, Leroy," Jack said softly, drawing his pistol. "I think we can see what they're up to now. We're going to get them from both sides, around the back. You go up that side of the building, and I'll go up the other. When you get to the end, pause for a count of ten, then give a whistle. We'll both come out and around at that point, and close them in."

"Pistols drawn?"

"Of course."

"Look... they've got their torch burning."

"That's a whiskey bottle full of coal oil with a cloth for a wick, and it'll set that store ablaze quicker than you can spit. Let's move."

"The Widow owns that store," Leroy said.

"No doubt that's why they aim to burn it," Jack whispered back. "Now let's move."

They headed toward the rear of the building, circling around as Jack had directed, pistols in their hands.

———

At last there was light. It streamed from the window of a house—Annie's house, in fact. Just like she'd said, she'd stayed home from the dance.

A shadow moved across the window. Annie moving around inside, going from one room to another. Matt suddenly felt cold and endangered. He wished he was in there, with Annie, talking and laughing, drinking coffee, nibbling on a sweetened biscuit or a bite of cake.

Ira paused, looking toward Annie's house. He craned his neck, peering through the window from a distance. Then he looked away, as if drawn in some other direction, but his head turned once again toward Annie's house. He moved in that direction, sneaking and quiet.

Matt's blood boiled. The sorry dog was going to *peep* at her! Watch a pretty woman in her own house without her knowing.

Matt muttered a silent curse and readied himself to make an arrest. The moment Ira knelt at that window, Matt would be on him, his pistol cracking down hard on his noggin just to make a point. He'd not knock him out. He'd just make sure he broke some skin and let a bruised skull-bone tell Ira Cornwell what the marshal of Stalker's Creek thought of Peeping Toms.

Ira sneaked toward the window, started to crouch.

A door opened on the far side of a nearby house. It creaked loudly on rusted hinges. Matt wheeled instinctively. He heard the slosh and splash of a bucket of dishwater being tossed out, then the door creaked shut again and thumped closed.

Matt turned his attention to Ira again, but Ira wasn't there.

Confusion struck, followed by panic. Had Ira gone inside? No, there hadn't been time, and Matt would have heard him enter. But he wasn't at the window. He had to be somewhere close by, shrouded by the darkness—

Matt stepped forward, not noticing that as he did so, he entered the perimeter of the area of light spilling out of Annie's window. Ira's form rose before him, looming up suddenly out of the darkness.

"Hello, *Marshall*," he said, spitting out the title with

ironic and hateful emphasis. "Down here looking for some Packard backside to kiss?"

Matt, startled, stepped back. He started to raise his pistol and tell Ira he was under arrest, but Ira was too fast. A heavy Colt swung up and struck Matt on the left temple, knocking off his hat, causing him to drop to one side and lose his grip on his own pistol.

Ira laughed, raised the Colt, and hit him again. Matt fell stunned, staring up at Ira grinning down at him, an evil grin. Ira's boot moved, kicking him hard with its pointed toe.

"Damned traitor!" Ira declared. "Taking Cornwell's kindness and repaying it by going to work for the damned *Widow*!" At the word "Widow," he kicked Matt again, harder. He cursed Matt bitterly, calling him every obscene thing he could think of, kicking him again and again... and Matt, the victor of a hundred barroom fights, found he couldn't react. Ira's initial blow had stunned him so thoroughly he couldn't even find his fists, much less use them.

"Ain't fit to live!" Ira said. "Down here following me around... or were you down here to peep through windows at the pretty ladies, *Marshal?*" Another kick in conjunction with the mockingly intoned word. Matt almost blacked out.

"Hell, I'm going to kill you," Ira said, growing drunk with his dominance over a man the entire Cornwell clan viewed as a Judas. "I'll blow your head off right here in the Widow's own town!"

Matt's half-focused eyes saw Ira raise the pistol, aim it at his face, squint down its length. The finger began to tighten...

Mercifully, Matt blacked out just as the loudest gunshot he'd ever heard, and the last he ever expected to hear, filled his ears like the voice of hell.

———

Ever since the death of her beloved Stalker, the Widow Packard had not slept well. She'd quit worrying about it long before, made peace with the fact that one of the bitter gifts of grief was the loss of rest. Many nights she lay awake, staring at the ceiling above her, willing to let sleep overtake her if it would but not despairing if it would not.

She spent those hours reliving in her mind the best days of her marriage to Stalker Packard, and talking to him as if he still lay beside her.

Tonight, though, she believed she would sleep. She was unusually tired, and unusually eager to escape the waking world. From down the street she could hear the music of a fiddle, the laughter and clapping of happy people. It reminded her of younger days in Arkansas, when she had loved a barn dance more than any other young woman for miles around. She'd been lithe, lean, and pretty in those days, nimble on her feet, able to swing and step and circle with the best of them, never even growing tired. She'd danced many such dances with Stalker. Once, years before that, she'd danced one with young Temple Fadden himself!

The echoes of the dance down the street tonight were painful reminders of a time she could not return to. She wanted to sleep and escape it.

She removed the cigar from her lips and stared at it, wondering why she did such an absurd thing as smoke them. It was because Stalker had smoked them, and she liked having the smell around her. Her eyes fell farther and took in the threadbare man's suit covering her ample form. How ridiculous she was! How Stalker would have laughed to see his wife dressing herself so! But yet she was compelled to do it. She would keep some part of him alive and with her, even if only his old, worn-out suits.

A thump, a bump, at her door...

The Widow was startled, backing up suddenly. Then she

felt ashamed. Just that stray cat, probably, rubbing up against the door like it always did.

She chuckled and headed for the door. There was milk in the kitchen, growing warm and soon to spoil. The cat would enjoy it and she would enjoy the company.

The Widow went to the door and opened it, pulling it back inside.

She gasped. There was no cat. Instead, McGeeter stood in the doorway, staring in at her... no, *through* her. His eyes were glazed, his posture odd...

He collapsed forward, revealing two things: the knife in his spine and the grinning man who had put it there, standing just behind where McGeeter had stood until he'd let him fall.

"Well, hello there, Widow!" Jimbo Cornwell said, his drunkard's breath assaulting her nostrils even from two yards away. "Looks like your little puppet boy's had his strings cut. Poor dead peg-leg!" Then he made a thrusting motion with his hand, as if stabbing with an invisible knife, and said, *"Ssscccritttcccccchhhhhh!"*

The Widow, too horrified to speak, backed away, staring at the Bowie probed deep into her dead employee's back.

"What did the damned old peg-leg think? Did he figure he could sneak up on a man in the dark with that leg just a thunking on the ground? Bah!" And he kicked the corpse. "It was easy, Widow. Just let him sneak on past, step up behind, and stick the old knife right into the backbone. He went down like a felled poplar, that peg-leg did! Another Packard dead and gone to hell!"

"He was not a Packard. He only worked for me... you murderer!"

"It's all the same in my book. Everybody in this damned town is a Packard as far as I'm concerned. And tonight, Widow woman, the Cornwells have come to Stalker's Creek to invite the Packards to dance! There's Cornwells spreading across this town, woman. We're going to set some fires, slice some flesh, even some old, old scores. Your murdering kin will dance to *our* tune tonight, old woman!"

"You're drunk... a drunk, murdering old fool!" she said. "You'll hang for this!"

"Oh, no, not me. No, ma'am. No, it's you who'll hang. We'll stretch your neck from a rafter, and then it'll be you who's dancing! You'll kick them fat legs while you choke out your life! You'll be joining your husband tonight, Widow. Do me a favor. When you see Stalker, tell him Jimbo Cornwell says hello... and that I hope the heat where he is ain't getting to him too bad!"

His hand rose, bearing a small pistol. "Come with me, Widow. I got some friends I want you to meet. They're out setting your store afire right now. When they come to put it out, they'll find you swinging on its flaming porch, sizzling just like old Stalker himself, down in hell! Come on ... let's move."

It was just then that they heard a gunshot. Not close, from across town, in fact, but loud enough to be noticeable. Jimbo turned his head for just a moment, reacting, and that moment was all the Widow needed.

She dropped with amazing speed and yanked the knife from McGeeter's back. Jimbo turned to face her again, starting to speak, starting to lift the pistol and fire at the big woman suddenly lunging toward him, right over the dead man... but he had time neither to fire nor to speak before the Bowie cut through the underside of his chin, almost back to the Adam's apple, and thrust up through his mouth, his sinuses, all the way to the base of his brain.

The Widow rammed it in hard, and deep, and let out a piercing scream of horror, grief, hatred, and terror as she did so.

Jimbo's body went limp, and for a moment literally

hung like a rag on the knife still in her hand, a hand now awash in fresh blood.

She screamed again, louder than before, and let go of the knife. Jimbo Cornwell fell across the corpse of the man he had murdered only moments before, slain by the same knife he had used to cut Thomas McGeeter's spine.

CHAPTER 29

"Hear that?" Leroy said. He was standing in front of the Widow Packard's store, pistol leveled on one of the two would-be arsonist Cornwells that he and Jack had just surprised as they were about to set the store ablaze. "That's the Widow's voice, sure as the world!"

"Why would she scream like that?"

"I don't know. I think that—"

They heard the blast of a shot at that moment, from across town.

"That came from the direction the marshal went," Jack said. "Good Lordy, what's happening in this town tonight?"

"What do you want to do with these two?" Leroy asked.

"Hang it... blast and blazes... ah, hell's bells, just let them go. Get on with you, both of you. Get out of Stalker's Creek, right now, and don't come back. Not ever. If you come back, I swear, I'll kill you myself. You understand me?"

"Yes, sir," one of the pair said. He sounded young and afraid, and from the smell of him, Jack suspected he'd peed his own britches at the moment the two deputies had surprised him and his companion. "We'll not come back, not at all." He lowered his hands and turned to run.

"Wait," Jack said. "What's going on here tonight? Why are so many of you Cornwells in town, looking for trouble?"

"It was Jimbo's idea," the man said. "He wanted to come and kill some Packards, and burn the Widow's store."

"And hang her from it while it burned," the other contributed.

Jack couldn't believe his ears. Had the feud really gone this far? "Why?"

"Because, well, the feud. Time to settle the score. That's what Jimbo said."

"There's been some Packards killed, too. The Widow's own son, not long ago."

"I didn't have nothing to do with that. Neither did he." He pointed at his companion.

"What about Jimbo? Or Bax or Will Cornwell?"

"No. Not that I know of."

"Get on with you. Run, and if you slow down or look back, you're dead men."

They did run. Jack watched them for a few moments to make sure his message had really taken. It had. They did not pause, did not look back.

"Come on," he said to Leroy. "Let's find out what made the Widow scream that way. Then we'll go investigate that gunshot."

"I hope they're alive."

"Who?"

"The Widow and the marshal."

"So do I. Dear Lord, what a night!"

They loped off in the direction of the Widow's house.

———

Annie Wolfe dropped the rifle and ran toward Matt, who was sitting up, wincing and deafened by the blast of the gunshot.

"Matt... Matt, are you all right?"

He grimaced and rubbed at his neck, then writhed his shoulders. "I'm... I think I'm all right." He gave his head a shake to clear it, then looked at the unmoving form of Ira Cornwell lying on the ground just beside him. "You shot him! Just as he was going to shoot me."

"I had to do it, Matt. He would have killed you."

"You saved my life, Annie."

The rusty hinges next door creaked again. "What's going on out there?" a male voice shouted. It sounded like an old man. "Who's shooting?"

Matt found his voice quickly. "Nothing, sir... just a little mishap. I'm the town marshal, just stay inside." Then to Annie he whispered: "I don't want anyone to see this. No one should know that you are the one who killed Ira."

"Why?"

"You've killed a Cornwell. They'll retaliate against you."

The man next door called again. "You're the who?"

"The marshal!" Matt shouted back. "Go on to bed! There's nothing you need to do!"

"It wouldn't matter if he came out," Annie said shakily. "He's old and blind."

"Give me your rifle, Annie?"

"Why?"

"So that if anyone bothers to look close enough to figure out Ira was killed by a rifle, I can have the rifle in my possession and say it was me who did it. I don't want the Cornwells blaming you for this, Annie. They're hateful and vengeful people."

"You needn't tell *me* that," Annie said quietly. "But no, Matt... I don't want to give you the rifle."

"Come on, Annie! It makes sense."

"No." She rose quickly, picked up the rifle from where it lay nearby, and held it close to her, away from Matt. She abruptly darted into her house.

Confused, Matt staggered to his feet and looked through her window in time to see Annie thrusting the rifle into a wardrobe. He got a clear view of the rifle for a couple of moments before the wardrobe door closed.

Annie returned and came to his side, helping him to stand. "You look dizzy."

"I am, a little. Dizzy I can handle a lot better than dead."

"Come inside. I'll get you something to drink. I want to see how badly hurt you are."

"Annie, if anyone asks, I killed him, not you. Do you understand me?"

"Yes."

"And if anyone brings up the question of the rifle, you can say I'd borrowed it from you, and gave it back after."

"Yes . .. that's good. That's what I was thinking we'd say. Now come inside. Sit down."

"Only for a minute, until I can clear my head," Matt said. "We've got a dead man here. I've got to deal with this. Why would he have come down here, Annie?"

"I don't know. Maybe he was going to Manse Packard's house. It's over that way, a quarter of a mile."

Matt nodded. That was probably it. Ira had been on his way to a Packard's house to kill or burn or whatever he'd intended to do, and then he'd been distracted by the opportunity to peep through the window of the house of an attractive woman.

Matt went inside, and Annie set about making coffee. But Matt remained seated only a minute or so, then rose and said, "Never mind the coffee, Annie. I've got to go. There are other Packards in town tonight. I need to go to Jack and my other deputized men, and tell them what's happened here. The trouble may not be over yet."

"All right," she said.

"I want you to help me move Ira, if you will. We'll put

him in your woodshed for the moment. I don't want him just lying dead out there to be found by whoever."

"I'll help you."

They went outside and did the task. Ira was heavy, hard to move, but they managed it. As they worked, Matt glanced at Annie's window and the wardrobe inside, and wished he could get in there, away from Annie, and get a closer look at that rifle. But there would be no opportunity tonight.

"Keep guard," Matt told her. "Others besides your neighbor may have heard that shot. Turn your light out, lock your door, and take your rifle to bed with you. But don't go to sleep. Keep alert in case any other Packards come looking for Ira. Don't respond to them. Make it appear your house is empty."

"You scare me, Matt."

"It's a scary night. But you'll be fine. Thank you for saving my life, Annie."

"I just did what I had to do."

"Thank God you did." Matt leaned over, kissed her forehead quickly, then turned and vanished into the darkness, heading back to find his deputies.

CHAPTER 30

I t was appalling, hardly possible to comprehend. When Matt learned of the attempt to burn down one of the Widow's businesses, he was shocked. When he learned of the violent death of McGeeter and the plan to kill the Widow, he was sick to his stomach.

"I hate to say such a thing, but I'm glad Jimbo Cornwell is dead," he said. "It's men such as him who have kept this feud alive."

"In truth, Matt," the Widow said softly, "all the Cornwell men are Jimbo Cornwell at heart. Some just manage to hide it a little better than others."

"Like Will."

"Yes. He can appear to be a very civilized fellow, a family man. But I know that when he was a young man back in Arkansas, he killed a nephew of mine by beating him to death with a club. It just never could be proven."

Matt could find nothing to say. That feeling of sickness in his stomach merely heightened.

There was only one good thing Matt could find in all of this, and that was that, amazingly, the series of tragic events had managed to play out without the notice of the public at large. Because most of the townsfolk were at the dance, there had been no one about to witness the capture of the would-be arsonists. The murder of McGeeter and the subsequent killing of Jimbo had not had witnesses beyond the Widow herself, and the blind neighbor who had heard the gunshot that killed Ira Cornwell had, of course, not seen anything and was easily persuaded that the shot had been a simple accidental discharge of a gun. The same story worked for those in the area of the dance who had heard the gunshot.

But Matt knew it would not remain hidden for long. The failed arsonists had gone free and were even now certainly heading back to Pactolas to tell what had happened. Not that they knew much. They knew they themselves had failed, that they had heard the Widow's scream, and that there had been a gunshot somewhere across town.

Things would become clearer, though, when Ira and Jimbo failed to come home. The Cornwells would demand answers... and come looking for them.

For the first time since taking his job, Matt began to wonder if he really had what it took to be a lawman.

———

Annie Wolfe shook her head. "I don't know that I want to stay somewhere else," she said. "Especially not at the Widow Packard's. Why can't I remain home?"

"Because we can't be absolutely sure that someone didn't see what happened. I don't think there were any witnesses, but the darkness can hide a thousand eyes. If word ever reached the Cornwells that you killed Ira, you would be in great danger here alone. At the Widow's we can keep an eye on you and her too, at the same time. I'm going to station Jack there to keep watch over both of you."

"You seem determined about this."

"I don't want you to be hurt, Annie. I'd never forgive myself if I let that happen."

She nodded. "Very well. I'll do it, then."

"Good. Pack your things. And bring that rifle of yours. You never know if you might need it."

She looked at him a moment, then nodded.

He sat in her little front room, waiting while she busied around, packing a bag with her meager possessions. When she came out of the back room at last, the rifle in one hand and the bag in the other, he noted that she had wrapped the rifle in a piece of cloth. He did not ask why, but a secret weight in his heart grew heavier, and the whole scenario became a little more unreal to him.

The Widow seemed to have aged ten years. A light of strength that had burned in her eyes before had died with the murder of her friend and employee McGeeter. And Matt felt responsible, for it was he who had deputized the man, he who had given him a task that ultimately cost him his life.

The Widow looked closely at Annie when the latter was brought to her. "This is the first time I've seen you close at hand, my dear," she said. "You are a lovely woman.... I've always thought so when I saw you walking in town."

"Thank you."

"Believe it or not, there was a time when I was beautiful, too. A time when even Matt's famous father thought of me as a great beauty. But not so great as you, I think." She paused. "You remind me so much of someone... but I don't know who. Someone from a long time ago."

Annie smiled, feebly.

"I understand we are to be staying together here," the Widow went on. "Welcome to my home. I'm sorry it is under such sad circumstances."

Annie nodded.

The Widow turned to Matt. "What will you do now?"

"I'm going to Pactolas," he said. "I'm going to talk to Bax and Will and tell them what has happened here. Annie, I'll tell them it was my shot that killed Ira, and from now on, that's the way we are to tell it. Even try to remember it that way, if you can. I killed him, not you."

Annie simply stared at him, eyes unreadable, blank.

"It will be dangerous for you to go to the Cornwells," the Widow said.

"More dangerous in the long run if I don't. If they learn that two of their own have been killed here and no one told them, these mountains will run with blood, most of it Packard blood. I have to go see if I can talk some sort of sanity into this situation."

"You'll not succeed," the Widow said. "There is no sanity among the Cornwells, no goodness of heart, no mercy or sense of justice except as it applies to those who hurt them."

Annie made an odd little sound and turned away.

"I'll leave as soon as Jack arrives," he said. "For now, nothing is to be said about these deaths, not even McGeeter's. I must see if there is a way I can keep this situation from growing worse."

"What will you do with the dead?"

"They are at the undertaker's—he'll hold them there for now, saying nothing about them. I've brought him into my confidence, and he agrees with the course of action I'm going to take."

"I don't agree with it," the Widow said flatly. "You are taking your life into your own hands."

"It's my duty, ma'am. It's what the town pays me for."

The Widow smiled at him and extended her hand. He shook it. Then he turned to Annie to shake her hand as well, but she did him one better. Leaning toward him, she kissed him squarely on the lips.

"I'm... honored," he said, stunned.

She looked at him sadly. "Be careful."

"I will be."

She nodded. "This is goodbye, then."

"I hope not forever."

She paused, then said again, "Goodbye."

CHAPTER 31

Matt wished he'd been more religious throughout his life. Here he was, riding out of the hills toward the house of Will Cornwell, and he needed to pray more than ever before. He was heading into a potentially murderous situation, and he had no assurance at all that he would come out of it alive and well.

He'd been seen already. He sensed it at first, then confirmed it from the corners of his eyes. Subtle movement in the woods around him. People watching, waiting for the return of Ira and Jimbo and being surprised to see Matt Fadden, traitor to the family who had aided him, coming back instead. Matt knew that at any moment he might be shot from his saddle. He could only hope that curiosity about why he had returned would keep that from happening.

Quietly, trying not to make too big a show of it, he pulled his Henry rifle from the saddle boot and laid it across his lap.

A man stepped onto the road in front of him. Matt recognized him as Ned Cornwell, one of the younger Cornwell men, still with peach fuzz on his face. He had that hard glint of hatred already well-aged in his eyes, though, and the shotgun in his hands glinted as well in the morning sun.

"Why you here, Fadden?"

"I need to talk to Bax and Will Cornwell."

"What do you want to say to them?"

"That's for their ears, not yours."

"You got some of our kin locked up in Stalker's Creek."

"Maybe I do." *Or maybe they're cooling on a slab at the undertaker's place.*

Ned nodded curtly, proud that he had—in his own perception, anyway—figured things out. "I reckon you'll be turning them loose real fast if you know what's good for you."

"I need to see Will and Bax."

"You're a lucky man. They're both in Will's house just now."

"Can I pass?"

Ned nodded him by and stood watching him with his best attempt at a haughty, fearless, dangerous look. It made Matt want to laugh, but he didn't.

The door opened as Matt was dismounting in the yard, but it was Jeff, not the senior Cornwells, who emerged.

"Hello, Jeff," Matt said. He held the reins of his horse in his right hand and the Henry in his left.

Jeff stared at him, silent. The look of hate in his eye was no different from what Matt had seen in Ned's. This time, though, it made him sad. He'd liked Jeff, knew that Jeff had liked him... but that was all lost now, lost to a feud of fools.

The door opened again and Will came out, followed by Bax. "Go back inside, Jeff," Will said, and Jeff complied, staring hatefully at Matt as he did so.

"You got brass, I'll say that for you," Bax said. "Not just anybody would be rash enough to come into the yard of folks who hate his damned guts enough to shoot him like a dog."

"You folks are good at hating. You got it down to an art. But I've got news you have a right to hear man-to-man, face-to-face."

"They're dead, ain't they," Bax said. "Jimbo and Ira."

"Yes. They're dead."

Bax didn't flinch, but Will gave a little jump like someone had struck him lightly from behind.

"How?"

Knowing how much these men already hated the Widow, Matt would not let them know she had killed Jimbo. "Jimbo attacked a man who works for the Widow. They managed to kill each other."

"The peg-leg?"

"His name was McGeeter. He was a good man."

"He was Cornwell trash. I'm glad Jimbo was able to kill the man who murdered him."

Matt wanted to scream at these men that the murderer was Jimbo, not McGeeter, but knew it would do no good. "Ira was killed by me, in self-defense."

"Then his blood is on your hands, and you bear the responsibility for whatever that leads to," Bax said.

Matt eyed his saddle, wondering how quickly he could get back into it. Ned and some others had already blocked the gate, so he knew he couldn't ride out the way he'd come in. He'd have to leap the horse over the fence. Whether this horse would do that he didn't know.

"Ira attacked me and was about to shoot me when I shot him. I'd caught him peeping through the window of a woman's house. Watching her."

"That's a lie. He'd not do that."

"He did. He had his pants down when I found him." Matt couldn't resist adding that one embellishment, because right now it was easy to truly despise these deluded, hate-driven men.

Will's face twitched and he reached beneath his coat.

Bax reached out and stopped him. "No. Don't kill him. He may be lying to us. It might be valuable to have him here with us until we know the full truth."

"The full truth is that a bunch of Cornwells came into Stalker's Creek to cause trouble, and instead trouble found them. They paid the price for what they did. The two who came home only got to do so because my deputies were forced to let them go so they could deal with a different situation."

"Deputies! Well, well! He's got him a full force of little Packard-loving helpers! Real big man, ain't you, Fadden!" Bax mocked.

"Big enough that you thought it was worth paying money for me to stand on your store porch and grin at people."

The window opened beside Will and a rifle barrel thrust out of the opening. In the shadows Matt saw Jeff's dark, frowning face peering down the barrel at him.

"No, son!" Will yelled just as Jeff fired.

Matt had managed to move just in time. The slug sang just past him, and clipped Ned Cornwell on the side of the thigh. He yelped like a pup and went down on one knee.

Will managed to yank the rifle away from Jeff and out through the window. By then Matt was on the run, abandoning his horse because he had no choice. He leaped the fence and headed for the barn.

He heard Ned yell, then flinched as another gunshot sounded. One of the Cornwells out on the road had fired at him. He glanced over his shoulder and saw Will, his savior a moment ago, now becoming his hunter, raising the very rifle he'd taken out of Jeff's hands. The rifle cracked and a slug plunked the dirt just behind Matt.

He veered into the barn and straight out the back, glad he had his Henry. This might come down to a fight to the finish, with him playing Crockett at the Alamo and the Cornwells playing Santa Anna's army.

Not if he could help it. He headed into the woods, intent on losing himself there and getting back to Stalker's Creek as soon as possible.

So much for working up a truce. Thanks to Jeff's shot, there would not even be any peace talks.

The impulse to hide was strong, but Matt knew that some of the Cornwells had dogs. They'd sniff him out in no time. He had to keep moving, find a creek to break his scent, then get across the hills on foot and back to Stalker's Creek.

What would happen after that he could only guess. Probably an outright war of the clans.

He heard them coming as he ran hard up a wooded slope. Another shot, another singing of a bullet. This one went through the treetops. He dodged right, then left, then found a ravine that gave him some additional cover as he made for the top of the ridge.

The next bullet struck very close. He couldn't resist a glance back to see who'd fired it. It was Bax. Hard-drinking, aging Bax apparently was the best shot of them all. As Matt looked he saw Bax's rifle burst powder again. The bullet actually clipped off part of the brim of his hat.

Matt ran harder, the ridge now only yards away. They were still coming, and Bax was readying to shoot again.

———

Jack rolled his cigarette slowly and carefully, not because he couldn't do it faster, but because he was very, very bored. It had been quite an experience, moving straight from the excitement of the horrific adventures of the previous night to the drudgery of sitting in a widow woman's front room, just in case somebody decided to try to kill her again.

At times he caught himself almost wishing something

dreadful would happen, just so he'd have something to do other than sit and smoke one cigarette after another.

Annie Wolfe could make things a little less boring, too, if only she would. Jack didn't get that many chances to talk to pretty women, but Annie was making herself scarce.

She'd taken the second upstairs bedroom, down the hall from the Widow's room, and hadn't emerged for more than a few minutes at a time. He supposed she was shaken up by having killed a man, but he wished she'd grow just lonely enough that she'd come down and pass some time with the bored deputy downstairs. A little beauty would brighten up this room a lot, and some conversation would make the cigarettes taste better.

Upstairs, the Widow was as silent and thoughtful as Jack, but she was far from bored. Her thoughts were disturbing, making her heart hammer. The fog of old memories was breaking under the light of remembrance.

She'd just recalled who Annie Wolfe reminded her of. Reminded her of so strongly that she couldn't believe it was coincidence. It was as if a ghost had returned.

A gentle, brushing sound at her door made the Widow start and turn. She stared at the knob and watched it slowly turn. The door opened, and Annie Wolfe stepped into the room. In her hands was her rifle.

The Widow stared at the rifle, which Annie pointed at her, then up to Annie's pretty but unsmiling face. "You are the very image of Mary Springer," she said.

"Yes," Annie replied. "I've been told that since I was a girl."

"Your grandmother?"

"My great-grandmother."

"It was a terrible thing that happened to her. I heard the stories. No one tells them anymore... but I heard them when I was a girl."

"Yes, it was terrible. Two wicked men, drunk, full of lust and wickedness."

"One a Cornwell... and one a Packard," the Widow said. "And the crime they committed against Mary Springer drove the families apart... and started the feud."

"You know all of this. Most claim to have forgotten."

"They make themselves forget. They don't want to look at their own family guilt."

"So we have each family blaming the other, when both are equally guilty," Annie said. "Making one evil turn into scores of evils ... and my poor husband, letting it burden him until it took him to his grave!"

"He was a Packard?"

"He was related to the Packards. His father was a good man who despised the feud and tried to end it. When he failed, he rejected his own family and left when my husband was just a boy. He taught his son to think like he did, to hate the feud and both families that keep it alive. We came here, my husband and me, to make a good home for ourselves. Then, after we were settled, we discovered that the feud that drove my husband's family out of Arkansas was suddenly all around us again. Cornwells in Pactolas, Packards in Stalker's Creek. Still hating, still accusing!"

"My husband began to believe he was truly under a curse, that fate had handed him the task of taking up his father's quest to end the feud. He didn't want that task. The weight of it ate away at his mind and made him sick. I believe it contributed to his death. And when I realized that, I knew I had a cause of my own."

"So the shootings over the past months... the ones the Packards and Cornwells have been blaming on one another..."

"Yes. It was me."

"Killing both Packards and Cornwells." The Widow's

eyes suddenly filled. "You killed my Henry, the poor sweet boy..."

"He was no 'poor sweet boy,' you foolish woman! Henry Packard once cut Emelia Cornwell with a knife, because of who she was, because of her last name. He very nearly sliced off her breast! She was fortunate to survive at all. You didn't know that, I suppose."

The Widow stared through tears at Annie, saying nothing.

"Henry Packard was as wicked as any of them, young as he was. He deserved to die. All of you, on both sides, you deserve to die, because you won't stop the feud. The poison is in the bloodstream of both families, and until one or the both of those families is gone, the fighting and hate will never stop."

"For the sake of heaven, Annie, don't you see that it's what you are doing that has made the feud so bad? A Cornwell dies or is shot at, and the Packards are blamed. A Packard dies, and the rest of them blame the Cornwells. Retaliation, back and forth... and the ones who suffer most are people like poor Tom McGeeter, who never should have died."

"There is only one way to end the feud, and that is to wipe out those who keep it going."

"Are you going to kill me, Annie? Because if you do, you're killing someone who only wants the feud to end. I *agree* with you about the feud! I hate it!"

"You are the living symbol of the Packard family. The Cornwells' focus most of their hatred on you. When you are gone—and when Bax and Will Cornwell are gone—the hatred will have fewer places to lodge and fester. I'm going to kill you, and when the chance comes, I will kill them too. I have to do it."

"This is wrong, Annie."

"It's the most right thing I can do."

"You forget that Jack Bail is downstairs. He'll not let you lead me out at gunpoint."

"Jack Bail is in no position to stop me."

"Oh, God help us, Annie... have you killed him?"

"He was asleep. I hit him, hard."

"We'll be seen."

"No, because we'll do nothing to draw attention, and we'll leave behind a bit of a distraction to make sure this town's attention is fully occupied."

The Widow could not summon the courage to ask what "distraction" Annie had in mind. "Where will you take me?"

"Into the woods. You'll die there like my great-grandmother died. Tied to a tree, and suffering."

"You're not trying to stop the feud, Annie. You're only causing it to go on. You know you can't wipe out two entire families."

"No, but I can make them wipe each other out. And the world will be a cleaner, better place for it. Sometimes the only way to put out a fire is to fan the flames until all the fuel is consumed. Now come on, old woman, and give me no trouble. It's time for this world to be rid of you."

CHAPTER 32

He was bruised, scratched, sore from head to toe, drenched in sweat... but alive. Matt could hardly believe it, and his prayers now had changed from pleas for survival to inners psalms of thanks. He had somehow evaded the pursuing Cornwells, and now, as he crossed one last ridge, Stalker's Creek came into view.

He paused, looking down on the squalid place that to him was now beautiful, a refuge. Yet he almost felt he could not enter the town. The Cornwells were still searching for him—he would not put it past them to actually follow him into the town and hunt him down like a dog. They might kill him on the very streets, and take other lives along with his.

So he stayed where he was, undecided what to do. Perhaps the Cornwells would not find him if he simply stayed put.

It was a weak hope, and he knew it. Yet he feared to enter his own town for dread of what the result might be.

It was his job to keep trouble away from Stalker's Creek, not lead it to it.

A few moments later, though, he knew that he would

indeed have to enter the town. His eyes grew wide with horror as he noted the black plume of smoke that rose from the center of town. He traced it from sky to earth, and saw that it came from the house of the Widow Packard.

"Annie..." he murmured.

Matt drew in a deep breath, hefted up his rifle, and began running, sliding, dodging down the rugged slope, and from its base ran on into Stalker's Creek.

———

The fire brigade was there, busy at work, tossing bucket after bucket of water onto a house that was going to burn despite their best efforts, and all of them knew it. Matt, tattered and torn, ran to the scene and found Jack seated on the ground, head in his hands.

"Jack, what happened? Where is Annie?"

"Gone, Matt. Gone. And the Widow too."

"Gone? You mean . .."

"Not the fire, no. They've just disappeared... Annie hit me, knocked me cold... I came to just in time to see her pushing the Widow out of the house at gunpoint. The fire was already burning. I think she set it, Matt. But why? Why?"

Despite the heat of the blaze and his exercise-heated muscles, Matt felt a chill. "Jack, I've been a fool. An outright fool. And I was too smitten by her to see it."

"What are you talking about?"

"I saw the rifle she had... I recognized it. And I figured out that... I realized she had... but I thought it was only the Cornwells she despised... I'm a fool."

"I'm the one who was hit in the head, and you're the one who's babbling."

"I can't explain it right now, Jack. I've got to go after them. Where did she take the Widow?"

"I don't know. The Widow was talking when she was being led out, talking in hope I would hear it, I guess, and saying something about the mountains and the woods."

Matt felt another chill. "Those mountains and woods are filled with Cornwells right now, Jack. Looking for me. If they get their hands on the Widow..."

Matt looked around and saw Kelsey the gun seller, walking up, drawn like scores of others by the fire. His appearance seemed providential to Matt, the chance to find an important answer. He approached Kelsey.

"I need to ask you something," he said. "I want you to give me a straight answer."

Kelsey looked at Matt's disheveled appearance and asked, "What happened to you?"

"I can't explain it now. I want you to tell me something, though: That rifle you had in your shop, not mine but the other one I asked you about... you told me it had come to you from some other gun seller, I think."

Kelsey looked like a trapped rabbit, eyes narrowing. "Yeah..."

"Was that true, Kelsey? I have to know."

"Why?"

"I can't explain now... It won't cause you a problem, Kelsey. I promise. I just need to know."

Kelsey shook his head. "No. I didn't tell you the truth. I lied because I didn't know why you were asking. That rifle was there because the owner had took a loan out from me and used the rifle to secure it. Then she came back later and repaid the loan, and I gave it back to her."

"Annie Wolfe."

"Yes... how did you know?"

"I saw the rifle at her house. That didn't mean much, because she could have bought that rifle from you right off your shelf. What did tell me something, but which I refused to let myself accept, was that she tried to hide the rifle from me. She wouldn't have tried to hide it if she hadn't known that I would recognize it. But she did know. So it had to be her who shot at Jimbo Cornwell over near Pactolas. She's the one who dropped the rifle, and watched as I found it, and hid it in the shed. She's the one who stole it back. I guess she hocked it with you sometime after that, then reclaimed it."

"I ain't sure I fully follow you."

"Never mind, Kelsey. I'll tell you all about it later on. Right now I have to head back to the hills. I've got some tracking to do, and God willing, a life or two to save."

Matt's energy was back, driven purely by his hammering heart and the rush of adrenaline in his veins. He'd found the track of the Widow, who had marked her trail by breaking a cigar and surreptitiously dropping fragments of it all along the way. But now, just as he felt he was about to find her and her captor, the Cornwells were nearly upon him.

Matt crouched behind a deadfall, struggling not to breathe too loudly, while one of the Cornwells who had guarded him in Will's yard stalked along nearby, shotgun in hand and eyes darting in all directions. He seemed to sense he was almost upon his prey. Matt readied himself to roll and shoot the Henry if he had to—if he was lucky he'd be able to get off a shot before the other man brought the shotgun into use.

The man paused just on the other side of the fallen log. He was so close now, and Matt squeezed so tightly up against the log, that he was hidden from Matt. His breathing, the scuff of his feet on the forest floor, even his nervous manipulations of the shotgun, were all audible to Matt.

After long, tense moments, though, the man swore quietly and began to walk away. Matt gave a silent prayer of gratitude as he listened to him moving farther and farther away. At length he dared to move from his hiding place and resume his tracking of the Widow Packard and Annie Wolfe.

"There he is!"

Matt winced as he heard the cry from behind him. He'd moved too quickly—another roaming Cornwell had seen him.

"You, Fadden! Stop or we'll shoot you down!"

Matt wasn't about to stop. He knew that he'd be shot down all the same. He ran harder and dodged into a stand of trees, making for some boulders nearby.

A rifle fired, the bullet spanging off one of the boulders ahead. Matt kept going. The next shot slapped into a tree, and the third thudded into the earth not a yard from his racing, sore feet.

———

Jeff Cornwell heard the shots and stopped, assessing how close they were and from which direction they had come. He gripped tightly the huge old Navy Colt pistol he'd dug out of a drawer at home after his father disarmed him of the rifle he'd thrust out the window.

He knew he wasn't supposed to be here. His father had ordered him to stay at home even as he and the others had set out after the fleeing Matt Fadden, whom Jeff now hated. But he couldn't stay behind. He was growing up, becoming a man, and it was time for him to take his place among the other Cornwell men and become active in the feud.

If he could, he'd gun down Matt Fadden on his own. He'd be proud to do it... and he hoped his father and Uncle Bax would be proud of him, too.

He heard another shot, and loped off in the direction from which it had come.

CHAPTER 33

The Widow closed her eyes, trying not to cry out in pain as Annie Wolfe tightened the bonds around her hands. The Widow was backed up against a tree, arms stretching around behind it and tied on the other side of the trunk.

She prayed hard—for a miracle to free her and save her life, and if not that, for a death that was quick and painless. She wished now that she had fought Annie Wolfe rather than giving in to her... but it was too late. She had let herself be trapped too deeply, just as Annie was trapped in her hate and apparent insanity.

Only one thing gave the Widow any hope: the gunshots that were exploding through the woods, growing ever closer to the place they were. She had no idea what was going on— it sounded like a small war in progress—but whatever it was had Annie Wolfe worried and distracted. It might keep the Widow alive.

Gunshots meant people, and people were witnesses. Even insane Annie had enough sense to realize she could not commit her crimes in the open. The fact she'd set the Widow's house afire as they left it was proof of that. She was deluded, bitter, vengeful beyond reason... but still cagey enough to hide her crime.

Annie finished tying the Widow, then went around and faced her, staring into her face. She held her rifle in hands that trembled, and at the sound of every new gunshot, blinked and glanced away.

"I was going to make you die slowly," she said to the Widow. "What my great-grandmother suffered was not quick and easy. It was ugly and obscene and cruel. But it appears I have no choice but to dispatch you fast, before others arrive."

"They'll know you did it, Annie. They'll track you down and you'll hang as a murderess."

"No one will know." Annie lifted the rifle and aimed it at the Widow's chest.

"No!" the Widow screamed. "No!"

Just over the nearest ridge Matt heard the Widow's yell, and from its tone knew that he had to react quickly. Something was about to happen to the Widow, obviously—but he was unable to leave the rock that served as his cover.

Will, hiding behind a tree two hundred feet away, was laying down a rain of gunfire that kept Matt pinned down.

He had to move, whatever the risk. The Widow obviously needed help, and besides, he'd just heard movement behind him. Another Cornwell or group of Cornwells arriving on the scene —and coming in from the back as they were, the stone would not protect him.

He came to his feet, slammed off a shot in Will's direction, and loped toward the top of the ridge.

Two things happened all at once. Will came out from behind his tree to take a better shot, and the source of the noise Matt had heard behind him revealed himself.

It was Jeff Cornwell, coming out of the brush. He moved fast, appearing just as his father squeezed off the shot intended to end Matt's life.

It missed Matt, but it did not miss Jeff. Will Cornwell's son took the slug from his father's rifle right through the forehead, and fell dead.

Matt topped the ridge just as he heard Will Cornwell scream, horror overwhelming him as he realized what he'd just done. From the corner of his eye Matt saw an exhausted Bax appear near Will, and other Cornwells as well. He saw Will turn his rifle upon himself, putting the muzzle of it in his mouth even as his older brother took in what was happening and tried to stop it...

It all went out of sight just as Matt went across the ridge, but he heard the blast of the shot that took off the top of Will Cornwell's skull. A self-inflicted shot, dealt out in punishment for the intolerable sin of having just shot his own son to death.

Matt felt an overwhelming revulsion at what had just happened, but there was no time to process the horror through his mind just now. He'd just spotted Annie Wolfe, taking aim at the Widow, who was tied to a tree...

"Annie!" Matt shouted, raising his Henry. "Stop it, Annie!"

Annie froze, then turned and glared at him.

Behind Matt, across the ridge, he heard Bax Cornwell's wailing voice, a man sobbing at the tragedy that his own foolish family had just brought upon itself. He heard other shouts and cries—the other Cornwells taking in the horrible scene and comprehending just what had been dealt to them by the feud they had all refused to abandon.

"I have to kill her, Matt," Annie said. "She deserves to die. All the Packards, all the Cornwells ... they deserve to die. They hurt people who have done nothing to them."

"Annie, on the other side of this ridge just now, Will Cornwell shot his own son to death, trying to kill me. That's Bax's voice you hear wailing. He's crying for young Jeff, but he's also crying for his brother, because Will just took his own life."

Annie took it in, then nodded. "Good," she said. "It's good."

"Good? How can you say that? If this is what you see as good, then you are an evil woman, Annie."

"You won't kill me."

"I will unless you drop that rifle."

"I won't drop it."

Emotion overwhelmed Matt. He wished he had never come to this territory, never heard of Pactolas or Stalker's Creek or either of the feuding families. He wished he'd never accepted the job of town marshal, and that he was anywhere else but here, at this time and place, faced with nothing but wickedness and death all around him.

"I can't let you kill her. I can't." Tears streamed down his face.

She saw the tears, and hesitated. Annie stared at him as if she'd never seen him before.

"Tenderness," she said. "I haven't seen it in so long. What an awful place this is, that you never see tenderness."

"Drop the rifle, Annie," he said.

She looked at the Widow, then back at Matt.

"Please drop it."

She nodded, and laid it on the ground. She turned and walked toward the next ridge.

"Wait, Annie, halt!" Matt said.

She kept going, up the ridge. Matt went to the Widow, hesitated, then laid down his own rifle and began trying to loosen her bonds. They were too tight. He dug for his knife to cut them.

Meanwhile, Annie kept going, vanishing over the ridgetop.

Matt cut the Widow's bonds and she collapsed.

"There's a cliff across that ridge," she said to Matt.

Matt nodded and raced up the same way Annie had just gone. He saw her, poised on the edge of the cliff, taking the locket from around her neck.

"Annie..."

She turned, smiled at him, and held the locket out toward him. He ran toward her, but she dropped the locket on the ground, closed her eyes, and threw herself over the brink.

He could not reach her in time. He got to the edge of the bluff in time to see her form plummeting down, striking stone and dirt, tumbling from there on, rolling like a limp and broken doll to a final stop amid the talus at the base of the escarpment.

Matt stared down at her corpse, then knelt and picked up the locket. He opened it. It bore inside a drawn image of an old woman with sad eyes. Written at the base of the picture, in the tiniest of letters, was the name "Mary Stringer."

Matt walked slowly over the ridge, then stopped at the top, seeing what initially was a dreadful sight. The Widow was still on the ground, trying to rise, and Bax Cornwell stood nearby her, rifle in hand. Matt began to lift his own rifle, ready to kill Bax if he started to harm the Widow... but instead Bax laid down his rifle, reached down, and helped the Widow to her feet.

Matt walked down to join them. Bax looked at him, his eyes vacant, like windows into the shell of what had before been a lively and robust man.

"Perhaps, ma'am, it's time we ended this fight of ours," Bax said to the Widow.

"High time," she said. "High time."

EPILOGUE

Matt shook Jack Bail's hand and admired the badge gleaming on his vest.

"You'll make a fine marshal for Stalker's Creek, Jack," he said. "I'm proud to pass the job on to you."

"I'm proud to take it. . . but I'd rather you be staying on."

"Nope. Too much heartache in the lawman business. I've had my fill."

"You've faced a situation so strange you'd never encounter another one like it between now and doomsday. Stay on, Matt. Keep on being the marshal here. I ain't looking for a promotion."

"Got to go, Jack. Got to go. Too many pains suffered here already."

"The feud's over."

"We hope. Sometimes hate dies a lot slower than people do. I can't take any more of this, Jack."

"So the son of Temple Fadden is running from a fight."

"From this fight, yes. Because it's just too senseless."

"What will you do?"

Matt shrugged, then raised his fists in a pugilistic stance.

"Back to brawling for money again."

"I reckon so."

"Glad to have got to know you, Matt Fadden."

"Same here, Jack. Good luck."

"Good luck to you."

Matt went to his horse and mounted up. He rode out of Stalker's Creek and toward the south, pausing at the edge of the cemetery to note the fresh grave there. Not many had wanted to bury Annie Wolfe in the same ground as their own loved ones, but the Widow, of all people, had intervened to make it possible.

Matt said his silent goodbye to her, to Stalker's Creek, and—he hoped—to all the tragedy he had witnessed here. Then he rode on.

GENESIS RIDER

To Rhonda

CHAPTER 1

SKINNER'S HILL, CALIFORNIA, 1851

Twenty years before, a boyhood accident with a log auger had cost Leroy Barth his right eye. As he shoved his bearded and sweating face close to that of Micah Ward, that dead eye was an ugly, ruined pucker that held Micah's gaze against his will.

The other eye, the good one, squinted at him, boring into him like a sort of auger itself.

"See this blind eye of mine, boy?" Barth growled, his breath like molded cheese in Micah's nostrils. "Know what that eye sees?"

Micah swallowed, pulling back, terrified. But Barth's grip was strong and held him.

"That eye sees nothing, boy. Not a thing. The same as your eyes seen that night at the old cabin. You know the night I'm talking about?"

Micah nodded. His throat was very dry.

"Tell what you seen that night, boy."

"Nothing ... nothing."

"That's right. Nothing. Just like this dead eye of mine. Did you see my brother there, boy?"

"Yes."

Barth shook him. "You answer me again! Did you see my brother?"

"No...no. I saw nothing."

"That's right. You didn't see him at all. Not a thing. And when they set your rump on that testifying chair and ask you that same question, you'll give that very same answer."

Micah was afraid he was going to faint. He was ten years old but just now felt as if he was hardly more than a baby, too scared even to cry.

"You seen nothing at all of my brother that night. Not hide nor hair. Right?"

"Right..."

"You seen no fight, no knife, no man killed."

Micah stared at the dead eye, fighting tears. Barth shook him. "No man killed! Say it!"

"No man killed."

Barth smiled and nodded, still gripping Micah's shoulders tightly. "There's the boy! The boy who seen nothing and who'll tell nothing! The boy who don't remember." He paused, then let go of Micah's right shoulder. Reaching down, he brought up a knife out of a sheath at his belt. He waved it menacingly under Micah's nose. "See that, boy? That's the thing that will make you keep on being the boy who don't remember."

Barth picked the end of the knife into the soft flesh beneath Micah's right eye. "See this eye of mine? Feel it? If you get in that witnessing chair and all at once decide that you did see something that night, and if you tell. I'll give you an eye just like mine. No, two of them. I'll cut your eyes right out of your head... you understand me?"

Micah couldn't squelch tears now. He nodded.

Barth picked him with the knife again, breaking the skin

a little. "Only difference will be, you'll have two eyes like mine, not just one. I'll blind you, boy. I'll blind you. And I'll kill that momma of yours, too. I'll do it, and don't think I'm lying."

Micah was afraid he might faint and collapse. He had no doubt that Leroy Barth would do everything he threatened and more.

Barth made a sudden grunting sound, moving the knife and making a quick thrust. Micah sucked in his breath and tried not to scream as Barth inflicted a small but painful cut straight down along his left jawline, then another horizontal one at the top. "There we go... my brother's initial. A nice T right there on your face.

It's just a reminder, boy. Just a reminder of all you didn't see and all you won't tell when they put my brother on trial."

Barth let Micah go at last. The boy stumbled back and fell on his rump. Blood ran down the left side of his neck. Micah looked around, hoping he might see someone else who'd witnessed what Barth had just done to him. But this was an isolated hollow, thick with trees. No one else was around.

"I'll kill your pappy, too, for good measure," Barth said coldly, sheathing the knife. "You remember all I told you, boy. And you keep your mouth shut. Not a word of what has happened here today to nobody. You tell your parents, and I'll know. I'll come cut your eyes out if you breathe so much as a word. You understand me?"

Micah nodded.

Leroy Barth stared down at him, then laughed with contempt. He turned and strode away.

Micah waited until he was gone before he allowed himself to break down completely. Rising, he ran, sobbing, deeper into the woods and hid. Shaking, terrified, he cried for a long time, holding his hand over the cut on his jaw.

Two hours later, he walked into the cabin that was his

home here in this Gold Rush mining camp. He averted his eyes from a certain building that was within view: a small building of heavy logs with no windows. This was the makeshift jail in Skinner's Hill and currently the lodging of one Tipton Barth, the brother of Leroy Barth. He was a man accused of the murder of another miner in a claim dispute...a knifing murder Micah had witnessed and which had haunted his dreams ever since.

Micah's mother, one of the relatively few women living in Skinner's Hill mining camp—a community that had sprung to life a year before and that would probably die as quickly once its streams and gullies had yielded up all their gold, saw the cut on his face at once. He'd hoped she'd not notice.

"Whoa, there, young man...let me see that face of yours."

Micah stopped and let her examine him. He could not, for some reason, let his gaze meet hers.

She looked at the cut with concern. "This looks like a knife cut, Micah."

"No, Mama," he said, trying to sound convincing and firm. "I scraped it on a nail."

"That doesn't look like a scrape, son. How would you get a scrape in that shape?"

"I'm not a bar, Mama!"

She pulled back, surprised at his forcefulness. Micah blinked and looked away from her.

"Alright, son. Whatever you say."

He went up to his loft room and lay down on his bed. This was something not generally allowable in the hard-working Ward household during daylight hours, but he felt the need for the childish comfort of his sleeping place. He dug deep beneath the covers and hoped he wouldn't cry again.

"Micah, are you in bed up there?"

"Yes, Mama."

"It's not even suppertime yet!"

"I'm feeling sick, Mama."

She came up the loft ladder after him and laid her hand across his forehead. "You don't feel hot."

"I'm sick. I'm not lying to you."

She looked at him in silent concern. Her eyes traced the line of the cut along his jaw. "I believe you, son," she said. "You rest until I call in your father for supper."

CHAPTER 2

M icah truly was feeling sick. His terror was deep, indescribable. He couldn't shake from his mind the horrible imagined vision of Leroy Barth cutting out his eyes.

He envisioned his face with dead eyes like Barth's own right eye. He imagined himself blind beside the graves of his murdered family.

Despite all the gentle but clear admonitions his father had given him, all the somber sermons about duty and courage, he knew he couldn't testify to what he'd seen Tipton Barth do to poor old Jim Sneed. If he did, Leroy Barth would do everything he'd threatened.

Micah ate no supper, did not even descend to join his parents at the table. His appetite was gone. He lay in his loft and listened to his parents eating and talking softly below in the cabin. His father's voice sounded tired, as always after a long day of mining.

After supper, Joseph Barth climbed to the loft to talk to his son. He sat on the edge of Micah's bed, a sturdy bed whose frame Joe had built himself from straight sapling logs and whose mattress he had stuffed by hand.

"Your mama tells me you got a scrape on your face today, Micah."

Micah briefly let him see the cut.

"Well, could have been worse," Joe Ward said. "It's a peculiar cut to have been made by a nail. Two cuts, really. Well, keep a watch on it to make sure it don't fester. You're feeling kind of sick now?"

"Yes."

Joe nodded. After a brief silence, he said, "Wouldn't be worrying about having to testify against Tipton Barth, would you?"

Micah couldn't answer.

Joe went on: "Because if you are, it'd be an expected thing. It's hard to do the right thing sometimes. But still, we got to do it. That's the way the good Lord wrote the rules, you know."

Micah hoped he wouldn't start crying again.

"All you got to do, son, is sit in that chair and tell the truth. We've got us no real nor official court up here, just a miner's court, but we want it to be a fair one. It's to the honor of the men of Skinner's Hill that they've chosen to have a real trial, not just a vigilante hanging. You understand the difference between vigilance committees and real courts?"

Micah nodded. He understood it well, from hearing his father's impassioned pleas with the other miners of this community to deal with the murder of Jim Sneed in as close to an orderly, law-abiding, systematic manner as could be achieved in a remote mining camp.

They'd agreed with Joseph Ward in the end and appointed a judge, a prosecutor, and defense attorney, and even a rotating squad of jailers to keep watch over Tipton Barth in his makeshift jail.

The prosecutor and defense attorney were real lawyers, one from Ohio, the other from Georgia. Attorneys were not hard to find in mining camps, where legal wranglings over mining claims and the like made their services valuable.

"That we're prosecuting Tipton Barth in a legal style makes it all the more important that nothing but the pure truth be told," Joe gently lectured. "That places a burden on your shoulders, son, for you are the only witness to the crime. And I know it's probably a heavy burden on your shoulders. Am I right?"

Tears welled despite Micah's attempts to stop them. He nodded quickly. If only his father knew just how heavy that burden was right now!

"I don't want you to worry about anything," Joe said. "Tipton is locked up. He's a mean man, but he can't hurt you. The men here, me most of all, will protect you from him. All that lies ahead for him is a trial, an almost certain conviction, sentencing, and a hanging." Joe paused somberly at that point. "Maybe I shouldn't have said the last part. I don't want you to worry about what sentence is carried out on Tipton Barth, son. That's not your concern at all, but that of the grown-up men. All your job is, is to tell the truth. You understand?"

"Yes, Pap," Micah managed to say.

"Good. Good." Joe patted his son's shoulder. "You want us to bring you up some food?"

Micah still was not hungry, but he nodded anyway.

When the food arrived, he managed to eat a little of it. Then he rolled over in his bed and pretended to go to sleep, but it was, in fact, a long and mostly sleepless night. When he did sleep, he dreamed that Leroy Barth had hold of him and was poking out his eyes.

Don't worry about Tipton Barth, his father had told him. But what about Leroy? He was in no jail, and he wouldn't hang. And he was an even meaner man than his murdering brother.

———

The court met outside. Tables were set up in a clearing, and a desk for the judge. Tipton Barth sat beside his attorney, arms crossed over his chest and a dark, contemptuous glower on his face. He was a big man, not quite as ugly as his brother because he had both his eyes. But he was scarred and rugged, touched by the marks of many past brawls.

Micah tried not to look at him. Glancing around at the encircling crowd, he saw at the rear of it Leroy Barth, staring at him, grinning cruelly. In that brief and unwanted moment when his gaze locked with Leroy's, Barth winked at him, then let the smile fade for half a moment, reminding Micah of what he was expected to do and what would happen if he failed.

The trial began. It was all an unheard, meaningless buzz to Micah, who stared at the ground. He felt an over-whelming sense of unreality, and in a way, it was as welcome as it was unpleasant. Best not to go through this with a clear head. Best to experience this as something not quite real, like the nightmare it was.

"Micah?" His father nudged him. "Didn't you hear? It's time for you to testify."

Micah jerked his head up. All eyes were on him.

"Come on, son," the judge said. "We need to hear from you."

"Are you sick, son?" Joe Ward asked. "You look a little pale."

"I'm... I don't know." Micah stood. He walked mechanically to his seat. They made him raise his hand, swear to tell the truth in the name of God. Micah had been taught to take vows seriously, especially those that evoked the name of God, for God was to be feared. But right now, he knew that he feared Leroy Barth much more.

CHAPTER 3

He never fully remembered all that followed. He answered questions, spoke up more loudly when told to, which was frequent, and saw the bewilderment on the faces of most. Only the Barth brothers looked happy.

Joe Ward had nothing to say to him when at last the ordeal was done, and he had returned to his seat.

He'd been afraid he might cry and embarrass himself when all this was done. Instead, he just felt numb.

Joe Ward climbed to the loft that night and sat down at the edge of Micah's bed. He filled and lit his pipe. Micah lay there looking at his silent father out of the corner of his eye, smelling the pipe smoke. He usually liked the smell, but tonight nothing could give him pleasure.

"Did you tell the truth today, Micah?" Joe asked at last.

"Yes, Pap." Micah felt his lie ring in his own ears.

"You sure? For what you said today, and what you'd said before..."

"I told the truth, Pap. I didn't see him kill nobody."

Joe wouldn't look at him. He puffed at the pipe, then nodded. "Very well, then. So you lied to us before."

"I didn't he..."

"You said before that you saw Tipton Barth kill poor old Sneed."

"I thought I had...I was wrong, though. I didn't really see nothing."

Now Joe did look at him. "Did someone get to you, Micah? Threaten you?"

It was hard not to cry. "No, Pap."

Joe nodded again. "A man walked free today who most were sure was a killer. I hope he truly is innocent, for if he's not, an injustice has happened."

Micah felt a weight descend upon him, wrap itself around him, root into him. This burden he would not easily shrug off.

"The Barth brothers have left," Joe said. "They rode out today after Tipton was cleared. Thank God they're gone, at least."

"Yes." It was a heartfelt agreement.

"Good night, son. I hope you sleep well."

"Thank you. You too. Pap."

When Joe was gone and crawling into his own bed below, beside his already sleeping wife, Micah buried his face in his covers and wept silently.

Then he slept, the deep and dreamless sleep of the emotionally exhausted, and for a time was free of that crushing burden.

———

But the burden was there when he awakened. He felt it as he rose, felt it as he ate a breakfast he did not even taste.

Later in the day, he found himself approaching the claim of Flavius Miller, who had come overland from Illinois right after the rush began.

Miller had no partners, working his claim alone. Some found him aloof, but to Micah, he had always been kindly.

He was a preacher, sometimes conducting worship services on Sunday mornings for those miners who wished to come. The Wards were generally among them.

He stopped working as Micah approached and greeted him.

"Hello, Micah. How are you today?"

"I'm fine... No. No, I'm not. There's something... I have this kind of feeling like a stone between my shoulders, and..." Micah trailed off, realizing he was talking nonsense.

Miller looked a little puzzled but seemed to take him seriously. "Got something on your conscience, son?"

Micah wondered if he knew. Everybody had known about the Barth trial and Micah's role. Everybody had been talking about how what Micah saw would send Barth to the noose. Then Micah had sat down in the witness chair and said he'd seen nothing at all.

"There's... I can't..." Micah trailed off again, realizing there was really nothing he could say. He had this sense that if he spoke, Leroy Barth would somehow instantly, mystically know. And he'd take his vengeance even now, with his murdering brother freed.

"Let's talk a few minutes," the preacher said.

Somehow, over the next hour, Micah managed to convey to the preacher his overwhelming pain, his sense of guilt, his fear, without expressly admitting what he'd done. If Miller figured out on his own what Micah had done, he didn't speak it.

They talked of many things that Micah had heard in church, about guilt and sin and forgiveness. Micah followed most of it.

When he was through talking, the preacher stepped inside his cabin and returned with a book. He handed it to Micah. It was a leather-bound Bible, the same one Miller held when he'd preach on Sunday mornings.

"I want you to have that," he said. "I've got another one.

You take that book, and you read it. What questions you have, you'll find answers in there."

Micah accepted the Bible. "Thank you."

"Son, I don't know just what this burden you carry is, though I suppose I could make guesses. Whatever it is, though, you look in that book for an answer. And don't stop looking until you find it. That book has given me peace for years and years. It can do the same for you."

Micah touched the leather cover, feeling its rough texture.

"You read that book starting tonight," Miller said. "Will you do that?"

"I will," Micah said.

CHAPTER 4

Micah Ward raised the Bible above his head and looked out across the congregation.

"And it was just as that mining camp preacher told me it would be," he said, winding down now to the conclusion of his sermon. "In this book, whose covers have nearly worn away from all the years I've pored over it, I found that peace I sought. And it's been my privilege for years now to share that same book and its message with such as you, my people, and my dear friends."

He paused and examined the faces of these people he loved. "Three years, three years this very day. That's how long you have given me the pleasure of being among you, being your friend and shepherd. The role of preacher was not one I had grown up believing I would ever hold. But God, as is so often said, moves in mysterious ways. Through tragedy, fear... through guilt... he builds avenues to reach those whom he will. And he reached me, changed me, and brought me to you. I thank you for the privilege of being your pastor."

He received nods and smiles. Micah's heart warmed. Truly he did love these people, and they loved him in return.

Micah glanced at his wife, Alice, who sat in her usual spot on the second pew. She gave him the smallest and most subtle of winks—her familiar signal that he had spoken well, that his sermon had been what he intended.

That wifely support meant much to him. He was no educated preacher, not formally anyway, and he'd entered the ministry with some trepidation. Did he really have the ability to do the task he believed he was called to do? How could such a man as he, with little schooling and no right to call himself a scholar, preach adequately to a congregation of people looking to him for leadership?

But he'd done it, and so far, it seemed, he was succeeding. Though preaching paid little, and he had to rely on farming to keep himself and Alice fed, he found it fulfilling.

There was not a day that passed that he did not thank God for the day that he'd been handed that Bible in Skinner's Camp. That was the start of it, the thing that set him on the path toward a new kind of life and the pulpit.

He lifted his hand. "Let's rise now and have our closing prayer. Brother Meadows, if you'd lead us, I'd be very obliged to you."

Micah leaned on the pulpit with his head bowed, listening to the deacon's prayer, but thinking mostly about the sermon he'd just preached. It had been a personally difficult one. In it, he'd come as close as he'd ever dared to telling the story of the Barth brothers and his failure, to tell the truth in that long-ago murder trial.

He'd prayed for forgiveness for that failure many times, for it had taken him a long time to believe God could ever forgive anyone for letting a murderer walk free. At last, though, peace had come, and he'd been able to put that event behind him.

He now seldom thought about the failure itself and

instead concentrated on the good things it had led to that visit to Flavius Miller, the gift of the Bible... the changing of his life.

He'd come close to telling the full story today, but no more than close. Not even his beloved Alice knew about the trial, the threats by Tipton Barth, his lie under oath. He'd not been able to bring himself to tell her, nor could he see anything to gain even if he could. He'd never told a living soul about what had happened.

When the prayer was finished, Micah made his way to the door of the church to shake the hands of his congregation members as they filed out. They complimented his sermon, gave him smiles and thanks, pats on the shoulder. He felt deeply happy.

Of all those who filed past him, only one was a stranger, but even he was someone Micah had seen before. He was a newcomer to Pardeeville who'd opened up a wagon-repair business in an old rented barn at the edge of town. Micah had seen him working about the place and had been told his name was Tower. Beyond that, he knew nothing of the man.

"Good preaching, Reverend," Tower said, smiling but somehow not managing to look convincing at it. Micah had noticed before that the man always looked sad.

"Thank you," Micah replied. "And good to have you with us. Mr. Tower, I think? The wagon man?"

"That's me. Jack Tower. Newcomer here."

"Are you a church member anywhere?"

"Belonged to a little Baptist church down in Texas. That's been some years back, though. I've moved around since then.... The truth is, I sort of let church and such get away from me for a few years."

"Well, that happens sometimes. The important thing is, you've come back. I'm glad you chose to be here." Micah paused, curious about the man for visitors to the church were relatively rare— but not sure how much he should ask. Western folks usually didn't take well to too much prying.

Micah decided to take a chance. "Have you got family, Mr. Tower?"

It was as if he'd just jabbed the man with a long needle. Tower actually winced a little, and it seemed to Micah that his eyes moistened almost instantly.

"No," Tower said tightly. "No family." He turned away. "Good day, Preacher."

Micah watched him walk away, heading for a buggy parked at the edge of the churchyard. Tower climbed into the buggy and drove away.

Alice came to her husband and gave him a kiss on the cheek. Except for their son, they were alone now.

"Wonderful sermon, Micah."

Thank you... but I think I just made a wrong move."

"What?"

He told her about the brief meeting with Tower and the fact he'd obviously stung him with his intrusive question. "I'm afraid he might not come back," Micah said. I shouldn't have been so inquisitive."

"It's hard to know how people will react to questions," Alice said. "If it concerns you, maybe you can go visit him and make amends. Isn't he the man who works on wagons over in town?"

"Yes." He watched as Tower's buggy disappeared over the low rise, dust boiling out behind it. It had been a long and dry autumn. "Maybe I will."

"Micah... your sermon today..." She trailed off as if hesitant to speak further.

He looked at her. "I thought you liked my sermon."

"I did like it," she said. "But you talked about things that make me... curious, I guess."

She'd said things like this before when he'd drifted close in conversation or sermons to the Barth incident.

"You want to know what happened to me when I was a boy," he said.

"Yes. I admit that I do, Micah. Whatever it was, obviously, it was something that terrified you and made you feel guilty. You're the man I love, so it's only natural I want to know."

"I understand. But it's not something I want to tell, dear. There's nothing gained by it. All you need to know is that it happened, that by the grace of God, I made it through, and the entire thing led me to a mining camp preacher and the beginning of a new life." He smiled at her. "So don't worry, and don't let this curiosity eat you up."

"Just tell me this: Were you hurt?"

For a moment, he felt the sting of that knife again, and his face gave the smallest of twitches. He fought back the impulse to touch the faint, T-shaped scar that still marked his face where Leroy Barth had cut him. His smile, though, remained. "No, not in any kind of significant or lasting way," he answered.

She wasn't satisfied, and he could tell it, but she made the best of it. "I suppose I'll have to just let it go, then. But maybe, Micah, someday... maybe you'll tell me?"

"Maybe." But in fact, he had no intention ever of doing so.

"Are you hungry?" she asked.

"Starved."

"The stew is ready," she said. "As soon as the corn bread bakes, well eat." She looked around. "Where's Flavius gotten to?" Flavius was their son, named by Micah after Flavius Miller, who'd given him the Bible and changed his life.

"Out running with his dog, I think," Micah said. "I'll go find him."

Micah finished his last bite of cornbread and pushed his plate away. He chewed slowly, deep in thought.

"What's on your mind, dear?" Alice asked.

"Hmm? Oh... just thinking about Jack Tower. Our church visitor. I think I'll give him some business."

"The buckboard wheel?" Alice said in a hopeful tone. The vehicle had been an inheritance of Alice's, left to her by an uncle who died without children, and she had always been proud of it because it was a fairly luxurious item, the sort she and Micah would never buy on their own. But the right wheel had recently been squeaking and wobbly to the extent Micah had been afraid for her to use the buckboard.

"That's right. It needs repair anyway, and it would be a chance for me to get to know him a little. Maybe persuade him to come back and visit the church again."

"I found a dead snake in the woods," Flavius announced in the abrupt manner of little boys.

"Oh, honey, don't tell us about it while we're eating."

Flavius shrugged and went back to his stew.

"Jack Tower carries heavy burdens," Alice said.

"How can you know that?" Micah asked.

"Can't you tell?" Alice said. "You can see a sorrow in him that is very deep indeed."

"If so, maybe I can be a source of help to him," Micah replied. "Flavius, send that cornbread this way."

"Mick Branchfield is going to fight Jimmy," Flavius declared in another sudden change of subject.

"How do you know?"

"He was saying so at church."

"And I'll bet you weren't supposed to tell it, either," Micah said.

"Why, Micah, he ought to tell such things when he

knows them," Alice remonstrated. "Boys don't need to be fighting each other."

Micah scooped a chunk of potato out of his stew and watched the steam rise from it. "No," he said. "They shouldn't. But you ought not tell things you hear in confidence, either."

"Oh, it wasn't in confidence," Flavius said sincerely. "He ain't confident about it at all."

Micah and his wife glanced at each other with little smiles.

"Not confident, huh?" Micah said. "Then why is he planning to fight?"

"He says he's got to. Jimmy won't leave him alone. He's been picking on him for nearly the whole year, and Mick's been trying to stay away from him, and that ain't working. So he says he's got to quit running away from it and face up to it."

"That sounds like Mick," Alice said. "When he talks, it's like hearing a grown-up talk. You ever noticed that about him, Micah?"

"I have. I've also noticed that he's about half the size of Jimmy. He's likely to get whupped."

"Mick knows that," Flavius said. "But he says he's got to show Jimmy he ain't afraid of him and that he won't run from him no more."

"Well, I admire his courage, anyway," Micah said. "Even though I can't condone fighting. The Bible tells us to turn the other cheek and to bless those who try to hurt us."

"What about that time Jesus ran them, bank tellers, out of the church house with that great big bullwhip?" Flavius asked.

"It was a temple, not a church, and I don't believe he had a bullwhip," Micah said. "I don't know that they had bullwhips back then. And they weren't bank tellers. They were money changers."

"Yeah, but what I mean is, sometimes there's times you got to just deal with things, ain't there? Without being nice about it?"

"I don't think you can draw a comparison between Jesus running the money changers out of the temple and Jimmy and Mick getting into a fight."

"I think you should tell Mick's parents he's planning to fight," Alice said to her son.

Micah spoke up. "Now, honey, he can't do that. Boys don't go tattling. It's kind of against the rules of being a boy." He winked at Flavius, who grinned back.

"Even if somebody can get hurt?"

"They're just two boys, Alice. They won't hurt each other."

Alice sighed and shook her head. "I swear, I don't understand men sometimes. Or boys. The way you think and act..."

"It's not hard, Ma," Flavius said. "It's just that, sometimes, a man or a boy just has to fight. Cause there ain't no other way. Right, Pa?"

"Right, son. Not often. But sometimes."

CHAPTER 6

T he sky was cloudy, the wind kicking up, the temperature dropping, and the buckboard wheel squeaking and wobbling worse than ever the next morning when Micah drove it into town. He'd come alone and was glad of it because he feared the wheel might break or simply fall off at almost any moment, and he never liked to go through such little disasters with Alice around. She tended to get overly worried about such things. There wasn't much to Pardeeville. It was a perfectly flat little community, laid out in a neat grid pattern because there were no intruding features of the landscape to create a need for any street to curve and break up the checkerboard pattern.

Jack Tower's wagon-repair business operated in what had been a barn at the south edge of town. Tower had done little to make the barn look like a place of business. He'd not even put up a sign. Only the various wagons parked around the front of it, in various states of repair, and the wagon wheels leaned against the barn wall, made the current use of the place evident.

Tower wasn't to be seen as Micah drove the wagon into

the lot. The barn door was open. Micah figured he was inside.

"Hello!" he loudly said as he pulled the creaking buckboard to a halt. "Anybody around?"

He heard what he thought was a reply from somewhere inside the barn. Tower's voice. But it had a harsh edge, and then a second voice spoke, more loudly, also harsh.

"Hello?" Micah said again, climbing down from the buckboard and heading for the door.

He heard Tower's voice again. "I told you I didn't think it would hold! I warned you that it would give way. But you insisted I not replace it."

"An axle should last longer than a week, and you know it!" the other voice replied, nearly shouting.

Micah recognized the speaker and winced. Henry Pierce, another local farmer, is renowned for his sour disposition, short temper, and tight-fistedness. Micah had never liked to be around him and felt guilty for his own secret gladness that Pierce was not part of his congregation.

"A new axle would have lasted as long as the wagon itself," Tower replied. "But you wouldn't let me give you a new axle. That's the whole damn point!"

Micah stopped at the edge of the door, frowning, sorry to hear Tower's swearing.

"This is a damn wagon-repair shop, ain't it?" Pierce shot back. "If I'd wanted a new axle, I could just buy myself a new wagon right along with it! I wanted my old axle fixed!"

"And fixed it was."

"It ain't fixed if it breaks within the week!"

"I told you, damn it all, that it wouldn't hold! And you wouldn't the hell listen!" Tower's voice had risen even more all at once, taking on a new, threatening quality. Micah actually backed away from the door a couple of steps. "Now, get your damned and sorry old hide out of this shop! Now! Before I break your neck like that axle!"

There was a brief pause, then Pierce said, "What are you doing with that? You put that hammer down!"

"I'll sink it in your worthless skull, you damned old fool!" Tower yelled back at him. "Get out! Get out of here, now!"

"I ought to have the law on you, threatening me like that!"

"Out! And don't come back here, you mealy-mouthed old devil!"

Micah heard Pierce storm out the back door of the barn. A moment later, he saw him circle back around through the side lot and head for the street, walking in a fast, angry stride. Pierce looked back toward the barn, and Micah noticed that his face was pale. The man was scared.

Pierce saw Micah standing there and paused. "There's your churchgoing types for you, Preacher!" Pierce called back. "Did you hear what he just said to me?"

Without awaiting an answer, Pierce turned again and stalked on up the street.

Micah decided to leave without making his presence known to Jack Tower. This obviously was not a good time to make a call.

But just as he turned back toward the buckboard, Tower appeared at the door. He froze for a moment when he saw the preacher there, and his red, angry-looking face lost a little of its color.

Micah and Tower looked silently at each other for a moment.

"Hello, Mr. Tower," Micah said.

"Preacher," Tower replied, barely audible.

Micah nodded, uncomfortable, tried to find something to say, and couldn't. He nodded again and headed back to the buckboard.

Climbing aboard, he drove off with the wheel wobbling and squeaking and did not look back at Jack Tower.

———

The sunset was a brilliant red. Micah, pausing from his labors with a hammer in hand, studied it and gave a quiet prayer of thanks for its beauty. Such sights exhilarated him.

This evening, though, he didn't respond quite as powerfully as usual. He'd been depressed ever since returning from Tower's wagon shop this morning, the buckboard still unrepaired.

Micah was not naive. He knew that, as a preacher, he generally saw people on their best behavior. Most folks grew quite righteous when he came into their presence, and he was quite certain that much of that righteousness faded as soon as he was gone.

Still, to hear Tower cursing and lambasting that unhappy customer had been unusually troubling. He'd assumed that, since Tower had visited his church, he was a different sort than that.

He chuckled at himself. Maybe he was naive after all. Hadn't Tower himself told him he'd drifted away from the church for years? Why should he assume the man would be some sort of saint just because he darkened a church door occasionally?

Micah lowered his gaze from the sky and saw a rider approaching from the direction of town. Micah squinted, trying to make out who it was.

He heard the side door of his house open, and Alice call him and Flavius in for supper. Flavius, who had been playing with his dog in the yard, hopped up and ran toward the house, but Micah called back, "I'll be in in a minute, dear."

He'd just made out who was approaching.

Jack Tower rode to the gate and stopped there.

Micah approached him, dusting sawdust and grit off his hands.

"Mr. Tower, sir. Welcome to my house."

"Hello, Preacher." He looked around. "Nice place."

"Thank you. It's small but sufficient. There's only the three of us here. Please, dismount and come over to the porch."

"I may have come at a time to interrupt your supper."

"Interrupt? No, no. In fact, join us."

"*I* couldn't do that."

"Sure you can. I insist. Alice always has more than enough food fixed."

"Obliged. And then, after... maybe you and me can talk in private a bit."

Micah had seen that one coming. As soon as he'd recognized Tower, he'd figured the man was coming to apologize to him for his behavior with that customer earlier in the day.

Alice was surprised but welcoming when Micah appeared inside with the unanticipated guest. She quickly laid out another plate and took Tower's hat and coat. Flavius, always glad for visitors, immediately began chattering at Tower, giving the man little chance to respond but also relaxing him, making him feel welcome.

The Wards and their guest ate slowly, talking about unimportant things. Alice apologized for the lack of a dessert, but Tower waved it off.

"The meal itself was dessert enough for me," he said. "I live alone, you see, and what I fix for myself ain't much worth having most of the time."

"Do you enjoy cigars?" Micah asked.

"I do."

"Then we'll make that our dessert. I've got a box of good ones, all the way from Chicago."

"So you're not a preacher who minds the use of tobacco."

"I enjoy a cigar every now and again," Micah replied. "I think the key is moderation. Let's step outside and enjoy a couple... moderately, of course."

O ut on the porch, with cigars nicely lit and flaring red-tipped in the darkness, Micah had to send Flavius back inside to allow Tower the opportunity to talk in private.

"You can probably guess why I came," he said, scratching the back of his neck uncomfortably.

"My guess is that you want to apologize to me for having cursed and acted as you did with that customer today."

"Yes. I didn't know you were there. I'd have controlled myself better if I had. Or I think I would have."

"There's no need to apologize to me, Mr. Tower. If you feel you acted in the wrong way, then apologize to the Lord and to the man you were speaking to."

"But you being a preacher and all..."

"I'll be forthright with you, Mr. Tower. One thing that sometimes can irritate preachers is the tendency of people to become all false and tense whenever the local clergyman comes around. As I said if you think you did wrong today, apologize to the ones you think you may have insulted, not to me."

"I will apologize. Although that fellow today ought to

apologize to me as well. He was quite belligerent. He insulted my work, and I don't abide that very easily."

"You men of business have to put up with a lot of nonsense from the public, no doubt about it."

"Indeed. It could try the patience of Job sometimes. There's days I wish I could just disappear."

They puffed on their cigars for a time, silent. Then Tower cleared his throat and spoke again.

"I'd like to tell you something, Preacher. Just so you'll know more about me and why maybe I sometimes don't act as I should, like I did today. What you saw there this morning wasn't my usual nature. Only over the last year or so have I tended to lose my temper that way."

"Why's that?"

"Because of what happened... to my family."

"I see. Something bad, I gather."

"They were taken from me, suddenly." He held a brief silence. "Murdered."

"Murdered!"

"Yes, sir. My wife's name was Angeline. My baby boy was Bradley, and my daughter was Nancy."

"You're telling me that all three of them were killed?"

"Yes. Back in Colorado, where we lived. I came to Kansas, fleeing the memories of it all. But I think they've followed me."

"I'm shocked, Mr. Tower. And horrified. What a terrible thing! I don't know what to say."

"There's no words that can help, really. It was worse than a straight-out murder, Preacher. My wife was... misused. My little Nancy, thank God, they left alone in that way, her being so young. But she fought them on behalf of her mother, and they struck her with a pistol butt and killed her."

Micah stared at his cigar, suddenly having lost all taste for it. He watched the coal slowly go dark as Tower continued.

"I was gone at the time it happened, away on business. Nobody exactly knows what happened. The best guess is that the pair of them came to my house and gained entrance on some pretext or the other. Angeline was always ready to feed a stranger or lend a hand. A fine woman she was. Your own wife's manner reminds me of her. Anyway, they got in and took advantage. When they'd killed them, they stole every kind of little thing of value they could from the house, Angeline's wedding ring and jewelry her mother had given her, and such. They set the house afire and left. The blaze went out, though. But not until it had smoked up the house so bad that my little baby boy, upstairs in his crib, died from smothering in it. Angeline and Nancy were already dead downstairs, Nancy from the blow to the head, Angeline from strangling."

Micah let the dead cigar fall from his fingers to the porch. "I'm sickened, Mr. Tower. And amazed you can even bring yourself to recount this to me so... dispassionately."

"You grow accustomed to it. Not accepting of it, not peaceful about it... just accustomed to the facts of what happened. There's nothing I can do to change it. And I wanted you to know why I might seem an odd man at times, Preacher. And not consistent. My emotions and such, you see, the state of my mind... it's all different because of the killing."

"I can understand that."

"I want to ask you, Preacher, not to share what we're talking about here. Not even with your wife. It's something I feel compelled to keep to myself. You're the first person here I've told."

"I'll say nothing." It would be hard to resist sharing such startling knowledge with Alice, but he'd keep his promise.

"Did they catch the killers?" Micah asked. "A posse caught up with one of them. He fought back, and they shot him dead on the spot. The other got away."

"Do you think he'll be caught?"

"I don't know. He should have been caught years before. That pair has killed others, you see. Many people over the years, from what I hear. All across the West."

"I don't know what to say to you about all this, Mr. Tower."

"Call me Jack. And there's nothing for you to say. What is, is. I just wanted you to know about it. I ain't making excuses for misbehaviors. Just giving an explanation. Before I lost my family, I wouldn't so much as whisper a cussword or yell at nobody. But now, sometimes, I grow like I was earlier today. I let outrage at folks who don't deserve it." He hesitated, then added, "Sometimes I even say blasphemous things to God. I want to curse him for having let my family be so mistreated. I curse myself for not having been there to keep my family safe. And I curse all the people who might have stopped the murderers before they ever got to my house and my family. They say that there'd been many times before that this pair had gotten away with crimes. They'd intimidate people away from testifying against them and so on. Or so they tell me."

That struck a little too close to home for Micah. He fidgeted and stood, pacing a little.

Tower took it as a sign he should move on and stood as well.

"Thank you, Preacher Ward. I appreciate you listening to me. And I pledge to you and to the Lord that I'll try to keep my temper better in the future and watch my language."

Micah said, "That seems a small thing now, knowing what you've suffered."

"There's those who have suffered more than me. And those who have suffered since me. The killer who got away has murdered two others; you see. One a town marshal, the other a fellow he murdered just to get his horse. I wish he could have been killed along with his brother."

242   CAMERON JUDD

"It was two brothers?" Micah asked.

"Yes. At least the one-eyed one is gone now. Well, good night. Thank your wife again for the victuals."

Tower turned and headed for his horse, which was still tethered at the gate.

"Jack..."

He turned. "Yes?"

"These brothers... what did you say their name was?"

"I didn't say. But it's Barth. Tipton and Leroy.

Leroy was the one killed by the posse. Good night again."

Micah tried to reply, but his voice was gone. He could hardly breathe.

He managed to remain standing until Jack Tower had mounted up and ridden away some distance, and then his knees buckled, and he sank to the porch, limp and weak and feeling he might become sick on the spot.

CHAPTER 8

L ong past midnight, Alice Ward rolled over in her bed and sat up.

Micah was out of bed, sitting in a chair by the window, staring out.

"Micah? Why are you up?"

"Couldn't sleep."

"Is something wrong?"

He did not answer.

"Micah? Are you sick? You looked pale after you came back in."

"So you already told me. No, I'm not sick."

"Come back to bed, Micah?"

"Later."

"But you need your rest."

"Later."

She knew better than to ask again. She watched his dark form there in the dark room, vaguely silhouetted against the window, and felt a deep, unsettling concern. She lay back down and waited for him to come to bed. He did not, and eventually, she drifted off to sleep again.

When she awakened in the morning, Micah was in bed

beside her, sleeping, but he woke up as she slipped out of bed, and a few minutes later, got out of bed himself.

He said hardly a handful of words all day. Alice didn't see him smile even once.

———

Two days later, Alice was in the kitchen, cutting up chicken for the night's supper and staring at the wall, thinking hard and feeling very troubled.

The door opened, and Flavius came in, head turned away to hide his face. He passed by her quickly and entered the next room, but as he did so, she saw him lift a hand and dab at his eye.

"Flavius?" she asked. "Is something wrong?"

He mumbled something back at her.

She wiped her hands clean and went after him. He was sitting in a chair, looking upset, and quickly turned his head away when she came in.

"Flavius, you're crying."

"I'm not."

"Come on, son. Tell me what's happened."

"It's Pap. He yelled at me. I was trying to help him, and I dropped the lumber. It was an accident, but he yelled at me."

"I'm sure he didn't mean to."

"He did. He was mad. He's been mad for days."

Alice sighed, walked over, and knelt beside Flavius's chair. "I don't think he's mad, exactly. He's just got something on his mind."

"Something I did?"

"No. I don't think it has anything to do with you. The truth is I don't know what it is."

"It started after Mr. Tower came and ate supper with us."

Alice thought about it and realized Flavius was right. She hadn't made the connection until then.

"Flavius, did you hear any of what they talked about on the porch?"

"No. Pap sent me away before that."

She frowned, silent. "Well," she said, "I'm sure everything will be all right. And I'm sure your father didn't mean to hurt your feelings."

"I'm worried about things, Mama. Something doesn't seem right."

"Everything is fine, son."

But she wasn't sure it really was.

———

The wind was up on Saturday evening, whipping across the Kansas plains, twisting into dust devils, and slapping the side of the house like a great hand.

Alice looked out the kitchen window. The sunset tonight was even redder than that brilliant one earlier in the week. Almost a bloody red.

She wondered where Micah was. He tended to be hard to find on Saturday evenings, usually off by himself studying for his sermon the next morning.

Alice went looking. He wasn't in the pantry or in his chair up by the bedroom window, two of his usual study retreats. She went to the porch and saw them there, sitting on the edge of the porch with his back turned toward her.

"Studying hard, Micah?" she asked, approaching.

He didn't answer. He was busy with something, and she was shocked to see that he was cleaning his pistol. It was a good pistol, a gift from her own father, who declared that any man west of the Mississippi was doing himself a disservice if he didn't own a good Colt revolver. Micah had always liked the pistol as an ornament and possession but generally ignored it, not being a man drawn to instruments of violence.

"I haven't seen you clean that pistol in months," she said, sitting down beside him on the porch's edge.

"That's why it needs cleaning," he said.

"I didn't know you'd fired it recently."

"I haven't. I fired it last maybe six months ago. I failed to clean it afterward."

"Are you planning to shoot it again soon?"

"A man should keep in practice with a pistol. He never knows when he might be called upon to use it. Bad things happen. Did you know that there've been families murdered by people who just stop by, asking for a meal or a drink of water?"

"What in the world has put such thoughts into your mind? You're the one who always says that our protection comes from God."

"Things happen, Alice. You can't be naive. You can't be complacent. You can't just sit and expect everything to be fine, for all the bad in the world just to fade away on its own."

"Micah, this doesn't sound like you. Why are you talking so sharply to me?"

"I'm not talking sharply." He rubbed on the pistol with a soft cloth, holding it up. The gleaming metal reflected the blood red sunset.

"Micah, something's wrong. You've not been yourself ever since Mr. Tower visited here."

"Not myself? Who else am I, then?"

"I don't know. A stranger."

He laughed without humor and shook his head as if she'd just said something foolish.

"Don't mock me, Micah. This isn't like you."

He looked at her, brows lowered.

"Micah, your eyes are red."

"If you're implying that I've been sitting out here crying, you're wrong. The wind is in my eyes, that's all."

"But there is something wrong."

"I've had something to think about lately."

"You can't tell me?"

He shook his head.

"When you're ready, Micah."

"Alice, I may have to go somewhere soon. Away."

"Where? Why?"

"Maybe to Colorado. I think I may have to deal with something. Correct a mistake I made once, a long time ago."

She held back the flood of questions that arose. She could not hold back her tears.

"I'm sorry," he said. "I wish I could tell you more."

"Does it have to do with Jack Tower?"

"No. Not really. Not directly."

She would press no further. Forcing a smile, she said, "What will you preach about tomorrow?"

"I don't know," he said. "So far, I've not been able to decide."

CHAPTER 9

M icah advanced to the pulpit slowly, clutching hard his beloved Bible. He'd sat silently through the hymns and prayers, hearing nothing. At the moment, he felt that, somehow, he wasn't really fully here.

He leaned on the pulpit and looked across the little congregation. Jack Tower was not present, and Micah was grateful. His presence would have only made this harder.

Micah cleared his throat, then said, "I must tell you, right now, that I have nothing to say to you today."

He paused while the congregation members glanced at one another. Alice looked back at him in open puzzlement. Flavius, as usual, had found something to distract him and seemed to hear nothing as he played about with a little stick he'd picked up on the way in.

Micah went on. "There are times when a preacher of the gospel can feel God speaking through him, flowing through him like water in a streambed. There are times when the flow dries up. This is one of those times."

He held up his Bible. "In this book, I've found the answers for my life. Now I find that it seems closed to me. I've read, I've prayed, I've meditated, and prayed some more.

And it seems clear to me that there's something I must do. Until it's done, there will be no more answers for me. And therefore, I'm telling you that as of today, I'm stepping down as your pastor."

He paused again, letting the realization sink in. Now even Flavius was paying attention.

"It's my hope that you will let me return later. It will be weeks at the least, maybe months. There's a task I must perform. Something I have to set straight."

Several people were looking at Alice as if to receive an explanation from her, but she had none to give. Her expression grew stony, and she gazed straight ahead, looking at no one, including her husband.

"I ask only one thing of you, and that is for your prayers," Micah said. "I don't know whether what I'm setting out to do is what God would have me do... I hope it is, but I don't know. And how I'll deal with the situation, I may encounter... I don't know that, either." He looked around at the confused faces. "I know this is difficult to understand. I know that you may not wish to have me remain your pastor when this is through. If not, I will understand. Maybe, by that point, I'll understand a lot more about many things than I do now."

Alice was fighting hard to maintain her statue-like expression. And Flavius, confused, was on the verge of crying.

"There's no sermon today," Micah said. "Well, maybe there is if only a brief one. It's this: Don't think the ghosts of your past will go away. They don't. They may hide for years, but they come back. And they call you to come face them. And now, that's what I've got to do. So, for now, goodbye, and amen. And while I'm gone, take care of my family for me. Thank you."

The people rose and crowded in on him as he left the pulpit, but he answered no questions. Alice stayed in her pew, and Flavius came to her side and wrapped his arms around her, clinging and looking at his father as if he'd become a stranger.

Micah went to them. "I'm sorry," he said. "Later, maybe, I can tell you more."

Alice looked away, and Flavius clutched her all the harder.

———

Flavius winced with the boom of each shot. He was in the house with his mother, looking out the window, watching his father in a field about a quarter of a mile away.

Micah was firing the pistol, aiming at a tree. He would fire until the pistol was empty, reload, and fire it empty again.

"Why is Pap practicing his shooting?" Flavius asked. "He never liked shooting before."

"I don't know," Alice replied.

"And why does he have to go away?"

"I don't know that either," she said.

"Will Pap tell us?"

"I don't think so. Not right away. Just pray for him, Flavius. Pray for him very hard."

———

Micah had owned the horse for three years and knew it to be skittish about entering enclosed spaces. The railroad crew had to fight hard to cajole the reluctant animal into the railroad car.

Alice had almost not come with him but had relented at last. She'd clung to him, begging him not to go.

"I have to go," he said. "There's something I should have done years ago and didn't, that I have to find a way to do now. If I can."

It was Flavius who broke Micah's heart. The boy comprehended this even less than his mother and wrapped his arms around Micah like he feared he'd never see him again. He pleaded with Micah to explain why he was going.

But Micah could not explain to another what he could barely understand himself.

Micah knew it would be best not to look at his wife and son as the train pulled out, but of course, he had to look. They stood on the station platform, expressions sad and, maybe, in Alice's case, also angry.

He waved at them, trying to make himself smile through the dirty window and only vaguely succeeding. He didn't feel like smiling. He wanted to weep aloud.

She was angry. It was easy to see. And he couldn't blame her. What sense did any of this make? How could he expect them to understand his behavior when he himself couldn't?

He didn't know why he was doing this... didn't even exactly know what he was doing. All he knew was that he had to go to Colorado and try to find a phantom from his past named Tipton Barth.

And then...

There's where it grew murky. What would he do if he did find Barth? Preach to him? Say a prayer with him? Give him a Bible?

Kill him?

It was a possibility. God help him; it was indeed a possibility.

There were those; he'd always heard who would not choose the right. Would not be changed. Would not be converted. Those were the ones; he'd been taught, for whom even God could do nothing except leave them to the consequences of their own actions.

Surely Tipton Barth was one of these. He'd lived his entire life as a killer. He'd never faced the consequences of it. Why would he ever turn away from it?

For the thousandth time in the course of a few days, Micah said mentally to himself: I should have stopped him long ago. It was given to me to see him brought to justice, and I failed out of fear. A boy's fear. Now I'm a man, and I must not be afraid.

He was afraid, though. Terrified. He knew nothing of manhunting, of capturing murderers, maybe even killing them, if it came to that.

He watched the train station fall out of sight behind him on the Kansas flatlands, then bowed his head and said a prayer for his wife and son.

Micah opened his red carpetbag, pulled out his Bible, and tried to read, but the rocking train made him feel woozy. At last, he closed the book and leaned back, staring at the ceiling of the passenger car and wondering what would happen next.

CHAPTER 10

The travel seemed endless, but the farther he got from his home, the more Micah relaxed. He'd not expected this, for the travel only brought him closer to Colorado and the manhunt for Tipton Barth. But the truth was that the farther this thing progressed, the more unrealistic it seemed. How likely was it he would find Barth? If the man was a murderer, he was probably not one to stay in one area long.

Micah had spoken to Jack Tower one time since Tower's visit to his property and found out exactly where Tower had lived while in Colorado. He'd done this in a way to arouse no suspicion on Tower's part, not wanting Tower to know what he had in mind.

Now it all seemed a little ridiculous. He'd reach the town of Greentree and discover that Tipton Barth was long gone. He'd ask a few questions, go through the motions of trying to find the man and return home with his conscience appeased. Then he could forget about Tipton Barth and events long past and get on with his life.

This whole thing really was foolish. He'd apologize to Alice when he got home and never do anything like this again.

Another passenger walked past and inadvertently kicked something out of the aisle way toward Micah. It was a discarded newspaper. Micah leaned over and picked it up.

When he unfolded it and saw the name, he curled his lip in vague contempt. This was a copy of the *American Crime Chronicle,* a rather sordid newspaper headquartered in Denver and published in a unique fashion across the nation. Correspondents across the country would gather and telegraph into Denver lurid, usually exaggerated stories of murders, robberies, kidnappings, rapes. The stories would be transcribed, quickly illustrated from a standing and ever-growing body of ready-made crime art created and constantly replenished by a pool of artists and published in first edition out of Denver.

Simultaneously, however, the stories would also be wired in turn to various other key locales across the country, where other versions of the same edition, slightly retooled depending on region, would be published, and distributed over the course of about a month. By the time the cycle was complete, it would be time for yet another edition, and it all would repeat.

Micah had little use for the *Chronicle* and had gone so far as to urge his congregation to shun it. He'd caught Flavius with an old copy or two before, gazing at the sensational illustrations, many of which featured women with exposed limbs, low-cut dresses, and so on.

Micah glanced over the copy of the newspaper, shaking his head. He tossed it aside. Any reading he'd do would be confined to his Bible.

————

By the time they reached the foot of the Rockies, Micah was extraordinarily weary of train travel. But the weather had grown much colder, and snow fell, blanketing the landscape and making it even more wildly beautiful than usual. Micah lost himself in the splendor and sang hymns beneath his breath.

So far, his fellow travelers had mostly left him alone, which suited him. What would he say if someone asked him why he was traveling into Colorado? Oh, I'm just trying to find a murderer whom I allowed to go unpunished many years ago, leaving him free to kill and kill again. Once I do find him, I'll either convert him or shoot him dead...

He wondered if he should simply turn around when he reached Greentree and ride back home again right away.

The train reached a steeper grade and curved up the side of a shining mountain. The wind whipped the snow into sharply slanting lines and made the black smoke from the locomotive dance and swirl in the snowy atmosphere. The mountains seemed vast, intimidating.

Micah was pleased when the train reached a more level area and began to slow for a refueling stop. He was nearly starved. By the time the train screeched to a halt at the train station of a little town whose name Micah did not know, he was already heading down the aisle toward the door.

There was no real cafe in the town, but a woman with a basket was selling sandwiches at the train station. Micah bought two of them and found a seat at the end of a bench on the platform. He positioned himself to avoid the worst of the wind.

He was startled by the sound of a loud collective whoop and burst of raucous laughter. Something small and bright flashed by his feet and launched itself over the edge of the station platform.

What remained of Micah's sandwich fell from his hand as he realized that what he'd just seen was a flaming rat.

He stood puzzled and horrified. To his right, a band of men appeared, five or six of them, all of them noticeably drunk, laughing and slapping one another's shoulders.

"That was a fast one, sure 'nough!" one of them said. "Never seen one run so fast!"

"There he is, down under the platform," another one declared, stooping and pointing. "See him burning? He ain't running now!"

They all seemed to find that funny and made an absurd show of bending and stooping to see the dying rat. All were so drunk that they could hardly keep their balance and stumbled about into each other.

Micah was appalled, partly at the drunkenness but mostly at the cruelty. He had no love of rats, but to kill one so viciously made him feel sickened and furious.

Though he wasn't forceful by nature, Micah was about to step forward and confront the group when the approach of another man, equally drunk, distracted them.

The newcomer yelled at the group. "Hey, gents! Got us a dog for this one."

Micah saw a small white dog struggling in the man's arms, and with a sickening feeling, realized what was intended for it. "Where's the coal oil?" one of the drunks bellowed. "Where'd you put the jar, Billy?"

One of the others produced a fruit jar with a clear liquid. Micah had taken it to be homemade whiskey but now realized it was indeed coal oil.

The man with the dog knelt, holding it, while the one with the jar squatted beside him.

Micah was frozen, unable even to breathe. He looked around. No one else seemed to be aware of what was going on.

Coal oil splashed across the dog, making it yelp and struggle harder. Micah saw one of the men fumbling with a box of matches...

"No!" he shouted, stepping forward. "Let that dog go!"

His shout was so loud that the squatting man with the

dog lost his balance and fell back. The dog broke loose and ran away, darting under the train station.

Micah took a deep breath, relieved.

A babble of curses rained at him from the gang of drunks. He hardly noticed. In his mind, he imagined the ugly image of that dog, flaming and running... It was intolerable. That such a cruel act would have even been considered by these men as a form of entertainment...

One of them was suddenly directly in his face, ranting and shouting, his breath reeking of whiskey.

Micah caught the man's words in midsentence. "...your own damned business!" he said. "What the hell you mean, running off my dog!"

Micah stared at the man, silent.

The fellow reached out and shoved him in the chest.

"Keep your hands off me," Micah said.

"You ran off my dog!" the man shouted.

"You were going to set that dog afire like you did the rat."

"And what the hell's that to you?"

"I don't stand by and let that happen."

"I'm going to beat the hell out of you!" the man yelled. His companions were moving in now, all of them with similar angry expressions. People were certainly taking notice now and backing away.

Micah realized what a predicament he had placed himself in. He was facing off a group of angry drunks... alone.

But when he thought about that dog, and what would have befallen it...

"If you want to beat me, go ahead and try," he heard himself say. "I'm not a bit sorry for saving that dog from the kind of cruelty you had planned for it!"

The man shoved Micah again, almost making him fall.

"That's enough," Micah said and struck the man in the nose with his fist.

He felt bone and cartilage crunch, heard the man suck in his breath in a great gasp, and saw him fall straight back like a felled tree. His drunk companions didn't even try to catch him but dodged out of the way. He hit the platform with a loud clump.

The drunks stared down at him, then up at Micah, and burst into laughter.

"What are you?" one of them asked. "Some kind of fighter?"

"I'm a preacher," Micah replied, looking down and wondering if he'd killed the man.

"A preacher? A preacher?" The man looked around at his companions. "Horace got knocked out by a preacher!"

They howled with appreciative mirth, gathering around Micah and slapping him on the shoulders. Micah kept looking at the fallen man.

"Is he alive?" he asked.

"Hell, it takes more than that to kill Horace! A preacher! Ain't that a hell of a thing!"

Micah was so bewildered that he grinned for lack of anything else to do.

"Have a drink, Preacher!"

"No. No, thank you. I don't touch it."

They treated him like an honored guest until he was back on the train again. He watched through the window as they helped their fallen friend come back around again and make it to his feet. His nose was bloody. But as the train pulled out, the man raised a hand and waved respectfully at Micah.

Micah was more bewildered than ever. He realized that, in a most unexpected way, he'd just gained respect from a breed of man he'd hardly had any dealings with. And he'd gained it in a way he would never have expected.

It grew funny as he thought about it, and he chuckled aloud.

But as the train moved on, he began to think more deeply about what had happened at the train station. He didn't believe in violence. Had he been advising anyone else about how to react to the kind of situation he'd just encountered, he'd have told him to turn the other cheek.

Maybe this time, though, he'd done a better thing by fighting back. He'd not done it intentionally—he'd struck the man purely by reflex—but it had solved a problem.

Maybe the world was a little more complex than he'd thought. Maybe, as the Bible said, there was a time for war as well as a time for peace.

He thought about Tipton Barth and what might lie ahead.

Lord, he prayed mentally. Whatever may come, if anything, be with me. And if I have to fight again, let me fight well.

CHAPTER 11

Micah was asleep when the crash occurred.

The jolt threw him out of his seat and caused his head to slam against the side of the seat across the aisle. He collapsed onto the floor of the passenger car, barely hearing the screams and yells of the other startled travelers.

The car tilted, rolling him, then leveled again, though it rocked like a boat for several moments as if it couldn't decide whether to tilt off the tracks or stay on. He came to rest against the base of another seat. Someone stepped on his arm, then was off him and gone. He groaned and tried to sit up. Someone else ran over him, knocking him back down.

He stayed there a moment until the train stopped rocking. Then he pushed up, groaning again, his head throbbing. He touched it gently, then looked at his fingers. There was blood, but only a little. Just a small abrasion.

The car was in tumult, people moving about, baggage scattering. Micah scooted himself into the space behind a nearby seat, trying to focus his vision and clear his head from the effects of his injury.

At last, he rose and headed toward the door. All other passengers by now had already exited.

Outside, he looked around. They were high in the mountains, snow falling, about five inches of it on the ground.

The passengers, many of them upset, were gathering around the railroad crew, peppering them with questions. Micah wandered over, hand clutching the tender place where his head had struck the seat. He was slightly dizzy.

He stopped when he saw the ruptured and derailed freight car in which his horse had been carried.

"What happened?" he asked a man standing nearby.

"We almost all got killed," the man replied in an angry tone. "The train hit something on the track, that there fell-over tree, I think and nigh got jarred clean off it. But that freight car there was the only one that actually derailed. We're danged lucky it didn't pull the rest of the train off with it."

"I had a horse being hauled in that car," Micah said.

"Uh-oh. You may have you a dead horse now."

Micah, ignoring his aching head, ran over to the shattered car and began peering around the wreckage, looking for his horse.

"Mister."

The speaker was a boy, blond-haired and shy-looking. Micah had noticed him earlier in the journey, seated with his mother.

"Yes, son?"

"You looking for your horse?"

"I am."

"It ain't in there. I saw it run loose, over that way." The boy pointed.

"Thank you, young man," Micah said. "I'll see if I can find him."

He headed off into the woods. Pausing, he looked back at the train. It would be a long time, he figured, before the train could be moved. He'd have plenty of time to find the horse if it was to be found at all. The only question was whether there would be some other place on the train in which it could be carried.

Micah hesitated, though. What if he got lost? These mountains were a far cry from the familiar Kansas flatlands.

He shook off the worry. The horse couldn't have roamed far. He'd find it quickly and get back to the train long before it moved off again. Micah moved on into the rugged mountains.

In his California youth, Micah had become a fairly proficient tracker. Thus it did not take him long to detect a sign of his horse, which he followed into the forested mountains. He felt certain he'd find his horse within a few minutes, check it over to make sure it had not been injured in the derailment, then take it back to the train, place it in one of the undamaged cars, and resume his journey.

After a while, however, he became less sure of the outcome. The sign seemed to vanish, and his horse was nowhere to be seen. He was surprised it had wandered this far in so short a time.

And how far, come to think of it, was this? He'd moved swiftly, concentrating on his tracking, and hadn't paid much attention to how far he'd come.

He paused, looking back toward the railroad. He could see nothing of it from here nor hear any sounds of work going on to clear the ruined car from the tracks.

Micah felt a pang of worry. Maybe he should forget about the horse and just go back. What if they got the track cleared and the train went on without him? His baggage was on that train, all his clothing, goods, even his pistol, and ammunition. He didn't want to be stranded out here with nothing in hand.

Yet he couldn't give up on the horse just yet. He wasn't a wealthy man. That horse had cost him a good deal. Besides, his wife and son were attached to it. He couldn't just sacrifice it. And what if it was injured? It would be cruel simply to abandon it out here in these mountains.

He pressed on, promising himself he would not go much farther.

Ahead, something had just moved on a hillside, going around an outcrop of rock just as Micah had glimpsed it. He wasn't sure, but it might have been the horse.

He advanced, picking his way along carefully, for the terrain was growing much rougher and steeper here. Gravel and other debris slid under his foot, and he fell with a grunt. He got to his feet again and proceeded even more carefully.

By the time he reached a position to allow him to see around the edge of the outcrop, whatever had created the movement he had seen had already vanished.

Micah felt a mounting irritation, not to mention a deepening worry. He'd come too far and now wasn't sure he was quite the tracker he'd thought he was. The sign he'd been following might not have been left by his horse at all, and if it had been, it didn't matter now. He'd lost the trail long ago.

And he'd traveled much farther than he should have. Time to give up on the horse and head back to the train.

He turned, and his foot slipped on gravel again. This time he fell at a different angle and rolled to a place where the hillside angled down at a very steep slope.

He tumbled down, rolling like a human boulder doing a one-man avalanche, pounding, and slamming against the stone in bruising fashion all the way to the bottom.

CHAPTER 12

Micah opened his eyes. He was lying on his left side, his body sprawled on stone, his cheek pressing against gravel. Blinking a few times, he tried to remember what had happened. Yes... he'd taken a tumble. Rolled down a slope...

Memory re-formed in his mind. The journey, the jolt on the tracks, the escape of his horse—he remembered it all now.

Cautiously he wiggled his toes, his fingers, then slowly sat up. His head hurt quite a lot. Turning slowly, he looked back up the slope down which he'd tumbled. Great day! Had he really fallen that far? He was lucky to be alive.

Micah said a brief prayer of thanks, then looked around, beginning to notice that something had changed about the landscape.

The light. It fell at different angles now and wasn't as bright as before. The sun was in the west, low on the horizon.

Could he really have lain there so long? He realized that he must have been unconscious. The day had passed, and the night was on its way.

The train...

Micah got up fast—and regretted it because of the way his head throbbed. He leaned against a sapling, letting a sudden burst of dizziness pass. Then he brushed off his clothing and made an assessment of his situation.

He was far away from the railroad tracks, and hours had passed. Either the train had moved on by now or his absence had been detected by the conductor, and some sort of search launched.

He hoped the latter was the case. But by now, as late as it was, such a search might have been concluded. The conductor might be miles away by now, writing up a report at some distant railroad station about a passenger who vanished, with his horse, after the derailment.

"They probably figure I just rode off," Micah said aloud.

He began to panic but got hold of himself. His situation was bad, no doubt about it, but not hopeless. He knew the direction in which the railroad lay. All he had to do was head south, and eventually, he'd run across it. He could find some shelter, pass the night. He could even hike up the tracks to the next stop if he felt up to it. He wasn't sure what the next stop was or how far it was up the track, but eventually, he'd reach it.

He wished he had his pistol with him, though. It was uncomfortable being out here without protection.

"Lord," he prayed aloud, "please watch over me. I've gotten myself into a real pickle."

No time to waste, he decided. The thing to do was reach the railroad. Who knows? Maybe he'd see a coming train and be able to flag it down, catch a ride. He'd probably find his baggage awaiting him at the next train station up the way.

Micah began hiking but hiking soon turned to climbing. There was no way for him to advance far without getting back up the slope down which he'd fallen. He moved along the base of the slope until he reached a place where it wasn't as steep and began clambering up.

Halfway to the top, he fell and rolled back down again. At the bottom, he lay there, stunned and scared, and wondered if he'd broken any bones this time.

He had not and said a prayer of thanks. But he felt greatly discouraged. It might take him until dark just to make it to the top of the slope again. He might have to spend a night out here in this wilderness alone and unarmed. And it was cold already, snow spitting down. He'd lost a lot of body heat lying on the ground as long as he had. At least he'd happened to fall into a place where the wind and terrain kept the ground mostly clear of snow accumulation. Had he lain directly in snow, he might have frozen to death.

He felt in his pockets...thank God! He had matches. At the very least, he could build a fire.

He revised his plan. He'd reach the top of the slope, find a sheltered area, gather some wood, and build a fire. He'd feed it all night, keeping it hot and bright. If by chance, there were searchers looking for him, they might see the blaze. If nothing else, it would keep him alive through the night and help avert predators.

Micah took a deep breath and made another go at the slope. He didn't allow himself to rush and thought out every step before he took it. The sky was beginning to darken in the east, which worried him, but he didn't let it panic him. He'd be fine as long as he could get to the top in time to gather some firewood.

This time he made it, but the light was dimming fast. He walked swiftly southward until he found a natural recess among rocks. There the wind would be deflected, and heat from a fire would reflect back off the surrounding rocks. Good.

Micah began gathering dead wood as much as he could find and carried it by armloads to his chosen camping place.

He knew he'd have to have a lot of it to make it through the night, so he worked hard until it was too dark to see. Returning with the final armload to the rocky nook, he set fire to twigs and bark fragments, then began piling progressively larger sticks on the fire until, at last, he had a fine blaze going. The heat was marvelous. He settled back against a flat stone and enjoyed the fire, feeling quite comfortable.

When the fire died down somewhat, he picked up more sticks and replenished it. He began to feel sleepy but decided to remain awake. It wouldn't be pleasant to let the fire go out and awaken to see himself facing off a bear or some other wild animal.

Hours passed. The fire burned, and the supply of wood steadily diminished. Micah worried that he might run out and lessened the size of the fire. At length, he grew confident that indeed he'd have enough wood to see him through until morning.

———

Despite himself, he did sleep a little. He'd open his eyes at the sound of wood snapping in the blaze and realize he'd been dozing. He wished he had a big pot of coffee right now. And biscuits dripping with butter. And a plateful of eggs, fried up just right like Alice always did them.

Whenever his next meal came, he'd enjoy it.

The fire was dimming again. Micah yawned and reached over, grabbing another stick. He tossed it into the blaze, then came to his feet.

What he'd just put in the fire wasn't a stick. It was a bone. A human one, it appeared. Perhaps a thighbone.

Reflexively holding his breath, Micah began looking around. He pushed the remnants of his firewood supply to one side and examined the ground beneath it. The firelight wasn't bright enough to give him a good view, so he threw on some extra wood, then knelt to get a closer view of the ground.

He yelled and jumped back up again when he realized that staring back at him was a yellowed, crumbling human skull.

Micah scrambled completely out of the rocky enclave. Standing there in the snow, he wondered what a man is supposed to do when he discovers a corpse out in the wilderness. His first impulse was to hide it, but then he realized how irrational that was. He had nothing to do with this man's death and nothing to cover up.

When his burst of panic had subsided, he returned to where he had been and began to examine the bones as best he could in the dim and flickering light of the fire. How had this man died? How long had he been here? Micah's impression was that it must be quite a long time, but he knew nothing about rates of decay.

Gradually losing his squeamishness, he began to pick about among the bones. There were quite a few of them, almost a full skeleton's worth, but badly scattered. Animals, he figured, had probably disturbed the corpse while there was still flesh on it upon which to feast. Thinking about that unsettled his stomach a little and caused him to make an inner vow never to die in the wilderness. Though he believed —and had declared in scores of sermons—that what happens to a body really doesn't matter because it is the soul that constitutes the true person, he had to admit that the thought of having his own bones scattered by beasts affected him more than he would have expected.

Micah put a little more wood on the fire and wished morning would come. He was eager to take a look at what he'd found with the full benefit of daylight.

Ten minutes later, he noticed a lightening of the eastern sky. The night had passed more quickly than he'd thought it would. He replenished the fire with the last of the wood and watched the sun rise, then set about to more closely examine the bones.

What drew his attention, however, was something that lay to the side of the bones, not visible until the daylight came. Micah knelt and picked up the holstered pistol he'd just spotted. It was a fine one, a Colt, with a bone handle gone slightly yellow. To his surprise, the holster had kept the pistol in good condition; there was hardly any rust at all. He checked and found it was loaded. The mechanism worked perfectly. Unloading the pistol, he snapped the trigger a few times.

He reloaded the pistol and noticed that almost all the cartridge loops on the gun belt were full.

"I don't know who you were, my friend, but I'm grateful to have found your pistol," he said. "I feel much safer for having it."

CHAPTER 13

Micah felt slightly qualmish about handling a gun belt that had been around the waist of a corpse, but under the circumstances, he was able to overcome it. The leather, having been exposed to the elements, was dark and stiff, but with some manipulation and rubbing, he managed to make it somewhat supple again.

Micah had seldom worn a gun and usually didn't feel very comfortable with weapons. He had nothing against a man owning a gun, knew it to be a necessity in the West, but never had felt that preachers with guns were a natural fit. In these circumstances, though, being armed was a good thing.

Micah examined the bones, determining that indeed almost the full skeleton was present, though scattered about. He found a rusted knife, a few folded pieces of paper that bore smudged, unreadable markings, a couple of coins, an old match case, an ivory toothpick. Nothing more. Nothing to tell who this man had been.

Though in Micah's theology, there was nothing to be gained by prayers for the dead, he felt the impulse to pray for this unknown person, this benefactor, in any case. He did so, interceding for the welfare of this man's soul and the comfort of whatever loved ones he'd left behind. Micah realized that these people, whoever they were, could not know what had happened to this man. He wished he could identify him and find some way to deliver the word of his death to those who needed to know it.

He considered burying the man but decided not to. There might be legalities involved here he didn't know about. Someday someone knowledgeable of such matters might be able to examine this body and locale and learn who this man had been. It would probably never happen, though. These bones would probably never be seen again, only lie and molder away to nothing.

Micah was tired, hungry, a little scared, but glad to be armed and on the move. He began to walk southward toward the tracks.

When a sudden whiff of wood smoke reached him, he stopped. His own fire was far behind him now and out. Where could this smoke be coming from?

Curiosity led him to turn north. He'd not roam far, just far enough to find the origin of the smoke. The smell was stronger now. What if there was a forest fire? How fast would it spread?

He crossed a ridge. The smoky smell increased. But it wasn't so strong that Micah seriously suspected a forest fire. This was more like the smell of smoke near a campsite or a town.

A town. Maybe there was a town back in these mountains, something off the rail line. He knew these mountains were home to many little mining communities, quick to rise and quick to vanish.

For the moment, he forgot about the rail line. Sniffing the air, going in the direction from which the smoky smell came, he wandered well off his chosen course. His stomach rumbled as he thought he caught the scent of cooking meat mixed with the aroma of the smoke.

Abruptly, he came upon a road. It surprised him so that he stopped in his tracks and just stared at it. It was a narrow road, little more than a wagon trail. It wound around a hill-side and out of sight. There were fresh wagon and horse tracks mixed with old ones.

Indeed that was meat he smelled. That could only mean that the town, if town it was, was not far away.

Having his feet on a real road was pleasing. He lost the sense of being lost and any immediate concern for returning to the railroad. He would visit this town, buy himself a good meal. Maybe he'd even find a room for the night and rest in a real bed. Sitting up in the snowy woods all night had worn him out.

He walked for less than a mile before seeing the first cabin. A man was chopping wood behind it and paused to look Micah over as he strode up the road.

"Good day, friend," Micah called. "How are you?"

"Fine enough," the man replied. He seemed a little wary but friendly as well. "And how are you?"

"Worn out, sir. I have some bad luck at the railroad." Briefly, Micah related his adventure, omitting the part about the corpse and pistol. "So here I am with no horse, no baggage, and my nose guiding me to whatever lies ahead. Is there a town around the bend yonder?"

"There is. Not much of one."

"What's the name?"

"Levi Hill."

"Can't say I've heard of it."

"Just a little mining town. Nothing much."

"Is there a cafe?"

"A slop shop. That's what most of us call it. Stew and biscuits and the like."

"Sounds good enough for me."

Micah walked on, soon rounding the bend. There he stopped and looked with some dismay on one of the most squalid towns he'd ever encountered.

There was no paint to be seen anywhere beyond that on a few crudely lettered commercial signs. Most of the bare wood buildings were splattered halfway up their fronts with mud from the rutted and pitted street. The street itself followed no clear line; it was more a muddy clearing between haphazardly located structures, all of which belched smoke from their stick-and-mud chimneys. The people were as dirty and colorless as the buildings. Even the horses tethered along the street seemed listless. The cleanest and most lively thing he saw, ironically, was a lone hog that wandered up the very center of the street.

Micah stepped aside to let the hog pass, then headed for the cafe. The smell of the meat was much stronger here, very heavy and greasy, nearly to the point of being unappealing.

At the edge of the cafe porch, Micah experienced a burst of momentary clarity. He realized how far from home he was, that in the course of this journey, he had already lost his baggage, his horse and saddle, and his own pistol. Thank God he'd found a replacement for that, at least.

He also realized the absurdity of his mission. Merciful heaven, it wasn't only absurd, but undefined! He was searching for a murderer, a ghost from his own past, without any clear notion of how he would deal with him once he found him. This was no new realization, of course, but the light in which it struck him was. He clearly saw how nonsensical his situation was. He was the Reverend Micah Ward, for heaven's sake! A young and capable pastor who lived surrounded by his own small but productive lands and loving family and by a congregation of devoted friends. What was he doing here?

He felt a sudden, overwhelming need to go home as quickly as possible. He would apologize to Alice and Flavius, then to his congregation. He would tell them he'd gone momentarily mad. He'd use his own foolishness as the source of a good dozen sermons.

But first, he'd eat. At least he could do that. He'd kept his money on his person, not in his baggage.

He ordered pork, eggs, and bread and wolfed it all down in less than two minutes. Then he ordered a second round and dined on it more slowly, taking time to examine his surroundings. Amazing how such things as cafes and shops and the like could spring up in the midst of nowhere. One day a wilderness, the next a town. This was the story of the American frontier, one that Micah had seldom taken time to ponder. Now that he did, he was quite struck by its significance. This transformation from wildness to civilization—of a sort—seemed to Micah, quite a good metaphor for the salvation of a soul. Yes, he could use that as soon as he got back to his home and his pulpit.

Someone slid into the chair across from him. A smiling face, feminine and beautiful, framed by curled, auburn hair. This stranger gave him an instant impression of childishness until he looked into her eyes. Despite her smile, her eyes were cold, hardened.

She laid a pistol on the table before him.

"You dropped this."

He looked at it. Indeed it was the pistol he'd found with the dead man.

"I'll be... I didn't know."

"It fell out of your holster while you were eating, and you didn't even notice. I never saw a man so wrapped up in his food. It made quite a clunking noise. Didn't you hear it?"

"I didn't," he admitted.

"A man who eats like that, I figure, must not have eaten for a long time."

"It had been a few hours."

She leaned a little closer and let her finger trail along the pistol. "Maybe a man who hasn't eaten in a long time hasn't done some other things in a long time, either."

The religiously centered life that Micah had lived had protected him from the side of fife that was now facing him, and for several moments he honestly failed to recognize what was happening. When the realization struck, his eyes widened, and he sat back. "Miss... I don't think it's at all appropriate what you seem to be implying."

Now she was the surprised one. "What?" She laughed. "What are you? Some kind of preacher?"

"As a matter of fact, I am."

She stared at him as if he'd just grown a second pair of eyes. "You lying to me?"

"No."

She laughed again, scooted her chair back, and waved toward Micah. "Did you hear that?" she said to the general population of the room. "He says he's a preacher!"

They all laughed. Micah was puzzled. It was funny, being a preacher? Had these people never encountered a preacher before?

Maybe they hadn't.

Lord, he thought, how sheltered have I been?

The young woman said, "Charlie, come over here and meet the preacher!"

A grinning, egg-bald man of indeterminate age came over, limping on a left leg that was a good eight inches shorter than the right one. He stuck out his hand at Micah. "Howdy, Preacher! Charlie Johnson."

Micah shook the hand. "Charlie."

"You really a preacher?"

"Yes."

"Well! Save my soul for me, Preacher!"

"I can't save anybody's soul."

"I thought that's what you preachers did. I thought you went around looking for sinners and saving their souls. Speaking of sinners, what do you think of Missy here?" He touched the girl on her shoulder. "Missy here knows sinning up and down. She can sin with the best of them, let me tell you! All for no more than a coin or two. She's the best sinner I ever—"

He cut off. His eyes had just fallen on the pistol lying on the table. The smile vanished, and he looked from the pistol to Micah and back to the pistol again, several times over. "I'll be damned," he whispered.

Micah was utterly confused now and also repelled. He wasn't accustomed to people or conversations of this sort. He reached over, took the pistol, and holstered it.

"That's your pistol," Charlie said, very serious all at once.

"Yes..."

"Has it always been your pistol?"

"No."

"The man you got it from... was he alive or dead?"

"Dead. Why do you ask?"

Charlie laughed again, but it was a very false laugh. Nervous, respectful, maybe fearful. Micah realized that Charlie was suddenly very mindful of not offending him. Charlie backed away, hands up with palms facing Micah, waving side to side. "Sorry I bothered you, Preacher. I didn't know... I thought you were, you know, a real preacher."

"What are you acting that way for, Charlie?" Missy asked.

"Come on, Missy. Come on. Let's leave this man alone. We don't want to be bothering him, no, no."

The girl looked confused as Charlie pulled her away. Micah watched as Charlie talked to her in a whisper in the far corner of the room. She kept glancing his way, and suddenly her expression changed. Her last glance his way was one of astonishment as if he were the president and she'd just recognized him.

Micah had had enough of this. He stood and left money on the table, then walked over to the proprietor. "Where might a man rent a room for the night in this town?"

"Well, there's a room with a bed upstairs. The lady who used to be in there run off a month ago."

"I'll take it if you'll give me a reasonable cost."

"Jimbo..." The speaker was Charlie, who came to the proprietor and briefly pulled him aside and whispered in his ear. The proprietor cocked up a brow and studied Micah with a look of surprise.

"I can give you the best kind of rate—no charge," he said.

Micah was befuddled. "Free?"

"That's right."

"Because I'm a preacher? Is that it?"

Charlie and Jimbo thought that one was funny. "That's it, sure enough. Because you're a preacher."

Micah smiled and nodded, said thank you, and headed up the stairs. It was morning, but he'd hardly rested the night before and was eager for sleep. And to get out of this rather odd and unexpectedly uncomfortable setting.

He'd stay in Levi Hill long enough to get a little rest, but after that, he'd move on as fast as possible.

CHAPTER 15

After Micah had gone up the stairs, a man who had been inconspicuously seated at a table in the rear corner stood and approached Charlie and Jimbo.

"Begging your pardon, gentlemen, but I'd like to talk to you," he said. He reached into his pocket and produced two business cards. "My name's Brandon Rhoton. I'm a writer for the *American Crime Chronicle*. I'd like to know a little more about what I just saw happening here."

"You write for the *American Crime Chronicle*, do you?" Charlie said.

"That's right. And I'm in a bit of a bind. I'm overdue in providing a story for the next edition, and I missed providing one at all for the past two months. So you can be sure, gentlemen, that I'm very interested in what I just witnessed." He paused and smiled. "Do I smell a possible story here?"

"You do... if you want to know about the man who killed Diamond Willie."

"Diamond Willie, the gunfighter?"

"Yep. You really do write for the *American Crime Chronicle*? No lying?"

"No lying." Rhoton produced a notepad from under his

coat and a stubby pencil. "I'd like to take a few notes for my memory. You're telling me that the man who just went up those stairs is the killer of Diamond Willie?"

Having someone taking notes of his words made Charlie feel important, and he took on an instant tone of authority. "Diamond Willie vanished a year ago. Nobody knew what happened to him, but Diamond Willie being Diamond Willie, everybody figured he'd been killed by some other gunfighter. He had enemies all over and a reputation that a lot of gunmen would like to take over for themselves."

"So what makes you say that man killed Diamond Willie?"

"Because I know Diamond Willie's pistol. I seen him showing it off a couple of times when he and me were in Denver at the same time. I played cards with Diamond Willie once,... almost was a friend of his. I know the pistol he carried. There was a mark he'd made on the bone handle."

"And that pistol..."

"Was the one that the preacher had today," Charlie said firmly.

"No question about it?"

"Nope. That preacher up there killed Diamond Willie."

"Which I'd say means he's no authentic preacher, surely."

"Most likely 'Preacher' is his gun fighting name. Like Diamond Willie going by Diamond Willie instead of whatever his real name was."

Rhoton chewed the end of the pencil, thinking. "So we've got a new gunfighter roaming around. Calls himself a preacher and uses the gun of Diamond Willie."

"Surely seems that way to me."

"Me too," Jimbo, the proprietor, threw in, not wanting to be left out of this story.

"And so we've got a mystery... just who is Preacher the

gunfighter? How and when did he kill Diamond Willie? And why has he waited this long to show himself?"

"Good questions," Charlie said.

"Yes," Jimbo agreed. "Good questions."

"And most of all, a good story," Rhoton said. "The best story I've run across in God knows how long."

"You're going to put this in the newspaper?"

"Oh, yes. Yes indeed."

"You going to talk to the preacher?"

"I just might." He laughed and slapped the notepad against the heel of his hand. "You know, I had a feeling I was right to come here! Something told me to search out this godforsaken little mining town! It didn't make sense, but I knew that I'd find the story I needed here. Just knew it. What's the day? What's the day?"

"Tuesday."

"No, the date!"

"The third."

"Good. Good. That gives me the time I need. I can talk to this preacher, get my story written, get to a telegraph station."

"You going to put my name in there?" Charlie asked.

"Of course." In fact, the weaselly Rhoton didn't care who Charlie was or plan to give credit to him in any way.

"Me, too?" Jimbo added.

"Certainly."

"I'll go up and see him," Missy said. She'd been listening to the conversation. "I can make him tell whatever you want him to tell."

"I don't think you're his type, honey," Rhoton said. "If you were, he'd have you with him already. Coffee. I want some coffee. I'm ready to start a little writing."

———

Micah rolled over in his bed and opened his eyes. He stared at an unfamiliar wall and window, through which a diminished light, like that of twilight, pierced dirty glass and even dirtier curtains.

Odd sounds and music came from below, muffled; he realized that it was this that had woken him. He felt quite confused for half a minute, then remembered that he was upstairs above a cafe in a remote Colorado mining town.

He sat up, grinning, and shaking his head. What an odd place for him to be! Once again, the whole unlikely nature of his mission struck him. He felt far away from home and lonely but not particularly unhappy at the moment. The rest had done him good.

A glance out the window, however, revealed that he had slept the day away. The sun was westering. It would be pointless to attempt to walk to the railroad tonight.

He'd have to speak to the proprietor about spending the night in this room. Not that sleep would be likely. He'd gotten hours of sleep already, and the cafe" downstairs would probably be noisy long into the night. He'd noticed the bar there earlier and surmised that what was a cafe by day was probably more a saloon by night.

He went to the mirror and combed his hair. He ran his hand across his whiskers and pondered his changing appearance. A few more days without shaving, a little more time on the road, and he'd hardly be recognizable as the Reverend Micah Ward.

Unexpectedly, that thought brought a twinge of excitement. He thought of the girl downstairs who had offered herself to him. In all his life, at least since his youth in the wild California mining camps, he'd never encountered a prostitute. Had never been around the sort of folks who drink and fight and talk crudely. He'd been in the protective circle of the church almost perpetually.

He stared in the mirror, thinking things he shouldn't as he gazed into the reflection of his eyes.

With an effort of will, he shrugged it off. No! No. He'd not let the occasion of isolation and separation from his family cause him to fall away. He'd resist temptation.

Still staring at himself in the mirror, he quoted scripture: "'There has no temptation taken you, but such as is common to man. But God is faithful and will not suffer you to be tempted above that which ye are able but will with the temptation provide a way of escape, so that ye may be able to bear it.'" He leaned closer to his own reflection. "In other words, Micah Ward, you've got no excuse to not behave yourself."

The noise below was growing louder. Sounds of revelry. The piano in the corner was hammering loudly, mostly out of tune. Unfamiliar sounds to a man who heard mostly hymns as piano music.

Micah was hungry. Maybe the cafe continued to function even after the saloon opened.

Straightening his clothing, Micah went to the door...

He thought of something and hesitated. "No," he said to himself. "I don't need it." He started to open the door again, hesitated another time, then gave in.

Need it or not, he'd feel better with the gun belt strapped around his waist. He worried about that. Was he losing his faith in God to protect him? Or was wearing a gun and dining in a saloon part of some game of pretend he was playing with himself? Was he enjoying toying around on the edges of a lifestyle he'd never known personally but preached against a hundred times?

"You think a little too much for your own good, Micah," he counseled himself. "You want to wear the pistol, wear the pistol. There's apparently no law against it in this town."

He walked down the stairs into the room below.

CHAPTER 16

H e noticed three things, one right after another.
The first was that the room was surprisingly crowded. A good dozen or more people, quite a group for such a small town, and three more entered even as he descended.

The second was that he seemed to attract much attention as he made his own entrance. He knew right away that he'd been discussed during his absence. Maybe it was a true novelty to have a preacher in this place.

The third thing was that he recognized two faces among the people. Two of the men who had been ready to burn that dog at the train station were here. The one whose nose he'd broken was not one of them; these were simply two of the ones who'd been with him. He saw that they recognized him even as he recognized them.

Micah descended the stairs and headed for the bar. He noticed that his pistol seemed to attract many glances. He couldn't figure out why; several of the men here bore side arms.

Micah went to the bar. "I'm looking for some supper."

"Cafe's closed. Sorry. We only run that during the daytime. If you want a drink, though..."

A man slid up to the bar beside Micah and said to the barkeep, "If this man wants supper, I'd suggest you change your policy and give it to him. I don't think Preacher here is a man to be trifled with."

Micah looked curiously at the stranger. "You know I'm a preacher?"

"I do, sir."

"And what are you?"

"I'm a writer, sir. For the *American Crime Chronicle*. Have you heard of us?"

"Oh, yes."

"Good. Good."

"How do you know about me?" Micah asked.

"I'm a journalist, sir. I listen to things. Ask questions. Put together surmises."

"And what have you surmised about me?"

"That a man in your profession wouldn't come to a place like this without a reason."

"Well, in a manner of speaking, I suppose you're right. I don't believe that anything happens without a reason."

"That may be true, sir."

"What's your name?" Micah asked.

"Rhoton."

"And mine is—"

"No! No. Don't tell me. A mystery is better. Always. The readers go for that, you see. Preacher. That's all the name needs. Just Preacher. Traveling the West, bearing that very special and significant pistol and doing what? Looking for someone, I'd wager."

"As a matter of fact, I am. But about my pistol, what makes it 'special and significant'?"

Rhoton threw back his head and laughed. "Don't we all know?"

"I'm not sure what you mean."

"When you took that from its former owner, he was dead, correct?"

"That's right."

"Quite a trophy."

"It wasn't a trophy. Just a useful and needed tool."

"Tell me, Preacher: How did you get that cross-shaped scar on your face? And who are you looking for?"

Micah wondered why this man was so curious about him. But experience had made him prone to be open about himself to encourage others to be open with him. "How I got the scar is something I'm not all that eager to talk about. And who I'm looking for, though it's no one else's business, is a man named Tipton Barth."

Rhoton's face changed. "Tipton Barth!" he said. "I'll be damned!"

"Not unless you choose to be," Micah answered, always ready to spread the message to which he'd devoted his life. "There's a way to escape that for all of us."

Two others stepped up, the pair from the train station. To Rhoton, they said, "This is quite a man you're talking to here. We both saw him down a man right on a train station platform."

"Do tell!" Rhoton pulled out his notepad and scribbled on it.

"Hello, Preacher," the man said to Micah.

"Hello," Micah replied, wary. Who would have imagined he'd run into any of the train station gang again?

Micah didn't quite understand all of this attention, particularly that of the journalist, and was ready to find some food.

"Is there a place around here that sells food?" he asked.

"Gerry James serves up supper on her back porch across town," the bartender said.

"I'll be going there, then," Micah said.

"He told us he was a preacher," the man from the train station said.

Rhoton laughed. "Oh, yes. Some kind of preacher a gunfighter is!"

Micah frowned at him. "A gunfighter? What gives you that notion? I am a preacher."

They laughed. Micah, puzzled, decided the explanation wasn't worth the effort.

He obtained directions to Gerty James's place from the bartender and left, feeling almost every eye upon him.

———

"I don't care what he says—he's a gunfighter, all right," Rhoton said after Micah was gone. "A man doesn't have the gun of Diamond Willie on him and not be a gunfighter. Mark my words: That man there gunned down Diamond Willie. And now he's looking for Tipton Barth, a man any sane man would do anything to avoid. He's a gunfighter, no question of it."

"He's good with his fists, too," one of the train station men said. "You should have seen how he busted Horace's nose."

"Busted his nose?" Rhoton said. "I thought you said he gunned him down."

"No, no. Just fists."

Rhoton swore. "Gunning down would be better for my purposes. What the hell? I'll write it that it was a gunfight."

"Write it? What do you mean?"

"I'm a journalist. A writer. I'm getting ready to reveal the story of Preacher, the killer of the infamous Diamond Willie, to the reading world."

"No lie!"

"I'll lie as need be. My kind of journalism doesn't exactly require devotion to the truth. Not completely, anyway."

"You say he killed Diamond Willie?"

"That's Willie's pistol he carries. How else would he have got it? Diamond Willie killed seven men in fair fights and that many more again in fights that maybe weren't so fair. Nobody would have been able to get Diamond Willie's pistol from him short of killing him for it." "You reckon he aims to kill Tipton Barth, too?"

"That would be my guess. That's what I intend to write. Why else would he be looking for such a one as Barth if not to kill him? I hope he succeeds. Barth is the worse scum you'll ever find. And besides, it would make a devil of a story."

"What if he really is just a preacher?"

"Hah! That's no preacher. I'll guarantee you that. That's a gunfighter, and I'm just about to make him famous," Rhoton said. "Half my story's already written. I'll wire it in tomorrow, and within a week, everybody who reads the *American Crime Chronicle* will be talking about Preacher, the mysterious new gunfighter with the T-shaped scar on his face who's roaming the mountains of Colorado and gunning for Tipton Barth."

CHAPTER 17

The food at Gerry's was delicious, though the filthiness of the woman as well as that of her place was enough to make Micah glad he hadn't watched the meal being prepared. Sometimes it was just best not to know.

The only other diners were two enormously fat men who, Micah gathered, were nightly customers of Gerty's informal restaurant, plus a couple of somber miners and an elderly woman Gerty called Aunt Hannah. Nobody except Gerty had much to say, and she had plenty. She jabbered throughout the meal, talking over a wide variety of news and opinions and rumors. Micah grew weary listening to her, then realized she might possess some knowledge that could help him.

"Beg your pardon, ma'am, but could I ask you something?" Micah asked during one of Gerty's rare pauses for breath.

"Why, speak on up!"

"Have you ever heard of a man named Tipton Barth?"

Gerty dropped into silence, and the others at the table all looked up at Micah.

"Oh, I've heard of that devil, yes sir," she said, solemn.

"Well, do you know where he might be found?"

One of the fat men said, "Beg pardon, friend, but why would anyone want to find Tipton Barth?"

"I... I didn't say I wanted to find him. I was just wondering if he really was in these parts."

"Are you a law officer?" the fat man asked.

"Not exactly. It's just a matter of interest to me. Curiosity."

"Are you a friend of his?"

"No. Anything but a friend."

"Thank the Lord for that. If you were friendly with that son of Satan, you'd not be a man I want to share a table with."

Gerty seized control of the conversation again. "That's right, sir. You're best not even to think of Tipton Barth. God only knows what kind of divine judgment was being done on this world when those two were created. One of them, Leroy, has gone on to his eternal punishment, thank God. But Tipton remains. Still, as foul and wicked as ever, they say, and a danger to every citizen. May God take him to join his brother soon."

Micah, who had nearly lost his resolve to go after Barth already, felt his resolve decline even more. "They tell me he is seen sometimes around Greentree."

"I've heard the same," one of the miners said. "They say he killed a woman and child there once. They say he and some of his ilk still linger in the area quite a lot. Like ghosts in the hills. Some folks are afraid to prospect around Greentree for fear of Barth and his gang."

"I can't say I blame them." Micah ventured a little bit of self-revelation. "I had an encounter with Tipton Barth many years ago, myself. In mining country, but not here, it was California, during the rush."

"That's a long time back."

"Yes. But Barth was then the same thing he is now. A

murderer. He killed a man named Jim Sneed and was put on trial for it. If he'd been convicted, he'd have been hanged."

"And why wasn't he convicted?"

Micah paused. "The story is that a witness who could have identified him as the killer was threatened by Tipton's brother. So he didn't tell the truth, and Tipton Barth went free."

They all thought about that. "Think of the lives that would have been saved if he'd been hanged."

"Yes," Micah said. "I have thought about that. Many times."

Aunt Hannah looked at him in a way that made Micah think she had read more between his words than had the others. "You ain't thinking of looking for him after all these years, are you?"

Micah's conscience wouldn't let him lie, but he didn't want to give a strictly straight answer, either. "It would take quite a strong motivation to want to find a man like that!" he said.

"Amen," said one of the miners. "I say let him stay far away from me. It's why I don't venture up toward Greentree. Them's dangerous climes. A lot worse than here."

"Well, I'll stay away. But... if somebody did want to find Tipton Barth, how would be the best way to go about it?"

"The best way... well, I reckon just get out the word that you're after him. Wanting to do him in, you know. He'd come looking for you then. The man's got a lot of pride in his reputation."

Micah finished his meal, telling himself he'd indeed best give up this notion of searching for Barth. He'd go back to his home and family and church and let things be like they used to be.

And when Jack Tower came around...well, he'd just not look him in the eye.

Micah rose to leave. Aunt Hannah lifted her withered

face toward him and said, "Young man... God go with you. You are the sword of the Lord. The sword of the Lord."

Micah mumbled an uncertain reply, paid for his food, and returned to the saloon. Passing through the barroom, he once again received many stares and evoked many whispers. He climbed the stairs to his room and took a glance back into the main room.

Rhoton was at a rear table, writing furiously on his pad, so lost in his creativity that he hadn't even noticed Micah's return.

It took a very long time for the noise in the saloon to subside and an even longer time yet for Micah to go to sleep.

———

Micah tried to pay the proprietor for his room the next morning, but the man continued to refuse it. Micah argued only briefly, then simply thanked the man and prepared to leave. He was ready to get out of this town.

"By the way, that story's been wrote, and Mr. Rhoton's gone on to wire it in as quick as he can get to a telegraph," the proprietor said as Micah was leaving. "You might run across him out on the road."

"That's interesting," Micah said, though really he wasn't much interested and hoped he didn't run across Rhoton on the road. He'd paid little attention to the scribbler, who seemed a pretentious and unimportant fellow. If Rhoton was a real journalist at all, he couldn't be much of one if he was hanging around backwater mining towns like this one.

Micah thought about the fact that he'd been mistaken for a gunfighter and smiled. Alice would think that was funny. But Alice was a long way off. His life back in Kansas was a long way off, too.

Here, where no one knew him, he could well be a

gunfighter, or a miner, or a lawman. He was just one more lone drifter, unknown to anyone.

But God knew him; he reminded himself. It was still his duty to behave as he should.

He left Levi Hill and walked back into the mountains. As he passed near the area where he'd found the skeleton, he realized he'd done nothing about officially reporting the find. There had been no law in Levi Hill that he'd seen, no official town structure of authority. Nothing he could do.

He trudged on, wondering how long it would take to reach the railroad.

A mile or so out, Micah stopped and turned. He thought he'd heard someone behind him. He waited to see if anyone would round the bend, but no one did, and now that he listened more closely, he could hear nothing.

Even so, he was sure he'd heard something. Maybe that journalist hadn't gone ahead after all but was behind him. That made Micah want to hurry on. He didn't want to become a fellow traveler of Rhoton's.

CHAPTER 18

T he wrecked railroad car was still there, lying beside the track. Micah looked around for his horse again, just in case it had wandered back this way. But it hadn't. Even if he did find it, his saddle was gone, along with his baggage.

Part of Micah was ready to head back to Kansas right now, but he hadn't made up his mind about what to do. For the sake of the baggage and the saddle alone, he felt compelled to go on toward Greentree. If his possessions were being held for him by the railroad, as he hoped, they probably were stashed up at the next railroad stop.

Micah walked up the track, which climbed up a steady grade and also curved around the side of a hill. The view was frequently spectacular, inspiring him to softly sing hymns as he trudged along. Eventually, he grew so out of breath that the hymn singing stopped, and he put his full concentration into his exertions.

Sometimes he would stop to rest, other times because he couldn't get over the notion that someone was traveling behind him. Yet he never spotted anyone. If he was being followed, his tracker was being careful not to get very close.

It was unnerving, and Micah hoped he was merely the victim of an overactive imagination.

———

The railroad tracks led him to a little whistle-stop named Borden. There was no town here, just a tiny train station with a water tank, a house or two nearby, and a small trading post that also sold sandwiches.

Micah went straight for the trading post and ordered food. He ate ravenously and drank several cups of coffee. All this walking made a man need plenty of fuel to keep going.

As he downed his last bite, he looked out of the trading post window and saw a man, bearing a rifle, come walking up the tracks the same way he had. Micah froze in mid-chew. So someone had been following him!

He looked closely at the man. He was some distance away and hard to see, but Micah was sure he'd seen that face in the saloon back at Levi Hill.

Micah wondered if he'd been truly followed or if he and this man simply shared the same route by coincidence. He hoped it was the latter.

After paying for his food, Micah left, took advantage of a nearby privy, then headed to the train station. The man from the Levi Hill saloon was on the porch, rolling a cigarette. He didn't glance up as Micah walked past him and through the door.

The station master was freeing a dead rat from a trap and cussing the fact that cold weather drove the rodents indoors. His listener was a man seated on a stool in the corner, reading a newspaper. Micah paid the fellow no heed.

"I'm looking for some baggage that might have been left off by the last Greentree-bound train," Micah said. "A carpetbag and maybe a saddle." He briefly explained the derailment and how he'd managed to become separated from the train.

"Matter of fact, there is a carpetbag," the station master said, wiping his hands on his pants to get off the essence of the deceased rat. "No saddle, though."

"I feared that," Micah said. It gave him a rather sickly feeling in the pit of his stomach. That saddle was one of his best possessions. Or had been.

"What color's the carpetbag?" the station master asked.

"Red. Solid."

"What color handle?"

"Black."

"All righty. Just had to check to be sure you and the bag really do go together. I've got it stowed in the back. Hang on."

The station master entered a large rear closet and began banging around in there, unseen but noisy.

A hand touched Micah's shoulder, startling him. He pivoted.

"Whoa, sir, sorry to startle you!" It was Rhoton, the journalist. "Just wanted to say hello."

"Right. Well... hello. What brings you here?"

"The telegraph line. It's my avenue of communication with my publication, you see. I wire in my stories."

I see.

"You've lost baggage, I gather?"

"That's right. But I think I've found it again."

The station master emerged with a red carpetbag in hand. "This look to be the one?"

"I think so."

Micah opened the bag and glanced inside. There at the top of the contents, was his gray shirt, just where he'd left it. It appeared the bag's contents had not been bothered.

"This is it," Micah said. "Thank you, sir."

"No problem. Sorry about the saddle. I can assure you if

it was took, it wasn't took by nobody associated with the rail-road. It may be you'll find it awaiting you at Greentree. There's a warehouse there where they store bigger items that get separated from their owners on trains."

"I see." Micah sighed. He'd been indecisive about contin-uing to Greentree or just turning back home and dropping his quest for Tipton Barth. Now it seemed he'd have to go onto Greentree simply to find his saddle.

"When's the next train to Greentree?" he asked.

"Not until tomorrow afternoon."

"Tomorrow—"

"Well!" Rhoton said. "That gives us plenty of time to talk!"

Micah glanced at him. Something about Rhoton, who wore a seedy suit and an even more seedy smile, annoyed him greatly. The idea of spending a day in conversation with him was not at all inspirational.

"Is Greentree the next stop up the track?"

"That's right. Ten miles."

"Micah pondered. He'd walked greater distances many a time, though admittedly not in the thin air of mountain country. "A steep climb?"

"Oh, no. We're on nearly the same level as Greentree right here. Just a shallow climb."

"Thank you." He'd made his decision. He'd walk the rest of the way and thus avoid an afternoon with Rhoton and the necessity of an overnight wait.

"Do you have some time to talk?" Rhoton said. He had his notepad out, and Micah recalled the fellow's illusion that Micah was some sort of mysterious gunfighter.

"I'm afraid not, sir," Micah replied. "I'm moving on."

Rhoton looked disappointed. "Well. In that case, I suppose I'll have to say farewell, then."

He glanced down at the pistol holstered on Micah's hip.

"The pistol of Diamond Willie! My, my. Can you at least tell me where Diamond Willie is now?"

"The man who last owned this pistol is in the hands of the Lord," Micah said. "Now, good day, and all the best to you." Micah turned and carried his carpetbag out the door, gladly leaving Rhoton behind.

The Levi Hill stranger was still on the porch, staring off at the mountains. Again he ignored Micah.

Micah strode out across the station yard to the tracks and began walking up them toward Greentree. He glanced back as he was about to go out of sight of the station.

The man on the porch was still sitting there, rolling another cigarette.

Micah was relieved. Apparently, he wasn't being followed after all.

CHAPTER 19

Refreshed by food and glad to have his bag again, Micah walked energetically for nearly two miles before he was at last forced to slow down. The mountain atmosphere certainly wasn't as rich as what he was accustomed to, and the blasted bag was growing heavier in his hand with every step. It felt as if it was loaded with bricks. Just what had he packed that was so heavy?

Ready for a rest, he veered off the tracks and sat down on a log, letting his breathing slow, and his heart quit hammering so hard. He sat the carpetbag at his feet, glad to be momentarily free of the burden.

A noise...

He turned, looking back down the track. He couldn't see far because the tracks made a curve, but it sounded as if...

No. Why would anyone follow him? Probably just some animal was crossing the tracks. He'd left that stranger still sitting on the porch at the train station.

Of course, he might have gotten up and followed as quickly as Micah was out of sight...

Micah listened again but heard nothing. No reason to

worry, he decided. He was just letting this Tipton Barth business get him edgy.

Micah picked up the carpetbag. It did seem overly heavy. Putting it onto his lap, he opened it and pulled out the shirt.

He looked inside. "I'll be!" he said aloud.

This wasn't his bag at all! It was of the same color and nearly identical design and happened to have been packed with a gray shirt on the top of the stack, but beneath that, everything was different.

And no wonder the bag was heavy. The most noticeable part of its contents was a revolver and a big box of ammunition. The revolver was small, the kind a man might carry in a shoulder-rig holster, but it was heavy. Micah pulled it out and studied it. It was loaded. He laid it down on the log beside him and continued to dig through the bag.

He found numerous personal items, such as a match case, a shaving kit, and a tobacco box. There was also a snap-latch money pouch, marked with the name "Johnny Cole" and seemingly quite stuffed.

Micah looked inside. The money pouch contained a thick roll of bills, tied up with a piece of twine. Micah slipped the twine loose and let the bills unroll themselves in his hand. Most of them were fifty-dollar bills, plus several hundred-dollar bills. There was at least a thousand dollars here.

Poor Johnny Cole, whoever he was. Micah had thought his own loss was significant, but Cole had lost a lot more than Micah had when this carpetbag went out of hand.

"Well! Looks like I'll be gaining more than just a famous pistol here today!"

Micah came to his feet, dumping the carpetbag on the ground in the process. The bills he clutched in his fist by reflex.

"That's a lot of money, Preacher," said the man Micah had last seen on the station house porch. "You steal that from somebody you gunned down? Diamond Willie, maybe?"

The stranger had a pistol leveled on Micah and a wicked grin on his face.

"What do you want from me?"

"Very simple. I want that pistol you carry. I want the pistol of Diamond Willie. So why don't you lose that gun belt, real slow."

Micah stooped slowly and laid the money on the ground by his feet. He then stood and unbuckled the gun belt.

"Toss it over here."

Micah complied, the gun belt plopping on the ground at the pistoleer's feet.

The man laughed. "Diamond Willie's own pistol! Imagine that! Diamond Willie killed a lot of men with that there pistol. It's a famous weapon. The man who carries it gains a reputation with it. Tell me this: Where did Diamond Willie die?"

"The man who owned that pistol lies dead in the wilderness not far from Levi Hill. Whether his name is Willie, I couldn't tell you."

"You must be some kind of gunfighter to have downed Diamond Willie. They say you couldn't see the man's hand move when he'd draw, so fast he was."

"I'm no gunfighter. And you don't understand. Diamond Willie, if that's who he was, was already—"

"Shut up. It don't matter now. It'll be me who gets the credit for killing Willie, and I'll make up my own story about how it happened. Diamond Willie ain't been seen in over a year that I know of, and I can tell any tale I want. Tell me this, though: Do you really call yourself Preacher?"

"I am a preacher."

"I'll bet you are. Did you say any Bible verses to Willie when you blasted him into hell?"

"My friend, you have a very wrong understanding of this whole situation."

"Do I, now? Well, like I said, it don't matter. I can make up my own story... once you're out of the way."

"What do you mean?"

"I intend to claim credit for killing Diamond Willie. There was a bounty on his head, you know. A big one. I produce that pistol, and I may stand a chance of gaining it. If nothing else, I'll gain the reputation that goes with killing so famous a gunfighter. But I can't very well leave you to go around telling your own version of the tale, can I?"

"Mister, I have a wife, a son. If you intend to harm me..."

"Harm? Not harm. I intend to kill you. We're all alone out here, Preacher. Nobody will know how it happened. Who knows? Maybe there's a bounty on your head, too!"

Instinct made Micah move. Somehow, a moment before it happened, he sensed that the man was going to pull the trigger. He threw himself to the left as the shot blasted, so close that he felt the hot sting of the expelled gunpowder. The bullet narrowly missed him.

The man swore and cocked the pistol again. Micah's hand swept down and scooped up the pistol he'd removed from the carpetbag and laid on the log. Still acting by instinct, he lifted it and fired, simultaneous with his attacker's second shot.

That second bullet also missed Micah, though it cut a little crease in the sleeve of his coat.

Micah's randomly fired shot, however, was more effective. It caught the gunman in the right hand, taking off two fingers at the top knuckles and making him fling his own pistol aside. It lay smoking on the ground while the man, howling in pain, gripped his bleeding right hand with his left one and staggered backward.

Micah, holding the pistol he'd just fired for the first time in his life, gaped, amazed at the shot he'd just pulled off. The

Lord surely must have guided that bullet, for Micah hadn't even had time to aim.

The man lifted a pallid face and looked at Micah with the expression of a man expecting to die at any moment.

"Just make it fast... that's all I ask. Don't gut-shoot me, please!"

Micah lowered the pistol. "I don't intend to shoot you at all. I wouldn't have shot you then if I hadn't been forced to."

"You ain't going to kill me?"

"No. I just want you to go away."

The man, despite his pain, laughed in relief. "Bless you, mister. Bless you! You ain't going to kill me, really?"

"Really. Just... just go away. Don't ever let me see you again." The preacher in Micah emerged for a moment. "And put this kind of thing behind you. You don't want to be a murderer. You don't want to kill a man for something so foolish as to possess some other murderer's pistol. Go on. Put sin behind you and turn to the Lord."

"You really do sound like a preacher!"

"I told you, I am one. How's your hand? You won't bleed to death, will you?"

"No. I got two fingers gone, though. God, it hurts!"

"Go back to the train station. They can patch you up."

"Bless you, Preacher. Thank you for not killing me. You shot off my fingers, but you could have just as easily put that bullet through my head."

It disgusted Micah to see a man who moments before had been ready to kill him and gloat about it now fawning and gushing before him.

"Get away from here. I forgive you for what you tried to do, but I have no desire to lay eyes on you anymore."

"Can I get my pistol that I flung over yonder?"

"I'm not that kind of fool, my friend. Just go on and be grateful you're still alive and not beyond hope."

"Can I look for my fingers?"

"They won't be useful to you now. Just go on."

The man, bleeding and holding his hand, turned and ran down the tracks and nearly out of sight. He turned, though, and called back: "What's your name, Preacher?"

Micah had no interest in this man, knowing who he was. He might have just told the fellow to shut up and keep running, but he was shaken by the realization he'd just shot a man. So he impulsively did something uncharacteristic: He lied. The name he'd found in the carpetbag flashed back to mind, and he called back, "Johnny Cole."

The man turned and ran out of sight.

Micah sat down on the log again, letting out a long, slow breath. He was shaking now, feeling faint. He thanked God he was still alive and wished he'd never left Kansas.

CHAPTER 20

The station master pulled his watch from his vest pocket and looked at it with a frown.

"Mr. Rhoton, sir, I think you've tied up my telegraph line long enough," he said, snapping the cover down again. "When will you be finished?"

Rhoton clicked the keys a few more times, stood, and tipped his hat. "All finished, sir. And I thank you."

"I'm not really supposed to do that, you know. Letting somebody unofficial use my telegraph, I mean."

"Would you have wanted to transmit so lengthy a story yourself?" Rhoton asked. He was feeling smug and satisfied just now. He'd just wired in a story—like most he wrote, one-third fact, one-third speculation, and one-third total fiction—that he was sure would revitalize his struggling career. A mysterious gunfighter, apparent killer of the infamous Diamond Willie, yet who also claimed to be, of all things, a preacher. What a tale! Add to that the fact that he was actually seeking Tipton Barth, another well-known killer. No doubt he intended to kill Barth, a speculation Rhoton had already included as fact in the story he'd just wired in. This was his greatest journalistic work, no doubt of it. And just the kind of thing readers of the *American Crime Chronicle* would eat up like candy. Within a short while, his editor would be reading over the story with a growing intensity of interest. This one was a prize, a cover story.

"You know, sir, I can't say I think much of your newspaper," the station master said. "Full of all kinds of nonsense and silliness. Why people want to read such, I can't imagine.

"And you don't read it?"

"Not much."

"But some."

"This job is lonely sometimes. A copy gets left here by somebody; of course, I read it."

"Disapproving all the while, of course."

"Your tone is a little sarcal... sarcis..."

"Sarcastic?"

"Yeah."

"Sorry about that. It's a bad tendency I have... I'll try... I'll be! What in the devil..."

Rhoton was looking out the window.

"What is it?" asked the station master.

"There's a man walking back this way, from up the track, and he's got a good amount of blood on him."

The station master was out the door a moment later. He stopped and watched the man staggering his way with one hand gripping another.

"That man was sitting on the porch a little earlier," he said. He stepped off the porch and headed toward him.

The wounded man stopped when he saw the station master nearing. Rhoton was only two steps behind.

"What happened to you, friend?" the station master asked.

"Got my fingers shot off," the man replied, his voice tight. "That gunfighter did it, the one who calls himself a preacher."

Rhoton shoved up close to the man. "What was that? The preacher?"

"Yeah... Johnny Cole. He told me his name is Johnny Cole."

A new fact. Rhoton grabbed his pad and pencil and scribbled.

"How'd he come to shoot you in the hand?" Rhoton asked.

"I think he was sparing my life... I'd drawn on him. I reckon, him being a preacher or whatever, he must believe in mercy. He shot me right in the hand, chopped off my fingers. I never saw nobody shoot like that."

Rhoton swore with delight, shaking his head and grinning. This story was growing bigger and better by the moment.

Tell me more," Rhoton said.

"Let's get this man patched up before you go pumping him for more of your damned nonsense!" the station master said.

Rhoton, though, was unrelenting. Even as the station master led the wounded man back to the station, and later as he did what he could to patch up his hand, Rhoton continued to interview the man. He wrote down much more on his notepad than what was actually said. Rhoton was a master of embellishment on the hoof.

"I'm afraid I'm going to have to ask you to use your telegraph line again, sir," he said to the station master when he was finished. "I've got to update the story I sent."

"Do I get paid for telling you all that?" the wounded man, his finger stumps now nicely bandaged, said.

"You're building a legend, my friend," Rhoton said, heading for the telegraph key. "The satisfaction of that surely should be pay enough."

———

Micah trudged slowly along, very weary and not particularly attentive to his surroundings because nothing here seemed worthy of more than one glance. He wondered whether Tipton Barth was here, somewhere, maybe in a barroom, maybe relaxing on one of the porches. Oddly, Micah hardly cared. He wasn't sure he'd even recognize Barth after all these years or that Barth would remember him. In any case, all he planned to do was go home and tell his family what a fool he'd been to leave in the first place.

But first, he needed a new pair of boots. During this last leg of his walk, the sole of his right boot had begun to flop, slapping against the bottom of his foot with every step. The left boot was in only slightly better condition.

Micah spotted a sign above a store: SMITH'S DRY GOODS AND SUNDRIES. Micah headed for the door.

It was dark inside, relative to the street, and pleasant. He paused, breathing deeply, thinking how tired he felt, and scanned the shelves, looking for boots.

"Do for you, sir?" a lazy-looking man asked, not even looking at Micah.

"I need a new pair of boots," Micah said, lifting a foot to show the flapping sole.

The man didn't even glance at it. He was absorbed in reading an outdated edition of the *American Crime Chronicle*. "Boots are over there."

"So I see. Thanks."

He spent fifteen minutes with the assorted boots and finally made his selection. He put them on, tossed his old boots into a corner, and walked over to pay.

The man was still reading his copy of the *Crime Chronicle*. He seemed irritated to have to interrupt his reading to take Micah's money.

"You enjoy that paper?" Micah asked, struggling to mask his irritation.

"Yeah."

"That the latest edition?"

"Yeah. But it's time for another one any day now. I've read this one through."

"Let me suggest you supplement your reading with the Bible."

The man looked up at him for the first time. "You a preacher?"

"As a matter of fact, I am."

"Yeah. Well, I ain't that much a reader. Except for the *Chronicle.*"

Micah walked back onto the street, enjoying the feeling of new boots but realizing he'd have to break them in before they really grew comfortable.

What now? The train station, maybe. A look for his baggage and saddle. Or maybe not. He was hungry. A restaurant was the thing.

He began his search.

H e found one that advertised flapjacks and sausage and entered into one of the best meals he'd had in quite a long time. It was so good, and he was so famished, that he ordered a second one. He felt extravagant, but the guilt was overwhelmed by the pleasure.

By the time he'd finished, the sun was edging down. Micah forgot about the train station for now and turned his attention to the local hotel.

"Room for one?" the man behind the counter said. "Any preference of floor? We've got four to choose from." The fellow seemed quite proud of this.

"In that case, I'll take the fourth floor," Micah said. "The better for the view."

"Indeed. And the rooms are fifteen cents cheaper because of the higher risk of dying should we suffer a fire."

"That's a true comfort," Micah said. "Thank you for mentioning that. I'll be sure to ponder that while I'm lying in bed."

Once in the room, though, he didn't worry much. There were porches at each level, spanning the full front of the structure, all of them connected by stairs. In case of fire, he could be on the street in moments.

He lay back on the bed, napping briefly, then decided to enjoy one of his relatively infrequent cigars on the porch. He stepped outside and settled down in a rocking chair, looking past the rooftops across the street and delighting in the beauty of the mountains, still lighted with the last glows of the sunset.

A splendid place was these mountains. Yet right now, he missed the flatlands of Kansas, his wife, his son. He thought about writing Alice a letter but put aside the idea with the happy realization that, if all went smoothly, he could probably reach home before the letter could.

"Goodbye, Tipton Barth," he said to the sky. "It was a righteous impulse, I suppose, that led me here to find you, but I'll search for you no more. There's nothing I can do about the crimes you've committed... and it's the role of the law, not a preacher, to protect the world from whatever crimes you may do again."

A part of himself questioned his own words, but right now, that particular voice was nearly silent. Micah Ward was glad, just now, to think of nothing but himself, his family, his impending journey home, the taste of his cigar, and the comfortable feeling of the rocking chair here on this lovely Colorado mountain country evening.

He opened his eyes abruptly. It was much darker, the cigar had dropped from his fingers to the porch and burned out, and he knew he'd gone to sleep.

Something had awakened him, though. He sat up straight.

"I'll beat the hell out of you, Starling!" a voice from below said loudly. "Come on. Smith, drag him around into the alley."

Micah stood and went to the porch railing. Below and across the street, a man was lying in the dirt, visible to Micah only because of the light coming from nearby buildings. Two other men were standing by him, looming over him threateningly. It was one of these who had spoken.

Micah examined the building directly behind the men. It was a barroom and gambling house, and he surmised from the general lay of the situation that the man on the ground had been rudely tossed out of that establishment by the other two.

The pair reached down and picked up the fallen man by his arms and dragged him toward a nearby alley. The man kicked and protested, but the pair treated him very roughly.

Micah couldn't see them well once they were in the alley, but he could hear their words, the downed man's outcries, and the thuds and thumps that told him a beating was going on.

He looked around on the street, hoping to spot some sort of policeman. There was none.

"Oh, Lord..." Micah whispered.

The sound of the beating was growing more horrific.

Something inside Micah told him to retreat back into his room and close the door and windows. Whatever was happening across the way was not his business.

Another voice, the one he knew was the right one to heed, told him to get down there right away and somehow stop what could be a murder in progress.

"Dear Lord, help me," he said. "Protect me and help me to protect this man below."

He headed for the stairs and began a fast descent to the street.

———

The sound of the beating was loud and sickening dull thuds, accompanied by grunts from both the beaters and the one receiving the beating.

Micah imposed himself into the end of the alley and said loudly, "In the name of the Lord, stop!"

They did stop and wheeled to face him, obviously astonished at his effrontery.

"In the name of the what?" one of them said.

"In the name of the Lord, my friend. I don't know what that man there on the ground has done to you, but I do see what you've done to him, and I'm telling you to stop."

"You and what army?"

"Me and the army of the Lord," Micah said. "Leave that man alone. You've done enough to him."

"Get the hell out of here."

"No."

"You want the same as him?"

"The Lord is my protector. You get to me; you'll have to go through him."

"You're loco. You're babbling like some damned pulpit screamer."

"I'm a minister of the gospel. And I'm telling you, on God's authority, to leave that man alone."

Micah expected the pair to come at him, but they didn't.

"That man there cheated us, insulted us, and tried to steal our money, right off a table," one said.

"Then he was wrong, and he deserves punishment... but if you keep doing what you're doing, you're going to kill that man. Is he worth hanging for?"

The pair of them glanced at each other. "Hell," the second one said. "We were ready to quit anyway."

"You can have him, Preacher," the other said. "Save his sorry soul, if you can."

They laughed and headed out the alley by its back entrance.

Micah went to the fallen man, who lay groaning. He'd vomited and was lying in it, the stench of it strong.

"They're gone now," Micah said. "I'll get you help, my friend."

"I'm... sick."

"You've been beaten. That's what's wrong with you. You need a doctor."

"No... just a bed. Rest... food. I need food."

"Is that why you took the money?"

"Yes. Starving."

Micah said, "Can you stand?"

"Don't know."

"Come on. Try. I'll get you to a doctor."

"No, doctor. Please. Only one doctor here; he hates me. Won't help me."

"Any good doctor would help you."

"I stole his horse, his buggy then sold them. I took silver from his house."

"You're a fine, upstanding citizen; I take it."

"Not... quite."

"We've got a lot of stairs to get up. But if you can try, I'll do my best to help you."

"I'll try. God bless you. God bless you."

"He has for many years. Now, come on. Let's give it a try."

CHAPTER 22

There were no broken bones, something Micah could account for only because the man he'd rescued was very drunk and therefore very loose and limber at the time he'd been beaten. Though he appeared destined for some severe bruising and soreness that would last for days, it seemed that the fellow would make it through.

But he'd not been lying when he said he was sick. Micah detected that the man had a strong fever. His body, covered with sweat, was dirty and hot, and stinking. Micah hoped the man wouldn't ruin the bed and draw the wrath of the hotel management.

His name was Starling Bright. Though he was too sore and sick to talk much, he was able to tell that much to Micah and also reveal that he was pretty much generally viewed as the town drunk in Greentree, Colorado. Also, a town thief. Bright made no attempt to hide the fact that he'd stolen many a dollar and many an item from places all around Greentree.

Micah wondered why the Lord had sent him such an unexpected find as this character.

Despite Blight's claim to be starving, he was unable to

eat much of the cafe meal that Micah fetched for him. He did relish the coffee, however, and thanked Micah profusely for saving him.

Micah, foreseeing a night on the floor while a stinking, sick, badly beaten stranger took up his bed, tried to maintain a good attitude about this turn of events.

"Lord, I know you devoted yourself while on earth to just such people as this one," he prayed in a whisper while Starling Bright slept. "Since you've sent one my way, let me do no less for him."

As he tossed and turned on a blanket on the floor that night, Micah wondered how long it would take Bright to get well.

He might not be going back to Kansas nearly as soon as he'd thought.

———

Five days later, Micah was still in Greentree, and Bright was still in his room. He was bruised, still in pain from his beating, but sober and cleaner. Micah had insisted that he wash himself up, had even condescended to help him do it, though less out of pure helpfulness and more to make the atmosphere inside the room more breathable.

He'd written that letter to Alice after all, telling her that he was well and safe and would come home soon, but exactly when, he couldn't say. He didn't tell her specifically about Bright, only that he'd encountered a situation requiring him to give some help where it was needed and that as soon as he was finished, he'd be home. He told her and Flavius that he loved them and missed them.

Then he headed to the street to mail his letter and bring back yet more food for himself and his unexpected roommate.

He posted the letter and meandered slowly up the street,

realizing that he'd not even given a thought to Tipton Barth since Bright came to him. He wondered if perhaps, oddly, it was to save Blight's life and to give him an opportunity to perhaps see his soul saved as well, that he'd felt led to come to this place. Maybe Tipton Barth had never been the point at all, but only God's mechanism for moving him to a place he was needed.

One thing was certain: Bright was a man with needs. He was a drunkard, a man unable to hold down work, a man who said his home was an abandoned privy. He'd begged Micah for liquor for the first two days but had quit doing that now and was beginning to talk of trying to give up drinking altogether. He'd been asking many questions about religion, faith, salvation... Micah couldn't say he was enjoying Bright's company, exactly, but he was feeling a certain fulfillment in believing he was bringing something good into the life of one of God's downtrodden creations.

A loud rumbling behind him made him wheel. A wagon, driven by a burly, bearded man in far too big of a hurry, was tearing up the street toward him.

Micah yelped in surprise and leaped toward the nearest boardwalk. The wagon barreled past, narrowly missing him.

"Watch where you're going, friend!" the man on the wagon yelled back at him.

Watch where *he* was going? For a moment, every bit of Micah's charity vanished. He was ready to go after that driver and tell him in far from ministerial terminology who it was who needed to be watching where he was going.

But Micah didn't do it. He'd learned to control his temper and so swallowed his anger and turned his attention back to buying food for himself and Bright.

The wagon stopped in front of a store building on down the street. The driver left his perch and circled to the rear of the wagon. He removed what looked like a bundle of newspapers and hauled them into the store. Moments later, he emerged, climbed back onto the wagon, went farther down the street, and repeated the same action again.

Micah grew curious. When the driver repeated the same routine yet another time, then drove on out of town, Micah decided to see what had been deposited in those stores.

He stopped in the nearest one, the same store in which he'd purchased the boots.

Just as he suspected, the fat man was behind the counter in the same position Micah had seen him the first time. He was reading the latest edition of the *American Crime Chronicle*. Micah looked at the newspaper bundle. Indeed it was the *Chronicle*.

He shook his head, marveling once again at the lurid tastes of the American reading public, and turned to go.

The fat man just then noticed his presence. Grumpily, he asked, "Can I help you?"

"No," Micah said. "Go on with your reading."

He went back to the street and headed for the cafe.

When Micah was gone, the fat man shifted in his chair and let the newspaper fully unfold. The upper half of the page was a garish illustration of a gunfighter with a T-shaped scar on one side of his face, gunning down a man identified, under the picture, as one Diamond Willie.

A big headline underscored the picture:

GUN-SLINGING PREACHER, KILLER OF DIAMOND WILLIE, ROAMING COLORADO TO QUENCH BLOODTHIRST FOR INFAMOUS TIPTON BARTH.

The fat man read a few more lines, then seemed to realize something. He flipped the paper over and looked at the picture, the scar on the face, then, with a frown, stared at the door through which Micah had just exited.

A scar, shaped like a T, a gunfighter who also was a preacher...

He came out of his chair and headed for the back, where an equally lazy fellow clerk was hiding in the storage area, smoking a cigar. He took the paper with him, eager to share his news.

———

The man in the cafe, whom Micah had come to know fairly well over the past several days because of his frequent trips to purchase food for himself and Starling Bright, had a copy of the *Chronicle* in hand when Micah walked in. He put it down slowly as Micah approached, saying nothing and looking at Micah in a way he never had before. Micah had the impression that his facial scar was getting a close examination.

"What's the matter, James?" Micah asked. "You look a little pale."

James swallowed. His eyes seemed abnormally wide.

"Seriously, James, are you sick or something?"

"I, uh, no. No. I'm fine. What can I do for you... Preacher?"

"Flapjacks. Two plates, packed for me to carry out, just like before."

"Whatever you want, Preacher. Tell you what... it's on the house this time."

"What?"

"Free. On me. In thanks, you know, for all the business."

"Mighty nice of you, James."

"I'm your friend. That's all. I'm your friend, and I want to show it. I am your friend, aren't I?"

"Of course you are. But I don't understand the way you're acting. Are you sure that nothing is wrong?"

"Nothing. Nothing is wrong at all." James forced a

laugh, glanced at the newspaper, and grabbed it quickly. He stuffed it out of sight behind the counter. "I'll get those flap-jacks right away."

Micah wondered what in the devil was going on. He sneaked a look in a mirror hanging on a nearby wall, just to make sure he didn't have something dirtying his face that he didn't know about.

When James came back with the flapjacks, he seemed even more nervous. Micah took the covered tray quickly, fearing James would drop it.

"I'll bring the dishes back as soon as we're through, like before," he said.

"No hurry," James said. "You just bring them back when you feel like it. Why don't bring them back at all if you don't want to."

Mere days before, James had given Micah a stern lecture about the importance of returning borrowed dishes promptly and undamaged. So this sudden reversal in attitude told him that something in the atmosphere indeed had shifted significantly.

"All right, James," he said. "I want to know why you're acting this way toward me."

James went white as milk. "Oh, Lord. I'm sorry. I wasn't trying to make you angry."

"I'm not angry. Why would I be angry?"

James seemed very relieved. "I'm glad to hear it. I wouldn't want to have you down on me."

Micah laughed. This was so puzzling; it was growing funny.

"I'm not down on you. You're one of the few folks in this town I can think of as at least somewhat a friend."

"I'm glad to hear it." James's eyes made a quick down-and-up flicker. "Not wearing your pistol, I see."

"No. Should I be?"

"I'd just figure you might be one to wear it all the time, you know. Just in case there was trouble."

"No."

"What if you saw Tipton Barth out there, unexpected, and you didn't have it?"

Micah frowned. He'd said nothing to James about his interest in Tipton Barth, an interest that had substantially declined to nothing by now, anyway. "How do you know about that?"

James, who did not know what Micah's attitude toward the *Crime Chronicle* story was or if he even knew about it, did not answer that question fully. "I just heard it said somewhere that you were looking for Barth."

Micah was surprised that something he'd discussed with relatively few would have made the rounds of local gossip so fast, or even at all. He was nothing but a stranger here and surely not that much of interest.

"I don't really have anything to say regarding Tipton Barth," he said.

James looked scared again, nodded, and went to work preparing Micah's food as quickly as possible.

Micah carried the tray toward the hotel, still puzzled and feeling vaguely disturbed. When he entered the lobby, he was glad to be off the street. Outside, he had an uncanny, skin-crawling feeling, like the entire town was watching him.

CHAPTER 23

A long wail heralded the approach of a train. Micah shook his head sadly at the sound. The day before, he had gotten around to visiting the train station to inquire after his baggage and saddle.

An exploration of the small warehouse behind the main station revealed plenty of interesting items but not Micah's possessions. He sighed, mentally giving up the baggage, regretting most of all the loss of his beloved Bible. He'd treasured it as long as he'd possessed it, and the likelihood of seeing it again seemed small.

As he walked back toward the hotel, he sorrowed over the loss of his Bible but also wondered if he might take it as a sign that he was to put the past behind him. He was certainly ready to take it that way. He'd lost all desire to encounter Tipton Barth.

Micah walked through the lobby of the hotel, bearing the tray of food. A young boy he'd seen on the streets a time or two happened to be inside. The boy had struck Micah as a tough type, probably living in a difficult family situation, the sort to be a bully and Hardcase. He'd sneered at Micah previously, as he apparently sneered at everyone, but this time he looked at Micah with an apparent combination of awe and fear.

Micah was slightly disturbed by this because he couldn't account for it. As he climbed the stairs, he puzzled over this and the other odd reactions he'd received.

As he was turning the key in the lock of his room, it hit him: The boy in the lobby had been holding a copy of a newspaper.

Possibilities began to click together in his mind. That *Crime Chronicle* writer he'd encountered, the way he'd been mistaken for a gunfighter because of the pistol he'd found...

Was it possible that the writer had actually put some kind of story in the *Crime Chronicle*?

The thought was chilling. Micah stood frozen a few moments, then shook his head. Too preposterous.

But he would try to take a look at that newspaper, just in case.

Starling Bright was seated in the corner when Micah entered the room. He was whittling on a cedar stick that he'd had in his pocket when Micah had brought him here. Chips covered the floor; the blade flashed back and forth furiously.

"Starling, what in the world are you doing?"

"Whittling."

"You're making a mess all over the place."

"I know. But I got to do something."

"Why?"

"Otherwise, I'd be doing something else."

Micah set the tray of food on the table. "What else would you be doing?"

"Drinking. The desire is mighty strong right now, Preacher."

"Then let's pray. You and me together."

"I'd be a hypocrite to do that, Preacher. I'm not a praying man. The Lord knows that."

"He does. He'd also like you to be one."

"How do you know?"

"The Bible, Starling. It tells us what we need to know. God loves you."

Starling whittled all the faster. Chips flew a good six feet. "I doubt that."

"Put your whittling down. We'll eat. And if you won't pray with me. I'll pray alone for you to have the strength to resist the temptation."

Starling did stop whittling and looked earnestly at Micah. "Temptation. I know about temptation, Preacher, and this is something that needs a stronger word to describe it. It's that way with liquor. For a time, you can just drink because you like it and because it makes you feel good. Then, before you know it, it's something you got to have. Like air or food. Except you want it even stronger than that."

"I've seen it do the same to others. I've also seen others escape from it through prayer and by taking it one day at a time. Or one hour at a time. But you've really got to want to do it."

Starling lowered his head. "I do want to, Preacher," he said.

"Then I'll do whatever I have to to help you. I think maybe it was to meet you and to help you that I was called to come to Greentree."

Starling looked up at him. "Do you really believe God himself told you to come to this sorry little town?"

"I think so. I was compelled to come here, it seemed. I just had a different reason to start with."

"Tipton Barth."

"Yes." Micah had already told Starling Bright some about how this journey had come about.

"But now you ain't looking for him no more?"

"I don't think I am. I think I've gotten past that."

"What would you have done if you had found him?"

"You know, crazy as it sounds, I don't think I ever really figured out the answer to that question. I just felt I had to find him and try to make up for a failure of mine a lot earlier in my life."

"You said something about that before, but you didn't explain."

Micah paused. He'd not ever told the full story to anyone. Oddly, he felt a desire to do so now. Starling Bright was a virtual stranger, unconnected with his life. Maybe it would be all right to tell him.

So he did. Succinctly, and with full honesty, he told Starling the tale of how he'd been frightened out of giving truthful testimony against Barth and how, as a result, Barth had gone free to kill many others, including the family of a lonely man who had wandered into Micah's own church, seeking relief from his pain.

"I'll be damned," Starling whispered.

"Starling, I wish you wouldn't say that," Micah said.

"Sorry... it's just that that's one hell of a... one deuce of a story." He paused. "God... you feel guilty, I guess."

Micah smiled vaguely. "You're forthright."

"I'm what?"

"Forthright? You say what you think without holding back."

"Is that good?"

"Yes. Most of the time, anyway."

"Then I'll tell you, forthright, that right now, it's all I can do to hold back from going out that door and finding myself a bottle of whiskey."

"I see. How would you pay for it?"

"With your money. I know where you keep it. I could steal some, and I wouldn't hesitate to do it. I've stolen plenty of times before." He paused, then grinned. "I'm being forthright again."

"You don't need to steal from me. I'll give you what you need if I can. But you don't need whiskey. You need the Lord, Starling."

"The Lord wouldn't want me."

"What if I could persuade you he did?"

"I wouldn't believe you."

"Let me pray with you, Starling."

"No. No. Not just yet. Maybe later."

"Don't try to put off what you know you need to do."

"Listen to me, Preacher. I ain't trying to play games with you. I want to be different. I want to be the kind of man like you talk about. But a man has to think, you know. He has to get used to things."

I see.

"I want you to tell me something, Preacher. Why have you helped me?"

Micah weighed his words. "Because... it's what I should do. It's what God would have me do. I told you... I think I was called here to help you."

"I'm sorry, Preacher. I can't believe it. I can't believe that God would care about me... nor any man such as yourself. There's no man that good. If you care about helping somebody like me, then you're a saint. And there ain't no real saints. None I've ever seen."

Micah didn't know how to respond and stammered for a moment. Then he said, "Starling, if I'm a saint, it's only through God's grace. And I tell you, all I am is a common man who wants to do the right thing. That's why I do care about you and why I want to help you."

Starling studied him. "I'd do nothing but disappoint you. Preacher. I'd just fail you. And the Lord. I'd make a show of repenting, and then I'd fail. That's who I am. And what I am."

"You can't do it in your own strength. That's why we have to turn to God."

Starling stared at him, saying nothing for a long time. Then he took a deep breath and said, "I'm hungry. I think I want to eat now."

Chapter 24

The ghost town of Genesis, north of
Greentree

The air was cold, and steam streamed from the nostrils
of the weary horse and those of its rider. When the
rider halted his mount and slid out of the saddle, steam rose
as well from the horse's heaving sides.

The rider paused long enough to pull a folded newspaper
from the saddlebag. He tied off the horse to a post and
headed for the door of the shack, which opened as he neared.

The man who emerged was graying and stout, his skin
heavily weathered and his eyes the color of cold flint. He
squinted at the newcomer.

"Was expecting you sooner, Jake."

The rider, out of breath, walked up to him fast and
thrust out the newspaper. "You got to see this, Tipton."

Tipton Barth reached out and accepted the newspaper.
"What the hell's this?"

"Open it. Look at the front."

Tipton Barth unfolded the paper as he stepped back
inside the shack, which was lighted only by the fireplace and

a couple of very dirty coal oil lamps. He squinted at the big etching of the gunfighter with the scar, then looked at the headline. His ever-present squint narrowed.

"Gunning for Tipton Barth, eh?" He laughed. "Well, now! That's interesting."

"Who do you think he is, Tipton?" Jake asked. "You ever heard of Johnny Cole?"

"Johnny Cole? That's his name?"

"That's what the story says. Read it!"

Tipton glanced at the columns of narrow type below the picture. He was a slow reader, hated to try, even though it embarrassed him to admit it. He cleared his throat, then said, "Tell you what, Jake. My eyes are hurting me this evening. Maybe you can read it for me."

"Surely, Tipton. I tell you, though, you won't like it."

Tipton Barth sat back in a wobbly chair, staring at the wall and chewing the stub of a burned-out cigar while his partner haltingly read the story. When he was finished at long last, Barth rolled the cigar to the other side of his mouth, gave it a final chew, and threw it into the fire.

"What do you think, Tipton? You know this fellow?"

"I never heard the name Johnny Cole in my life."

"But he's got to have some reason to be coming after you. The story makes it sound that way, anyhow."

"Don't you know nothing, Jake? That rag is mostly nonsense and lies. There may not be no Johnny Cole."

"But it says he wears Diamond's old pistol."

"Could be another lie."

Jake thought about it. "So maybe I came riding all the way up here for nothing."

"Maybe." Barth pulled out a new cigar, this one fresh. He stared at it. "But there's one thing in that story... something that rings a bell."

"What's that?"

"That scar. Shaped like a T letter. Something about that is familiar. But I can't put a finger on it."

"So what happens? What if this Johnny Cole ain't a he? What if he shows up, gunning for you?"

"Let him come. I ain't afraid of him."

"But if he's gunman enough to have shot Diamond Willie..."

"Let him come. I've killed aplenty men in my day. One more won't matter." He stopped speaking long enough to light the cigar from one of the lamps. He puffed it into a good flame, then said, "Besides, it would give me a good chance to see that scar, and maybe remember what it is I can't just now."

"Tipton, your eyes ain't what they once were. You know that. If this fellow is young..."

But Tipton wasn't listening. He puffed the cigar thoughtfully, then took the newspaper and spent the next half hour in silence, studying the fanciful picture of the gunfighter with the T-shaped scar on his face.

———

That night, Micah dreamed about Alice, Flavius, and home. The images were vivid, enticing in one way, but accompanied by odd and uncomfortable feelings. He awakened to find a lamp burning in the room and Starling standing beside his pallet, looking down at him.

"You're sick," Starling said. His image swam in Micah's vision. "I'm afraid you've caught whatever I had."

Micah only half-understood him. "I'm not sick."

"You been moaning over here like somebody's sliced your leg off. Come on. Let me help you up. I'm moving over here on the floor, and you can have your bed back."

Micah was aware of nothing more until morning when he awakened. He was in the bed, feeling very sick. Starling

Bright was gone. Micah felt too weak and disoriented to wonder where he had gone or if he was coming back.

He did come back with food. "I took some of your money," he said. "I wasn't stealing it, I swear. You can count it if you want. It's just that now that you're sick, I figure it's my duty to take care of you."

Micah just didn't have it in him to say thank you. Nor to eat. His food went untouched, and he slept fitfully.

An indeterminable time later, he awakened thirsty and asked for water. Starling was there and brought him a cup. Micah drank all he could, then went to sleep again. He had just enough lucidity about him to know that he was fevered, and at the moment, fully dependent on Starling. This was an odd reversal of roles. Micah wondered how reliable his nursemaid was going to be.

The next morning he felt much better, though he was so weak he could hardly lift his head from the pillow. Starting was there, faithfully tending him and seeming proud to be doing so. Micah realized that, for the first time perhaps, Starling Bright had someone depending on him and something to motivate him other than his own urges for alcohol.

But Micah worried. His money had been running very low and probably was gone by now. Most likely, Starling was now using the money that had been in the baggage of Johnny Cole, whoever he was. This seemed to Micah the moral equivalent of theft, however unintentional. He wished he'd turned the Cole bag back in at the railroad station. He'd intended to, but if he had, how else could he have paid for this room?

Too much to think about. He let it go and rested, eager to get his strength back.

It was time to go home.

As Micah ate his supper that night, sitting up on the bed, Starling came to him.

"I done it," he said.

"What?"

"I prayed... I done what you told me I should do. I got myself straightened out with God."

Micah smiled. "You mean it, Starling?"

"I do. I've turned away from all my sinning. I've asked the Lord to take me over and forgive me."

Micah reached out a weak hand and shook Starling's trembling one. "I congratulate you. That was the best decision you'll ever make."

"No more drinking, Preacher. Not for me. I've asked God to take that away from me, and he has."

"Starling, listen to me. Every answer won't necessarily fall right in place just because you prayed that prayer. It may be hard for you to turn away from liquor after all these years."

"But I asked God to take the desire away from me.

"I hope he will. Sometimes it happens that way. But not always. You can't just assume it will."

Starling laughed. "I'll show you, Preacher. I'll show you."

Micah lay back and closed his eyes. "I hope you will, Starling. Truly I do."

———

As Micah slept that night, Starling slipped out of the room and out onto the street. He prayed as he walked along, praying that the craving that had crept strongly upon him an hour before would miraculously disappear, praying that some force beyond himself would turn his path away from the saloon that was his intended destination—for he surely lacked the will or even the true desire to turn away on his own—and praying that God would forgive him for the sin he was about to commit.

He found it far too easy to walk through the saloon door and to the bar, his pockets bulging with the cash he'd found in the carpetbag. It had been far too easy to take that, too, even though he knew what his secret intentions for the money were.

Surely the Lord would understand, just one drink. A man couldn't throw his sin out without at least a fond farewell, a glass raised in salute to times past.

He had enough money to settle his tab and buy a full new bottle besides. He took it, feeling guilty, praying even as he sinned, but not intending for a moment to give the sin up. Not tonight.

He found a table in the corner and worked the cork out of the bottle. Closing his eyes a moment, he whispered words to the sky and poured the first shot into the glass.

CHAPTER 25

The whiskey took over quickly, and the remorse set in soon after.

Starling Bright, still drinking, wept silently over his failure. He'd failed himself, his repentance, his Lord... and Micah Ward. The only man who'd ever shown any interest in him or taken one step to help him when he needed it, he had betrayed.

Starling didn't know if the Lord would ever forgive him for this. He'd certainly not forgive himself.

But he could find a way to make it up to Micah.

Starling glanced toward the right. On an empty table lay a newspaper, a copy of the *Crime Chronicle*. Starling wasn't much of a reader, though, at times, he did enjoy reading the *Chronicle*. He stood and staggered over to the copy and tried to pick it up. It slipped from his fingers and onto the floor. He stooped uncertainly to pick it up.

He held the posture for several seconds, staring at the picture on the page. A gunfighter, shooting down another man. And on the gunfighter's face was a scar just like the one on Micah Ward's cheek!

This was surely the oddest of coincidences, and it

intrigued Starling even in his present impaired condition. He picked up the paper and sat down again, looking at the headline, beginning to read...

It took him nearly half an hour to get to the end of the article, but by the time he did, nothing was clear anymore. The story he'd just read could surely be about no one else but Micah Ward. How many preachers with T-shaped scars and a quest centering on Tipton Barth could there be roaming around in Colorado?

Yet the name in the story was Johnny Cole, not Micah Ward. Who was Johnny Cole?

Starling pondered this question until an answer began to come. If Micah Ward really was a gunfighter rather than a true preacher, then he might use an alias at times. Gunfighters were known to do that. Maybe Johnny Cole was simply Micah Ward's alias... or vice versa.

Johnny Cole... something familiar there. Recently so.

He remembered. The name was in the preacher's baggage.

The question was answered. Johnny Cole and Micah Ward were indeed one and the same. Two names, one man.

But also two quests, it seemed. The version of the man as presented in the *Crime Chronicle* depicted a vengeance-bound gunman, determined to see Tipton Barth killed. But the Micah Ward Starling knew was a gentle man, a man of true faith, one who didn't seem much interested in even finding Tipton Barth now, much less killing him.

Still drinking, Starling pored over the mystery, trying to reconcile it. Bit by bit, he began to draw a conclusion.

Micah Ward, if that really was his name, was probably a man who had to present to the world a false front in order to protect himself. A gunfighter was hunted everywhere he went. What better way to hide who he was than to pretend to be a man of peace and faith?

Maybe it wasn't even pretense. Starling was not a man

who understood much about right and wrong, religion, duty, and so on. Maybe there was no contradiction in it at all. After all, could it really be wrong to gun down men like Diamond Willie and Tipton Barth, hardened killers who deserved no better?

Micah had told Starling the story of his boyhood experience with the Barth brothers in California and how that had motivated his present journey to this place. But the more Starling thought about it, the more unlikely the story seemed. Would a man really do such a thing because of something that happened that long ago? Well, maybe. Old resentments and old scores sometimes had long lives. But Micah had seemed uncertain about what he would have done if he did find Tipton Barth. And that, Starling, decided in his alcohol-driven brain, raised some questions.

No man would travel as far as Micah had without exactly knowing what he intended to do, Starling decided. So if Micah had declared that he didn't know his own intentions, that was surely just a cover tale.

Starling reached his conclusion, accepting it with more firmness than it might have seemed to merit in a sober moment: Micah Ward indeed was a gunfighter, but one with a gentle and almost contradictory side to himself. His harder side was driving him to find and kill Tipton Barth, while his gentler side compelled him to hide that fact from others. In particular, he'd sought to hide it from Starling himself, not wanting to admit to a man he hoped to see saved that he himself had a violent and darker side.

Starling took a drink to his own cleverness in figuring all this out. He picked up the newspaper and nodded.

He knew now what he could do to make up to Micah Ward for this failure, this return to drinking right on the heels of his professed conversion. It would be dangerous, difficult, but if he tried hard and proceeded carefully, he could probably do it.

Starling took another drink, this time to steel his nerves. He wasn't accustomed to making big decisions, and here he'd just made two of them, one after the other. First, he'd decided to get religion.

Now he'd decided—he was almost sure—to kill an outlaw.

If getting rid of Tipton Barth was what Micah wanted, then that was what Starling Bright would do for him. Micah had helped him. Now he would help Micah in turn.

———

Tipton Barth walked alone, deep in thought and anger burning along with a touch of secret fear.

He'd remembered. It had come to him in the middle of the night and made him sit upright in his bed.

The boy, years ago, in California, when he was on trial for the murder of that fellow... what was his name? He couldn't remember.

It was that boy, the one witness who could have convicted him, who had the T-shaped scar on his face.

At that time, of course, it wasn't a scar but a fresh cut inflicted by Leroy. But there was no doubt that the fellow would have a scar today. Leroy had a way of cutting that ensured that; he'd always been proud of it.

Tipton laughed. The letter T, standing for his own name, was carried around by that fellow ever since that trial. It was funny. A joke of Leroy's that had outlasted Leroy himself.

Tipton's smile faded, though, as he considered the possibilities. What if that boy really had grown up to be a gunfighter? What if he really was such a fine gunman that he'd shot down the infamous Diamond Willie?

What if he really was in Colorado, looking for the man whose initial had marred his visage most of his fife?

Tipton sat down on a log, thinking through his situation. He knew he was a wanted man in many states and territories. Yet he'd never been much worried about it, even though it was no secret that he tended to hide out in the remote mountains around the old, dead town of Genesis. Not many bounty hunters or lawmen had tried to come after him. Those who had had not lived through the effort.

He'd made examples of them all, leaving then-bodies where they could be found, usually in a condition that sent his message quite clearly: Don't come looking for Tipton Barth.

Tipton pulled out the now-crumpled copy of the *Crime Chronicle* and studied the story and illustration one more time. Would this Cole fellow really come after him? How dangerous was he?

It would take a dangerous man indeed to kill Tipton Barth. Then again, it would have taken a dangerous man to kill Diamond Willie.

Tipton stood, swearing. Maybe he should leave the mountains for a time. It had been too long since he'd had a taste of city life. Generally, it suited him to hide away from the world, descending from his hiding places only long enough to rob, drink a little, and enjoy the company of women. Now might be a prudent time to make such a journey. Let this Cole fellow come and go. He and his partner Jake, who had filled the companionship void left by the death of Leroy, could have a fine time in the bars and brothels far from this wilderness and not worry about sneaking gunmen.

But it galled him to think of running. He'd never run from anyone. And this was certainly not the first time someone had come gunning for him.

Yet this one was different. There was something about this so-far-unmet enemy that scared Tipton. He was ashamed to admit it to himself. Maybe it was because he was a preacher;... it gave the stranger a kind of mystical aura.

Barth swore, standing. He decided right then that he would not run. Let this scar-faced manhunter show up—if he even existed. The *Crime Chronicle* was known for its loose grip on the truth. It had written lies enough about Barth himself over the years.

If this tale turned out to be true, though, Tipton Barth would be ready for whatever came.

In the meantime, he'd maintain a sharp lookout and have Jake do the same. He wished there were more than just the two of them here at the moment. Sometimes, depending on the degree of heat from the law in the world below, there were as many as seven or eight fellow desperadoes holing up here at this ghost town. Too bad it wasn't that way just now.

CHAPTER 26

T he night passed without the return of Starling Bright, and Micah arose the next morning very worried.

He was still weak, not really ready to emerge into the world, but he was tired of this room, of this illness. He wanted to get out of this hotel and this town and get back home to his wife and son.

But first, he wanted to know what had become of Starling. The man was—at least allegedly—a convert under Micah's influence. He couldn't just walk away without knowing what had become of him.

Micah washed himself and put on his freshest clothing. He strapped on the Diamond Willie pistol, packed his bags, and walked down to the lobby of the hotel.

"I'm leaving here," he said to the oddly wide-eyed desk clerk. "I need to know what I owe you."

The clerk swallowed hard and looked at the books. "You're paid up, sir," he said.

"That's impossible," Micah replied. "I've overstayed my original booking by days."

"No charge," the clerk said. "It's our pleasure to have you, sir."

Micah was mystified. "Why are you looking that way? Why are you giving me free lodging I didn't ask for?"

"Sir, it's our pleasure. You're a special guest. Please accept our hospitality with our compliments."

Micah was already digging in his bags for money. But he stopped when he realized that the money was there no more. He looked up at the clerk, then said, "I... I thank you."

He walked out of the hotel.

Outside, he sat down on a bench on the porch, surprised and saddened. Obviously, Starling had taken his money. All he had left was a few dollars that he'd hidden in his boot and which Starling had not found. He wasn't sure it was enough to get him home.

Micah shook his head, disillusioned. Apparently, Starling's conversion hadn't run very deep.

Well, he had all the more reason to find the man, then. Maybe some of the money was left, and he could get it back. Maybe he could figure out who Johnny Cole was and where he lived and get the money, most of it anyway, back to him someday.

Micah stepped out into the street to begin his search for Starling. Where would a fellow like him be? Probably in a saloon, sorry to say. And here, the saloons ran around the clock.

Micah headed for the nearest one, thinking how odd it was for him, a preacher, to be deliberately visiting such a place of vice. But no stranger than breaking a man's nose and shooting the fingers off another! What a strange journey this had been!

When Micah entered the saloon, it grew stranger yet.

———

It was too early in the day for anyone to be drinking, but a couple of men apparently hadn't been told and were halfway through glasses of beer.

When Micah walked through the door, one of those men stood, abandoning his glass, and headed out a side door. Others simply stared at him, and the barkeep went pale.

"Howdy, folks," Micah said.

"Howdy, Mr. Cole," the barkeep said.

Mr. Cole? "Begging your pardon, but that's not my name," Micah said.

"Whatever you say, sir."

Micah laughed. "What's this all about? I seem to be getting this kind of reaction wherever I go."

"It's just respect, sir. Begging your pardon for me saying so, but any man who could gun down Diamond Willie and take his guns right off his corpse deserves respect."

"Well, maybe so. Unless he happened to find, Diamond Willie lying dead in the woods, like I did."

"What? You didn't shoot him?"

"No. I don't even know it was Diamond Willie I found. All I found was bones and a pistol that was in good working order. But tell me something: Where did you hear my name was Cole?"

"The story, sir. In the *Crime Chronicle?*"

Oh, no. Maybe that wild suspicion Micah had harbored was true, after all. Maybe, Rhoton, the journalist, had meant business with that interviewing and note-taking.

"Just what does this story say?"

The barkeep answered by reaching under the bar and bringing out a copy. Micah took it, unfolded it, looked at the picture, the headline, the story itself.

"Lord have mercy," he said. No wonder people had been treating him like an object of fear and awe. No wonder he'd been given free lodging.

"It's true, that story?" the barkeep asked.

"No. There's a shadow of truth behind some of it, but by far more lies."

"You're name really isn't Johnny Cole?"

"No. My name's Micah Ward."

"You're not gunning for Tipton Barth?"

"I was looking for Barth at one time, not gunning for him. I didn't know what I'd do when I found him... It's a long story."

"You're not a gunfighter?"

"I'm a preacher. From Kansas."

The atmosphere was changing, people relaxing, the awe and fear going away. "So, how did this tale get printed?"

"It's a long story. I happened to talk to a journalist who obviously was more interested in a lurid story than the truth. I didn't really believe he'd write anything."

"Well, he did."

One of the beer drinkers said, "You'd best hope that Tipton Barth doesn't see that story."

Micah thought about that. It wasn't pleasant. Indeed it was time to go home.

He tossed the newspaper down. "I can't do anything about what somebody else has printed, and I can't worry about Tipton Barth," he said. "Right now, the only person I'm looking for is a fellow named Starling Bright."

"Starling? The drunkard?"

"Starling the convert. He's turned to the Lord."

The laughter was riotous.

"Starling, a convert? He didn't look none too converted last night when I saw him loving on his whiskey bottle at the Silver Pistol Saloon."

Micah had feared as much.

"Where is he now?" he asked.

"Couldn't tell you."

Micah left the saloon feeling both astonished and dejected, astonished that his simple trip to Colorado had found its way, in radically distorted form, into a sensational-ized crime journal and dejected that a man he had hoped might really have changed was not changed after all.

He looked up and down the street until he found the Silver Pistol Saloon. This one was one of the few in town that actually closed in the morning hours, but a man was sweeping up inside and answered Micah's knock.

"Ain't open until this afternoon," he said.

"I'm just looking for information. Somebody told me Starling Bright was in here last night. I'm trying to find him."

"Does he owe you money?"

"In a way."

"Well, you're looking for him at a good time. He had enough money last night to pay off his whole tab. I figure he stole it somewhere."

Micah could have told him just where, but that wasn't the point at the moment. "Where is he now?"

"I don't know. All I know is that he was talking big talk when he left."

"What kind of big talk?"

I don't know. Some mission he was going to do for a friend of his. He was talking like a manhunter. It was funny, to tell you the truth. He was drunk as he could be." The man stopped suddenly and stared at Micah's scar. "Damnation! Are you that preaching gunfighter who's after Tipton Barth?"

"I'm not after anybody. I'm not a gunfighter. What did you mean? Starling was talking like a manhunter?"

"Hold on. Let me ask Joe. Joe talked to him more than I did."

The man yelled back into the rear of the building. A tired-looking man with garters on his sleeves emerged, with a glass in one hand, being swabbed clean by a cloth in the other. "Yeah?"

"What did Starling say to you last night?"

The man chuckled. "Said he was heading off to Genesis to get Tipton Barth. Said he was doing it for his 'friend.'"

Micah felt weak. "Genesis... the mining town?"

"Ghost town now. That's where Barth hides out. Everybody knows it, the law included, but nobody bothers him. Except for Starling, I guess." He laughed.

"You don't think he'd really go up there?" Micah asked.

"No. No. He was drunk. He's a drunk, but he's no fool. Hell, not go after Barth."

"Why would he have said something like that, then?"

"He was reading in that newspaper about the preacher with the scar who is—" The man cut off.

Micah said, "Yes, yes, I know I've got the scar on my face. Yes, the story was about me, sort of... but it was lies and misunderstanding for the most part. But if Starling read that story, and if he decided that I really *was* after Tipton Barth..." Micah turned to the barkeep. "Where can a man borrow a horse around here?"

"Well, you can rent one over at Smith's Livery."

"Cheap?"

"Cheap enough."

"Then I thank you, gentlemen. And I'd be obliged to know the way to get to Genesis."

"Genesis! Why do you want to go there?"

"Because I think Starling did, and I can't have him getting killed trying to fight my battle for me."

"I don't know what you're talking about, my friend."

"It doesn't matter, as long as you can point me in the right direction."

CHAPTER 27

Starling Bright was on his hands and knees, heaving and hurting. His horse, "borrowed" from its place at a hitching post the night before, stood nearby, cropping dried grass that poked up through the snow and occasionally casting a wary eye on its unhappy former rider.

Starling had begun this journey before morning, heading out while fully drunk. He didn't remember taking the horse and wasn't even sure why he was here. He was moving past intoxication now, becoming sick and tired. And all he wanted was to go back down to Greentree.

When he'd heaved all he could, he sat upon his haunches and took several deep breaths. Why had he come up here, anyway? He only remembered that he'd had a very good reason for it.

As the clarity of mind returned to a degree, he realized how foolish he'd been. Not only had he risked passing out up here and freezing to death, but he'd also ridden almost to the town of Genesis, the very hideout of Tipton Barth and his occasional gang of fellow scoundrels.

Why in the world would he have done that?

All at once, he remembered and almost felt sick again.

"Lord bless me for a fool indeed!" he whispered. "And get me safely home again, quick as I can!"

He wondered how he ever could have drunk enough to make him think he could manhunt the likes of Tipton Barth. He hoped he never got that drunk again.

He was nearly to his horse when a gunshot made him yell and duck, covering his head. The horse whinnied and ran off, over the hill, leaving Starling there alone.

He uncovered his head and looked up.

Tipton Barth, whose face he'd seen depicted on wanted posters in the *American Crime Chronicle* and in at least two photographs, was looking back at him. At his side was a man Starling had never seen before.

"Hello, friend," Barth said.

"Hello," Starling replied weakly.

"What's your name?"

"Starling Bright."

"Where you from, Starling?"

"Greentree."

"Why are you here?"

"No reason, sir. I just rode up."

Barth said, "Do you know who I am?"

"I think... I believe, sir, that you may be Mr. Tipton Barth."

"I am indeed. And this is my mountain. See that building yonder? That's the southern edge of Genesis. It's a ghost town now, but it's my town,... and I don't take to being disturbed in my town."

"I'm mighty sorry, sir. I'll go."

"And do what? Tell that you seen me up here?"

"Oh, no, sir. No. I'd never."

"I can't know that, can I!"

"Please, sir, you can trust me. I give you my word. I'll never tell nobody I saw you."

"I got a policy, Mr. Bright. I never trust a stranger's word."

Starling's panicked mind began working fast. His resolution to reform and convert held no sway with him now. He merely wanted to survive. "You don't want to hurt me, Mr. Barth. I came up here to warn you about something."

"Warn me?"

"Yes, sir. There's a man gunning for you. A preacher. He's down in Greentree right now, and he might come up here after you." Down inside, something of Starling was dying, suffering... He knew that what he was doing was immensely selfish and wrong and could endanger the only man who had ever demonstrated any practical concern for him. But he'd started now and couldn't stop. "His name is Micah Ward, and he's got a scar on his face shaped like a T, and it's your initial, sir. It was carved onto Micah Ward's face when he was just a boy by your very own brother. He told me all about it."

"Micah Ward. That's right. I remember now. The name was Micah Ward. Just a scared little runt pup sitting there in a witness chair and saying he never laid eyes on me killing a fellow. But the truth is, I did kill that fellow. Did it just like this."

He drew his pistol, leveled it at Starling, and fired.

Barth holstered his pistol. "That was a bit of bother."

"You heard what he said, didn't you, Tipton? That story's true, about the preacher."

"Mostly true, anyway."

"So, what are you going to do about it?"

"Wait for him. If he comes, we'll be ready for him. And maybe leave him a sign to welcome him."

"What kind of sign?"

"Got your knife on you?"

"Always."

"Let me have it. I'll show you."

———

Micah had been a praying man so long that prayer required no conscious thought. Today, though, his prayers were deliberate, a continuing conscious stream, because he knew the danger into which he rode.

The snow had begun to fall again, covering up the tracks he'd been following. The tracks of Starling's horse, he figured. Hard to believe the man had actually come up here looking for Barth. What could account for it?

Though Micah, as always, had a strong sense of being accompanied by God everywhere he went, at the moment, on the more merely human level, he was conscious of being very alone. He wasn't sure how far away Genesis was or whether Barth would be there when he reached it. His prayer was that he would not, but that Starling would. He would fetch him back safely to Greentree and then make his own way back to Kansas for good.

He halted, peering through the falling snow. Something had caught his eye.

A church belfry! He'd not expected to see such a thing out here. Yet there it was, bell still in place, a carved wooden cross before it, on the peak of the porch roof. A closer look showed, though, that the place was in quite an ill repair. The belfry roof was almost gone, the bell hanging cockeyed and bound soon to fall, and the cross broken off at the top like a great splinter.

Micah knew he had reached the ghost town of Genesis. He only hoped, and prayed, that Starling would be easy to find there if he was still there at all.

He rode on, cutting through the trees and entering the edge of the town.

It was a place of ruin, much worn away by the years and lack of occupation. There was no evidence of life at all here, which under the circumstances, Micah found encouraging.

Maybe Tipton Barth didn't frequent this ghost town at all. Perhaps it was just one more rumor in a West rife with them.

He halted. There was no sound but wind, the faint rattle of the snow against trees and buildings, and a faint creaking of something moving in the wind.

The creaking increased as the wind gusted, and Micah tracked the sound. Turning to the right, he saw something at the edge of an alleyway, moving and turning, hanging there.

He dismounted, frowning, and drew closer.

"Oh, Lord," Micah whispered. "Oh, Lord, look what they've done to poor Starling!"

He was hanging there by a rope tied around his wrists. Blood covered his chest, and he was obviously dead.

A cut in the shape of the letter T had been carved into his right cheek.

CHAPTER 28

"Well, now! Micah Ward, is it?"

The voice echoed across the abandoned town. Even after all these years, Micah knew it. He turned, trying to find the place it came from. His hand moved as if on its own to touch the butt of Diamond Willie's pistol, holstered on his right hip.

"Thinking of shooting me, Micah? Or have you come to save my soul? Which are you, gunfighter or preacher?"

Micah could not find the place from which the voice came. "Where are you, Tipton Barth?" he called, hoping he sounded braver than he felt.

"Why, maybe I'm everywhere, like the good Lord himself! Maybe I'm here and there at the same time!" Barth laughed.

Another laugh answered him, coming from a different direction. So there were two, at least, Barth and someone else.

"Why did you kill this man?" Micah called, gesturing at the pitiful corpse of Starling Bright. "What harm did he ever do you?"

"Harm? Why he wandered into my town! That's no

small offense to Tipton Barth, young man. This is my town! I can't just have any old fool walking into it, can I? Right, Jake?"

The voice from elsewhere called, "That's right, Tipton."

Micah caught its direction and the tiniest motion. Jake, whoever he was, was atop a false-fronted building to Micah's left, hiding behind the front wall, which stood higher than the flat roof, like a solid railing.

Micah kept that building in the corner of his eye while at the same time looking for cover in case he had to make a quick dive.

"So answer me: Which are you, preacher or gunfighter?"

"I'm a preacher, Tipton Barth. One who at last felt compelled to come set right what I should have set right years ago but was scared out of doing!"

"Set right, you say? And what do you mean by 'set right'?"

"That's a good question, Barth, one I don't know I can answer. All I know is, I think my path has been led across yours by a higher hand than yours or mine. And now that I'm here, I want to offer you something. A chance to erase your guilt, to start again. To be forgiven."

"What? Are you preaching to me, Reverend? Did you hear him, Jake? What do you think of that, him preaching at me?"

"I'd take offense at it if I was you, Tipton!"

"And so I do. So I do."

There! Micah picked out where Barth was, the church belfry.

At least he knew where they were and where he stood: a bad place. Either one of them could drop him in his tracks, and there was no handy place where he could take cover.

That's why they'd hung poor Starling's body where they had, to draw him to the right spot. They'd probably been watching him from the time he came into view of the town.

"Come down and talk to me, Barth," Micah called, resting his hand on his pistol now. "Let me tell you how your life can change."

Barth didn't reply, and Micah sensed that something in the atmosphere was changing. The banter was ending; in moments, he might very well be as dead as Starling Bright.

Who would shoot first? Micah put his bet on Jake, who was positioned somewhat better than was Barth, to get in a clear shot.

Micah closed his hand around the pistol butt. "Lord," he whispered, "I cannot hope to hit that man from here. Guide my aim, God. I can't do it on my own."

"Tipton?" Jake called. "Now?"

"Now!" Tipton called back.

Micah had the pistol out and lifted even as Jake lunged up, in view now, and aimed his rifle over the storefront. Micah didn't try to aim. He merely pointed the pistol as he might point his finger, thumbed back the hammer, and pulled the trigger.

Jake yelled, dropped his rifle, and staggered. He stood there, blood emerging, and watched Micah Ward run back toward the abandoned church. Then he closed his eyes and fell forward, off the roof and to the ground below. He did not move again.

Micah, inside the church, looked for a way up to the belfry. There it was—a staircase, very rickety but obviously strong enough to have supported Tipton Barth.

"I'm coming for you, Barth!" Micah called. "You have the choice—throw down your weapons and talk to me and let me tell you how you may yet save your sorry soul... or you die."

The words hardly seemed Micah's own. He did not plan them, heard them as if they were spoken by another. Nor did he consciously follow any plan. He simply felt compelled to move up that staircase, without hesitation and despite the danger. Maybe God was guiding him, or maybe some previously untouched warrior's instinct. Whatever the explanation, he yielded himself and moved fast, knowing that this was the very thing Barth would not anticipate. Knowing that at this moment, the murderer Tipton Barth was probably as scared as Micah himself had been many years ago in California.

The stairs held under Micah's weight. He ran up them, pistol drawn and burst into the belfry.

Barth was there, armed but seemingly paralyzed in fear. Micah stared at the familiar, though much aged, face for less than two seconds before advancing again, pistol before him.

"Drop your weapon, Barth! And get on your knees! You have the choice to hear me out as I give you the word of the Lord or the choice to die! Which will it be?" Micah stepped forward, hardly two yards away now, intense in manner, pistol ready to shoot. "Which, Barth? Choose! Choose!"

Barth roared and snapped the trigger of his rifle.

It clicked dead. A misfire.

"God is protecting me, Barth! God is protecting me so that I can tell you his truth. You can be forgiven. You can escape the consequences of your own evil! Will you hear me out, Barth? Or will you die?"

"Go to hell!" Barth yelled. He squeezed the trigger again. Another misfire. With a roar of fury, he swung the useless rifle like a club. Micah ducked it.

"Drop it, Barth! Drop it, and let's talk, you and me!"

Barth backed up against the edge of the belfry railing now. He swung the rifle again, throwing himself off balance. He flailed, eyes widening, and fell back out of the belfry with a scream. There was a terrible, tearing sound and a dead thud, and the scream cut off abruptly.

Micah advanced and looked out of the belfry.

Barth was looking back at him with dying eyes. A sharp wooden shard was poking out of his chest, bloody and gruesome. He'd fallen back atop the broken cross, piercing himself clean through, his body pinned on the splintered cross like a bug impaled on a needle.

The light in Barth's eyes was fading fast. Micah looked at him. "You could have been saved," he said. "You could have listened."

Barth's head fell back, and his stiffened body relaxed.

Micah holstered his pistol and slowly descended from the belfry. He felt like he might collapse at any moment, weeping like a child, but once outside again, he simply stood on the street in the falling snow, numb and for the moment unable even to pray.

At last, though, he did pray. His prayer was simple, not a request, not a plea, but simply a statement.

"Lord, I want to go home."

He did not leave immediately. First, he removed the body of poor Starling Bright and laid it out safely in a nearby building. He'd notify someone in Greentree and send them up to fetch him. As for Jake, he dragged his body to the abandoned church, atop which the corpse of Tipton Barth still dangled, pinned on the broken cross.

He set the church house ablaze just before he rode out of Genesis. It flamed and smoked behind him as he departed, but he did not look back.

His eye was turned toward Kansas, and he would not turn it away again until he was home.

A Look at: The Gallowsman and Henry Kidd, Outlaw
Two Full Length Western Novels

Cameron Judd's ability to capture the spirit of adventure and promise of the wild frontier with writing that is powerful, authoritative, and respectful of America's frontier traditions is on full display in these two, full-length standalone novels.

In *The Gallowsman*, Ben Woolard is a man ready to start over. The life he's leaving behind is none too pretty, filled with ghosts and pain. When he lost his wife and children, he took to the bottle so hard he almost couldn't find his way out again. And his career as a Union spy during the war still doesn't sit quite right with him, even if the man sent to the gallows by his testimony was a murderer. But now Ben's finally sobered up, moved west to Colorado, staked out a claim, and put the past behind him.

But sometimes the past won't lie still. Sometimes it just won't stay buried. And, as Ben learns when folks start telling him that the man he saw hanged is still alive and in town—sometimes those ghosts come back.

Henry Kidd, Outlaw: In the waning days of the Civil War, a Unionist farmer is brutally murdered, leaving behind a wife and three daughters—and his only son. The family gives young Marsh Perkins a grim duty. He is to track down Henry Kidd, the man who killed his father, and either kill him or bring him back to face justice.

Young Marsh is the best hunter in the mountains, and there is no one else to do the job, so he sets out alone, from Tennessee through Arkansas and Texas, one young man on the trail of a ruthless outlaw. And Kidd's trail is easy to follow—wherever he goes bodies tend to be left behind. But what will Marsh do when he finally catches up with Kidd? Will he be able to avenge his father's death, or will he become just another body in Henry Kidd's wake?

"Judd is a fine action writer." — Publisher's Weekly

ABOUT THE AUTHOR

Cameron Judd is the author of more than fifty published novels of the American frontier, two of his works having been national finalists in the Spur Awards competition of the Western Writers of America. He has written under his own names and pen names including Judson Grey, Tobias Cole and Will Cade. A native and lifelong Tennessean, he has three adult children. He and his wife, Rhonda, share their Northeast Tennessee home with a cornbread-loving dog named Lola. He is a former award-winning newspaper journalist and editor.